Praise for LORD SOMERTON'S HEIR

"...an easy read that had me interested from the start. Set in the Regency period this story is part romance part "who dunnit" mystery. It's well written and well paced with enough drama and information to keep you enthralled without feeling boring or drawn out..." *(Beauty and Lace Book Club)*

"...Alison Stuart takes you on a journey of discovery, love and mystery. There is elegance, and treachery with handsome men and beautiful ladies. She writes a beautiful setting that comes alive as you read and I love the character development and storyline that goes along with it. A great read!" *(Beauty and Lace Book Club)*

"This is the Regency romance you read when you want something a bit different because it also brings you a nice, but not too scary murder mystery... If you want a well written Regency romance that is not run of the mill because it has a little bit extra, then this is for you. It definitely was it for me." *(Sara Goodreads)*

LORD SOMERTON'S HEIR

A romantic Regency suspense

ALISON STUART

LORD SOMERTON'S HEIR

© 2014 by Alison Stuart

First Published 2014

Revised Australian Paperback Edition First Published 2021

ISBN (Print) 9780975640791

This edition: Oportet Publishing 2025

Cover Design: Jennifer Peters

This is a work of fiction. Names, characters, places, and incidents either are the product of the author's imagination or are used fictitiously, and any resemblance to actual persons, living or dead, business establishments, events, or locales is entirely coincidental.

No part of this book may be reproduced in any form or by any electronic or mechanical means, including information storage and retrieval systems, without written permission from the author, except for the use of brief quotations in a book review.

No AI Training: Without in any way limiting the author's [and publisher's] exclusive rights under copyright, any use of this publication to "train" generative artificial intelligence (AI) technologies to generate text is expressly prohibited. The author reserves all rights to license uses of this work for generative AI training and development of machine learning language models.

Spelling and styles throughout is **UK/Australian English**.

Discover other titles by Alison Stuart at

Author website: http://www.alisonstuart.com

About the Author

Alison Stuart writes historical romances and short stories set in England and Australia and across different periods of history. She is best known for her English Civil War stories and also for The Women of Maiden's Creek series set in the Victorian goldfields in the 1870s.

She also writes historical mysteries as A.M. Stuart, and her popular Harriet Gordon mystery series is set in Singapore in 1910.

Alison lives in Melbourne, Australia. In a past life, she worked as a lawyer across a variety of disciplines, including the military and emergency services. She has lived in Africa and Singapore and, when circumstances permit, travels extensively (for research, of course).

To discover more about Alison Stuart visit her website (alisonstuart.com) or follow her on any of the social media accounts below.

DEDICATION

This book is dedicated to my mother, MPT, my rock and my best friend.

Prologue

BRANTSTONE HALL 11 DECEMBER 1814

In the light of the lanterns held up by the stablehands, the glossy hide of the great, black horse reflected fire. The animal shivered, breaking the fire into golden sparks. The handsome head bobbed, testing the hold of Thompson, the head groom, while the huge eyes, white against the dark-fringed lashes, scanned the crowd of faces.

Isabel, Lady Somerton, clutching her shawl around her shoulders against the cold, dark winter morning, stopped short of the horse, her hand going to her mouth.

No saddle—no rider.

'What's happened?'

The words were forced through lips that refused to move.

'His lordship went out on Pharaoh last evening, my lady.' The head groom, Thompson, swallowed. 'We found the 'orse in the stable yard this morning. We've no idea how long it's been here.'

Pharaoh pulled at the restraining reins, rearing up, his great ironclad hooves raising sparks as they returned to the cobbles.

'Get the horse inside the stable and see to him,' Isabel

ordered. 'We must order a search party. My husband is lying out there, injured.'

And in this cold.

She shuddered, dismissing the thought that they may be too late.

Thompson thrust the reins at his son. 'See to the 'orse, boy.'

Peter Thompson seemed dwarfed against the enormous animal, but Pharaoh went meekly at his touch, head lowered as if exhaustion had claimed him and he wanted nothing more than a warm stall and a basket of oats.

Thompson looked at Lady Somerton. 'Do you know where he was bound, my lady?'

Isabel swallowed.

'Lady Kendall,' she said. 'He was intending to visit Lady Kendall.'

Thompson nodded. 'Aye. We'll take that route first. To me, all of you.'

Thompson gathered his hands around him. The staff, still rubbing the sleep from their eyes, were fetched from the house, and the men of Brantstone Hall set out on foot to search for the missing Lord Somerton, leaving Isabel standing alone in the stable yard in the cold, grey light of dawn. She would have stood there all morning if Mrs. Fletcher, the housekeeper, had not fetched her inside, sitting her down in the blue parlour with a tray of tea and buttered bread.

Isabel sat unmoving, staring out at the winter landscape of the Brantstone Park as if she expected Anthony to come galloping down the carriageway. The tea, in its delicate porcelain cup, sat undrunk and cold, and the bread curled and dried as the little clock on the mantelpiece ticked away the minutes.

She knew, even before Thompson knocked on the door and stood shifting from one foot to the other, his shapeless felt hat clutched in his hand, that Anthony was dead.

Isabel followed the head groom back out into the stable yard. She looked at the farmer's manure cart that had been dragged into the yard and with her head held high, she walked across to it. Thompson interposed himself between her and the inanimate object that lay in the filthy dray.

'Are you sure, my lady?' he asked.

She nodded, and Thompson flicked back the sacking that covered the shapeless lump in the back of the cart. Anthony lay, stiff with rigor mortis in the slimy filth, and Isabel stared down into her husband's face, into his open, staring eyes, already opaque in death. An ignominious end to his life, she thought.

'We found him over by Lovett's Bridge. He'd taken the hedge intending the shortcut across the Home Farm fields,' Thompson was saying. He jerked his head at the saddle, the beautiful, hand-tooled saddle that had been tossed into the cart with its owner. 'Looks like the girth strap broke, and he came off. Broke his neck in the fall. He'd not have known anything about it, m'lady.'

Her gaze rested on the saddle. It had been her gift to Anthony on his birthday only a few months earlier. Now it was the cause of his death. It stood as a symbol of everything that had gone wrong between herself and her husband.

Aware of the anxious faces that surrounded her, Isabel swallowed. They expected her to break down. They wanted her tears, but she had none to give. She had expended too many tears over Anthony, Lord Somerton, while he lived to spare any for him now that he was dead.

She turned on her heel and walked back to the house with her head held high. With every step, the enormity of Anthony's death sank in.

She was free, but at what price came that freedom?

Her back straightened, and her lips tightened.

To attain freedom, first she had to find Lord Somerton's heir.

Chapter One

LONDON 28 JUNE 1815

'Are you certain he's here?' Isabel—Lady Somerton—asked, her voice muffled by the lavender-scented kerchief she had pressed to her nose and mouth.

The pathetic piece of muslin did little to conceal the stench of unwashed bodies, blood, corrupted wounds, and worse that pervaded the makeshift hospital. The price Wellington had paid for the victory lay crowded on filthy straw mattresses on the makeshift hospital floor of an old warehouse in Battersea.

The wounded of Waterloo had been crowded together, so many of them that only a curtain separated the officers from the other ranks. Most still wore the tattered remnants of the uniform they had worn in battle over ten days ago, and it looked to Isabel as if the rough bandages over their wounds had not been changed in days.

A young boy, hardly older than Peter Thompson, the stable boy at Brantstone, screamed for his mother. Her heart stopped at the heartrending sound, and she turned and knelt beside him, smoothing the hair back from his burning forehead. The child had probably been a drummer boy, caught in the horror of the battle.

He clutched her hand, looking at her with unseeing eyes, and she murmured to him, the sort of platitudes she imagined a mother would use with an ailing child. His breathing steadied and then stilled; the hand clutching hers fell away.

Her companion, Bragge, the Somerton man of business, touched her shoulder.

'Come away, my lady.'

She stared down at the child on the cot.

'But ...'

'He's dead, my lady.'

Bile rose in her throat, but she swallowed it down. She could not show weakness, not now. She needed all her strength.

She rose slowly to her feet and cast the dead boy one last look, her lips moving in silent prayer for his soul and the mother who would grieve for her son.

Beyond the curtain, the conditions for the officers were little better. At least they had cots, not straw-filled bags, but those who had survived the rapid evacuation to England were in a poor state.

'The orderly over there said he's in that corner, m'lady.' Bragge's voice carried no conviction, and he looked as green and sickly as she felt.

He held the lantern higher to illuminate the man they had sought for so many months.

He lay on his left side with his back to them. A torn and stained scarlet jacket with yellow facings and a captain's epaulets had been thrown across his shoulders, and a ragged blanket covered his torso and legs. All Isabel could see of the man was dark, matted hair.

Isabel held back for a moment, wondering what she would say. She had rehearsed a pretty little speech in the coach, but now, as she looked down at the man, known to the world as Captain Sebastian Alder, the words deserted her. How would he take the news? It could not be every day that the humble son of a country parson found himself elevated to the peerage. Would he rejoice or rail against his mother, who had kept the secret of his parentage from him?

Doubt seized her. What manner of man would he turn out to be? Surely a parson's son would have some education, but would he be capable of running the Somerton estates? For the first time since hearing the news that they had found the heir to the Somerton estates, a niggling doubt caught her.

'M' lady?'

Bragge's voice broke through her musing, and she took a deep breath. Steeling her nerves, she reached out a gloved hand, touching the man on the shoulder.

'Captain Alder?'

Her uncertainty caught in the rising tone.

When he did not stir, she looked up at Bragge, her heart sinking.

'Are we too late?' she ventured.

'Try again, my lady.'

She bent down and closed her fingers on his shoulder, shaking him.

With a speed that took her completely by surprise, a hand grasped her wrist as the man rolled onto his back, hot, angry, feverish eyes seeking out the person who had disturbed him.

'Who the hell are you?' he demanded.

Isabel gasped, taking a step back, but he did not release her wrist.

'I'm sorry! I didn't mean to startle you ... or hurt you,' she added, seeing pain in the tightened lips and sunken eyes.

Slow comprehension softened the unshaven face, and he released her wrist. His eyes closed, and he let out a softly aspirated breath.

'My apologies to you, lady. I didn't mean to scare you. Just a soldier's instincts,' he said.

Rubbing her wrist, she looked down at the man and caught

her breath. There could be no denying this man was a Somerton. He had his cousin's finely chiselled cheekbones and well-shaped mouth, but his jaw had a strength to it that Anthony had lacked.

'Are you ...' she began, quelling the uncertain quaver in her voice. 'Are you Captain Sebastian Alder, son of the late Marjory Alder of Little Benning in Cheshire?'

His eyes opened again, but all the fight had gone from him. Beneath the stubble on his chin, his face looked grey, the eyes feverish and sunken in his skull.

'My mother has been eighteen years in the grave. Why do you want to know about her?' His gaze flicked to Bragge, and he frowned as if he were trying to bring them both into focus. 'Who are you?'

'I am the dowager Viscountess Somerton, and this is my late husband's man of business, Bragge. We have been looking for you for over six months now.'

He frowned. 'Looking for me? What do you mean? What is your business with me?' His voice rasped with the effort of speech.

'We've come to take you home,' Isabel said.

His mouth quirked into a humourless smile. 'That is a nice sentiment, Lady Somerton, but I doubt I would survive such a trip. It's nigh on two hundred miles to Cheshire.'

'Oh, not to Cheshire. We are taking you to your new home: Somerton House in Hanover Square.'

The man ran a hand across his eyes. 'This is a jest or some strange fever dream that I'm going to wake from. Lady Somerton, or whoever you are, I do not live in Hanover Square. I told you, my home is in Cheshire.'

'It's no jest, Captain Alder. You are now the Viscount Somerton of Brantstone, first cousin to my late husband and, as such, the heir to his estates.'

To her surprise, Alder covered his face with his hands and laughed.

Ignoring him, she continued, 'The doctors said you would be

all right to be moved such a short distance, and I have arranged the best doctor to see to you.' She glanced at Bragge. 'Please go and fetch the coachmen.'

Bragge inclined his head and turned away, leaving Isabel alone with the new Lord Somerton.

Alder removed his hands from his face and watched her with puzzlement in his eyes—brown eyes, she noted, a soft, warm brown, not the cold grey of Anthony's.

She looked around the ward and shuddered. 'This is a terrible place,' she said, more to herself than to him. 'I'm surprised anyone survives it.'

'They don't.'

The man on the pallet tried to sit up, falling back with a groan.

"Ere! Who are you then?'

A strident cockney voice caused Isabel to turn on her heel. She was confronted by a soldier of Alder's regiment, judging by the yellow facings of his jacket. He carried a bowl of water and some cloths, and he looked at Isabel as if she were some ill-intentioned assassin.

Isabel straightened.

'I'm Lady Somerton. Who are you?'

'I'm Bennet, Corporal Obadiah Bennet, and you ain't got no business with my captain. He ain't strong enough for visitors.'

Alder's hand clutched at his corporal's sleeve. 'Lady Somerton is just leaving, Bennet,' he croaked.

Isabel glanced down at the sick man. He had to come with her. Without him, she would be lost. It was not his choice. He had obligations and responsibilities to assume. Didn't he understand that?

'Why do you want to take him away? I can take perfectly good care of him 'ere,' Bennet said.

Isabel looked around the stinking ward. The dead boy still lay unregarded on his mattress, his sightless eyes staring at the ceiling.

'No! I can't leave without you.' She heard the rising hysteria in her voice as she looked down at Sebastian Alder. 'You will die here. At Somerton House we can look after you properly. I can get the best doctors ... A nurse ...'

'And why would a grand lady like you want to do that?' Bennet sounded derisive.

'Because,' she lowered her voice, aware that their little contretemps was attracting attention, 'your captain is the new Lord Somerton and he should be taken home where he can be looked after properly.'

'What?' Corporal Bennet stared at her and then down at his officer. 'Is this lady stark, staring mad? I've known you since you was sixteen years old and you may be many things, but you ain't no lord.'

Alder waved a hand. 'I think you need to explain yourself, Lady Somerton, and then leave me in peace.'

'It's true, Captain Alder. Your father was James Kingsley, my late husband's uncle.'

Bennet scoffed. 'His father was the Reverend Alder of Little Benning in Cheshire and a right decent gentleman too.'

Isabel glared at the little man, tempted to rebuke him for his insolence.

'The Reverend Alder was his *step*father.' She looked down at the wounded man. His eyes were open but unfocussed, and she wondered if he could even hear what she was saying. 'According to my information, your mother married him when you were two years old. How many times must I repeat it? You are Lord Somerton's heir.'

Alder frowned as if trying to reconcile what she was saying. He raised a hand and ran it across his eyes. 'It sounds an incredible tale, but, Lady Somerton, I don't have the strength to argue with you. If it means that you are intent on removing me to somewhere more pleasant than this charnel house, I can do no more than be much obliged.'

She crouched down beside him, instinctively straightening

the blanket and the ruined jacket. 'I know this is a shock. I promise you the full story when you are stronger. For now, we must get you away from this place.'

Sebastian Alder laid a grimy hand on her arm. 'Do whatever you want with me, Lady Somerton. I am yours to command.'

'What about me?' Bennet protested.

'Bennet comes too.' Alder's fingers closed on her sleeve, his voice now so weak she had to bend to hear him. 'He's been my batman for fifteen years now. I'm not leaving him.'

'Of course.' Isabel glanced at the little corporal. 'Bennet comes too.'

She smiled at the new Lord Somerton and put her hand over his, gently laying it back on his chest. His eyes were closed and he appeared to be asleep or unconscious.

Rising to her feet, she beckoned Bragge and the coachmen who had pushed past the curtains, one carrying a stretcher. She prayed they were not too late. Even the most innocuous of wounds could kill if not treated properly and she needed the new Lord Somerton to live.

Chapter Two

Sebastian found himself once again on a dusty road in Portugal. Above him, distant black shapes circled in the colourless sky. Sebastian caught his breath, knowing only too well what those ominous birds portended. Somewhere, ahead of them, death had passed this way.

Beside him, his friend, Major Harry Dempster, put out his hand to catch Sebastian's reins. 'Alder... no!'

But Sebastian put his heels to his horse and charged ahead of the patrol. He heard the thundering of hooves as Dempster raced to catch him, but it was too late.

His horse shied at the sight of the first body lying sprawled in the roadway, the uniform of Colonel Aradeiras barely visible beneath the film of dust. This man had almost escaped, but they had caught him, a French sabre nearly decapitating his head in one clean slice.

Dempster was once more by his side, but Sebastian barely registered his presence.

'Go back, Captain Alder,' his senior officer ordered.

Numbly, Sebastian shook his head. He now knew what lay around the bend in the road, why the carrion birds circled above their heads.

Her father had sent a message to say Inez had left Lisbon with an armed party of his own handpicked men as an escort. In his lodgings, his landlady had prepared his bedchamber with flowers and clean linen, excited at the prospect of the *senhora*'s arrival.

The wedding and their few precious days together had been a lifetime ago. Now, to a man, Colonel Aradeiras' escort lay dead in the dusty road around the broken carriage, no match for the rifles and sabres of the French raiding party. The coach lay on its side, the horses dead in the traces.

Sebastian flung himself off his horse, running blindly towards the broken coach, and found it empty, the upholstery ripped no doubt in a frenzied search for gold.

The breath stopped in his throat. Where were the women? Where was Inez and her maid, the elderly and patient Maria?

Beyond the coach, he stopped on the side of the road, looking down an incline into a grove of olive trees, too shocked to take in the terrible tableau the French had left for him.

The raiding pary had not spared the women, even Maria who must have been touching seventy. The two women lay sprawled on their backs, their clothing rent from their bodies and blood... the blood...

Sebastian started towards them, only to find himself pulled back. He fought the restraining hands of Harry Dempster and Sergeant Pike.

'She's dead, Alder. There's nothing you can do for her,' Harry was saying.

But the blood roared in Sebastian's ears, and he could see only a red haze before his eyes. Inez, he had to get to Inez.

He had promised to protect her with the last breath in his body, but he had failed her, failed her in the worst possible way a man—a husband—could. He had not been there when the French had attacked. He had not fought off the ravaging wolves that had used his wife's body for their own pleasure before bayoneting her. An animal howl of pure despair tore from his throat and, still in Pike's grip, he went down on his knees in the dust.

The world faded and turned black, and he was falling, falling, falling into that black morass of despair from which he knew he would never recover.

᠃

ISABEL AWOKE WITH A START AT THE SOUND OF CRASHING china. She rose from her bed, lit the night candle, and, pulling a loose robe over her nightdress, stepped out into the corridor. She came across Bennet at the head of the stairs, cleaning up a broken bowl that had, from the liquid that now spilled across the dark, polished wood, contained water.

He looked up at her, dark, sunken circles under his eyes. Even though she had employed a nurse, this man had borne the brunt of the nursing and had not left his captain's side for the last three days.

She laid her hand on his shoulder.

'Enough, Bennet. Finish cleaning up the mess and then go and get some sleep. You're exhausted. I'll wake the nurse.'

Bennet rose to his feet. 'She's useless, beggin' your pardon, me lady, and the Cap'n can't be left alone. The fever's got a right hold of him.'

'Then I'll sit with him a little while, and if I need help I will wake you both.'

Exhaustion turned to horror. 'Oh no, my lady, that would hardly be proper.'

'Pish to propriety. No one needs to know except you and me. You've done a sterling job but you are no good to anyone, let alone your captain, in your current state.'

When Bennet continued to look doubtful, she drew herself up and said in a firm tone, 'I insist. Good night, Bennet.'

She turned on her heel and walked into the room that had been her husband's bedchamber. Isabel set the candlestick on a table and approached the bed. She paused, taking a moment to accustom herself not only to the odour of the sickroom but to the fact that it was not Anthony whose long frame occupied the finely carved bed.

Sebastian Alder's dramatic arrival at Somerton House had been met with remarkable calm by the servants, who seemed to take it for granted that when one Lord Somerton died, another took his place—although they were not generally carried in through the front door on a stretcher.

The doctor had told her that Sebastian had taken a musket ball just beneath his right ribs. The ball had passed through and, while it appeared to have missed anything major, the wound had become infected, and the lack of proper care and attention in the days since the battle had contributed to a nasty mess and a wound fever.

Isabel knew from reports from Bennet and gossip from her own maid, Lucy, that Sebastian had barely been lucid since his arrival, and it had frustrated her that propriety forbade her interference.

'Pish to propriety,' she repeated to herself, looking down at the man who lay sprawled in the large bed, one of Anthony's nightshirts open at the neck and twisted around his chest, a testimony to his restless state.

Even though the nightshirt had been made with plenty of room, it seemed too tight across the shoulders of this man. She attempted to untangle the garment, but Sebastian pulled away from her, muttering incoherently.

She walked over to the shuttered window, throwing it wide. The cool night air rushed into the room, and she paused for a moment, her hands still on the casement, letting the breeze tumble her hair before turning back to the room. The fire flickered in the draught, and she bent over it, scattering the logs with the poker. The room would be cool within a short time.

Returning to the bed, Isabel pulled back the heavy blankets, leaving only a sheet covering the feverish man. The material clung to his body, revealing a broad chest tapering to narrow hips, with strong horseman's thighs. She swallowed. The only man with whom she had such an intimate acquaintance had been her husband and those were memories she pushed away.

To distract herself, Isabel looked around and saw a bowl of water with a cloth sitting on the nightstand. She wet the cloth and folded it into a pad, laying it across the man's burning forehead and then his wrists. She kept this up until he calmed and settled into a fitful sleep.

Isabel pulled up a chair and set herself to watch.

Sebastian Alder's right hand lay outside the covers, palm up, the fingers curled. Something in the vulnerability of the gesture touched her, and she reached out and laid her hand on his. Even in the candlelight, she could see the calluses and scars of his years of soldiering and the grime of the battlefield still ingrained around his fingernails. She thought of Anthony's soft, white, immaculately manicured fingers and shivered.

His fingers tightened on hers, and he turned his face to her, his eyes wide and dark in the light of the candlelight. He mumbled something and she leaned in close to hear him.

'*Inez. Você precisa voltar para mim,*' he murmured, his voice hoarse with fever.

Beyond the name Inez, she understood nothing and wondered if he spoke in Portuguese or Spanish. He began to speak rapidly in the same foreign language, his fingers tightening on hers with urgency, his eyes beseeching her for an answer she could not give.

In the end, she ventured the one Spanish word she did know. 'Si, Sebastian,' she said, adding in English, 'I am here.'

His eyes closed, the grip on her hand relaxed, and he slept at last.

Chapter Three

Sebastian lay very still, listening to... silence.
He screwed his eyes tighter shut. In the dark of his fever, Inez had come to him, her long hair falling around her shoulders like dark satin, and her brown eyes full of love.

He had begged her to come back to him, and she had replied in English, 'I am here'.

He knew it had been a dream. Inez lay buried in the brown earth of her native Portugal, her death forever on his conscience, and he was... where?

Surely if he opened his eyes, he would find himself back in the fetid ward of the hospital with no beautiful ladies spinning strange stories, but the fine linen and soft bolsters beneath his head told a different story.

Hardly daring to breathe, he opened his eyes and found himself looking up at an embroidered bed hanging. He picked out a myriad of brightly coloured flowers jostling together in a heavenly cluster above him. When he turned his head, he saw an elegant tallboy standing against richly patterned wallpaper beside a heavy, mahogany door. Perhaps he had died and this was heaven?

The sound of familiar whistling from outside the door caused a smile to catch at the corners of his mouth.

No.

Heaven would never admit Corporal Bennet.

'Oh, so you're awake?' Bennet entered the room carrying a tray. 'Doctors said now the fever's broken, you'd be hungry, so I took the liberty of bringing up some broth for you.'

He whipped the cloth from a steaming bowl. The scent of chicken broth rose into the air. Sebastian's stomach growled in anticipation, and he tried to pull himself up in bed, realising that his efforts were as pathetic as those of a newborn lamb.

Without fuss, Bennet was there to assist. A custard of some nondescript appearance and taste followed the broth.

Invalid pap.

He told Bennet that next time he wanted real food. Bennet just clicked his tongue and shook his head.

'Doctor's orders, Cap'n,' he said. 'We nearly lost you and it's goin' to take some time to build up your strength again.'

'It will if you keep feeding me that swill,' Sebastian observed. He looked around the room, noting the expensive furniture and thick rugs on the floor. 'Where am I?'

'You're at Somerton House in Hanover Square, and very grand it is too. I've counted twenty bedrooms.'

'Why am I here?'

'Don't you remember?'

'Some strange woman with a tale about me being Lord Somerton?'

'Aye, that's right. Seems like she's right too. You are Lord Somerton.'

Sebastian lay back on his pillows and looked up at the bed hangings again.

'I cannot possibly be Lord Somerton. I've never even heard of Lord Somerton.'

Bennet shrugged. 'Well, her ladyship's got the proof. So you'd better start getting used to it... m'lord.'

Bennet swept him a deep bow and, had he been stronger, Sebastian would have thrown a pillow at him. As it was, he could do nothing except suggest in strident terms that Bennet leave him in peace.

A few minutes later, the door opened again. Sebastian gathered his strength to snarl at Bennet, but subsided when he saw his visitor was a woman—a woman who looked vaguely familiar.

'Good morning, my lord,' she said.

He managed a smile. 'Good morning, madam. You will forgive me not standing but I fear I would fall over.'

'As you undoubtedly would. You have been very ill, Captain Alder... my lord... but it seems you are now on the mend and as soon as your strength is sufficiently recovered, you will travel to the Somerton estate at Brantstone in Lincolnshire.'

Somerton estate?

Oh yes, he remembered her now. The woman from the hospital.

He pulled himself up in the bed, flinching as the wound caught.

'Ah, so I didn't dream it. Please remind me—who are you, madam?'

She advanced and stood at the end of the bed.

'I am the dowager Lady Somerton, the widow of your cousin, Anthony, who died in an accident just before Christmas.'

Sebastian looked away, absently pleating the heavy linen sheet between his fingers.

'I recall you mentioned that at the hospital. My father...' his voice cracked as he corrected himself, 'my stepfather was the late Reverend Alder of Little Benning. My mother never...'

His mother had never breathed a word about the identity of his real father. When he was old enough to understand these things, he had asked, but she had turned away, tears in her eyes and he had never asked again.

Your father is dead, Bas. That is all you need to know.

He had assumed himself to be a bastard, and she had taken

the knowledge of his father's identity with her to the grave. He swallowed, remembering how he would pass men in the streets and wonder if any of them could be his real father.

He squared his shoulders and looked up at Lady Somerton, embarrassed to see she had been watching him.

'So tell me, Lady Somerton, as you seem remarkably well informed on my antecedents: who, then, was my true father?'

'James Kingsley, the younger son of the late Lord Somerton, my husband's grandfather. He eloped with your mother and was cut off by his father. I believe he died shortly after your birth. I have the necessary proof that the marriage was legal. You and my husband, Anthony, are... were... legitimate first cousins.' She paused and seemed to clear her throat before continuing, 'Anthony and I were not blessed with children, and, as the closest male in the direct lineage, you are the heir to my husband's estate. It is quite simple.'

Sebastian passed a weary hand over his eyes. 'Simple for you, perhaps, Lady Somerton, but I swear to you this is the first I have heard of the Somertons. My mother never thought fit to mention any such connection. Even on her deathbed.'

'It's not for me to gainsay your mother's reasons for withholding that knowledge from you.' Her tone held a sharp edge as if she were losing patience with him. 'If you still doubt me, I have the evidence of the marriage, Captain Alder, and of your birth and your father's death. It has all been duly notarised. Nothing more is needed.'

She folded her hands in front of her, and the import of what she had said finally sank in. He, plain Sebastian Alder, son of a parson, an officer in the Fortieth Regiment of Foot, was now a viscount and the inheritor, he presumed, of some vast estate.

'I knew that the Reverend Alder was not my father,' he hastened to reassure her. 'He took us both in when my mother was in dire need. He was a good man and I could not have asked for a better father.'

He glanced at the ironbound box that stood in a corner of

the room with the name *Alder* stencilled in chipped and fading letters on the lid. The sum total of his possessions fitted in that pathetic box. Surely this had to be some sort of cruel jest, and someone would appear to tell him that it had all been a mistake and he was still plain Captain Sebastian Alder, a wounded officer of His Majesty, now on half pay.

'I believe you have a brother and sister still living in Little Benning?' Lady Somerton enquired with an arch to her eyebrows.

He nodded. 'You are well informed, Lady Somerton. Matthew and Constance are the children of my mother's marriage to the Reverend Alder.' He frowned. 'Do they know of my... change in fortune?'

'I believe that should be a task for you, not I,' Isabel said.

'I will write to them.' He gave a hollow, unwise laugh that made his wound catch. 'I doubt they'll believe me.' He shook his head, imagining Connie and Matt reading the letter in the parlour of the little cottage. 'I don't believe it myself.'

'You will find all you need in the desk.' Lady Somerton indicated a mahogany desk in the window embrasure. 'I will leave you to rest. Is there anything you need?'

Sebastian looked around the sumptuous bedchamber and then returned his gaze to Isabel with a rueful half smile. 'Some decent food?'

Lady Somerton unbent enough to smile, softening the severe effect of her sombre clothes and hideous matron's cap, and he wondered if he could lure more smiles from her on better acquaintance.

'I'm not sure Doctor Sandler will approve, but I will see what can be done. You're tired. I will leave you in peace.'

He sank back against the feather bolsters that threatened to engulf him in their downy depths and lifted a hand to detain her.

'One last thing: would it be possible to see the London broadsheets?'

He wanted to see the casualty lists. So many friends lay dead on that bloody field. He thought of Major Heyland and the letter his friend had written to his wife on that last night. She would be a grieving widow now, his last words clutched in her hand. He prayed that Waterloo had ended the carnage.

She nodded. 'Of course. You are Lord Somerton. Whatever you wish, you just have to ask.'

With that, she closed the door behind her.

He closed his eyes and considered that statement. *Whatever he wished, he just had to ask.*

Chapter Four

Sebastian ran an appreciative hand over the tooled green leather of the inlaid mahogany writing desk and took a steadying breath. He could hardly bring himself to believe that this desk, like the house itself, now belonged to him. He picked up the pen and drew a sheet of thick cream paper towards him, wondering how to begin this all-important letter to his brother and sister.

Despite Bennet's protestations, he insisted on rising from his bed and dressing in his one set of civilian clothes. His jacket now hung on him, reminding him that once again he had diced with death.

As he had lain in the hospital his only thought had been how they would survive on half pay now that the war was truly over. Some strange fate had, for the first time in his life, dealt him an unexpected hand.

He traced the embossed crest with its five-pointed stars at the head of sheet with his finger—the Somerton coat of arms, he presumed – dipped the nib of the pen in the inkstand, and began to write.

My dearest Connie and Matt. I know Bennet sent word to you that I had been wounded at Waterloo and returned to England. I write now to reassure you that my wound, while unpleasant, is not as bad as last time, and I am well on the road to recovery. However, I have to admit to you that my recovery is due in no small part to a dramatic turn of events that will astonish you. I have been informed that I am the heir to Lord Somerton of Brantstone in Lincolnshire, who died some months ago. He was, it appears, my cousin, and my father his uncle. I have been provided with solid evidence of my parentage, and I am now resident in the London abode, a small, pleasant house of only some 20 bedrooms (Bennet has counted them). When the doctors declare me fit for travel, I intend to travel to the family estate at Brantstone Hall and as soon as I am settled I will send for you both to join me but I think it prudent that you allow me a little time to become accustomed to this change in our fortunes and see what needs to be done to make proper provision for you both, and, of course, Mrs. Mead. I am sure this comes as much a shock to you as it does to me. My soldiering days are done. I must learn to be a gentleman of the aristocracy. Until we meet, S.

He sanded the letter and folded it, sealing it with wax. A seal, engraved with the same coat of arms, had been placed on the silver stand beside the wax. He picked it up and applied it to the wax, shaking his head in disbelief as he inspected the impression of the Somerton coat of arms.

Rising carefully from the chair, his hand going to his side as the barely healed scar caught, he limped over to the door. Beyond it, a wide gallery circled around from a broad, sweeping staircase. Using the balustrade for support, he took the stairs with care, cursing the infernal weakness of ill health.

When he reached the ground floor, he found himself in an elegant, circular entrance hall with a floor of black and white tiles. He turned a slow circle, taking in the elegant Grecian statuary in the alcoves and the fine paintings on the walls.

A number of closed doors, all of which were now his to open, led from the hall. He took a deep breath, hesitating and, for a moment, closed his eyes. Surely this magical world would vanish, and it would all be revealed as a fevered dream. But when he opened his eyes, a white marble statue of Diana and her hounds beamed back at him. He smiled and put his hand to one of the doorknobs.

The first door revealed a dining room dominated by a long, polished table and the second a handsome reception room. The third revealed a bright, cheerful parlour—a woman's room, he thought.

'Captain Alder!'

Lady Somerton rose from a small escritoire as he entered, her eyes wide with surprise. She wore the same gown of black silk that he had seen her in the previous day, unrelieved except for a white collar, fastened by a black mourning brooch and narrow white cuffs at her wrists. Her honey-coloured hair had been scraped away from her face and concealed by an ugly cap. The effect leeched any colour from her face and made her look years beyond her true age, which he guessed to be much of his own years.

Even in the summer light, she appeared pale and forbidding. To effect such severe mourning, he supposed she must have loved her husband very deeply.

'My apologies, Lady Somerton. I should have knocked. I didn't mean to intrude.'

He turned for the door but she took a step towards him her hand outstretched.

'No, no, you are not intruding. Come in and I shall send for some tea. I am only surprised to see you up and about so soon.'

He lowered himself into the chair she proffered, regretting his impetuosity at venturing so far. He had, as usual, overstretched the limits of his body.

He held up the folded paper.

'I have a letter to send.'

Isabel took it from him without glancing at the address.

'I shall put it with my letters and it will go this afternoon.'

He thanked her and leaned his head back against the chair, closing his eyes as he gathered his strength to face the stairs again.

'I sent Bennet on a mission to do some shopping for you, and, if you are up to it, we will arrange for the tailor to come tomorrow,' Isabel said.

Sebastian opened his eyes and looked down at the frayed cuffs of his only civilian coat. He bit his tongue against the protest that rose to his throat.

Every spare penny of his captain's pay went to Matt and Connie, leaving nothing for himself. Despite Bennet's best efforts, even his dress uniform was second-hand and prone to moth holes.

Captain Sebastian Alder had no money to spend on new clothes, but Lord Somerton could hardly appear in public in a coat so old that the black of the fabric had turned to verdigris.

He looked around the bright, sunny room. A glazed door led out into the walled garden he could see from his bedroom window and he longed to throw it open and stride out into the fresh air.

'Now that you are on the road to recovery, I will arrange for Bragge to meet with you,' Isabel said.

'Bragge?'

'You may not remember him from the hospital, but he was Anthony's man of business and his father's before him. There is nothing he can't tell you about the Somerton estate. The lawyers also wish to meet you to explain the details of the entail. You will have plenty to occupy yourself until you are fit to make the journey.'

Sebastian frowned. 'Please forgive me, Lady Somerton, but do you mind if I ask how my cousin died?'

Her lips tightened and she looked down at the cup she was holding.

'A riding accident. The girth of his saddle broke as he was taking a hedge and he fell. He broke his neck.'

'I am sorry.'

'Thank you,' she responded in a flat voice. A lock of dark blonde hair escaped from her cap, but Isabel made no attempt to restore it or to raise her eyes.

Sebastian considered her for a moment. His concern was with the living, not the dead. Was it grief or something else? Anthony was dead, just as Inez... He pushed that memory to the dark corners of his mind. The recent fever had resurrected the old pain, and it gnawed at him like a wound that would not heal.

'Can you tell me more about yourself, Lady Somerton? Did my cousin leave you provided for?'

She raised her head, regarding him for a moment with clear, grey eyes.

'Thank you, Lord Somerton, I have a jointure and the use of the dower house. I shall be quite comfortable and indeed, it is my intention to vacate Brantstone Hall once you are settled.'

'You'll continue to live in the dower house?'

She nodded and her eyes brightened.

'As soon as some urgent repairs are complete but I assure you I shall be quite well occupied and do not intend to be of the least bit of trouble to you.'

He smiled, seeing the excitement light up her eyes. 'And what is it you will be doing to keep yourself so busy?'

'Now I have my own income, it will be the means of financing a school for the daughters of mill workers in the town I came from.'

As she spoke, he heard an animation in her voice he had not heard before. Something within her seemed to come to life, and a flash of the beauty she could have been, were it not for the drab clothes and severe hairstyle, flashed across her oval face.

When he didn't respond, the light in her eyes died, and her chin rose in defiance of the objection she no doubt expected him to raise.

'That sounds like a splendid plan. I look forward to hearing more about it,' he said, rather too quickly, but, in truth, he had neither the strength nor the interest to pursue the subject further at present.

If the woman wanted to start a school, who was he to argue with her? She seemed ideally suited for the role of school ma'am.

He looked at the pale liquid in the delicate cup she had given him. The cup looked absurd in his large hand. He set it down.

'Lady Somerton, I assume that my sudden elevation comes with corresponding duties and responsibilities. Apart from yourself, of course, are there others at Brantstone I should know of?'

She straightened in her chair. 'Firstly, my lord, let me assure you, I am not your responsibility. As to the others, Anthony's impoverished cousins, Mr. and Miss Lynch, are residents at Brantstone but you owe them no duty or responsibility. Then there is your grandmother ...'

Sebastian raised his head. 'My grandmother?'

'On your mother's side. She lives in the village. There are also three aunts and a large assortment of cousins.'

'My grandmother?' Sebastian repeated.

'It was through her we learned of the possibility of your existence. Finding you was another matter. Is something the matter?'

Sebastian stared at her.

Family? He had family of his own?

He recovered his manners. 'Forgive me, Lady Somerton. In all my life there has only ever been myself and my brother, and my sister. I can't even begin to imagine what it will mean to Connie—my sister—to find she has a wider family.'

Isabel looked down at her hands. 'Having no family of my own, Lord Somerton, I can imagine what a joyous surprise this must be for you.'

'No family?'

She raised her face, and her gaze met his. 'None. My parents died when I was a child, and my uncle and aunt, who raised me, are now dead.'

Sebastian thought he should say something, but the words stuck in his throat. He wanted to assure this woman that she would always be welcome in his home and that she was, in his mind anyway, family and under his care and responsibility.

Isabel rose from her seat and fetched an elegant ebony cane from a corner of the room. 'I found this in a cupboard. It belonged to Anthony. He carried it everywhere. He carried it for affectation, but it seems quite sturdy. I thought you may find it useful in your recuperation.'

Sebastian took the cane, inspecting the carved ivory handle bearing the Somerton coat of arms.

'That is a kind thought, Lady Somerton. If I am going to go about like a man of eighty, I may as well look the part.'

Isabel smiled, and again he caught an elusive glimpse of the person behind the severe hairstyle and dark dress. As quickly as it had come, it vanished.

He had a dim memory of thinking her the most beautiful woman he had ever seen. In the right gown and with her hair softened, Lady Somerton had the potential of a rare beauty. He swallowed and reminded himself that, whatever his change in fortune, she would always be the widow of a viscount and he a simple soldier.

With the aid of the cane, he pulled himself to his feet. 'Lady Somerton, thank you for your kindness to me over the last week.'

She turned back to her desk. 'Purely self-interest, my lord.' She looked back at him. 'If the weather is fine, and you feel up to it, it is my custom to take a walk in Kensington Gardens around four in the afternoon. Would you care to join me?'

'In a day or two, perhaps,' Sebastian replied and, with an inclination of his head left her to her letters.

Back in his room, Sebastian found Bennet. The little corporal had laid out his purchases on the bed and stood back with a pleased grin, like a dog expecting praise for fetching a stick. Sebastian eyed the stockings, gloves, drawers, shirts, and neckcloths without interest. As he subsided, exhausted, onto a chair, Bennet poured a glass of port and lulled by the warmth of the fire and the alcohol, Sebastian fell asleep.

Chapter Five

As Isabel and Sebastian strolled the well-kept paths of Kensington Gardens, Isabel wondered why she chose to inflict this particular form of torture on herself. Habit, she supposed. She had chosen to cut herself off from genteel society, and rumours as to the reason abounded. She knew the gossip. The truth would go with her to the grave.

Beside her, Sebastian walked slowly, leaning heavily on the walking stick she had given him, and, behind them, her maid and Bennet kept a respectful distance. Isabel had been out of society for so long that very few people she passed acknowledged her, although a few curious glances were thrown her way. Those who did know her gave her nothing more than a peremptory greeting and expression of feigned sorrow over Anthony's death and waited with an expectant look to be introduced to Sebastian. They went on their way, disappointed.

As they turned a corner, a man and a woman walked along the path towards them, arm in arm, the woman leaning in towards the man and giggling at some private joke. The man looked up and recognition sprang into his face as his gaze fell not on her but her companion.

'Alder! By all the gods, fancy meeting you here.'

The man beside her stiffened.

'Good God! Harry Dempster!'

The two men clasped hands, theirs a fraternity born of long acquaintance, Isabel guessed.

'Alder! I hardly recognise you. How long has it been?'

'Not since you left the regiment, Dempster.' Sebastian turned to Isabel, 'Lady Somerton, my old friend and comrade, Colonel Dempster.'

The woman with the colonel turned to Isabel and she recognised Elizabeth Langmead, wife of Sir John Langmead. Sir John must be absent on one of his diplomatic missions, she thought. A fool to leave his much younger wife alone, prey to every rake in London.

'My, my, Lady Somerton. I thought you resided in the country these days?' the woman said, dropping into a curtsey so slight it bordered on insolent.

'Lady Somerton.' Colonel Dempster bent over her hand. 'I have seen you from afar, but we've never formally met.'

'You've heard of me? Do we have a mutual acquaintance?' Isabel enquired.

'My sister, Georgiana—sorry, Lady Kendall—has a place close to the Somerton estates in Lincolnshire.' He paused. 'She told me the bad news about your husband. I knew him. My commiserations, ma'am.'

This man was Georgiana Kendall's brother? Surely the fates could not be so perverse.

Isabel took a deep breath and forced a smile. 'Thank you. What a small world, Colonel, but you are obviously not acquainted with Captain Alder's news?'

Dempster turned an enquiring eye on his old friend.

'Captain Alder is the new Lord Somerton,' Isabel said.

Harry Dempster stared at her and then at Sebastian. 'You dark horse. I didn't know you were kin of the Somertons.'

'I didn't know myself until recently,' Sebastian said. He glanced at Isabel. 'Still not sure I completely believe it.'

Lady Langmead looked the new Lord Somerton up and down, no doubt taking in the shabby coat with its fraying cuffs and the unbarbered hair that skimmed the top of a badly knotted stock. It would be all through the fashionable salons by tomorrow, Isabel thought.

'I don't think we've had the pleasure, sir,' Lady Langmead said, holding out her hand.

'Lord Somerton,' Isabel said, pointedly addressing Sebastian first, 'may I introduce Lady Langmead?'

Sebastian bowed awkwardly.

Elizabeth Langmead's lip curled slightly, but she did at least do him the courtesy of returning a curtsey.

Harry Dempster spread his arms in an expansive gesture.

'But this is incredible news! Congratulations, Alder. You deserve good fortune, if anyone does. Lady Somerton, where did you find him?'

'Among the wounded of Waterloo, Colonel,' she replied.

Harry turned back to look at Sebastian, his face grave.

'You were there? Was it as bad as they say?'

'Worse,' Sebastian replied, and a look passed between them, the deep understanding of two men who have fought together on the field of battle.

'I'm glad to be out of it.' As if only just recalling the presence of the two women, Harry straightened. 'Alder and I served in Spain together.'

'Another time best forgotten.'

The hard edge to Sebastian's voice made Isabel turn to look at him. She knew so little about this man, beyond the neatly written report on his antecedents provided to her by Bragge. *Served in the Army of the Peninsula 1807 – 1809*, it had read.

'Are you in London for long?' Sebastian addressed Harry.

'No, damn it. Father has summoned me home and I'm off in the morning, but I shall make it my business to escape to Lincolnshire as soon as I can. My sister is much better company than the old man. Are you going up to Brantstone soon?'

'As soon as Lord Somerton is well enough to travel, Colonel,' Isabel responded before Sebastian could reply. She shot the new Lord Somerton a sharp glance. 'He is barely out of his sick bed.'

'Well, perhaps I could call on you. Tonight—?' Harry began but was cut short by his companion.

'Tonight you are engaged to escort me to the Duchess of Rutland's soiree, and we must be on our way,' Lady Langmead said, her lips curling into a petulant pout.

'I am indeed. Then it will have to be Lincolnshire as soon as I can escape the pater. I shall look forward to catching up with you there, Alder... Sorry, Somerton.'

'And I.'

Sebastian leaned on the cane and watched the rapidly retreating back of his friend as he was all but dragged away by Lady Langmead. He closed his eyes, his mouth tightening.

'You're tired. We must get home,' Isabel said.

He nodded and, as they turned back towards Somerton House, he paused and straightened, looking down at Isabel. His lips curved in a smile and he crooked his elbow.

'Would you do me the honour of taking my arm, Lady Somerton?'

She hesitated, but her eyes met his and she found herself smiling in response, as she tucked her gloved hand into the curve of his elbow. Beneath the jacket, the muscles of his forearm tightened at her touch.

'I must leave tomorrow to ensure all is in readiness for your arrival at Brantstone,' she said.

'So soon?'

'Now you are on your feet, my lord, you don't need me. Bragge will see to anything you require.'

He nodded, but without enthusiasm. 'I'm sure he will. Thank you for your kindness, Lady Somerton.'

She glanced up at him and said with absolute honesty, 'Pure self-interest, Lord Somerton. I am pleased to hand over the responsibility of Brantstone to its rightful master.'

Back in the house, she waited until Sebastian had retired to his bedchamber, with Bennet snapping at his heels. Removing her gloves and bonnet, she handed them to her maid, Lucy, and turned for the stairs. As she heard the door to the bedroom close, she allowed herself to smile.

Not long now. Once Sebastian Alder was safely installed at Brantstone, she would be free.

It was all she could do not to bound up the stairs two at a time, while a voice in her head whispered, '*Free! Free!*'

Chapter Six

Sebastian stood at the window, his hands behind his back, looking down at the bustling London street. A blackened chimney sweep passed the time of day with a butcher's boy towing a cart of bloodied packages. Two drunken soldiers lurched past, their arms around each other's shoulders, dark bottles clutched in their hands. Sebastian recognised the facings of their uniforms as belonging to the 59th Regiment of Foot.

Probably *Veterans of Waterloo*, he thought grimly. Soon they would be put out on to half pay, probably forced to beg for a living. Some grim times coming for England's heroes.

A coach stood at the front of the house, the Somerton arms emblazoned on the door. As he watched, Lady Somerton descended the front steps with a quick, firm step, a black feather in her bonnet waving jauntily, at odds with the deep mourning she affected. She handed the bandbox she carried to her maid and allowed one of the footmen to help her into the coach.

Intriguing woman, Sebastian thought, and, as if he had called out to her, she glanced up. She must have seen him at the window and, while her gaze held his for a moment, she did not in any other way acknowledge his presence before the coach drove away. With her departure, he felt oddly cast adrift, as if she had been the one familiar person anchoring him to this strange new life; a life that was proving to be even stranger than he could have imagined, if there was truth in what the lawyer in the room behind him was saying. The Somerton man of business, Bragge, and the lawyer had laid out a complete accounting of the Somerton inheritance.

What inheritance? Sebastian had thought with mounting anger as Bragge and the lawyer revealed the full extent of his cousin's inept management.

It had all gone, expended on clothes and horses and who knew what else besides. There were large, unexplained monthly payments, which Bragge suggested were probably gambling debts, and a foolish investment two years earlier in a gold mine in Guinea, based on a prospectus issued by a group calling themselves *The Golden Adventurers Club*. It was this last bit of idiocy that had taken every last penny, including, it seemed, Isabel's jointure. Brantstone and the London house were mortgaged.

The lawyer's nasal voice ceased, and, Bragge loudly cleared his throat, summoning Sebastian back to the business at hand. He turned around in time to see a quick, uncertain glance pass between the two men. They had every right to be nervous.

Sebastian regarded the man with cold eyes.

'I blame myself,' Bragge said. 'His late lordship was not disposed to confide in me. I had no idea that he had...' The man swallowed, wiping his upper lip with a large kerchief. 'If I had known... In fairness, the damage to the estate should have been more readily ascertainable.'

Any man of business worth his pay should have known to the penny the extent of his master's debts at any given time, regardless of other concerns. Sebastian regarded the man without sympathy. If he had been his quartermaster, Bragge would have been flogged. As it was, he may well find himself looking for a new employer before this day was out.

'Does Lady Somerton know that her jointure is gone?' he enquired.

Bragge shook his head. 'No, my lord.'

Sebastian thought of Isabel's shining eyes as she spoke of her school. How long had she been nurturing this dream? How was he to tell her that all her dreams were dashed because her foolish husband had squandered her money? *Her* money.

'How did he get his hands on the jointure?' Sebastian demanded of the lawyer.

The man swallowed. 'It seems he forged her ladyship's signature on the documents.'

Reprehensible, Sebastian thought, *if not criminal*.

The more he learned of his cousin, the less he liked him. But Anthony was dead and, for some perverse reason, it had fallen to him to clean up the mess.

'Recrimination is not going to restore the fortunes of this estate. I suggest that, for the moment, we do not burden Lady Somerton with this news,' he said, suddenly desperately tired. The sheer effort of trying to digest the figures laid out before him had been exhausting.

Bragge looked at him. 'She should be told, sir.'

'In time,' snapped Sebastian.

Sebastian dismissed the man, unflogged and with his employment still intact, and sat down at the desk. He turned back to the neat rows of figures, trying to find some reason for hope.

Somehow, the money needed to be found to reimburse Isabel for her lost income, but after a while, he shut the books and leaned back in his chair, pressing his fingers together as he concluded that the Somerton inheritance was a tainted privilege.

In some ways he was no better off than he would have been if he had remained a penniless officer of the line on half pay. At least then, he only had his siblings and himself to worry about. Now he had a household and an estate, all claiming pennies from a purse that looked decidedly the worse for wear.

Where had it all gone and how, in God's name, was he expected to restore the family fortunes? If his cousin had walked into the room at that point, Sebastian may well have had to be constrained from breaking the man's neck himself.

Chapter Seven

BRANTSTONE HALL 15 AUGUST 1815

Sebastian waited with mounting impatience for the footmen to set down the steps of the coach before descending. He knew this moment would set the tone for whatever his life would be from now on and if he exited the Somerton coach without a proper degree of dignity all respect would be lost.

The soles of his new boots crunched on the fine gravel, and he looked up at the Palladian mansion with its portico supported by tall columns that soared above him. He hoped his face did not betray the apprehension he felt. From the coach box, he heard Bennet's muttered 'Cor blimey' and smiled. His thoughts exactly.

Lady Somerton waited on the top step, her hands clasped in front of her severe black skirt, her hair concealed within a cap of the type his mother had once favoured. She looked as cold and forbidding as the columns that flanked the portico. However, as he approached, a smile twitched at the corners of her lips.

'Welcome to Brantstone, Lord Somerton,' she said.

'Thank you, Lady Somerton,' he replied with an answering smile.

He leaned heavily on the ebony cane to catch his breath. He probably should have remained in London for another week, as the doctor advised, but he was anxious to pick up the reins of his new life.

'Allow me to introduce you to the staff,' Lady Somerton said. She stood back and followed him into the house.

The front hall of the house in London was only an echo of this magnificent entranceway, around which the entire staff of the house had been assembled to meet their new master— everyone from the steward and the housekeeper to the lowliest kitchen hand.

A young girl stepped forward with a posy of flowers, which she presented to him with a shy curtsey. Sebastian stooped to the girl's level. He took the flowers and asked her name.

'Matilda, my lord,' she said in a small voice, her wide, surprised eyes meeting his as if she couldn't believe he would deign to address her.

'Where do you work?' He asked.

'In't kitchen, m'lord.'

He straightened and smiled at the child. 'Thank you, Matilda.'

He went around the circle, making a point of greeting every staff member, asking their name and position, and hoping he would remember. He had always made it a point to know the name of every man in his company, and he did not consider a household staff much different. He had thought the matter through in the tedious hours in the coach and decided that if he thought of the task ahead as being akin to a sudden promotion to colonel of a regiment, it did not seem so daunting.

The greetings done, the staff dispersed, leaving only the housekeeper, introduced as Mrs.. Fletcher, and a footman who helped him off with his travelling coat and new hat.

'Would you care to take a cup of tea?' Lady Somerton enquired, indicating a door to her left.

Sebastian thought longingly of a comfortable bed and a tankard of beer. Instead, he ignored his body's protests and mustered a smile. A tankard of beer would probably be thought indelicate, and rest could wait. He had dispatched Bennet to the bookshops of London to seek out some books of instruction in etiquette. Although he had found these most instructive, he had so much to learn.

He was not a complete stranger to the ways of the upper echelons of society. As the Reverend Alder's eldest son, he had been a frequent visitor to the 'big house' at Little Benning, being deemed a suitable companion to Sir Richard's sickly son. The boy had not lived to adulthood, and, to ease his grief, perhaps, Sir Richard had been kind to the young Sebastian, even purchasing his commission as an ensign. But Sir Richard, too, had followed his son to the grave, and with him went his patronage. From that moment, Sebastian had been on his own.

The old, rambling home of a baronet bore no comparison to this mansion. Money, and plenty of it, had built Brantstone. He wondered what nefarious practices his forebears had indulged in to allow the purchase of such an ostentatious building.

He followed Isabel across the black and white tiles towards a heavy door. Before he could reach for the door knob, a footman sprang forward and opened the door admitting Sebastian and Isabel into a pleasant parlour, the windows hung with blue velvet curtains. As he crossed the threshold, a young man, who had been sitting on a well-upholstered chair, sprang to his feet. A heavy lock of bright fair hair fell across his face in his haste, and he brushed it back with a delicate hand as he advanced to greet Sebastian.

'Lord Somerton... cousin... if I might make so bold.' He thrust out a hand. 'Welcome, welcome, welcome.'

In the face of this effusive greeting, and more out of reflex than politeness, Sebastian took the proffered hand and shook it.

'Thank you, er ...' He glanced at Isabel.

'My apologies, Lord Somerton. I mentioned Mister Lynch and his sister, who are guests here at Brantstone,' she said.

'Frederick Lynch, your servant, sir.' The young man bowed. 'And may I present my sister, Frances. But please, as we are kin, Fanny and Freddy to your lordship.'

A young woman, who had been reclining on a brocaded daybed, rose to her feet and curtsied, holding out her hand.

Two eyes the colour of cornflowers looked up at him from a small, peaked face framed by ringlets the same shade as her brother's hair. He could not take his eyes off the rosebud mouth, which his brother officers would have described as 'eminently kissable'.

'Please sit,' Lady Somerton said, indicating a chair. 'I will pour tea.' As she handed Sebastian a bowl and saucer, she said, 'As I explained to you in London, Mister and Miss Lynch are cousins of my late husband.'

The two Lynchs smiled at Sebastian. Frederick was one of those young men with classical looks who could be any age— high cheekbones and dark, soulful eyes with a full, soft mouth and a receding chin. Sebastian had seen his sort in the army, often the younger sons of the aristocracy with purchased commissions and no idea of how to lead men. More at home in a drawing room than on a battlefield, they generally died in their first action.

Fanny took a sip of tea. 'Cousin Sebastian, I do hope you are recovered from your terrible wound?'

Sebastian made the mistake of looking at her and, once again, found himself drowning in a pair of the bluest eyes he had ever seen.

'Er, yes, thank you,' he stuttered.

'We've been simply dying to meet you ever since we received word of your existence and then dear Isabel saw your name in the casualty lists and went flying off to London,' Fanny continued, apparently oblivious of the effect she was having on him. 'It's just been too, too exciting. Now here you are.'

'Excellent,' Freddy put in for good measure. 'We despaired of ever finding an heir, didn't we, Cousin Isabel?'

Sebastian glanced at Isabel. Her face, as appeared to be her custom, betrayed little, and he wondered if she kept everything so tightly contained that one day it would just burst from her.

'We did indeed,' she agreed, lifting the cup to her lips and taking a sip. As she set it back in the saucer, she said, 'Tell me, Lord Somerton, what did your brother and sister make of the news?'

He smiled at the memory of Connie's reply to his letter. It had been filled with scratching out and exclamation marks and demands to know when she and Matt could join him.

'I don't think they believe me. My sister's letter was almost unintelligible.'

'Oh, you have a brother and sister,' Fanny declared. 'How marvellous. Are they Kingsleys too?'

'No. They are my half-siblings. My brother, Matthew, teaches at the local grammar school, and my sister, Constance, is an artist. She paints miniatures.'

Fanny blinked. 'They work?'

The comment brought Sebastian up with a jolt. Of course they worked. His captain's pay alone was barely enough to support them. As soon as Matt had been old enough, he had taken a teaching post at the village school. Any thought of Oxford had been out of the question. Connie's choice of profession had been her own. She had told him in no uncertain terms that she wished to contribute to the household, and her considerable artistic talent would be otherwise wasted. For someone so young, she had already garnered several lucrative commissions.

'When will they be arriving?' Isabel cut in before Sebastian could respond.

Sebastian's gaze drifted to the window and the wide expanse of parkland beyond. His land, he presumed.

'I thought it best to wait a little while. At least until I've found my feet.'

Fanny gave a small cry of distress, her hand flying to a well-endowed bosom that threatened at any moment to burst free of the low-cut neckline of her dress.

'Oh, but you simply can't leave them to moulder in some dreary little corner. You must bring them to Brantstone.' She reached across and took her brother's hand, looking up at him with a fond smile. 'Freddy and I have been talking, and we think you should hold a ball. The neighbours must be simply dying to meet the new Lord Somerton and what better way than a ball?'

'A ball?' Isabel set her cup down, the cup rattling in the saucer.

'Oh! With your agreement of course, Cousin Isabel,' Fanny said. 'Any earlier would have been quite improper, but you did say you would be moving to the dower house as soon as the new Lord Somerton was installed.'

'The dower house is not quite ready and I am still officially in mourning,' Isabel said. She paused and glanced at Sebastian, 'Although for once, I must agree with you, Fanny. I think a ball would be an excellent way to introduce the new Lord Somerton to our society.'

Fanny clasped her hands together. 'Oh, dear Isabel, I'm so glad you are in agreement.'

Sebastian glanced at Isabel, looking for rescue, but he seemed to be on his own.

'I'm not sure a ball—' he began.

'Somerton,' Freddy broke in. 'A ball at Brantstone will launch you into society. It will be the talk of the county.'

'I don't need to be launched into society—' Sebastian began to say, but Fanny had already moved ahead.

'Freddy and I are set on the first week in September. Aren't we, Freddy?'

'Absolutely,' Freddy concurred.

Sebastian cast another desperate look at Isabel. This time she returned a sympathetic smile.

'That's only six weeks, Fanny,' Isabel observed.

'Plenty of time. Please don't concern yourself, Lady Somerton. I know you will be quite busy enough with the dower house. Freddy and I are happy to organise it all and it will be marvellous to be of some use.' Fanny shot Sebastian a smile of such incredible sweetness that his opposition to the very idea of a ball melted. 'And of course, Lord Somerton, I hope that your brother and sister will be here by then. It will be a wonderful welcome to them and set you up in fine form for the season. You can't say no, dear Cousin Sebastian.'

They both returned his horrified look with hopeful smiles.

He cleared his throat and tugged at his neck cloth. 'If you think that it is an appropriate way for me to start this new role, then so be it. But don't expect me to dance, Miss Lynch.'

Fanny blinked. 'Not dance? But why ever not, Cousin Sebastian? Oh dear, do you have a bad leg? Remember, Freddy, poor Miles Otterley could not dance because he had a French musket ball lodged in his knee.'

'Oh yes, poor fellow, walked with a dreadful limp,' her brother concurred.

Sebastian opened his mouth to protest that, while he did have a 'bad leg', he had his own reasons for not dancing that had nothing to do with a French musket ball, but Isabel cut across him with a comment about the weather.

Chapter Eight

Isabel glanced up at the clock on the mantelpiece and across at the new Lord Somerton, noticing the pinched look around his nose and mouth. An hour with the Lynchs when fully fit would be an ordeal. Now he just looked exhausted.

She rose to her feet, prompting the two men to stand.

'If you wish, Lord Somerton, allow me to show you the house,' she suggested.

He reached for the ebony cane. 'I think, Lady Somerton, that can wait. For now I would be thankful for the opportunity to rest before supper.'

'Of course. I will show you to your rooms.'

He turned at the door and inclined his head. 'Mister Lynch, Miss Lynch.'

As they made their way up the stairs, Sebastian asked in a low voice, 'Forgive me asking, Lady Somerton, but who exactly are those people?'

A fair question, Isabel considered. 'They are cousins of Anthony's on his mother's side, so no blood kin of yours.' She turned to look at him. 'You owe them no obligation at all. Anthony found them in straitened circumstances about a year ago, and they have lived here on his grace and favour ever since.'

'Did he make no allowance for them in his will?'

'No,' she said shortly.

'What am I expected to do with them?'

They had reached the top of the stairs and Isabel turned to look at him.

'It is not for me to say. You are Lord Somerton. It is your decision as to whether you throw them out or make some sort of settlement on them.'

He stared back at her. 'Throw them out? I can hardly do that, Lady Somerton.'

Isabel swallowed the scathing retort that rose in her throat. They had been uninvited guests in this house long enough. Freddy was quite capable of making his own way in the world, but chose not to. As for Fanny, lack of a respectable dowry, or indeed any dowry, lessened her attractions on the marriage market. She was reaching an age when she could be considered unmarriageable and should be grateful for any offer she received, but Freddy seemed set on a 'good' marriage for his sister and had resisted suggestions of suitable husbands for Fanny. '*Nothing less than a title, my dear Lady Somerton,*' he had said. '*It's what she deserves.*'

She changed the subject. 'When your sister arrives, you will have a lady to grace your table, Lord Somerton. It is my hope that the work on the dower house will be complete and I will take my leave of you then.'

Before he could respond, she threw open the door of the bedchamber. Sebastian stood in the doorway and looked around the magnificent room that occupied the end of the west wing of the house, running the full depth of the building.

He leaned on the cane with both hands and shook his head. 'I swear, Lady Somerton, the entire contents of my cottage would be lost in this room.'

'It is a little ostentatious,' Isabel agreed.

A huge four-poster bed, draped with green silk hangings, dominated the room, which had been decorated with a green silk wallpaper that matched the bed hangings. Sebastian reached out to trace the design of herons that fluttered across the pale fabric.

'Of course, you may decorate to your own taste, my lord,' Isabel said.

He turned and gave her a half smile. 'I wouldn't know where to start.'

A discreet cough came from behind them. Both Sebastian and Isabel turned.

'My lord, welcome to Brantstone Hall,' said a ponderous voice.

'And you are?' Sebastian enquired.

'Pierce, my lord. I am your lordship's valet. I apologise for not being downstairs to greet you. I was detained in ensuring all was in readiness for you.'

'Valet?' Sebastian glanced at Isabel.

"Ere, what about me?' Bennet had appeared in the doorway, carrying Sebastian's battered campaign trunk. 'He don't need a valet. I've been his batman these fifteen years past.'

'And I have been valet to the last two Lord Somertons.' Pierce looked down his nose at the interloper into his kingdom.

Sebastian turned to Isabel and she read the look of mute appeal in his eyes.

'I think for the moment—Pierce, Bennet—we should all leave Lord Somerton to get some rest. And might I suggest, Pierce, that his lordship takes supper in his rooms tonight?'

'Very good, m'lady. I shall tell the kitchen.' Pierce bowed and made off at a stately pace.

Isabel excused herself and closed the door behind her.

Returning to the parlour, she found Freddy and Fanny engaged in a game of Piquet. Freddy suggested a game of Pope Joan, but she declined, picking up her embroidery frame.

'Oh, my dear Isabel,' Freddy said, without moving his eyes from his cards, 'we will have our work cut out with our new Lord Somerton.'

Isabel looked up. 'What do you mean?'

'My dear, the way he talks. And his clothes! He has no idea, does he?'

Isabel stiffened. 'I think he will soon adapt, Freddy, and if I may make an observation, I do not think he will take kindly to any instruction from you.'

Freddy swivelled in his chair to look at her. He placed a hand on his chest, a frown creasing his forehead and a pained look in his eye.

'What do you mean?'

'May I remind you, he is no kin of yours, Freddy. You would be advised to start looking to your own future.'

'Oh, he wouldn't throw us out, would he?' Fanny declared, her blue eyes wide.

Isabel stabbed the needle into the cloth. 'It is not for me to say what Lord Somerton will do.'

Out of the corner of her eye, she caught the quick look that passed between the siblings. Was it fear?

Chapter Nine

Obadiah Bennet took the cup proffered by Mrs.. Fletcher, the housekeeper, and stretched out his legs. He had been invited to take a chair beside the fire, which burned due to the unseasonable cool of the evening, and here he was taking tea with Mrs.. Fletcher and Mr. Pierce.

It had not taken batman and valet long to settle their differences. At the age of seventy-five, Pierce told Bennet he would be pleased to teach the younger man the fine art of being a 'gentleman's gentleman' and Bennet had agreed with alacrity.

'That's a fine cuppa,' Bennet told the housekeeper, who acknowledged the praise with a small bob of her head.

'It is such a relief to have Lord Somerton here at last, isn't it, Mr. Pierce?' she said. 'He seems like a steady sort of man.' She leaned forward. 'So tell me, Mr. Bennet, is he a single gentleman?'

Bennet hesitated. 'He is, Mrs.. Fletcher.'

'Oh, but he's a fine-looking man,' she persisted. 'Surely there's been a woman in his life?'

Before Bennet could respond, Pierce cleared his throat. 'My dear Bennet, you hear and see things as a valet. The first lesson is: discretion.' He tapped his nose. 'One does not question or gossip about one's master.'

'Of course,' Bennet agreed.

The terrible fate of Mrs.. Alder, as he liked to think of her, was no one's business but his captain's, and he, Bennet, would carry it to his grave.

Mrs.. Fletcher sat back in her chair, clearly disappointed.

'The late Lord Somerton was not easy,' she said with a heavy sigh. 'Never knew his comings and goings.'

'Not a happy man,' Pierce conceded, apparently contravening his own first rule. 'Lovely wife, estates, money and still not content.' He shrugged.

'It was the child's death,' Mrs.. Fletcher said.

'Child?' Bennet asked.

Mrs.. Fletcher sighed. 'Aye, such a bonny boy he was too. Nursemaid found him dead in his cradle just over a year ago. Broke her ladyship's heart. She's worn mourning ever since. And then his lordship went only a few months later. That's enough sadness for anybody to have in their life.'

Bennet, born in the slums of London, had seen too many children die to take anything more than a pragmatic view of such events.

'Drove his lordship back to his wicked ways in London,' Pierce said with a shake of his head.

'Still, he didn't deserve to die the way he did.' Mrs.. Fletcher took a delicate sip of her tea.

''How did he die?' Bennet enquired.

'It was a riding accident. The girth on his saddle snapped when he was taking a hedge. He broke his neck in the fall and they found him cold and dead in the morning,' Mrs.. Fletcher said. 'Of course, what he was doing out at that hour of the night, and visiting a lady no less...'

Bennet pricked up his ears. 'A lady?'

Mrs.. Fletcher's lips tightened. 'That Lady Kendall. Three

husbands she's had, they do say.' Her lips pursed. 'For all her fine ways, she isn't any better than she ought to be.'

'Now, now, Mrs.. Fletcher. That's enough,' Mr. Pierce chided.

The door of the servant's hall opened, and a man and a woman entered. The staff around Bennet immediately stiffened. The man, a big fellow with a round, unformed face like a bowl of dough, looked at Bennet. His companion, a young woman with a crooked eye, gave him a humourless smile.

'This 'ere must be the new lord's man,' she said.

Bennet stood up and held out his hand. 'Bennet, pleased to meet you ...'

Neither the man nor the woman moved or responded.

'This is MMr.Jenkins and his sister, Sally,' Mrs. Fletcher said. 'They serve Mr. and Miss Lynch.'

The man grunted something unintelligible, jerked his head at his sister and turned away, his sister following. As the door shut behind them again, Bennet subsided back on to his seat.

'Strange cove,' he commented.

'Mute,' Pierce said. 'He had his tongue cut out. Don't know what for, but it's a horrible sight. You don't want to annoy him.'

'So who are these Lynchs?' Bennet asked.

Mrs.. Fletcher shrugged. 'Cousins of the late lord. Came here as guests about a year ago and have never left.'

Bennet jerked his head at the door. 'And did those two come with them?'

Mrs.. Fletcher nodded. 'God knows who is paying them. The Lynchs don't have a penny between them, but the Jenkins are nothing if not loyal.' She straightened. 'Another cup of tea, Mr. Bennet? And can I tempt you to a slice of cake?'

Bennet settled back with a contented sigh. He'd had his fill of soldiering and the new turn of events gave him great hope for a comfortable future. No more flea-ridden billets and starvation rations. A comfy bed and three meals a day for the rest of his life.

Bennet was a truly happy man.

Chapter Ten

True to his soldier's habit, Sebastian woke with the first light of day. He rose feeling stiff from the long coach ride, but otherwise better than he had felt in weeks. He knew Bennet would be firmly of the opinion that he should rest, but if he had to endure being cooped up in his bedchamber for any longer, he would start looking for someone to kill, beginning with Bennet.

He dressed himself, not bothering with a neckcloth, pulled on his old boots, and, feeling like a fifteen-year-old playing truant from school, tiptoed out of his room and down the back stairs.

He passed the kitchens, which were a hive of activity, unnoticed and escaped into the cool, clear air of what promised to be a beautiful summer day. Swinging the ebony cane, he took a deep, grateful breath and set out down the long, winding driveway, scattering sheep who had strayed on to the path. As he passed the gatehouse that stood to one side of the magnificent gates, surmounted with the now familiar Somerton crest, he paused to greet the gatekeeper, introduced himself to the astonished man and his wife, and asked the directions to the village.

A few hundred yards past the gate, he entered the village of

Brantstone. The residents had begun to stir and he stopped at the inn, interrupting the publican who was .rolling empty wine barrels out of the front door. The man gave his name as Wilkins.

'My lord, 'tis early, but will you step into the parlour for some breakfast?'

Sebastian knew he probably should have refused, but the smell of frying bacon wafted out into the street.

Wilkins preceded him into the cool interior with a bellow of 'Mrs. Wilkins! Put on some extra bacon. We've a guest.'

A red-faced woman poked her head out of the kitchen.

'Good mornin', sir,' she said. ''Tis early for a traveller.'

Sebastian opened his mouth to introduce himself, but Wilkins was ahead of him.

'This ain't no traveller, Martha. This 'eres the new lord.'

The woman dropped into a hasty curtsey. 'Oh sir, I should have known. One look at you and I could sees you're a Somerton. You take a seat in the parlour and I'll bring you a breakfast to remember.'

Sebastian ducked his head to enter the parlour, his heels ringing on the spotless flagstones. Wilkins pulled out a chair at the table and Mrs. Wilkins appeared almost immediately with a pot of small ale in one hand and a heaped plate in the other.

'You won't get better up at the Hall,' she said. 'We heard how as you was wounded at Waterloo, and may I say you still look a mite peaky. A good breakfast'll set you straight for the day.'

Sebastian tucked in with relish. He indicated for Wilkins to sit with him while he ate and the publican complied.

'Tell me about the village,' Sebastian asked.

'Depends what you want to know, sir,' Wilkins responded.

'Mr. Bragge has given me the formal facts and figures but I want to know about the people.'

He wanted to know about their lives, their children, their concerns, and who better to inform him than the landlord of the pub?

Wilkins seemed happy to comply and chattered on while Sebastian ate his meal. As Sebastian mopped his plate with a hunk of still-warm bread he asked about his cousin's accident. The landlord leaned back in his chair.

'Ah, 'twas a sad business with his late lordship. I was in the search party that found him.'

'Tell me where the accident happened.'

'His lordship liked to take a shortcut across the fields. He'd done it a hundred times afore.'

'I heard the girth broke.'

Wilkins nodded. 'Saw the saddle myself. It had come off, of course, when he fell. Brand new it was.'

Sebastian leaned forward. 'And Lord Somerton? What were his injuries?'

Wilkins pulled a face. 'His neck was broken, you could see that as soon as look at him. Not a pretty sight, but you're a soldier, my lord. I don't need to tell you ...'

'Quite,' agreed Sebastian. 'Were there any other injuries?'

'Broken leg and... no... I think that was it.'

'What are you gossiping about now?' Martha Wilkins swooped down on the table. 'I tell you, m'lord, he's worse than an old woman.'

'His lordship was asking about the late lord's death.'

Mrs.. Wilkins shook her head. 'That was a terrible shock. God's punishment for his wicked ways, I say.'

'Now then, Mrs. Wilkins ...' the landlord protested, but Sebastian ignored him.

'What do you mean?'

Mrs. Wilkins bridled, smoothing an imaginary crease from her spotless apron. 'I'm not one to gossip but they do say he was over visiting that Lady Kendall. A frequent visitor, from what I hear, and he's not the only one. Like bees to honey ...' She shook her head in approbation. 'Three husbands she's had and not content that she's got to have someone else's husband.'

'That's enough now, Mrs. Wilkins.' The landlord pushed his chair back and stood up, signalling the end of the conversation.

Sebastian, too, rose to his feet, narrowly avoiding bumping his head on one of the low beams.

'Thank you, Mrs. Wilkins. That was the best breakfast I've had in a long time. You may see me on an early morning stroll more often.'

Mrs. Wilkins picked up the clean platter and smiled with satisfaction.

'My lord, you are more'n welcome and I won't think of taking payment for it,' she added huffily as he set some coins down on the table.

'Well, save it for someone who needs it,' Sebastian said. 'Thank you both for your hospitality. Ouch!' he exclaimed as he failed to miss the door lintel. 'I fear your inn was built for shorter people.'

'You are uncommon tall for these parts, m'lord,' Wilkins observed. 'Just like your father. He was a good six fingers taller than his brother.'

A familiar sense of regret at the mention of a father he had never known tugged at Sebastian. As he strolled past the pond, he wondered if there had been any likenesses of James Kingsley preserved up at the hall, among the gallery of ancestors that seemed to line every wall. He made a mental note to ask Lady Somerton.

A pretty church built of the local grey stone with a single, squat Norman tower stood on the far side of the village green. Despite the early hour, the door to the church stood partly ajar. He pushed it open and stepped inside, allowing his eyes a moment or two to become accustomed to the gloom.

A woman knelt on the steps of the sanctuary, scrubbing the well-worn stone. She started at the sound of his boots and rose to her feet, turning to see whom the intruder could be.

'My apologies, madam, I didn't mean to disturb you,' Sebastian said.

The light from the window fell on her face and he took a step back. For a moment, just a fleeting moment, he thought he had come face to face with the ghost of his mother. The instant passed, and he saw just a small, middle-aged woman whose grey hair had escaped her sensible cap with the exertion of her work.

The woman stared at him and then, as if recovering herself, dropped into a curtsey.

'You're not disturbing me, my lord.' She set the cloths down and approached him, her eyes not leaving his face. 'You are the new Lord Somerton, aren't you?' Seeing him in the light, her hands flew to her face, and she gasped. 'You're so like your father.'

She reached out as if she intended to touch his face and then dropped as she remembered her place. Sebastian held his breath. Another person who not only knew his father, but probably his mother as well.

She smiled and, for a moment, he caught again that flash of something very familiar in her face as she read his thoughts.

'I knew them both, my lord. Your mother and I shared a bed from the time we were small girls. I'm your aunt, Margaret, but the family calls me Peggy,' the woman replied to his unspoken question.

So he had not been mistaken about the family resemblance. Something lost within him had told him that this woman was related to him. Isabel had told him that his mother had left behind a large family.

How did one greet long-lost aunts? Kiss them, hug them, shake their hands? He settled for a foolish grin.

'I've been expecting you!' his aunt chided. 'Ever since we heard they'd found you, we've been waiting for this day. After all 'twas mother and I who told Mr. Bragge about you and set them off on the search.' She held out her hand to him. 'Come and meet your gran. Marjory was always her favourite.'

'It's too early... I'm not dressed.'

Sebastian groped for excuses. Accidental encounters with long-lost aunts was one thing, grandmothers quite another.

Peggy took his hand. 'She'd not care if you came in rags,' she said. 'She's been waiting more than thirty years for this day.'

Sebastian followed his aunt out of the church to the gate of a small cottage only yards away from the church. She paused and turned to look at him.

'My father—your grandfather, that is—died ten years ago, and the old lord granted us a grace and favour cottage. It's not much, I know, but it does us well enough.'

The wicket gate opened with a protesting squeak and he followed her up the gravel path to the front door. Peggy opened the door and turned back to him.

'You wait here,' she said, and then, as if remembering who she addressed, she added with an embarrassed smile, 'if you don't mind, my lord. I need a moment or two to make sure Ma is ready.'

While Sebastian waited, he could hear Peggy's low voice in the parlour. He went over in his mind what he should say to this long-lost grandparent, and it seemed an age before his aunt appeared, standing back to admit him to the little room. Once again, Sebastian ducked his head to avoid the low beams and wondered if the entire village had been constructed by midgets.

An elderly woman sat in a chair beside the fire, looking just as he had imagined a grandmother should look. Fluffs of white hair escaped from her neat lace cap and milky blue eyes looked up at him from a face that looked as fragile as tissue.

'Lord Somerton, Ma,' Peggy announced, unnecessarily.

'You'll have to come closer, boy,' the old woman said. 'My eyes aren't that good.'

'She's all but blind and quite a bit deaf, so you'll need to talk clear,' Peggy whispered in his ear.

Sebastian went down on one knee at the woman's feet and took her hand. He kissed it, the delicate skin like paper beneath his lips. When he looked up, she had tears in her eyes. Her hand went to his hair, caressing him as if he were a small child.

'I never thought I'd see the day when Marjory's boy would come to me,' she said as her gnarled fingers moved to his face, lightly touching his eyes, his nose and his mouth as if the touch would in some way produce a picture in her mind. 'You've a good strong face,' she said and smiled, cuffing him lightly on the cheek. 'And you have come out without shaving. That will never do!'

'He's as like his father as he could be,' Peggy said.

'Oh, he was a good boy, James,' his grandmother said, 'but headstrong like our girl.'

As he straightened, Sebastian found himself completely bereft of the well-rehearsed words. He coughed to disguise the unfamiliar prickling sensation at the back of his throat.

'I ... I... have a brother and a sister. Your grandchildren, too.'

The old lady looked in the general direction of her daughter.

'Oh, Peggy. All these years and we never knew.' She turned back to Sebastian, her fingers found his and she squeezed them tightly as if afraid to let go. 'Your grandfather, the Reverend, was undone by her eloping with the lord's son. He forbade letters from Marjory. If she ever sent them, he threw them unopened into the fire.' Her voice shook with emotion as she said, 'We only heard she was dead by sheer chance. That good man, the Reverend Alder, passed a message by word of mouth to a friend, and he whispered it to me when he came to visit.' She shook her head as if trying to vanquish the memory.

Sebastian lowered his head. If it hadn't been for the kindness of the Reverend Alder, both he and his mother would have ended up in the workhouse—or dead. Such unspeakable cruelty by her own father beggared belief.

As if answering his unspoken words, his grandmother continued. 'You mustn't judge your grandfather, lad. Marjory was promised to marry a young clergyman from over Grantham way. He's a bishop now. Her running off like that, jilting her intended, and with the lord's son doing the same to his young lady, and him with not a penny to his name after his father cut him out.' She shook her head and lowered her eyes. 'It brought terrible shame to this house.'

So that was how it had happened. His parents had both been betrothed to other people, facing two loveless marriages or the fleeting chance of happiness together, even with the approbation of family and society. Whatever happiness they had enjoyed had been short lived. He wondered if his mother had appealed to her father after James had died. If she had, it sounded like her cry for help fell on stony ground. So much for Christian charity.

He glanced out of the window at the solid respectability of the church building and shook his head. These were matters that belonged in the past. His mother's second marriage to the Reverend Alder had been a happy one and she had died greatly loved and greatly mourned.

His grandmother echoed his thoughts. 'Those are sad memories we must leave in the past. You are here now, where you rightly belong, and I know your mother and father would be proud of you. A hero of Waterloo, Peggy tells me.'

Sebastian laughed. 'Hardly a hero, grandmother. Merely lucky to still be alive.'

'But you were hurt?' She frowned. 'Are you recovered?'

'I am,' he replied. 'Lady Somerton ensured I had the best of care.'

'Ah, Lady Somerton! She's a good lady.' His grandmother nodded with approval. 'Not like that good-for-nothing husband of hers.'

'Mother!' Peggy reproved.

'I'm too old not to speak my mind, Peggy, and you know it. The late lord did more to undo this estate in a few short years than his ancestors had spent in building it up. And the way he behaved after the baby died... Disgraceful.'

'Baby?' Sebastian asked, but his grandmother didn't hear.

'Edie!' The old woman called, and a young maid appeared at

the door, bobbing a quick curtsey and colouring when she saw the two ladies had a visitor.

'Edie, some tea, and bring some freshly-baked bread and our strawberry jam. His lordship looks like he needs feeding up.'

Sebastian opened his mouth to protest that he had already had a large breakfast, but the maid had vanished. He was desperate to ask about the baby, but he had to curb his impatience until Edie reappeared with a tray of tea and bread and jam.

Only after his aunt had ensured that he had been served a doorstopper-sized slice of bread and had a hot cup of tea did he feel he could return to the subject.

'Grandmother,' he said, noting that she coloured with pleasure at the new mode of address, 'what were you saying about a baby?'

Peggy answered for her mother. 'You don't know? Well, I suppose you wouldn't unless her ladyship has told you, which she obviously hasn't.' She took a sip of her tea and settled in to impart the gossip. 'After all those years of marriage, her ladyship had a baby boy. William, they called him. A bonny little lad he was, wasn't he, Ma?'

'Oh, he was. All smiles and chuckles during his christening... His mother and father just doted on the boy. Never seen them really happy together, but the baby seemed to heal the rift. You go on, Peggy.'

'It was so sad,' Peggy continued. 'When the babe was only six months old, the nursemaid found him dead in his cradle. Not a mark on his little body, she told me, just cold and dead.'

Sebastian set his empty cup down, recalling Isabel's words. *'As Anthony and I were not blessed with children, you are the heir to my husband's estate ...'* She had been blessed, but for such a short time.

'When was this?'

Peggy frowned. 'It would be about a year ago now. They both took the death hard, in their own ways. Her ladyship became ... well ... as you see her now, and his lordship went back to his wild ways. Drinking and gambling, so they say ...' Peggy continued.

'Now, Peggy, that is gossip,' her mother said.

'It's fact, Ma. We all know who he was visiting the night he died. That Lady Kendall—'

'Peggy!'

That Lady Kendall again, thought Sebastian. He would like to make the acquaintance of Harry's scandalous sister. As he took a bite of the still warm bread and the tastiest strawberry jam he had ever eaten, he thought about Isabel and her dowdy clothes and severe hairstyle and realised that she did not wear mourning for her husband but for her child, barely a year in the grave.

Peggy sniffed and glared at her mother. 'I'm sorry Lord Somerton had to die like that but if it meant a good man, our Sebastian, came home, then that is God's will,' she concluded.

Sebastian brushed the crumbs from his breeches.

'Are the Somerton family graves in the church?' he asked.

'Only the old ones. Your great-great-grandfather, had a mausoleum built on the hill looking over the Somerton lands. 'Tis that white building beyond the lake. 'Twas he that built the hall, earned his money trading in slaves,' Peggy added with pursed lips that indicated her disapproval.

Sebastian agreed with her. His fortune, such of it as had been left to him by successive generations, had been built on the misfortune of others. It was indeed a tainted inheritance.

'Enough dark talk,' his grandmother said. 'Tell me about your brother and sister while Peggy pours us another cup of tea.'

Sebastian told them about Matt and Connie and their life in the vicarage at Little Benning before his stepfather's death. His aunt and grandmother sat in silence, hanging on his every word. Peggy, in her turn, told him about his aunts and the veritable tribes of cousins. It was only when the clock on the shelf chimed ten that Sebastian jumped to his feet.

'They'll be wondering where I am,' he said. 'I must go. We will... we must... you must...'

He struggled to find some words to say that he wanted them to come to the hall, to visit, to live, to be with him. They were his real family. Not outsiders like Fanny and Freddy.

Peggy put a hand on his sleeve. 'All in good time, my lord. We're content, more so for knowing you are here. You will bring Matthew and Constance to see us, when they arrive?'

'Of course, and I will visit again.'

As he walked away from the little cottage, a knot of emotion gathered in his chest and he found he had to choke back unaccustomed tears.

Chapter Eleven

'Where's Sebastian this morning?' Fanny enquired as Isabel sat down at the table for breakfast.

Isabel raised an eyebrow at Fanny's peremptory tone and the familiar use of Lord Somerton's forename. 'While it is no business of yours, *Lord* Somerton is probably feeling the effect of the long journey and, if he has any sense, he will spend a few days resting and recuperating.'

The door burst open, and Sebastian strode in. His appearance caused even Freddy to lay down the broadsheet he had been reading.

Isabel took a breath. Far from resembling the languishing invalid whose portrait she had just painted, Sebastian had a good colour in his unshaven face. It didn't look as if a comb had seen his hair, and he wore his shirt open at the neck with no neckcloth, under a long, green coat. In this dishevelled state he exuded energy.

In their short acquaintance, she hadn't seen him looking so—she struggled for a word—alive.

'Breakfast?' Fanny enquired, staring at this apparition.

Sebastian glanced at the groaning board. 'Er, no. I've already eaten. I was looking for the London broadsheets. Parker said they had arrived. Ah... you have them, Lynch.'

Freddy folded the papers and, as he handed them over, he remarked, 'My dear fellow, you haven't been out looking like that?'

Sebastian looked down at his ensemble. 'Looking like what?'

'My dear Somerton. Unshaven... no neckcloth.' Freddy's mouth formed a moue of disapproval.

'I've been for a walk. I didn't intend on social calling but as it happened, I had a long talk to Wilkins the publican, and I met my aunt and grandmother.' He glanced at Isabel. 'A delightful surprise. And as every woman in the village seemed intent on fattening me up, I have no room for anything more to eat. No thank you, Johnson,' Sebastian waved aside the footman with a proffered dish of kidneys.

Freddy's knife clattered on the plate, and he glanced at Isabel. Isabel read the horror in his eyes. One *never* acknowledged a servant by name. She picked up her napkin and dabbed at her lips to hide the smile.

As Sebastian turned to leave the room, Freddy straightened in his chair. 'You're probably unaware, Somerton, that now you have arrived at Brantstone, there will be a veritable parade of the county notables all leaving their card for you. The local mamas will be simply dying to introduce you to their darling daughters.'

Sebastian looked back at him. 'What do you mean?'

'He means you are the most eligible male in the county,' Fanny said, turning her blue eyes on him. 'That is why this ball is so important. We have to launch you properly into society and find you a suitable bride.' She smiled.

'As you said you didn't dance, I have arranged for Monsieur Fromard to attend on you tomorrow morning,' Freddy said.

Sebastian's mouth tightened, but he responded pleasantly enough. 'And what does Monsieur Fromard do?'

Freddy shot him a frosty look. 'Dancing and deportment, dear fellow.'

Sebastian drew himself up to his full, formidable height. 'I am an officer of the Duke of Wellington and quite well schooled in all the usual dances one would expect at such an occasion, but let's get one thing quite clear, Lynch: I don't dance.' His tone dripped ice.

'Oh, were you at the Duchess of Richmond's ball on the eve of Waterloo?' Fanny clapped her hands together.

'A mere captain of the line?' Sebastian gave her a withering glance.

'But you're Lord Somerton. How rude of the Duchess.'

Isabel looked at Fanny with amazement. 'Fanny, neither Sebastian nor the Duchess were acquainted with his antecedents.'

Sebastian cast Fanny a look of sheer exasperation. 'Miss Lynch,' he said, employing a tone of polite patience. 'Have you not noticed that I walk with a limp? A French musket ball ended my dancing career. Trust me, whatever my inclination towards a cotillion, I make a most difficult dance partner. I therefore choose not to dance on these occasions.'

'Cousin Sebastian,' Fanny adopted a wheedling tone, 'how do you hope to find an eligible young lady if you cannot dance? There are expectations ...'

Sebastian stalked towards the door. With one hand on the doorknob, he turned and said, 'There may well be expectations from every mother with an eligible daughter in the county, but I'm not some prize steed and I am not, I repeat, *not* in the marriage market!' On the last he opened the door. 'Now please excuse me, Lady Somerton, Miss Lynch, Mr. Lynch.'

Fanny stared at the door as it shut behind him with a firm bang. 'Well, really!' she said in a huffy tone.

'No breeding,' Freddy said, primping the corners of his mouth with his napkin. 'What can you expect? Can you imagine Anthony strolling around the village looking like a veritable ruffian, hobnobbing with the tenants? Oh, my dear Lady Somerton, what have you brought home?'

Freddy rose to his feet and huffed out of the room.

Chapter Twelve

'Am I disturbing you?'

Sebastian looked over the top of the broadsheet as Freddy slid into the chair across from him, a slim leather volume held in his hand.

His jaw tightened with annoyance. He had sought out the library in the hope of finding a quiet corner. For a house this size, it seemed remarkably busy. The walls of this fine room, with a magnificently painted ceiling sporting nymphs and cupids, were lined with high, heavy bookcases, filled with an impressive array of leather-bound books, and seemed to provide a sanctuary of male solidity.

'Are you a reader of the poets, sir?' Freddy enquired, with a slight curl of his lip as if he anticipated the answer.

'I rather enjoy Lord Byron, but I find Shelley a bit flowery for my taste. I prefer the older poets such as Donne,' Sebastian said, retreating back behind his paper.

Freddy cleared his throat. 'Well, cousin, it is encouraging to know we share something in common.'

The possessive use of the familiar 'cousin' had begun to grate on Sebastian's nerves. His fingers tightened on the edges of the broadsheet.

'I understand from Lady Somerton that we are not blood relatives,' he said, without lowering his paper.

'Well not *blood* relatives, dear chap, but surely cousins by marriage?'

Sebastian folded his paper and set it down on the table beside him. 'I wouldn't presume upon a relationship that does not exist in law.'

'Presume? Oh, my dear chap, I presume nothing. Fan and I are just your humble servants.' Freddy looked down at the quizzing glass that hung from his neck, produced a kerchief and began polishing it. 'Fact is, we have nowhere else to go. My late father left me with debts, dear chap. If it were not for dear Anthony's kindness, we would be on the street. With poor Anthony now gone, we will, of course, make other arrangements, but I do crave a little leniency to allow us time to find suitable alternate accommodation.'

Sebastian considered the man. He could not, in good conscience or Christian charity, throw them both out if they had nowhere else to go, and maybe some sort of settlement would be required.

'Of course. You are welcome to stay for as long as it takes,' he said with little warmth.

'Oh, you are too kind. You have my assurance that we will be gone as soon as is possible.' Freddy folded his hands across the front of his waistcoat and smiled expectantly.

When Sebastian resumed his reading of the broadsheet and did not initiate any further conversation, Freddy said, 'I suppose you are one of those chaps who spends his time hunting and shooting?'

'I was brought up in the country. I both hunt and shoot, but I have spent too many years hunting and shooting our enemies,' he said. 'I am happy to let foxes and pheasants live in peace.'

If he hoped his words would deter Freddy from continuing the conversation, he was mistaken.

'Cousin Anthony's stable was judged one of the finest in the county,' Freddy continued and Sebastian felt obliged to lower his paper and give him his attention. 'Anthony knew his horseflesh and as for the fairer sex...' He leaned forward in a conspiratorial manner and said in a lowered voice. 'Pity he was a little less choosy about his wife.'

Sebastian bristled and the paper crackled in his hand. 'I will not have Lady Somerton spoken of in that way.'

Freddy's eyes widened and he held up a deprecatory hand. 'Lady Somerton is a fine woman but not... Anthony's sort. He liked his women with a bit more spirit in 'em. They weren't exactly what you might call a match made in heaven and, to be honest, would you take with a woman who dresses like such a dowd? I mean, my dear, the child's been dead well over a year and dear Cousin Anthony nearly as long.'

The child again.

'My dear chap, there's only one reason a fellow like Anthony would marry a woman like Isabel: money. She was an heiress. If he hadn't married her, he'd have lost Brantstone. Just like my late, unlamented father did our estate,' he concluded with ill-disguised bitterness.

'I see,' said Sebastian.

So the fine horses in the stable, which he was yet to inspect, and the elegant surroundings were courtesy of Isabel, and what had Anthony left her? A *'comfortable jointure and use of the dower house'*. It seemed like a poor exchange, and now even that had gone.

'What do you know of Anthony's death?' he said, deflecting the topic from Isabel.

'It was an accident,' Freddy said with an expressive lift of his eyebrows. 'Just between us chaps, Cousin Anthony was on his way home from visiting a certain lady. I guess that he'd fuelled himself on a bit too much of the good lady's late husband's wine stock. Took a hedge and came off. Snapped his neck. They found him in the morning, cold and stiff.'

'So, between us chaps, was Anthony unfaithful?' Sebastian enquired.

Freddy looked genuinely startled. 'I suppose... yes, of course he was. Got no comfort at home, if you know what I mean. Told you he liked the company of women with a bit of spirit to 'em.'

Sebastian looked past Freddy, gazing out of the window. He tried to imagine Isabel's lot in life, tied to a man who apparently had only married her for her money, preferring the company of light skirts. Their only child dead before his first birthday. No wonder she sought the peace and serenity of the dower house. Brantstone Hall could hold precious few happy memories for her.

Sebastian sat back in his chair and contemplated the elegant fop sitting across from him.

'Forgive my curiosity, Lynch, but can you be a little more specific about your relationship to my cousin?'

Freddy blinked. 'Have I been remiss in not informing you of my antecedents? Why my mother was second cousin to dear Anthony's mother.'

Sebastian found the relationship somewhat remote. 'And how exactly did you come to be here at Brantstone?'

Freddy rolled his eyes to the ceiling. 'My father was the very worst of gamblers. He lost everything on horses and then took his own life, leaving poor Fan and I quite on our own in the world. Dear Anthony offered us shelter and comfort when we needed it most. He promised, *promised*, to leave us provided for in his will, but, as you know, there was no such provision for us and the estate devolved to you.' He paused, his fingers playing with the ribbon of his quizzing glass. 'What a happy day that must have been for you, Sebastian.'

Sebastian regarded Freddy over his steepled fingers.

He sighed. 'Look, Lynch. Whatever my cousin's intention towards you and your sister, I am conscious that I cannot, in all conscience, disregard an obligation, but until I can liquidate some more assets and have a better idea of the extent of the estate, I cannot make you any promises.'

Freddy twirled his quizzing glass.

'That is very kind of you, and more than we deserve. Now we are friends again, perhaps I can divert you with a small game of cards?'

Sebastian rose to his feet. 'You must excuse me, Lynch, but I am a little weary after my walk this morning.'

He shut the library door with a deep, thankful breath. He could have sworn the man was doused in some sort of fragrance. If Freddy haunted the library, he would have to find another room in the house to call his own.

As he passed the blue parlour he peered in through the half open door. Isabel sat at a desk, pen in hand. He knocked and entered.

She looked up and smiled. She seemed to be unbending a little in his presence and the smile softened her features.

'Can I help you, my lord?'

Remembering the talk with his grandmother, his gaze swept the walls of the parlour on which hung a large number of portraits, large and small.

'One day you need to take me through the rogues' gallery,' he said.

Isabel smiled. 'Well, there are a couple of rogues here in this room that you may be quite interested in.' She rose to her feet and walked over to a medium-sized portrait of two young men in powdered wigs lounging under a stylised oak tree. A dog and a hunting rifle completed the picture.

'The younger man is your father,' she said, 'and the older his brother, George, Anthony's father.'

Sebastian joined her, staring at the first likeness of his father he had ever seen.

'Everyone I met this morning says I look like my father,' he said. 'I can't see it myself.'

'You're at least ten years older than the James in the picture but, yes,' Isabel considered him, 'there is a strong resemblance.'

'What about Anthony? Is there any likeness of him in the house?'

Isabel's chest rose as she seemed to take a deep breath. 'I have a small picture painted last year,' she said. 'Do you want to see it?'

He nodded. 'It helps to be able to put a face to a name. I'm not good at just names.'

'Wait here. I will fetch it.'

While he waited for her to return, Sebastian studied the bucolic painting of his father and uncle, searching for the character of the men in the stylised representation. James lacked the robust physique of his older brother, and he thought he could sense a dreamy nature in his father's eyes, but perhaps that was just artistic licence.

He heard Isabel's footsteps behind him and turned to face her. She handed him a portable leather-bound folio. He raised the little latch, opening it to reveal a small but exquisite portrait of a man standing behind a woman seated on a low chair. His hand rested lightly but possessively on her left shoulder. The woman held a baby in her arms.

He glanced up, noticing a line between Isabel's eyebrows, a sure sign of the rigid self-control she imposed on herself.

'I know about the child,' he said quietly.

She let out a breath.

'My aunt and grandmother let it slip,' he said.

She nodded. 'That was painted when William was three months old. It is a very good likeness of Anthony.'

And you, Sebastian thought.

There could be no mistaking Isabel, even dressed in a light blue gown with her dark hair worn in a soft, flattering style. In her painted smile and the ease with which she cradled the child in her right arm while her left hand was raised, touching that of her husband, he saw genuine happiness. What had changed?

He turned his attention to Anthony. He looked very much as Sebastian had expected. The word 'fop' came first to his mind. Anthony wore his dark curled hair fashionably long with the long sideburns similar to those affected by Freddy Lynch. In further emulation of Freddy, his waistcoat appeared to be expensive brocade worn with a high starched collar and intricately tied neckcloth. He was no judge of male beauty, but he guessed that a woman might consider Anthony, Lord Somerton, a handsome man with his high cheekbones and well-shaped mouth. He scanned the face looking for something that might give some indication of character, but he found nothing. It was as if the man's handsome features were a mask.

What was he hiding?

'Do you think we are much alike?' Sebastian commented, handing the precious folder back to Isabel.

'You mean in looks? There are moments when I think there is a superficial similarity, but in all other respects you are as unlike as two men could possibly be.' She looked down at the folder in her hands for a moment before raising her face, her expression grave. 'Trust me, Lord Somerton, that is a good thing.'

For a long moment, they stood quite still, looking at each other. There was such unguarded pain in her eyes, he had to resist taking her in his arms. It was the death of her child, not her husband, which had robbed this woman of light and life. He wondered what it would take to bring her back.

Isabel glanced away, her shoulders lifting as if she remembered herself. When she looked back at him, the mask was back in place, calm and implacable.

'Is there anything else you wanted to ask me?'

Sebastian cleared his throat. 'Tomorrow is Sunday. What time is the church service?'

Isabel's eyes widened. 'Nine-thirty,' she said.

'Do you attend?' he asked.

'Of course, but...'

He frowned, 'But?'

'It's just that Anthony rarely—'

'I am not Anthony,' he said in a tone that even to his ears sounded sharp.

She regarded him for a long moment. 'Well then, if you care to accompany me, it is my custom to walk to the church directly after breakfast.'

He nodded. 'Thank you. I would like to do that. Now I think I should rest or I will have to answer to Bennet.'

'I will have dinner sent up to your room.'

He nodded and left her standing in the parlour, clutching the precious portrait to her chest.

※

Isabel waited until she heard Sebastian's boots on the hall tiles before closing the door to the parlour. She opened the little portrait and set it on the escritoire. She kissed her forefinger and touched the painted face of the small baby in her lap.

This was all she had to remind her of that brief moment in time when she had been happy, completely and utterly happy, and she clung to the memory, taking it out, like the portrait, holding it in her hands, feeling its warmth sustain her for a little longer.

She wondered what it was about Sebastian Alder that had prompted her to show this likeness to him. He seemed to invite confidences and that thought unnerved her.

Taking a steadying breath, she picked up her pen, trying to concentrate on a letter to Lady Ainslie.

Lord Somerton's heir had been found, saved from near death and installed at Brantstone. Her responsibility was done. The rest was up to him. She, Isabel, had other plans that did not involve him.

She picked up her pen and dipped it in the inkpot.

'*My dear Harriet,*' she wrote. '*The new Lord Somerton is now at Brantstone and our plans for the school, so long delayed, can now proceed ...*

She paused and looked out of the window at the long sweep of the drive and the church spire rising above the trees. If she craned her neck to the right, she could make out the chimneys of the dower house. Her heart leaped with excitement. Her own home, freedom and a chance to make something of her life.

... Lord Somerton is a contradiction. Of course, it is but his first days here, and while he is doing everything wrong, treating the servants and the tenants with too much familiarity, yet it only seems to make him more endearing. Even in the short time he has been here, I can see in their eyes for all his rough edges, the staff appear to have accepted him. I do not expect he will change. However simple his upbringing has been, the one thing the Reverend Alder seems to have instilled in him is a great trust and respect for his fellow human beings, however humble...

She played with the feathers of the pen for a moment, remembering how he had stooped from his great height to ask a little kitchen maid her name. That had been the moment that had set the stamp on Lord Somerton's heir.

... When the opportunity presents, I am looking forward to talking to him at greater length about our plans for the daughters of the mill workers in Manchester. I expect a more sympathetic audience than my late husband would have given me.

She put her elbows on her table and covered her ears with her hands as if she still heard Anthony's mocking laughter.

'*My dear Isabel. You may as well throw money into the pigswill than try and educate the lower classes. Those girls who won't go into the mills will end up on the streets. You are wasting your time and* my *money.*'

She couldn't save the world. She wasn't trying to, but even if she could give half a dozen young girls a better start in life, then she would have accomplished something.

No, Sebastian Alder wouldn't laugh at her as Anthony had done. He would listen with grave, approving eyes. She looked down at what she had written, scrawled a few lines of general gossip and signed her name. As she sealed the letter, she smiled. She picked up the travelling folio and shut it, hooking it closed.

That part of her life was over, and a new life was beginning, filled with meaning and purpose.

Chapter Thirteen

The bells of the village church chimed across the parkland, summoning the faithful from the estate. Isabel stood in the hall, pulling on her gloves. As she reached for her bonnet, held out by her maid, a clattering on the staircase made them both look up.

Sebastian had not been at breakfast and she wondered if he had slept late. He had, no doubt, left his bedroom immaculately dressed by Pierce, but in the short distance to the bottom of the stairs, his neckcloth had come askew. Isabel wondered if he ever looked tidy and decided his charm lay in his insouciance. She hoped he would never learn how to wear a neckcloth with the same dash as Anthony.

'Am I late?' he enquired as he reached the bottom of the stairs. 'I heard the bells...'

'No, you're not late. The rector will not start without you.'

He carried his hat, cane, and a small book, which he laid on the table as he tugged at the recalcitrant neckcloth. The effort only worsened it.

Isabel shook her head.

'Let me,' she said.

He obligingly stood still as she reached up and tucked the

wayward ends of the cloth back where Pierce had intended. He smelled of fresh soap with a faint spicy tang to it. Her fingers brushed the freshly shaven skin of his neck, and the muscles in his throat contracted. A warm flush rose to her face and she withdrew her hand, hastily pulling on her gloves.

He ran a finger around the edge of the neckcloth.

'You don't tie it as tightly as Pierce. Thank you, Lady Somerton. Where did I put my hat? Oh, thank you, Johnson.'

As the footman collected Sebastian's hat and cane from the table and handed them to him, Isabel picked up the small, battered book, a copy of the Book of Common Prayer.

'Your prayer book looks well worn,' she remarked as she gave it to him.

He looked down at the book in his hand. 'It was my father's... my stepfather's,' he corrected himself. 'I have nothing of my father's except this.' He raised his eyes to the painted dome. 'The Reverend Alder gave the prayer book to me when I joined the army.'

'Can I see it?' Isabel asked, holding out her hand.

He shrugged and held it out for her. She flicked through the dog-eared pages, covered in annotations written in pencil in a crabbed hand that she suspected had been that of the Reverend Alder.

On the end pages and crammed into the margins were tiny drawings, mostly caricatures or hasty sketches of people, a curious anomaly to find in such a book. She doubted the Reverend Alder had turned his prayer book into a sketchbook. She looked up at Sebastian and noticed a flush of colour in his face.

'Did you do these sketches?'

'Just something to pass a tedious sermon,' Sebastian responded with a croak.

Isabel traced the caricature of a chaplain's ruddy, self-satisfied face with her finger.

'But it's so good. I can almost hear him pontificating.'

Sebastian held out his hand, and she gave the book back to him. He stuffed it unceremoniously into his pocket.

'Connie's the artist in the family. I just scribble.' He glanced up at the stairs. 'I take it we will not be joined by the Lynchs?'

Isabel shook her head. 'I don't think either of them has set foot in the church, except for funerals, in all the time they've been here.'

As they stepped out into the light of another glorious day, he swung his cane and turned his face to the sun. 'I love this time of year.'

Isabel drew her shawl around her shoulders and tried to match her stride to his. He slowed with a rueful apology.

As they walked, he said, 'I have written to my brother and sister and told them I will send the coach for them as soon as they are ready to leave.'

Isabel glanced up at him in time to see a flicker of yearning cross his eyes.

'That's good news. I look forward to meeting them. I am sure they will love their new home.'

He gave a rueful smile. 'I don't think I could restrain them from coming. I suspect Connie is already packed.' He clasped his hands behind his back and said in a wistful tone, 'I still have trouble thinking of anywhere except Little Benning as home. It will be strange to have them here.'

'I am sure they will accustom themselves quickly enough,' Isabel said with certainty. Surely, the two young people would have no difficulty in accustoming themselves to such a comfortable life.

She had turned down a path that ran away from the driveway, a well-trodden shortcut that took them through the woods.

'This is a much more pleasant route to the village,' Sebastian remarked. 'I took the road yesterday. Tell me about the incumbent of the parish. Is it my living?'

'It is. Your grandfather only died four years ago, after forty years in the parish. Poor Reverend Dunn is still referred to as the "new vicar".'

'And he will probably always be referred to that way,' Sebastian observed, correctly.

Isabel glanced at him. 'I forget you are, after all, the grandson and indeed the son of a parson.'

He squinted into the trees above them. 'God and I have not always been on the best of terms. Indeed, there was a time when I stood on the precipice of hell and considered it quite a viable alternative.'

She checked her stride and looked at him in consternation. It went against everything she thought she knew about this man.

'No. I cannot credit that,' she said.

'There was a time in Spain—' He stopped himself abruptly and began again. 'I was wounded at Talavera, and they sent me back to England. I... had seen some terrible things, Isabel. I stopped having hope.'

She looked up at him. 'To lose hope is surely to lose the will to live, Sebastian. What changed?'

He looked down at her, and his mouth quirked into a self-deprecating smile. 'My father reminded me that there is still great goodness in this world.'

'The Reverend Alder sounds a remarkable man,' Isabel observed.

'He was, and I could do with his wise counsel now.'

They had reached the village, and a sizeable crowd, all dressed in their Sunday best, gathered at the door of the church.

'I see the church attracts quite a congregation.' Sebastian straightened, his hand going to the knot of his cravat.

'I don't think the Reverend Dunn can claim any credit, my lord. You are the attraction today,' Isabel observed.

They encountered Sebastian's Aunt Peggy at the lychgate. Seeing Sebastian, she coloured and dropped into a wobbly curtsey.

Sebastian tipped his hat. 'Good morning, Aunt. How is your mother today?'

'She is too frail to attend the service anymore,' Peggy said. 'The Reverend will call in later.'

Sebastian held out his arm. 'May I escort you into church?'

Peggy's eyes widened and darted to the right and left. The colour in her cheek deepened.

'Oh, I couldn't...'

'I insist,' he said.

Peggy took his arm. Isabel put her hand to her mouth to conceal the smile that crept onto her lips as Peggy's social elevation provoked a murmuring from the gathering crowd.

As they walked up the path towards the door of the church, Sebastian tipped his hat in response to the greetings, the rustle of petticoats from the curtseying ladies accompanying their progress into the church.

'The Somerton pew is at the front,' Isabel whispered, indicating the pew at the left-hand side of the church aisle, beneath the pulpit.

'After you, Lady Somerton,' Sebastian smiled, removing his hat. 'Aunt ...'

'Oh, my lord, I can't,' Peggy whispered, her fingers plucking at his sleeve. 'Not the lord's pew.'

'Of course you can. You are my family and this is my family pew,' he whispered back.

'Beg pardon, my lady,' Peggy said as Isabel made room for her. 'I hope you don't mind, but his lordship insisted.'

'Of course I don't mind,' Isabel responded with a welcoming smile.

A rustle stirred the congregation and Isabel glanced around to see the cause of the disquiet. Isabel caught her breath as a woman wearing a fashionable dress and pelisse of Sherwood green, with a matching green hat topped with a jaunty feather, walked confidently down the aisle to take her place across from the Somerton pew. As she seated herself, the woman glanced sideways, catching Sebastian's eye, and inclined her head, causing the curls of chestnut hair that clustered beneath the bonnet to bounce. Despite the veil Isabel did not miss the tantalising smile and the inclination of her head directed at Sebastian.

Sebastian acknowledged her with a nod and the woman's glance moved to Isabel. Isabel pretended not to have noticed the woman's attention.

'Who is that?' Isabel heard Sebastian whisper to his aunt.

'That's Lady Kendall,' Peggy replied. 'We don't often see her in church. She lives at Fairchild Hall, about two miles over towards Grantham.'

Isabel looked down at the prayer book in her hand and drew a steadying breath. Nobody present could be under any illusion as to what had drawn Lady Georgiana Kendall to the service of divine worship, and it had nothing to do with God or Reverend Dunn's sermon.

The Reverend, pink with pleasure, publicly acknowledged Sebastian's presence, welcoming him to the parish.

Isabel cast a glance at Sebastian. He sat quite still, his back arrow straight, his profile carved from the same stone as those of his ancestors, whose tombs filled the corners of the old church. He looked as if he had been born to the role. The weight of the expectations that pressed in on him did not seem to bother him in the least, but she suspected that the still waters that were Sebastian Alder ran very deep.

Isabel bowed her head and said her familiar silent prayer for the soul of her dead child.

Chapter Fourteen

With his eyes firmly fixed on the fine window above the altar, showing the crucified Christ, Sebastian let the familiar words of the morning prayer pass over him. Just like the manner of his arrival at the hall, this morning would set the tone for his stewardship of the Somerton estate. Everything he did or said would be noted, dissected, and conclusions drawn about him that would be hard to erase.

His common upbringing could either serve to set him apart or give him empathy with his tenants and neighbours. His fingers tightened on the prayer book as he willed his stepfather to send him some sort of divine guidance. In the absence of inspiration, he fell back on what he knew best. He straightened his shoulders and assumed the countenance of a man about to do battle.

As the sermon dragged on, he tried not to steal a glance at Lady Kendall. Even across the aisle of a church, he sensed the powerful attraction of this woman who wasn't 'any better than she should have been', as Bennet, relating his conversations from below stairs, had described her.

He looked forward to meeting Harry's wayward older sister, Georgiana. There had been many a night in Spain when Harry had read of his sister's antics in back copies of London gossip sheets. His brother officers had chivvied him and demanded introductions. Had someone said she had been through three husbands? A shiver of anticipation ran down his spine.

The congregation rose for the last hymn, and he could hear Lady Kendall's clear, rich soprano rising into the ancient beams of the church. He had every intention of making himself better acquainted with the mysterious, and possibly scandalous, Lady Kendall as soon as the service ended. The thought caused the blood in his pulse to quicken.

Everyone, it seemed, had cause to linger after the service and, as Sebastian emerged with his aunt on his arm, a noticeable flutter seemed to go around the small groups gathered near the graves. His intention of speaking with Lady Kendall was thwarted by the veritable bevy of pretty young ladies of good standing in his path, eager to make his acquaintance. He looked to Isabel to effect the introductions and managed to stutter out some polite conversation about the weather and the sermon.

Only as the woman in green approached. Beside him Isabel stiffened, drawing back a little. He cast a quick glance at Isabel in her dowdy clothes and unflattering black bonnet and felt a tinge of guilt. The serene, oval face did not betray her emotions. In the circumstances, she must find such encounters difficult but there could no avoiding the woman with whom Anthony had allegedly spent his last evening.

Lady Kendall curtsied and pushed back the veil from her hat. Sebastian drew a quick breath. The fleeting glimpse in the church did not disappoint: High cheekbones, large, green eyes and full, red lips that invited a kiss.

'Lady Somerton.' Lady Kendall acknowledged Isabel with a quick bob. 'How do you do on this beautiful morning?'

'Lord Somerton,' Isabel said with absolute politeness, 'allow me to present Lady Kendall.'

'Welcome to Brantstone, my lord. I believe you are

acquainted with my brother, Harry?' Her voice had a deep, husky tone that reminded Sebastian of warm honey.

Lady Kendall held out her hand and he took it with a polite bow. 'Lady Kendall. It is a pleasure to make your acquaintance, and yes, Harry is an old comrade in arms.'

As he straightened, she smiled at him with her head tilted as she had done in church. Her eyes were the colour of emeralds and, like the jewel they resembled, they glittered.

'The parish is simply dying to make your acquaintance,' she said in a lowered tone. 'Your coming has been anticipated for some time.'

'Well, I hope the reality does not disappoint,' Sebastian managed.

'Not at all. Harry has spoken often of you.'

Ignoring Isabel, Lady Kendall tucked a small, gloved hand into his arm and looked up at him.

'Would you do me the honour of walking me to my carriage?'

As she had already begun to propel him down the path, he could only offer a short apology to Isabel and the others.

'Indeed,' Lady Kendall said as soon as they were out of earshot, 'I am sure you are everything the good mamas of the county would wish for.'

'And what is that?' Sebastian asked.

'A title, a fortune and unwed,' Lady Kendall replied.

Sebastian gave a snort of laughter. If only they knew how illusory the 'fortune' had proved to be.

'You know you are very like your cousin to look at,' she said.

'So I've been told, but I assure you that is where the resemblance ends,' Sebastian replied. She invited a bit of gentle sparring so he countered, 'I believe you were well acquainted with my cousin.'

Lady Kendall laughed and her gaze met his in perfect understanding.

'Yes, we were indeed... quite well acquainted.'

A barouche waited by the lychgate and, as Sebastian handed her up into the carriage, she smiled down at him.

'I shall look forward to our next meeting, Lord Somerton. You must come and take tea with me.'

'It would be a pleasure, Lady Kendall.'

She leaned forward to instruct her driver, but suddenly straightened.

'There he is, the rogue!' She stood up and waved as a man on a roan horse trotted towards them. 'What kept you, Harry?' she demanded, resuming her seat.

Harry Dempster slid from the saddle and, looping the reins over his shoulder, walked over to the barouche.

'Sorry, George, I overslept.' The man turned to Sebastian, and a grin split his face. 'Alder? Good God, I hardly recognised you from our encounter in London.'

'Dempster! It's good to see you.'

The two men grasped hands, slapping each other on the shoulder.

'I'm staying with my sister, Georgie.' Harry indicated Lady Kendall who smiled in response. 'I only got in yesterday. Georgie was bursting to tell me that there was a new Lord Somerton who had been plucked from the obscurity of His Majesty's finest.' He slapped Sebastian on the shoulder again. 'And just for once I was able to enlighten her. None other than my old comrade, Bas Alder!'

Lady Kendall sighed. 'What a happy reunion. I suppose you two are going to catch up on old times? I shall leave you to it. Drive on.'

The barouche lurched forward at a pretty pace, the green feather in Lady Kendall's bonnet bobbing as it rounded the corner.

'My lord, we really must return to the hall shortly.'

At the sound of Isabel's quiet voice, Sebastian tore his eyes away from the departing carriage as Harry turned to Isabel. He took her outstretched hand and bowed over it.

'My dear Lady Somerton. How are you?'

'Well, thank you, Colonel. Excuse me, gentlemen, I must speak with Mrs. Bryan before we leave,' Isabel said.

She turned away to talk to a stout woman in a blue gown who had been trying to get her attention.

'Fortune has smiled on you at last, Alder,' Harry said.

Sebastian held up his hands. 'I scarce believe it myself.'

'Well, I'm glad! You've earned it. I didn't hear the full story when we met in London so please enlighten me. How did this change in fortunes come about?'

Sebastian recounted the family antecedents and the tale of waking up in Somerton House to the news.

Harry shook his head. 'Well, you hear these tales, but I never thought to put much credence in them. So, how does it feel to be the new Lord Somerton?'

'Can't say I've come to terms with it yet. Between us, my late cousin has left me with a pile of debt and trouble.'

'Doesn't surprise me. An interesting chap, your cousin,' Harry said.

'How well did you know him?'

Harry shrugged. 'Reasonably well. Met him through Georgie and we shared a few good dinners and rounds of cards, in London mostly. You know the sort of thing. I always found him hard to judge. A bit mercurial if you know what I mean.' Harry's cheerful face became serious. 'What are you going to do about it?'

Sebastian shook his head. 'Sell off some assets.'

Harry's face brightened. 'If you are considering selling any of the racehorses let me know.'

'Ah yes, the racehorses. I have to confess I haven't even seen the stables yet. I found some pedigree books in Anthony's papers. He seemed to know what he was doing.'

'Your cousin may have been a fool in some ways, but he knew his horses,' Harry agreed.

Sebastian shook his head. 'I had better not get too attached to them then. What about you? I haven't seen you since you left the regiment in '09 or was it '10?'

'I got out in '09. Had enough of bad food and hard beds, and my father was nagging me to show some interest in the estates.' He rolled his eyes.

'Well, I'm glad to see you. Glad of a familiar face, truth be told.' Sebastian smiled with genuine pleasure. 'Will you join us for dinner?'

'Unfortunately, I must get back to London for a few days, but I'll return by the end of the week,' Harry said. 'And now, if you don't mind, I'd better follow Georgie home, or I'll never hear the end of it. Give my regards to Lady Somerton.' He tipped his hat in Isabel's direction.

'It's always good to see an old friend,' Sebastian said as Isabel rejoined him. He had an ally now, someone with whom he could be himself.

'I can understand that,' Isabel said. 'My own friend, Lady Ainslie, lives too far away for us to meet often, but when we do, it is as if we have only been parted a few days.'

Sebastian offered her his arm. She hesitated before slipping her hand into the crook of his elbow, a comfortable and familiar gesture. He glanced down at her, frustrated that her bonnet obscured her face. While Lady Kendall had the power to invoke instantaneous lust, he found this woman far more intriguing.

She remained silent as they retraced the path through the woods. He swung the cane he still carried.

'Harry used to talk about his sister,' Sebastian said at last, breaking the silence between them. 'She would be a few years older than him.'

Not that you would think it to look at her, he thought privately.

Isabel stopped in the path, withdrawing her hand from his arm. 'Lord Somerton, I think there is something you should know about Lady Kendall. Indeed, I am surprised you haven't been apprised of the choicest piece of gossip concerning my late husband. He had been visiting Lady Kendall the night he died.'

Sebastian cleared his throat. 'I had heard that.'

'You should know that he was, in fact, a frequent visitor to her home. Lady Kendall occupied a very particular position in my husband's life. She was his mistress.'

Sebastian tried to look surprised but could see from the tightening of Isabel's mouth that he had failed.

'I'm sorry,' he mumbled. 'I had heard the story. I should have been more careful of your sensibilities.'

She looked away, the muscles in her neck taut as she swallowed. 'Brantstone Hall is your home, Lord Somerton and Lady Kendall is your friend's sister. I can raise no objection if you wish to entertain her, and her brother, of course, but do not ask me to play at being the gracious hostess in her company.'

'I understand.'

She looked back at him, an almost wild desperation in her eyes. 'Do you?'

Before he could respond she set off at a brisk pace. He joined her, but they walked back to the hall in silence.

Chapter Fifteen

Isabel would have been appalled if anyone had accused her of flouncing. Nonetheless, she arrived back at the hall feeling uncharacteristically out of sorts and irritated.

She went straight up to her bedchamber and stood by the window, unbuttoning her gloves while she thought about Georgiana, Lady Kendall. Really, the woman just had to flutter her eyelashes and men fell helpless at her feet.

How did she do it?

Isabel tugged impatiently at a small pearl button, tearing the silk threads that held it to the fine kid. The button fell to the floor with a soft ping and rolled under a chair.

'Oh, curse it!' Isabel said aloud, consigning this small domestic inconvenience to the long list of grudges she held against Lady Kendall.

What concern was of it hers if Lord Somerton succumbed to the obvious charms of Lady Kendall?

Going down on her hands and knees, she searched around for the little button, retrieving it from behind her chest of drawers.

She sat back on her heels and caught her refection in the

long mirror. Who was that woman with the haggard face and dark circled eyes that looked back at her?

'Lucy!' she summoned her maid who appeared at the door.

'My lady?'

'Find my riding habit and tell the stables to saddle Stella. I am going for a ride before dinner.'

Lucy's eyes widened. 'A ride, my lady?'

'I need exercise and fresh air.'

'But m'lady—'

'Now, Lucy.'

Standing before her mirror, pleating the fine pleating the fine woollen skirt of her riding habit between her fingers, she understood her maid's reluctance. The deep bottle-green habit, fashionably trimmed with black frogging, had been her last purchase before William's death and now it hung on her. When had she become so thin?

Experimentally, she pulled a few stray curls from the severe coil of hair on the back of her head, noting how they softened the hard angles of her face, a parody of the fashionable hairstyles she had once favoured.

Impatiently, she poked the unruly curls back. Why was she indulging in such foolishness? She had no one to impress and yet, if Sebastian could see her as she had once been, he might be pleasantly surprised. No one had ever called her a beauty, but, in the right clothes and the right company, she had been known to turn heads. The queen of the London drawing rooms had reduced herself to black rags and hideous caps. Something unsettling was stirring in her heart, bringing her back to life, and it frightened her.

She stood up and reached for her hat, pinning it to her head and settling the veil over her face, pulling on her gloves, she left her room.

In the stable yard, her usual mount, the star-faced bay mare called Stella, stood saddled and ready. With the boy's help she mounted, kicking the mare into a trot and then a canter, clearing the stables and the house, her ride taking her more by instinct than design to the grand mausoleum on the hill.

Only when she reached the small grove of trees did she pause, slipping off the saddle and securing Stella's reins to the nearest oak. Tripping over her skirts, she ran towards the mausoleum and flung herself down on the step, pressing her cheek against the cold marble.

With her finger, she traced the letters of the carved, gilded name.

WILLIAM ANTHONY CHARLES KINGSLEY
Born 3 August 1813 Died 29 May 1814 Suffer Little Children.

Below William's name was that of her husband, but Isabel hadn't come here to think about Anthony. The death of her child sat heavily on her heart. The horror of the morning they had found William dead in his crib, still twisted like a knife in her heart. Every day she walked up this hill, and every day she wondered if the hurting ever became any easier.

She drew her knees up to her chin and wrapped her arms around them. A cold breeze stirred the dry grass around the crypt and the smell of freshly cut hay rose in the wind.

The grass should be scythed. Anthony would hate to have his tomb in such an untidy state.

Chapter Sixteen

On his return to Brantstone after church, Sebastian spent the time until dinner, avoiding Fanny and Freddy by shutting himself in his own bedchamber with the London broadsheets.

He sat in an overstuffed armchair covered in the same silk as the walls and bed hangings and surveyed the room. When Connie arrived he would consult her about redecorating. She had a marvellous eye for what suited the occupant of a room. All he knew was that the pale silk wall coverings and matching bed covers and elegant gilded furniture was *not* his style. However redecorating was a luxury he could ill afford.

He rose to his feet and looked out the window. It still lacked an hour until dinner, so he decided that a long overdue visit to the stables would be in order. He found a side door and circled the house until he reached the magnificent buildings built in the same style as the house and entered under an elegant clock tower.

Thompson, the head groom, had been included in the introductions on his arrival and came out to meet him, hastily pulling a coat on over his shirtsleeves. Sebastian greeted him by name and asked to be shown over the stables.

'Honoured, my lord,' Thompson replied.

The man escorted him through the immaculate stable block, stopping at each stall to introduce the occupant as if they were favoured tenants. Sebastian followed, enthralled and a little awed that all these magnificent beasts were now his. Freddy had been right. Whatever else his cousin lacked, there was no denying he knew his horses. A dozen racehorses, handsome beasts with long legs and powerful hindquarters, strong and beautifully matched carriage horses and an assortment of saddle horses filled the stalls. For the first time, Sebastian felt a cousinly bond with the late Lord Somerton. Anthony may have had no interest in the house and the estate but he understood horses and knew their value.

He stopped to admire a magnificent black stallion. The animal watched him, ears swivelling with curiosity at the sound of his voice as he approached. Sebastian opened the door of the stall and stepped inside, running an experienced hand down the arched neck of the horse.

'More than a little Arab in this one,' he remarked,

Thompson nodded. 'That's Pharaoh. You've a good eye, my lord.'

'I'd like to ride him.'

Thompson looked dubious. 'He's a handful, my lord.' He hooked his thumbs in his belt and rocked on the balls of his feet. 'To be honest with you, his late lordship was riding 'im when he had the accident.'

Sebastian gave the handsome beast a thoughtful look.

'Has anyone ridden him since?'

'I've had him out a few times, my lord, but you know how 'tis when a horse—' He broke off.

Sebastian knew he had been going to add: 'becomes a killer'.

'There's some as would have had him destroyed,' Thompson continued

'That would have been a pity. From what I know of my

cousin's demise, it was hardly the fault of the horse. Get him ready for me, Thompson. I'll take him out now.'

Thompson hesitated as if about to say something, but thought better of it and inclined his head.

'As your lordship wishes.'

Sebastian continued the rest of the stables tour by himself. As he reached the end of the row of stalls, past a pair of matching bay carriage horses, he heard the soft tone of a woman's voice. In the very last stall, a small, heavily pregnant piebald mare was being fed withered carrots by no less a person than the dowager Lady Somerton.

She'd not heard him approach and it gave him the luxury of a moment to stop and watch her as she caressed the little mare's nose and whispered in her ear. The mare seemed to lean against her, nickering softly in answer to Isabel's voice.

Isabel wore an elegant green riding habit, completely at odds with the dreadful, shapeless black gowns she seemed to favour. A long strand of hair, the colour of dark honey, had escaped the jaunty hat with its green and black feathers and black netting.

No one would describe Isabel as beautiful, but here, when she thought no one was watching, she had a lovely serenity to her regular features, normally glazed in a mask of polite indifference. In profile, the intelligent brow, strong, slightly pointed nose and a determined little chin gave her the appearance of a different woman to the one he had come to know.

He cleared his throat, and she turned around with an expression that was at once startled and annoyed. Seeing Sebastian, she tucked the loose strand of hair under her hat.

He whipped his hat off and indicated the little pony.

'Is the mare yours?'

She nodded. 'This is Millie. I know she's not much to look at, but she's my last link with my uncle. He gave her to me for my sixteenth birthday. She has the sweetest temperament of any horse I have ever known.'

Sebastian entered the stall and ran a hand down the mare's nose and nodded.

'You can see that in her eyes,' he agreed, running an expert hand over the mare's swollen belly. 'She's not far off foaling.'

Isabel nodded. 'Only a matter of days. Lucky girl,' she addressed the horse, 'you're going to be a mama again.'

'Your husband kept a good stable,' Sebastian said.

She nodded. 'Horses were his life and he enjoyed more than a little success at Newmarket. One of the few things he was good at,' she added.

She gave the mare one last pat on the nose, brushed her hands on her skirt and walked out of the stall. Sebastian followed her out into the courtyard where a couple of the stable boys were grooming two of the racehorses. One of the animals fidgeted under the boy's ministrations and Sebastian gave it a cursory glance, taking in the twitching of its ears and how it pulled against the boy's hand, the whites of its eyes showing. A nervous beast. Not one he would trust.

Thompson waited by the mounting block, holding Pharaoh by the bridle.

Isabel stopped and looked up at Sebastian.

'You're not going to ride Pharaoh, are you?'

Hearing the genuine apprehension in her voice, he looked at her, seeing fear in her eyes. 'Why not?'

'Didn't Thompson tell you—'

'That this was the horse Anthony was riding the night he died? Yes, he did. I don't blame the horse for what happened.'

'But, Lord Somerton, you are barely out of your sick bed!'

Sebastian ignored her protest and swung himself up into the saddle, wincing as the barely healed wound caught. *This might not have been a good idea*, he considered, as Pharaoh recoiled from the unaccustomed weight on his back, going down on his hindquarters, his eyes rolling. It took all of Thompson's strength to hold him.

Sebastian took the reins, feeling for the horse's mouth.

'Let him go, Thompson,' he ordered.

The groom obeyed. Pharaoh responded by rearing. Failing to dislodge his rider, he danced sideways, tossing his head. Sebastian held him firmly, talking to the horse, calming him. Only when Pharaoh had settled did he put his heels to the horse's side, taking him on a slow circuit of the stable yard. He tapped his heels and the horse responded obediently, moving into a graceful trot and then a canter with only the slightest urging.

Sebastian brought the creature back to where Isabel and Thompson stood, approval written on Thompson's face and relief on Isabel's.

Thompson stroked the horse's nose. 'You see, old fellow? The new lord ain't so bad, is he?'

Sebastian wondered if he was talking to him or the horse. Either way, he appreciated the grudging praise.

Isabel added. 'The new lord is not quite so hard on a horse's mouth, either.' She turned to the groom. 'How is your wife today, Thompson?'

'Fair ta middling. Kind of you to enquire, your leddyship.'

The lilt of a girl's voice singing a country song made them all look up. Young Matilda, the kitchen maid, had entered the yard carrying a bucket from which carrot tops poked. Seeing the new Lord Somerton, her singing died away, and she stopped in the middle of the gateway, her eyes wide with alarm, staring past the group at the mounting block.

At the sound of a horse whinnying, they all turned to see what had taken the girl's attention. The stable boy holding the nervous racehorse gave a sharp cry as the plunging beast shook his hold. It whirled around on its hindquarters, rolling eyes fixed on the gateway where Matilda stood.

Isabel cried out a warning, but Matilda did not move. She stared with wide eyes at the horse and dropped her bucket, scattering carrot tops. Without thinking, Sebastian pulled Pharaoh around, putting his heels to the horse's side. He reached Matilda seconds before the runaway, leaning down from Pharaoh and scooping her up as the racehorse crashed past them, making for the park.

Safe in his arms, the young girl pressed her face into his coat. He put a protective arm around her shaking shoulders.

'You're safe now, Matilda,' he said, and turned Pharaoh back to the mounting block where he let Matilda down. She sat down on the block and buried her head in her hands. Isabel pulled the sobbing child towards her and held her close, making hushing sounds. Sebastian watched her, seeing not the child but the woman who should have been a mother.

Now the danger had passed, a familiar stabbing catch in the wound and, more worryingly, the warm stickiness of blood on his skin reminded Sebastian that the exercise had been foolish. Making sure he had the animal positioned so that he could dismount on the offside to the bystanders, he slid off, grimacing in pain under the pretence of adjusting the stirrup.

He thanked Thompson, who had taken the reins. Isabel looked up from Matilda, and he inclined his head. Without another word he walked out of the stable yard, only his stiff back and tight mouth betraying the fact that each footstep sent shafts of fire jarring through his body.

He made it to his bedchamber without a break in his stride. Once there, he looked around for a chair, but the elegant silk-covered seats and oriental rugs did not invite the risk of a bloodstain. Finding nothing suitable, he rang for Bennet and sat on the windowsill.

He got no sympathy from his corporal.

'What were you thinking, sir?' Bennet chided, removing the ruined jacket and bloodstained shirt. 'That exit wound is barely scabbed, and you've gone and broken it open again. Sorry, sir, I'm going to say it: you're an idiot.'

'I should have you whipped for your impudence,' Sebastian said between gritted teeth. *If I didn't happen to agree with you.* 'Just patch me up.'

'Patch you up so you can go off careening around on 'orses

again? I don't think so. You're going back to your bed,' Bennet said in a voice that brooked no argument.

⁂

As Isabel ascended the stairs, she passed Pierce. The old man carried a pile of clothing and was muttering to himself as he stomped past, barely acknowledging her. She caught the words 'ruined' and 'never would've happened in the old lord's day'.

She put a hand on his arm to waylay him. 'Whatever's the matter, Pierce?'

'It's his lordship,' Pierce said. 'Only gone and ruined a perfectly good set of linens. Not to mention his new jacket. I've no idea how I'm going to get the blood out.'

'Blood?'

Pierce indicated the shirt. The red-brown stain on the back of the new linen told its own story.

'Soak it in cold water,' Isabel suggested. Gathering up her skirt, she hastened down the corridor to Sebastian's room.

She found him sitting in a large, winged chair wearing a pair of loose trousers, a clean shirt and a loose green brocade banyan that she recognised as one of Anthony's. Underneath the shirt, she could see the tell-tale ridge of heavy bandaging. He had placed his slippered feet on a stool and had his nose in a book. He looked up as she entered.

'Don't stand!' she said as he reached for the arms of the chair to haul himself up.

As he subsided back into the chair with a grimace, she opened her mouth, but something flashed in his eye and she thought better of it.

'My dear Lady Somerton, if you're here to practice your schoolroom manners and lecture me on the foolishness of riding horses when I am barely out of my sick bed, spare yourself,' he said with a rueful smile. 'I have been lectured by Bennet and disapproved of by Pierce.'

Relief sharpened her tongue. 'I am naturally concerned for your health, my lord. It would be most inconvenient if you were to die on me now.'

She tempered the words with a smile as he shut the book with a thump.

'I assure you, Lady Somerton, I have no intention of dying.'

'I'm relieved to hear that.'

She wanted to tell him what a remarkable thing he had done, but something in his demeanour discouraged discussion of what had occurred in the stable yard.

He held up the book he had been reading. 'Tell me, are all the books in the library like this?'

'Like what?'

He flicked the pages. 'Uncut.'

Isabel took the book from him. John Milton's *Paradise Lost*, exquisitely bound in Moroccan leather and embossed with the Somerton coat of arms, its uncut pages smelt as if they had come straight from the printer. A letter opener sat on the table next to Sebastian's chair, along with a decanter of whisky and a glass.

She handed it back to him. 'Your grandfather purchased the library. The books were for show, not for reading.'

He opened it to the page he had been reading and, without looking up at her, said, 'Please excuse me from joining you for dinner. I am under orders from Bennet that I am not to set one foot outside this room.'

Isabel allowed a smile to catch at the corners of her mouth.

'You tolerate a great deal of insubordination from your batman, Captain Alder.'

He looked up at her and she saw no humour in his eyes.

'I owe Bennet my life. He can be as insubordinate as he likes. Thank you for your concern about my health. Now you have satisfied yourself that I am not at death's door, I will see you tomorrow, Lady Somerton.'

Dismissed, Isabel left the room, closing the door softly behind her, just as the gong rang to announce dinner.

Chapter Seventeen

Bennet disliked horses. A Londoner born and bred, he had no understanding of them, considering them four-legged dangers to health and happiness. Unfortunately, it fell to Bennet to brave the stables and retrieve his lordship's brand new hat, which he had mislaid during his latest hare-brained escapade.

Picking his way across a stable yard scattered with horse manure, he met a boy coming out of the main door of the stable, carrying a saddle. He stopped the youngster and enquired after the missing hat.

'I've got it safe in the chaff room.' The boy's face brightened. 'Are you Corporal Bennet?'

Bennet stiffened. 'Mister Bennet now, lad.'

The boy smiled. 'I'm Peter Thompson. No one's ridden Pharaoh like his lordship did today. Even his late lordship never quite...' Realising he may have spoken out of turn, the boy turned pink. 'What's it like in the army? I'd give anything to join the cavalry.'

'Would you, lad? Couldn't imagine anything worse meself. I prefer to have me own two feet firmly on the ground.'

The boy's eyes darted to the door of the stable. 'I can't leave Pa by himself. Not now Ma's sick and Amy's gone.'

'Amy?'

'My sister,' the boy said with a downward turn to his mouth. 'She... she died last autumn. Pa's got no one but me now. It was a bad winter. First Amy and Ma... then we could scarce believe when his lordship had his accident.'

Bennet's interest piqued. 'I 'eard he had an accident. Do you know how it happened?'

Peter hesitated. 'It isn't my place to say.'

'It's all right. You can tell me,' Bennet invited.

'His lordship went a-visiting up at Lady Kendall's,' Peter said. 'Near as we know, he took the hedge over by Lovett's Bridge and the girth broke.' The boy's face took on a sullen, defensive cast. 'It weren't our fault. It were a brand new saddle. Her leddyship had given it to his lordship for his birthday only months afore and he used it all the time. We checked it regular.'

Something in the boy's voice caused Bennet to pause. 'Did you look at it after the accident?'

Peter's eyes darted around the stable yard, and he jerked his head at the door.

'Come wiv me and I'll get his lordship's hat.'

As Bennet followed the boy into the long building, his nose wrinkled at the smell of horse—many horses. Apparently impervious, the boy led him down the line of horse stalls. He stopped at a door at the end of the row and looked back at Bennet.

'Her leddyship told us to destroy the saddle.' The boy shifted his weight and looked around. 'It seemed a shame to destroy such a beautiful thing when all it needed was a new girth strap.'

Bennet looked at the boy, who shuffled his feet as his eyes slid sideways.

'It's all right, lad. It's only me, you won't get into trouble,' he said.

'I put it away somewhere safe.'

'So you still have it?' A small spark of curiosity flared in Bennet.

The boy opened the door. 'Aye, 'tis in here.'

''Ow about you show me?' Bennet suggested.

The chaff room was lined with large wooden bins where the horses' oats and feed were stored. Peter went to the furthest bin and lifted the lid. On first sight, it appeared to be full of chaff. Peter leaned over the edge of the bin and rustled around in the chaff. With a grunt, he pulled out a large, awkward sack and set it on the table.

He pulled off the covering to reveal an elegant, modern saddle. The leather around the pommel had been heavily tooled and bore the Somerton arms. Bennet recognised the stars, from escutcheons all around the house.

As Peter watched, Bennet turned the saddle over. He may not have liked horses but he knew enough to recognise the girth strap, which still hung buckled to the saddle. It had broken high up beneath the saddle flap on the off side. Bennet held up the torn edges. In his hands, the leather still felt new and firm. Even he could see there should have been no reason for the girth to fail. Unless ...

He drew a deep breath as he looked more closely at the broken ends.

To the casual observer, the strap appeared to have torn, but now, as he looked at it, he was not so certain. The first half-inch on both sides of the strap betrayed a clean cut—a knife cut. He turned the strap over in his hands, looking at the underside. Unless he was very much mistaken, the underside of the strap had been scored with a knife as well. It meant that the girth strap had been severely compromised and, put under any kind of stress, would have failed.

Bennet frowned, letting the implication of his discovery sink in. Someone had cut the girth strap. Someone had intended for it to fail. Someone had intended Lord Somerton to suffer a serious fall. He ran his hand over the embossing on the pommel.

Someone had intended for Lord Somerton to be injured or … killed. His blood ran cold.

'It didn't seem right,' Peter said. 'I thought if anyone asked the question…' He tailed off.

Bennet nodded. 'You did the right thing, boy.'

'What should I do with it?'

'Just you put the saddle back where you've been hiding it,' Bennet said.

'Are you sure? Do you think his lordship should know?'

Quite possibly, Bennet thought.

'Just put it back and I think we will keep it our secret for now, lad.'

He watched as the boy returned the parcelled saddle to the bottom of the feed bin. As the boy turned around, Bennet looked around the room.

'Now where's his lordship's 'at?'

❦

Bennet stamped into the bedchamber carrying Sebastian's hat. Sebastian set his book to one side and considered his batman from over his steepled fingers. He knew Bennet's moods as well as he knew his own. And something troubled his batman.

Bennet stood by the window, absently brushing chaff from the beaver skin.

'Something on your mind, Bennet?' Sebastian enquired.

Bennet started as if he hadn't noticed Sebastian.

'Beg pardon, m'lord,' he said.

Sebastian raised an eyebrow and, taking his silence as it was intended—an invitation to talk—Bennet set the hat down and crossed over to Sebastian's chair.

'Mind me speaking out of turn, sir?'

'When has that ever stopped you? What's troubling you?'

'Well, you know as how the late Lord Somerton died?'

'Girth broke and he came off his horse.'

Bennet nodded. 'I... No, it don't make sense.'

'What are you talking about, Bennet?'

'I've just seen the saddle and the girth strap was cut.'

Sebastian stared at him. 'Are you sure?'

'As certain as I am standing here talking to you.'

Bennet took a breath and recounted his interview with young Peter Thompson. When he had finished, Sebastian sat back in the chair and let the enormity of what Bennet had told him sink in.

Anthony's death was no accident. Someone had intended, if not to kill him, to at least cause a serious injury. He glanced at the door and thought about the residents beyond it.

Someone in this house could be a murderer.

Chapter Eighteen

Sebastian faced Bragge across the large mahogany desk in the study. He liked this room. While Freddy Lynch seemed to be in possession of the library, filling it with the nauseating cologne that he wore, this room, with its leather inlaid desk and resolutely masculine furniture, made him feel welcome.

He and Bragge had been on an inspection tour of the estate, an excursion undertaken from the back of one of the more docile saddle horses. Even so, he felt stiff and sore and out of sorts.

The state of the farms had horrified him. No money had been spent on their upkeep for years. Little wonder the returns were so low.

'It is time for some economising. Is everything in order for the auction on Friday?'

'It is, my lord.' It had not taken Bragge long to organise for the sale of the racehorses, setting up an auction to be held at the hall. 'We should do well. There are years of work invested in those beasts and they have a good reputation.'

'Then they should be worth something to someone whose business it is to understand these things. Personally, I have no interest in racing,' Sebastian said. 'Far better they go to someone who will pay us well for them.'

'What about the rest of the stable, sir?'

Sebastian thought of the matched bay carriage horses and the elegant grey pair used for the phaeton. He could not bring himself to sell those—not yet.

'Just the racing horses.'

Bragge scribbled in his notebook.

'Now about this ball that Miss Lynch is hell bent on holding ...' Sebastian began, his hand straying to a small, steadily mounting pile of invoices that seemed to be associated with the soiree.

'Well, it does seem rather an extravagance, my lord, but on the other hand, it is an excellent way of meeting the county. I used to say to his late lordship that the importance of one's acquaintances was not to be underestimated.'

'And he ignored your advice?'

'He was wont to ignore my advice on most matters, my lord.'

Bragge's tight lips betrayed his thoughts on the subject of the last Lord Somerton.

Sebastian heaved a sigh. 'The ball remains but between us, Bragge, what am I to do with the Lynchs? They've been costing my cousin a fortune.'

The drain on the purse caused by those two individuals showed up in the accounts as a hefty monthly allowance paid to Freddy. The sum did not, of course, include the free board and lodging he and his sister also enjoyed. He would talk to Lynch about the ridiculous allowance his cousin had been paying. It should have been sufficient to keep him and his sister in modest comfort in their own accommodation without the necessity of living on Somerton grace and favour.

Bragge looked surprised. 'Your lordship doesn't owe them anything. They are no relations of yours.'

'I know that, but I feel some moral obligation towards them.'

Bragge averted his eyes, cleared his throat, but said nothing.

Sebastian leaned back in his chair, thinking about Freddy Lynch.

'Tell me, Bragge, has anyone ever looked into their claim to be who they say they are?'

Bragge shook his head. 'His lordship vouched for them. That was enough.'

'I am not my cousin. I think before I make any decision about a settlement, I would like their claims investigated. Good reconnaissance, Bragge, is the key to a successful campaign.'

'Do you have reason to doubt their veracity, my lord?' Bragge ventured.

'There is something about them that is not quite...' Sebastian trailed off. It was not so much a word he sought as a nagging feeling of distrust, honed by a lifetime of rubbing shoulders with every sort of man. Something about Freddy Lynch did not ring true.

Bragge nodded. 'I know a man in that line of work, my lord.'

'Excellent. See to it and, while you're at it, can you find out more about this *Golden Adventurers Club*—the lucky recipient of my inheritance? If for no other reason than I hope to meet one or more of them and give them a bloody nose!'

Bragge's eyebrows rose, but he made no comment, just appended a note in his book. He looked up.

'There is one last matter, my lord.'

'That is?'

'Her ladyship. Have you broken the news of her jointure to her yet?'

A heavy weight settled on Sebastian's shoulders. 'No.'

'It is just that she has tradesmen working on the dower house. Those bills must be paid.'

'Have them sent to me.'

Bragge hesitated for a moment. 'As you wish, my lord.'

He bowed and left the room.

Sebastian stood up and walked over to the window, which afforded an excellent view out across the garden and parkland.

He could see the chimneys of the dower house rising above the trees. He would never let Isabel suffer for the sake of her husband's foolishness. While he was Lord Somerton she would live comfortably, but the matter of the charity school that she had mentioned remained. He knew he had to talk to her, and the sooner the better.

Chapter Nineteen

Isabel sat at her desk penning a letter in reply to Lady Ainslie. Her friend had written that suitable premises had been found for the school and Harriet was keen to sign the lease.

'May I disturb you?'

She looked up as Sebastian entered the parlour, sliding the letter beneath the blotter. She rose to her feet and gestured at one of the chairs. He sat down heavily on one of the elegant gilt seats and she heard an ominous creak from the protesting furniture. Sebastian flushed and, to cover his embarrassment, Isabel picked up a second cup from the tray that had just been brought in to her.

'Would you care for some tea?' she enquired.

'Thank you, Lady Somerton.'

As she handed him the cup, his hand shook slopping tea in the saucer. He upended the contents of the saucer into the cup. Her mouth fell open but, before Isabel could compose herself, he looked up at her with a rueful smile.

'The bad habits of a lifetime are hard to break, Lady Somerton,' he said.

'Unfortunately, it is those little habits that you are going to have to break,' she observed.

She took a dainty sip from her cup and and set it down, folding her hands neatly in her lap. The fingers of Sebastian's right hand drummed the delicate arms of the chair.

'Is there something troubling you?' she enquired.

He brought his clear, strong gaze up to meet hers.

'I have spent the day with Bragge,' he began. 'We're not quite in the workhouse, but I'm going to have to make some serious economies. Were you aware of the position of the estate?'

She shifted uncomfortably and gave a small shrug, wondering what this conversation was leading to.

'I had my suspicions. Like his father before him, Somerton was a profligate spender, and I knew the money didn't all come from his success at the races.'

'No, it didn't,' Sebastian said. He leaned forward, clasping his hands together on his knees. 'Lady Somerton, I have some bad news to impart to you.' He took a deep breath. 'It is about your jointure. Your late husband...'

She stared at him, the implication of what he was saying beginning to dawn on her. Surely not her jointure. She put a hand to her mouth as her life shattered at her feet.

'It's gone?' she said.

He nodded. 'He forged your signature on the papers.'

That knowledge twisted like a knife in her heart. He had forged her signature. What else had he done?

'What did he spend it on?' Every word came out with an effort.

Sebastian shrugged. 'Apart from his gambling debts at Whites, it seems a large portion went on a gold mine venture in Guinea.'

She let out a heavy breath, fighting tears.

'And what charlatan got him to invest in such a venture?'

Sebastian shook his head. 'I don't know. It was called the

Golden Adventurers Club but who its members were, I have no idea. I have asked Bragge to look into it further.'

She looked away, her hand to her mouth and her heart hammering as she battled her emotions. It had all gone and with it her freedom, her dreams... the school... What would she tell Harriet?

With difficulty, she brought her attention back to Sebastian, seeing the concern in his eyes.

A good man, she thought, *but how could he possibly even begin to understand?*

'I want to assure you, Lady Somerton, that it will be my responsibility to ensure you want for nothing. The dower house is yours, and I will provide a monthly allowance—'

'The dower house?' She heard her voice catch, and she rose to her feet. Swallowing, she managed to say, 'It is not the dower house, Lord Somerton... it is my life. Please excuse me.'

Without looking backwards, she left him and barely made the sanctuary of her own bedchamber before the flood burst. She fell face down on the covers of her bed, curling into a small ball as her heart broke.

Just when she thought Anthony could hurt her no more, he had reached from the grave and stolen the last of her dreams from her.

Chapter Twenty

The day of the horse auction dawned bright and clear. From early in the morning, a large crowd began to gather in the grounds, where Sebastian, at Freddy's suggestion, had obligingly arranged for the erection of a large marquee and light refreshment. In discussing the plans over dinner, Freddy had pointed out that a crowd that had been fed and watered with a pleasant ale would be more likely to be feeling in an expansive mood when the bidding began.

Sebastian had twelve horses to sell and, to judge from the crowd, they would fetch a pretty penny. Not for the first time, he considered that Anthony's eye for horses could have been the man's one redeeming feature. It may well be the saving of the estate.

As he circulated among the crowd, he noticed Lady Kendall in conversation with her brother as they inspected a handsome bay mare. They both looked up as he approached. Lady Kendall smiled as Sebastian took her outstretched hand.

'Do you have an interest in horses, Lady Kendall?' he enquired.

Her eyes crinkled at the corners. 'Indeed I do. My last

husband owned several winners at Newmarket and I rather enjoy carrying on his tradition.'

'Are there any horses here that take your eye?' Sebastian indicated the magnificent beasts being paraded around the crowd.

'I rather fancy that chestnut with the white sock on his off foreleg,' Lady Kendall said.

'I don't believe he has any wins to his name,' Sebastian responded.

'Not yet,' she said. 'What about you, Harry?'

'My man is bidding on the sorrel filly,' Harry said.

She nodded. 'Excellent choice, but I doubt Father will be quite so sanguine if you are successful. Now I really must go and talk to my own man about the chestnut.' She dipped a curtsey, and smiling sweetly at both men, excused herself.

Sebastian stared after her as the crowd parted to let her through. Although it was predominantly a male occasion, a few wives and families had accompanied their menfolk, no doubt, Sebastian considered ruefully, hoping for a chance of an early encounter with the new, and eminently eligible, Lord Somerton.

Out of the corner of his eye, he saw one of the county mamas, with her clutch of eligible daughters in tow, bearing down on them.

'Come inside and join me in an ale,' Sebastian said, grasping his friend by the elbow and propelling him bodily towards the house.

Inside the cool hall, they encountered Fanny tying on her bonnet.

'What a crowd,' Fanny said. 'Who would have thought such a boring thing as selling horses could be such a social occasion? I thought I should like to join Freddy and see the bidding.'

Harry bowed low over Fanny's hand as Sebastian introduced her.

'Enchanted. Of course, Mr. Lynch and myself are acquainted, but Alder never mentioned you were cousins.'

'Well she's not actually *my* cousin,' Sebastian pointed out. He nearly added, *I appear to have inherited her with the estate*, but refrained.

'Are you a friend of dear cousin Sebastian's?' Fanny enquired, tucking her hand around Sebastian's arm.

His jaw clenched at the unwanted intimacy and the assumption of ownership the gesture entailed.

'We served together in the same regiment, my dear,' Harry said.

'Oh, then you must have some wonderful stories to tell about Seb—Lord Somerton.'

Fanny flashed Sebastian her prettiest smile but he had become inured to her charms over their short acquaintance.

As Harry opened his mouth to speak, Sebastian shot him a warning glance and Harry said, 'Just boring military stuff. Nothing of any interest to a pretty young thing such as yourself.'

Fanny giggled, covering her mouth with her free hand and patting her curls.

She cast a dimpled smile at Harry. 'I do hope you will be attending the ball, Colonel?'

'What ball?' Harry cast an enquiring eye at Sebastian.

'Some ghastly soiree Fanny is organising to allow me the opportunity to meet the neighbours,' Sebastian replied, removing the clinging hand from his arm. 'Although, by the look of this crowd, I think they're all here today. They seem hell bent on introducing themselves to me and I'm damned if I can remember a single name.'

'Cousin Sebastian is being quite churlish about it,' Fanny pouted.

'Sebastian Alder? Churlish about a ball? Never!' Harry said with a wink.

'As I have explained to Miss Lynch, a certain French musket ball ended my dancing days.'

'Nonsense. You hardly limp. I don't see why you can't dance,' said Harry unhelpfully.

'I am certain an invitation has been sent to your sister, so I do hope you will come as well,' Fanny continued.

'Wouldn't miss it for the world, if only to see Bas here in dancing slippers!' He glanced at Sebastian and winked. 'I've got no immediate plans that would take me away from Lincolnshire.'

'I think that is the auctioneer's bell,' Sebastian said.

'You're not going to watch?' Fanny pouted.

Sebastian shook his head. 'No. Bragge can give me the good news later.'

After Fanny left the house, Sebastian shook his head and clapped his friend on the shoulder.

'You have just set your cap at the silliest female it has ever been my misfortune to meet.'

Harry grinned. 'Just a bit of fun, Alder.'

'Odd pair, those,' Sebastian remarked. 'You said you know Lynch?'

Harry shook his head. 'I've met him a few times, in London. Always happy for a hand of cards. I must confess she's a pretty thing, though.'

'No dowry, no pedigree that I am aware of and one of the most foolish females I have ever met.'

Harry shook his head. 'Alder, you are too quick to judgement. Apart from the lack of dowry and pedigree, she may well have other redeeming features.'

Sebastian admitted Harry to the peace of the study and the two men subsided into the masculine leather chairs that stood by the empty grate. Johnson brought two stout ales on a silver tray. The absurdity of the gesture did not escape Sebastian. He caught the footman's eyes but, beyond a slight quirk of the mouth, the man was too well trained to react.

'I can't tell you what a relief it is to have a familiar face here,' Sebastian said.

Harry smiled. 'It's good to see you too. Not sorry to miss the fun at Waterloo.'

Sebastian laughed without humour. 'Oh, trust me, you missed

nothing. The rain and the mud for starters... and when the Imperial Guard charged us, I thought my day had finally come.'

'Ah, but you stood up to them, Alder.'

'The square held but Heyland—you remember him?—died in my arms. We took La Haye Sainte farm but I got hit in the process. We lost a lot of good men that day.'

Harry nodded. 'You look to have made a good recovery.'

'I have Lady Somerton to thank for that. She's the one who found me. If I'm honest, she probably saved my life.'

'Ah yes, the formidable Lady Somerton,' Harry said. 'I can imagine she let nothing stand in her way when she thought she had found Lord Somerton's heir.'

Sebastian regarded his friend for a long moment. 'I've heard that it was not a happy marriage.'

Harry took a draught of his ale before replying. 'A more mismatched couple you would never meet, but they tried.'

This was news to Sebastian. 'What do you mean?'

'In the early days of their marriage, they were the centre of quite an influential circle of the *ton*. The house in London was the place to be seen but his eye started to wander and the marriage soured.' Harry drained his cup and seemed to contemplate the empty vessel for a moment before he said, 'Lady Somerton retired to the country. I don't think she's been seen in London much in several years.'

'And Anthony?'

Harry swilled his beer. 'I don't think he was seen much at Brantstone.'

'Tell me about Anthony. Did he have any enemies?'

Harry frowned. 'Enemies? A man like that is sure to have enemies. Possibly a few cuckolded husbands, certainly cheated card players, but no one in particular comes to mind. Why do you ask?'

Armed with the information Bennet had given him, Sebastian had slipped unseen into the stables and inspected the saddle for himself. The cut had been subtle but the evidence damning.

The saddle had been tampered with in such a way as to cause a rider serious injury ... or death.

'I think ...' Sebastian voiced, for the first time, the thought that had been growing in his mind since Bennet first told him about the saddle. 'I think he may have been murdered.'

Harry's eyes widened. 'Good lord! What on earth makes you think that?'

'I've got evidence,' he said.

'What sort of evidence?'

Sebastian shook his head. He'd said too much, even to Harry, whom he would have trusted with his life.

'I'm probably seeing shadows where there aren't any. Take no notice of me.'

Harry shook his head in disbelief. 'You must be mistaken, Alder. God knows he could be irritating and he certainly owed money to all and sundry, but I can't think of anyone who would want to *kill* him.' He paused and laughed, raising his glass to his lips again. 'Apart from you, that is!'

'I didn't even know he existed and, besides, I have an impeccable alibi.'

Harry frowned. 'Be sensible, Alder. Who would want to kill him?'

'That's what I was asking you.'

Harry laughed. 'No, you are seeing shadows. Somerton broke his neck taking a hedge. Accidents happen. It doesn't mean there is anything sinister about it.' When Sebastian didn't respond, Harry's face sobered. 'You surely don't suspect someone in this house capable of such a thing?'

Sebastian had considered that question. It seemed to be in Freddy and Fanny's interest to keep Anthony alive. The servants? It seemed ludicrous that a servant would kill their master unless they had very good reason to do so.

To the best of his knowledge, the only person with motive enough to want to see Anthony dead may have been Isabel. But why? It certainly seemed to have been a loveless marriage but that was not generally motive for murder. Money? Murder seemed an extreme measure for finding the finance to start a school. He pushed the thought away.

'The man had enough creditors,' Harry said. 'Maybe one of them ...?'

Sebastian shook his head. 'They'd have wanted him alive. A dead debtor is of no use.'

Harry set down his empty mug. 'No, it seems too far-fetched. I can't believe it, Alder.'

'Your sister was possibly the last person to see him alive. Has she said anything about the night he died?'

'Georgie? Good God, no. Why?'

'I have heard rumours that he had ...' Sebastian searched for the right word, 'an involvement with your sister.'

Harry regarded him for a moment. 'Look, she's my sister and I adore her, but I'm not immune to her faults. She likes to marry old, rich men and likes to take the young, good-looking ones to her bed. Somerton was one of the latter. so yes, it's quite likely they formed some sort of attachment. I'm not privy to my sister's private life.' He gave a shudder. 'In fact, I deem it in my own best interest not to know, but if it puts your mind at rest, Alder, I was there that night and nothing untoward happened. He came for supper and left. That was it.'

'Was he drunk?'

Harry shrugged. 'He'd had a few wines but he was in control if that is what you are asking.' He laughed. 'Forget it, Alder. It was an accident. They happen. And on the subject of my lovely sister, I give you fair warning that you may need to watch your own honour. I've seen the way she looks at you.'

Sebastian laughed. 'As if she would eat me for supper?'

'Preferably covered in a sugar glaze with an apple in your mouth,' Harry said. 'Dangerous woman, my sister.'

'I can see the attraction, Dempster, but no... I assure you I can resist her blandishments.'

Harry leaned forward, his brow creased. 'It's none of my

business, Alder, but it's been seven years since Inez. You've got responsibilities now. Time to find yourself another wife.'

The back of Sebastian's neck prickled as it always did when Inez was mentioned.

'I've always had responsibilities, Dempster.'

'But now you need an heir.'

Sebastian rose to his feet and walked over to the window. Outside, the crowd was beginning to drift away. The auction had concluded. His heart clenched, the pain as raw and bitter as it had been the day he had found his wife's battered and violated body.

He heard Harry rise to his feet and join him at the window. They stood together in empathetic silence.

'I'm serious,' Harry said at last. 'You have to overcome thinking of yourself as plain Captain Sebastian Alder. You are now Lord Somerton, and the world and all the beautiful women you have ever dreamed of are at your feet. Take in the London season, play the field. You never know.'

'Playing the field has little interest.'

'What about the widow?' Harry suggested.

'Isabel? Good lord, Harry! I hardly know her.'

Harry just shook his head. 'No one says you have to love the woman you marry. You just want two things, a good dowry and a good breeder.'

Sebastian shot his friend a look of disgust.

'That's how it's done,' Harry said with a shrug.

Sebastian stared out of the window, horrified by his friend's cold, calculating approach to marriage.

Was that how it had been for Anthony and Isabel? he wondered.

Chapter Twenty-One

Isabel woke to a gentle knocking on her door and her maid's voice at the keyhole.

'M' lady, m' lady...'

Sitting up, she bade Lily come in and the woman, clad in her nightdress with a shawl over her shoulders, crept into the room.

'Sorry to disturb you, ma'am,' Lily said, 'but young Peter's downstairs. Millie's foaling and it isn't going well. Thompson thought you would want to know.'

Isabel swung her legs out of the bed as she ran her hands over her face in an effort to wake herself up.

'Of course I do. Quick, Lily, find me some warm clothes.'

Clad in an old dress of blue wool with a tartan shawl wrapped around her, her hair still tied in a loose braid down her back, Isabel hurried from the room, letting the door slam behind her.

'What's going on?'

She had reached the stairs and turned to see Sebastian standing in the doorway of his bedchamber, his green banyan pulled haphazardly over his nightshirt. His hair stuck up in spikes.

'I'm sorry, I didn't mean to wake you,' Isabel said.

'I wasn't asleep,' Sebastian growled, although his dishevelled hair and heavy eyes gave a lie to his words. 'I'm a light sleeper,' he added.

'It's Millie,' Isabel said. 'She's having difficulty with the foal.'

'Wait there. I'll just find some clothes.' Sebastian turned back into his room.

'Really, my lord, there is no need,' Isabel said, but the door had already shut behind him.

She joined the boy in the hallway. Peter shifted from foot to foot with impatience until Sebastian, looking like he had grabbed the nearest clothes he could find, joined them.

They hurried out of the house to the stables. The little piebald mare lay on the clean straw bedding of her stall, lathered in sweat and clearly in distress. Her terrified eyes rolled towards her mistress, and she uttered a faint nicker.

Thompson, his sleeves rolled up over his elbows, knelt on the straw at her rear. He looked up as they entered the stall and shook his head, his mouth a grim line. Isabel sank to the floor, holding the mare's head in her lap and whispering in her ear while Sebastian ran a hand over her heaving flank. One tiny hoof protruded from the birth canal.

'This is not good,' Sebastian said.

Thompson nodded. 'I reckon he's stuck.'

'The foal will have to be repositioned,' Sebastian said.

Thompson looked up at him. 'I'll have to get the boy to try, sir. I cut my hand this morning.' He held up a bandaged right hand.

'I've done this before,' Sebastian said, stripping off his jacket and shirt, and when Thompson looked doubtful, he added. 'I've been around horses all my life, Thompson. Isabel, can you get her to stand?'

Isabel tried not to let her eyes linger on the impressive expanse of chest above the heavy strapping. Not for the first time did it warrant favourable comparison with her late husband whose pampered lifestyle showed in his physique. This man had obviously lived a vigorous outdoor life. The years of soldiering were written on that hard, muscular body. The tan did not stop at his neckline but extended down his powerful chest and shoulders, contrasting with the white bandage that still bound his recent wound.

Her heartbeat quickened in a way she had not experienced. *Damn the man!* The unexpected reaction to the sight of Sebastian's torso astonished her, as if a part of herself she had kept shut away tapped at the door to her consciousness.

'Isabel? Lady Somerton?'

Realising he had asked her to get the mare to stand, she nodded and rose, urging the mare to come with her. Millie did not want to cooperate. It took the strength of both men and a great deal of coaxing from Isabel to get the little pony to her feet. The mare stood on shaking legs while Sebastian washed his right arm thoroughly before covering it with a foul-smelling grease Thompson had produced.

Isabel watched, the unspoken words forming on her lips to stop him, conscious, even if he was not, that he was in no physical shape for this sort of exertion. She held her peace. Millie needed help and he was the only person who could provide it, so she held the pony's head while Sebastian slid his arm inside the mare.

He grimaced and then smiled. 'Come on little fellow,' he said. 'Out you come. Thompson, tie that bootlace to the hoof and pull down—gently.'

Thompson complied.

'Isabel, let her go,' Sebastian ordered.

Isabel released her hold on the halter and the mare went down on her knees, rolling over on her side. The pony groaned and shuddered.

On his knees beside the horse, Sebastian looked up at Isabel and grinned.

'Here he comes. Well done, Millie.'

Isabel stroked the mare's neck as the second hoof protruded

and, with one gigantic contraction, the nose and head of the foal appeared.

Sebastian sat back on his heels as Peter, following his father's instructions, gently eased the little creature out, the boy's face shining with wonder. Millie gave a great shuddering sigh and relaxed under Isabel's hand.

They sat in awe as the mare and the little foal rested from their travails. Isabel stole a glance at the new Lord Somerton, seeing the smile on his face as the mare's head swung around to look at her baby. It would have been beneath Anthony's dignity to have attended the stable, let alone participated in a foaling. He loved horses, but Anthony liked to keep himself away from anything remotely dirty or unpleasant. That had been Anthony's loss. Nothing could have been more wonderful than seeing a new life come into the world.

With a grunt, Millie rose to her feet. The foal also struggled up, standing on shaking stick-thin legs. The foal nickered and it was Sebastian, not the head groom, who instructed Peter in guiding the baby's questing mouth towards its mother. It took a couple of attempts but it latched on and began suckling greedily, its little tail beating in pleasure.

Isabel's heart melted both at the sight of the little creature and the smile on Sebastian's face. Hardened soldier or not, the experience of the foal's birth clearly affected him and tears started in her own eyes. She dashed them away before he could notice and think her foolish.

Thompson looked up at the window. 'It'll be dawn soon.' He turned back to Sebastian. 'Thank you, my lord. You missed your vocation as a stable hand.'

Sebastian smiled as he rose to his feet. 'Oh, I had plenty of practice. As a boy, I used to haunt the local squire's stables. I'll leave you to it and have a wash down outside.'

Isabel picked up his shirt and coat. 'I'll bring these,' she said.

He looked down at his hands and grimaced.

'Thanks.'

'Ye'll find soap by the trough,' Thompson said and turned back to the horse.

The first grey streaks of dawn lightened the sky as Sebastian and Isabel stepped out into the courtyard. A water-filled trough stood to one side of the door, soap balanced on the rim, and a rough towel hung on a rusty nail.

Sebastian plunged his arms into the trough with a sharp exclamation at the water's temperature. He picked up the soap and began scrubbing vigorously. Standing to one side, holding his shirt and coat, Isabel found her eyes fixed on his broad shoulders. His muscles rippled beneath the brown skin and once again her heartbeat quickened. She took a deep steadying breath.

As the sky lightened, she could see that there were other scars marring the brown skin.

'You seem remarkably careless of your life, Lord Somerton.'

He glanced at a long, white scar that ran down his bicep. 'I've been a soldier a long time, Isabel.'

A flush of pleasure rose to her cheeks at this invitation to familiarity. Being alone with a half-naked man in the early hours of the morning did not call for formality, neither did it reflect well on her reputation. She glanced around the stable yard, but they were quite alone.

He straightened and began towelling off. The grey light of the early dawn flattened the planes of his face, leeching the colour from his skin and eyes, but she could see the lift of humour curling the corners of his mouth as he caught her watching him, and the heat rose to her face as she thrust his shirt at him.

He pulled it over his head and took the coat from her, his eyes not leaving her face. As he buttoned the coat he tilted his head to one side.

'I've been trying to work out what is different about you this morning. It's your hair.'

He reached out and touched the loosely tied, heavy braid

that hung over her shoulder. His finger brushed her cheek, leaving a burning trail across her cool skin.

'What about my hair?' Isabel stuttered.

'I like the way you have bits of it around your face,' he withdrew his hand and looked away. 'Now I am being personal.'

Given his previous state of undress and the fact that they were alone together, a personal remark seemed the least of her concerns.

'I'll forgive you this once.' She took a step back from him. 'I must be getting back to the house.'

Before someone sees us together like this.

Sebastian looked at the sky. 'It's going to be another lovely day. I think I'll go for a walk.'

Isabel lingered in the gateway to the stable, watching him stride away from her into the early morning mist. He moved with purpose and strength, and she felt sure, had she been a soldier, she would have willingly followed where he led.

Chapter Twenty-Two

Sebastian strode into the breakfast room. He did not look like a man who had spent the early hours of the morning assisting with a foaling. Freshly shaved and with a neatly tied, white, starched linen stock, he looked like a man who had slept long and well. A lock of dark hair fell damply across his forehead, and Isabel could smell the tang of fresh soap.

She, on the other hand, felt—as her late aunt would have said—like she had been dragged through a hedge backwards. With only a few hours of sleep, the dark circles dragged her eyes into her head. Her hair lacked lustre and fell in lank locks from the harsh bun into which she had screwed it that morning.

Freddy looked up from his cup of tea.

'My dear Somerton, you look very pleased with yourself this morning.'

Sebastian sat down. 'We had a very successful day yesterday,' he said. 'I can now clear some of the worst of my cousin's debts, and,' he glanced at Isabel, 'we now have a new addition to the stable. Has Lady Somerton told you?'

Two pairs of eyes turned on Isabel. She swallowed her mouthful of tea.

'Millie foaled last night,' she said. 'A lovely little colt.'

'Oh, I must go and visit after breakfast!' Fanny clasped her hands together under her chin. 'I love baby animals.'

'Of course you do,' Freddy simpered.

Isabel glanced at Sebastian and caught the twitch of his mouth. It was all she could do not to laugh.

'Your mail, my lord.' A footman with a silver salver bearing the morning mail appeared at Sebastian's elbow. Sebastian took the letters and the proffered letter opener and sifted through the missives.

'My brother,' he said, selecting one and consigning the rest to the table.

He slid the knife beneath the seal and opened it with a smile. However, as he read through the note, his brow darkened.

'Is something amiss in Little Benning?' Isabel enquired.

Sebastian ran his hand through his damp hair, making it stick up on end, and rose to his feet with such speed that his chair toppled backwards, skilfully retrieved by Johnson before it hit the floor.

'I have to go home,' he said.

'Home?' Fanny asked, her eyes wide with astonishment. 'What do you mean?'

'Cheshire.' Sebastian looked at Isabel. 'My sister has been taken ill and is in a high fever. Baker—' he addressed one of the other footmen, who visibly jumped.

Sebastian had apparently made it his business to learn the name of all the household staff and made sure he addressed them by their names. As this was unheard of in his cousin's time, it was little wonder that the poor staff looked startled when his lordship spoke to them.

'My lord?'

'Take a message to Thompson that I want Pharaoh saddled and ready within the hour.'

He turned and strode out of the room. Isabel rose quickly and caught up with him in the front hall. She interposed herself between him and the stairs, standing on the second step to bring herself level with him.

'You cannot possibly consider riding Pharaoh to Cheshire,' she said.

'Indeed, I can. Please stand aside, Lady Somerton.' He placed a foot on the first step, meaning to go around her, but she responded by laying her hand on his chest.

'You are barely out of your own sick bed,' she said.

Sebastian stepped back. 'What do you mean?'

'I mean, if you ride hell for leather to your sister's bedside today, you will be more likely to end up tearing your wound open again and risking a fever. Let me order the coach for you.'

'The coach,' he repeated and ran a hand across his eyes. 'I forgot that I own a coach.'

'I shall order it to be brought around to the front door in an hour. That will give me enough time to pack a few things myself,' Isabel continued.

He frowned up at her. 'What do you mean?'

'I shall accompany you.'

Sebastian stared at her. 'That is very kind, Lady Somerton, but really there is no need.'

'There is a young girl who needs a...' she paused, struggling for a word, 'a friend.'

'I assure you, she is well cared for. My housekeeper, Mrs. Mead—'

'Can hardly manage a household and a sick girl, Lord Somerton. Trust me, I have some experience in these matters. I will be of more use to you there than here,' she said in a voice that, she hoped, brooked no opposition.

Chapter Twenty-Three

As the coach rolled out of Brantstone's great gates, Isabel looked across at Sebastian, slumped in the diagonal corner, resting his head on his hand as he stared out of the window, his concern for his sister written in the downward turn of his mouth and the furrowed brow.

So long used to concealing all emotion, a forgotten place in her heart stirred and she reached out and laid her hand over his.

'Sebastian,' she said, using his first name without conscious thought, 'we will be there by the morning. There is nothing you can do for her and worrying won't help.'

He made no effort to withdraw his hand.

'I should have been there... I shouldn't have left them... I should have brought them with me.' The words, heavy with responsibility and guilt, rolled out.

She tightened her fingers around his. 'You did exactly the right thing. Even if you had been there, your presence would not have stopped Constance taking ill. It is probably nothing more than a fever. It will pass and you can bring them back to Brantstone with you when she is strong enough.'

He looked up at her, his face contorted with distress. 'They are the world to me, Isabel. My mother passed away when

Connie was born, and my stepfather died when they were still young. I am all they have and I have been neglectful of my duties to them.'

She smiled, trying to instil some confidence in him. 'No brother could have done more. I look forward to meeting them.'

He looked down at her hand and his fingers tightened on hers. 'Thank you for coming. You are a good friend, Lady Somerton—Isabel.'

Even through the soft kid of her gloves, she could feel the strength in his fingers. Her breath quickened as his gaze met hers, and he released her hand and returned to his contemplation of the passing countryside.

Isabel leaned back against the leather squabs and closed her eyes. On one hand, it pleased her to be thought of as his friend, but, somewhere deep inside, did she seek more than friendship? Is that why she had offered to come with him? A selfish opportunity to spend time alone with him, away from the many eyes at Brantstone?

No, she told herself. Her concern was for Constance. If she had a motive it was purely selfish. She needed to ensure Sebastian's sister was well and capable of taking on the responsibility of the house. Bringing Constance to Brantstone had to be achieved before she would be free of the last of her duties.

'Do you have any family, Isabel?' Sebastian's voice jerked her out of her reverie.

She opened her eyes and shook her head. 'No. My parents are dead and none of my siblings survived their infancy. The climate in the West Indies is unforgiving for the weak.'

He turned away from the window to look at her. 'The West Indies?'

'My father made his fortune in sugar, and I was born in Jamaica. A tropical fever carried both my parents off when I was nine, and I was sent home to England to be brought up by my aunt and uncle.'

'Where was that?'

'Near Manchester. My uncle was a mill owner.'

'And were they kind to you, your aunt and uncle?'

For a moment she didn't answer—couldn't answer. Memories of the beatings and the dark cupboard under the servants' stairs, where she had been confined for real and imagined infractions against the iron rule of her aunt, still haunted her nightmares.

'They were childless.' She paused. 'My uncle was kind but my aunt had her own ideas about how to bring up a child. When I was not at school I helped with the local charities she supported. I suppose I should be grateful to her. Through that work I saw how bleak the life of the working women could be.' She bit her tongue before she added, *Any woman's life.*

He studied her face for a long moment.

'And how did you come to marry my cousin?'

'My aunt sent me to London for a season and we were introduced. I imagined myself in love with him.'

Madly, deeply, wildly in love. She had begged her uncle to permit the marriage. He had tried to warn her but she would not hear a word against him. Anthony had offered for her, her aunt approved, and her uncle could only agree. Like the smuggled romances she had read at school, she would marry Anthony and live happily ever after.

'Anthony needed an heiress and he got what he wanted: a wealthy wife with a good dowry.'

'And you?'

'I escaped my aunt's cold house for a gilded cage of another making.' She could not keep the bitterness from her words.

When she raised her eyes to look at him, she saw the undisguised shock in his face and said with a hollow laugh, 'That is how it is done, Lord Somerton, and if you have any sense you will do something similar. Find yourself a wealthy wife and restore the fortune of the Somertons. I think I know you well enough to know you will not squander the windfall the way Anthony did.'

She could hear the acrimony in her voice but felt powerless to prevent it.

He frowned, his gaze burning into hers through the gloom of the carriage as he said, 'When I wed, Lady Somerton, it will not be for the sake of a convenient business arrangement.'

'Then you are a romantic, Sebastian.'

Once she had been a romantic. At the school for young ladies she had been sent to, like the other girls, she had sighed over distant, unattainable young men and buried her nose in unsuitable novels, but after a few months of marriage, she had turned her thoughts to loftier ideals. If there was nothing to be done about her marriage, perhaps in some small way, she could help other women.

Now she sat in a coach with a man who professed that he would only wed for love and wondered what real love was. How did it feel? How did you know when you were in love? She knew it had not been the breathtaking desperation she had felt when the devilishly handsome Anthony Kingsley sauntered into a room.

Had it been the happiness she had known in those months after William's birth when Anthony had sloughed off his veneer of callousness and indifference and had been attentive to her every wish? There had been no visits to London. He had stayed at Brantstone. They had laughed together and, once again, her heart lifted when he walked into the room.

William's death had ended all of that. When she had needed him the most he had withdrawn from her, retreated to London and his old life. On the few occasions he had returned to Brantstone, the visits were marked with deliberate cruelty and long visits to Lady Kendall.

'Isabel?' Sebastian's voice jerked her out of her maudlin reverie. 'Did I say something out of turn?'

She shook her head. 'I was just thinking that love did not help your parents, Lord Somerton. Your father disinherited, and your mother cast out of her family.'

He rested a long finger against his cheek and leaned on his hand.

'I cannot answer for my parents, Isabel. I never knew them together but I do know my mother found both love and happiness with the Reverend Alder. That was the pattern of my childhood, and that is all I ask for my children. To be brought up with two parents who both love and respect each other.'

'You ask a lot, Sebastian.' Isabel shook her head. 'In my experience, romantic love is a foolish concept.'

He tilted his head to one side. 'My cousin has a great deal to answer for, Isabel, to have left you so wounded and bitter.'

Was it so obvious?

She straightened her shoulders and shrugged. 'No, Sebastian, you're wrong. I have a title and status in society, even if I have no money to my name. As for love, I've nothing to compare. Even when they lived, my parents spent little time in my company. In Jamaica I was raised by the slaves and then an aunt and uncle who kept their distance. That was my lot in life, and I accepted it. Had Anthony not died when he did, I would have endured.'

'Endured? Endured is what I did on the Peninsula, Lady Somerton. It is not my idea of marriage.'

'It is marriage in our class, Sebastian. And it is as well you learn that now or you will find yourself equally as cynical before long.'

His mouth tightened. 'If that is indeed what I am to expect, it is a bleak outlook and it is as well that I was not raised of your class. I do know what it is to love and be loved. My wife—' His voice caught and he looked away.

She looked up at him, remembering his fevered cry for Inez.

'Your wife?' she prompted, inviting his confidence.

He responded with a brusque, 'She died.'

'I'm sorry,' she said.

It seemed an inadequate response for what she took to be a deep and gnawing loss.

He took a deep breath and glanced back at her. 'It was a long time ago.'

She let the silence stretch between them, wondering if he would venture any further information, but he remained staring out of the window.

'Whatever the price, Lord Somerton, I have paid my dues,' she ventured. 'Anthony is dead and, whatever you may think, legally I am now free to do as I wish.'

He shifted, bringing his gaze back to her and relaxing a little as he leaned back against the plush upholstery. He crossed his arms and stretched out his long legs. Her gaze rested momentarily on the strong, well-muscled leg that now intruded on her space.

He regarded her for a long moment before he asked, 'And what is it you wish to do now you have earned your freedom, Lady Somerton?'

She took a breath. 'I know my jointure is gone but I intend to continue with my plans for the charity school.'

He raised an eyebrow. 'And how will you finance it?'

'My friend, Lady Ainslie, has a modest income, so I cannot ask her for money, but I have thought about it and I believe if I start a school in the dower house...'

He sat up straight. 'Start a school in the dower house? What sort of school?'

'A school for young ladies. Daughters of men who can afford to pay for the things that a lady of quality can give them.'

'So you intend to live out your life playing governess to the bored, indolent daughters of the aristocracy? Hardly worthy of you, Isabel.'

She flushed. 'No! But as I no longer have an independent income of my own, except what you can spare, it is a means to an end.'

He leaned back against the dark blue velvet of the coach seat. 'And you think the fees from a school at Brantstone will accomplish this?'

'If I live simply, then yes. Lady Ainslie is, like me, a widow. We have been planning this venture since we were schoolgirls ourselves.'

'No,' he said.

For a moment she thought she had misheard.

'I said, no,' he repeated.

She sat bolt upright. 'No? What do you mean, no?'

'While you may live in the dower house for as long as you wish, I cannot allow you to turn it into a school.'

Heat rose to her face. 'How else am I to raise the funds for my charity school? Would you have me hire out my services as a companion for young ladies wishing to enter society? For that is my only alternative. There are those who seek out impoverished titled ladies to ensure their darlings meet just the right man.'

His mouth tightened into a hard, grim line. 'No, Lady Somerton. I have no wish for you to do either.'

'Then what will you have me do?' she seethed.

He straightened, filling the space in the coach with his presence. 'I will not have you hiring out your services like a... like a... common doxy.'

'A doxy!' Her voice had risen an octave.

He raised a hand. 'That was a poor choice of words. Please, Isabel. You mistake me. If there is a way I can right Anthony's misuse of both you and your fortune, I will do so, but you need to give me time.'

She glared at him through narrowed eyes.

'You want to make it right?' She laughed bitterly. 'It is all gone. Anthony had no such care for either me or my fortune.'

He nodded. 'I know. I just ask for a little patience.'

Isabel subsided in her seat and, with her chin on her hand, looked out of the window without seeing the passing countryside.

'I'm sorry. I spoke harshly. What I am trying to say is that it is my intention that you can continue with your plans without the need for you to resort to teaching the daughters of the indolent wealthy.'

'Hmm,' was all she could think of in response.

He chuckled. 'I think you will like Connie. She has an independent mind, like yours,' Sebastian said.

She brought her attention back to him. 'Well, she is fortunate to have a brother to encourage her in independent thought.'

'I'm not certain that I encourage her,' Sebastian said, 'but if I thought my sister would choose to meekly stay at home keeping house, then I was sorely mistaken. She is a talented artist and has... had...' Isabel heard the quick change in tense. Whatever future Constance had been making for herself had changed with her brother's fortunes. ' Had begun to make her own way in painting miniature portraits.'

'And will she take to the life at Brantstone?'

Sebastian looked up at the roof of the coach. 'I am not sure. It will be hard for her to give away her independence, but you, above all, should understand that.'

Her gaze was drawn to meet his and she struggled to understand what it was in this man that compelled him to protect every living thing he felt some responsibility for. Such a way in this world could only lead to hurt and disappointment.

THEY STOPPED FREQUENTLY TO REST AND CHANGE THE HORSES, and Sebastian, frustrated by the slightest delay, was not content to sit quietly in the inn. He paced the stable yards, chivvying the ostlers along while Isabel took refreshment.

They took a hasty supper at a coaching inn, changed horses again, and, with the lanterns lit, travelled on into the night. The roads became increasingly rough and the coach had to slow to a walking pace as the coachman navigated the treacherous potholes in the dark.

Wakeful and impatient, Sebastian gritted his teeth as the

coach plodded on. Across from him, Isabel had nodded off to sleep. She curled in a corner of the darkened coach, her face no more than a pale oval.

Since their discussion of the morning when he had forbidden her to use the dower house as a school, Isabel had fallen into silence responding to his attempts at conversation with monosyllabic responses. Sebastian had not intended to be quite so blunt with her, and he knew he had upset her, but the thought of her selling her services as a teacher, governess, or companion, or whatever it was she had planned, horrified him.

He reflected on what she had told him of her life and thought he could understand her a little better now. There had been precious little love or happiness in her privileged life. Far better, he thought, to be the penniless child of a parson and grow up in a happy home full of laughter and music.

He wanted to support her venture. He admired the idea—if he was honest, he admired Isabel—but he could make no promises until the state of his finances became clearer.

A lock of hair had come loose and fallen across her face. He leaned across and lifted it, gently tucking it behind her ear. She stirred but did not wake and he let his hand linger just above the soft curve of her cheek.

She didn't have Lady Kendall's striking beauty, but there was a soft vulnerability in her face that she masked in her waking moments. He sat back in his corner with his arms crossed as he contemplated the sleeping woman. She had known so much hurt and bitterness. His cousin had much to answer for.

The coach lurched, throwing Isabel from her seat. She gave a sharp cry as Sebastian caught her. He held her for a moment. Beneath his hands, she seemed to have the fragility of a bird. She went rigid and pushed away from him.

'Steady, Lady Somerton,' he said, and, to his surprise, she stilled in his embrace.

For a moment she seemed to relax and he took a deep breath, drawing in the essence of rosemary and lavender, a scent so different from Lady Kendall's exotic perfumes. All he needed to do was draw her into his arms and he could kiss her. The thought that he wanted to do just that startled him.

The same notion must have occurred to her, and she stiffened. He released his grip and she fell back into her own place, righting her skirts and patting her hair back into place with muttered apologies for inconveniencing him. Once more, the composed and distant Lady Somerton.

He smiled to himself. For all her outward calm, she sounded breathless and flustered. Perhaps Anthony had not completely killed the romantic girl, and there was hope she could learn to love—and trust – again

He laughed, hoping it would put her back at her ease. 'No apology necessary. We should be there soon. We've made good time.'

She looked out into the dark night. 'What time is it?'

He shook his head. 'It must be nearly midnight. I'm sorry. You must be exhausted. I should have let you stop for the night.'

She shook her head. 'Not at all. I have slept quite well.'

'I sent a message on ahead at our last stop, so they will be expecting us.'

The coachman knocked on the roof, and Sebastian pulled down the window.

'Village up ahead, sir.'

He sat back and closed his eyes. He was home.

Chapter Twenty-Four

The coach drew to a shuddering halt and Isabel lifted the leather curtain to peer out of the window. In the dark she could make out little except the outline of a small cottage. Lights burned in one of the downstairs windows, and above the front porch, light glimmered between curtains.

The front door opened, and the silhouette of a young man appeared on the threshold. He held up a lamp, illuminating his face, and stared at the magnificent coach with undisguised awe.

'Matt!'

Without waiting for the footman, Sebastian flung open the door of the coach, jumped down, and raced towards the door like a schoolboy.

The two men met on the garden path and embraced.

Remembering Isabel, Sebastian turned as the coachman handed her down from the coach. With one arm across his brother's shoulder, he guided the young man forward.

'Lady Somerton, allow me to present my brother, Matthew Alder.'

Matthew bowed low over Isabel's hand.

'Welcome to Little Benning, Lady Somerton. I only wish it was in better circumstances.'

He smiled at her, and she found herself unable to resist a smile in response. Even in the light of the coach lanterns, she could see he was a good-looking young man, half a head shorter than his brother, his hair a few shades lighter. His eyes crinkled at the edges, and his mouth seemed to be lifted in a permanent smile. If he had not already broken every heart in this village, he soon would.

'How is Connie?' Sebastian asked.

The humour drained from Matt's face, and he shook his head.

'The doctor's bled her again this evening but he says if the fever does not break by the morning...'

'Then let me see her.' Isabel began walking down the path, removing her gloves.

At the door, an elderly dame who wore the cap and apron of a servant met them. The woman bobbed a curtsey, holding out her hand for Isabel's hat, cloak, and gloves.

'Lady Somerton, this is Mrs. Mead, our housekeeper,' Matthew affected the introduction.

'Lady Somerton?' The old woman turned to Sebastian, her expression one of surprise and confusion.

'The *widowed* Lady Somerton.' Isabel made the correction herself.

Mrs. Mead cast a curious glance at Sebastian, who ducked his head to enter the cottage. He bent to kiss the woman.

'Mrs. Mead, as I asked in my message, did you arrange the best room for Lady Somerton at the White Swan?' he asked.

Isabel turned to him with the unspoken question on her lips.

'There's no room here and you must be exhausted after the journey,' Sebastian said, spreading his hand apologetically.

'The White Swan has no rooms tonight,' Matt said. 'But we have made arrangements for Lady Somerton to have my room. I'll share with you, Bas,' Matthew said.

'Thank you, Mr. Alder. Your room will do me fine and I will be more use here than living in splendour at the inn.'

'You haven't seen the White Swan,' Matt murmured under his breath.

'My lady, we live very simply,' Mrs. Mead said, a frown creasing her brow.

Isabel held up a hand. 'Mrs. Mead, I am here to help, not to be entertained. Now, shall we go up? I know Lord Somerton would like to see his sister.'

'Help? What help is a fine lady like her going to be?' Isabel heard the old lady whisper to Matthew as they climbed the narrow stairs to the upper storey of the cottage.

Four doors led off the tiny landing. The unmistakable fug of a sickroom permeated the close atmosphere as Sebastian opened one of the doors, again ducking his head to enter the room.

A fire burned fiercely in the hearth, making the room unbearably warm. Obscured by the piles of bedding, a young woman tossed feverishly in the bed. She had thrown the bedding off, and Mrs. Mead, hurried forward, pulling the blankets up again.

'Leave them,' Isabel said.

'Doctor said she had to be kept warm,' the old woman said.

'Fiddlesticks!' Isabel said.

The old woman stiffened, her eyes wide with shock.

Isabel met her gaze and continued, 'Damp that fire immediately and open the windows.'

Mrs. Mead looked at Sebastian.

'Isabel?' Sebastian raised a quizzical eyebrow.

She returned his gaze with unblinking evenness. 'Trust me, Sebastian. I know what I am doing.'

He turned to Mrs. Mead. 'Please do as her ladyship has asked, Mrs. Mead. Her methods are unorthodox, but I know from personal experience they seem to work.'

Isabel looked at him, and her heart lurched as he smiled and winked at her. Did he remember that night in London when she had nursed him through his fever's crisis?

The old woman gave a sharp intake of breath. 'But, my lord, the doctor was most insistent...'

Isabel bit back a retort about the wisdom of the doctor and said, 'Please, Mrs. Mead. I do have some knowledge in these matters.' She glanced at Matt. 'Mister Alder, can you fetch me a bowl of water? Cold from a well, if possible. And some cloths.'

She flung back the curtains and shutters and opened the windows, filling the room with the cool night air. The girl on the bed took a shuddering breath and her eyes flickered open.

Sebastian perched on the edge of the bed, taking one of her hands in his.

'Connie. I'm here,' he whispered.

'Bas?' The girl turned bleary eyes to the sound of his voice.

'I came as soon as I heard you were ill.'

'Don't leave.' Her voice cracked and she flung her head to one side, again lost in delirium.

Sebastian did not relinquish her hand as Isabel rolled her sleeves up and began folding back the voluminous bedding. She ignored the squeak of alarm from the housekeeper and picked up Connie's free hand, running her fingers lightly over the bandaged wrists. Spots of blood marred the white sheets.

She looked up at Sebastian.

'Little wonder she's so weak.'

'Of course she's been bled. Doctor's been every day,' Mrs. Mead's voice quavered. 'He said it would purge the bad humour that is affecting her.'

Isabel looked up but bit back the caustic remark that rose to her lips.

Matthew appeared at Isabel's elbow with a large basin of water.

'Straight from the well, as you ordered.'

'Set it on the nightstand.' Isabel dipped one of the cloths Matthew had also brought with him into the water and began to sponge the girl's face and hands.

'Oh, you'll kill her,' Mrs. Mead said at last, wringing her

hands together. 'The fever must be sweated out of her. The doctor was most insistent ...'

Sebastian frowned. 'I don't recall Dr Neville being an advocate of bleeding. In fact, I seem to remember his thoughts about the treatment of fever were much the same as Lady Somerton's.'

'Dr Neville moved to Chester last year. We have Dr Llewellyn now.'

Sebastian rose to his feet. 'Then I will send the coach to Chester for Neville in the morning.'

'Cap'n Alder, you can't...' Mrs. Mead began and then broke off in the realisation that he could, and he would.

Isabel stood up and laid a hand on the old woman's arm.

'The fever will kill her if she is layered up with so much heat. In the place where I was born, I was taught that to bring a fever down you must keep the patient cool. Mrs. Mead, can you take a cloth and help me to sponge her? I'm sorry, Lord Somerton, but could I ask you to leave?'

Sebastian rose to his feet and, with a last glance at them both from the door, he left the room, pushing his brother before him.

The two women worked on the girl through the night, taking it in turns to bathe her with cold water and beneath their gentle hands, Connie fretted and shivered in the soon sodden, blood-specked sheets. As the first grey streaks of dawn began to lighten the sky, they ceased their ministrations.

Mrs. Mead changed the girl's sheets and nightdress and, as she pulled the bedding up, she looked at Isabel, her face puckered with concern.

'My lady, I'm sure you mean well, but it doesn't seem to have made a blind bit of difference.'

Isabel looked down at the girl, who had fallen into a fitful sleep, and for the first time, a qualm of fear at her high-handed disregard of the doctor's instructions gripped her.

'It's a new day, and she is still alive, Mrs. Mead. That is as much as we can hope for.'

Mrs. Mead's lip trembled. 'I hope you're right, my lady.' She stooped and stroked Connie's face. 'She's as dear to me as my own darling could be. It would break my heart to lose her.'

She stood up with a grimace and straightened her crumpled apron. 'Now you must be all done in after travelling all day and then sitting up all night. The bed's made up next door. Go and get some rest... my lady.' Two spots of colour appeared in her wan cheeks as she remembered this woman's status.

Isabel smiled. 'I will do just that. Wake me at midday and I shall sit with her while you rest.'

In the little bedchamber she barely had the energy to strip down to her chemise before falling gratefully into the soft embrace of the mattress.

Chapter Twenty-Five

Isabel woke to the clattering of pans downstairs. She washed and dressed in a clean gown and made her way down the narrow, uneven stairs to the kitchen.

To her surprise, she found Sebastian in his shirtsleeves with no neckcloth, apparently engaged in preparing a meal. Seeing her, he reached for his jacket, pulling it on.

'Please excuse my state of undress,' he said.

She shook her head, and it was on her lips to remark that she had seen him in a greater state of undress on at least two occasions, but refrained.

He clattered around the kitchen with a confident familiarity, setting out a rough lunch of soup, cheese, and bread.

'I'm sorry it's such plain fare,' he said with a smile, the lines in the corners of his eyes crinkling.

Despite the circumstances that had led to them being in Little Benning, for the first time in their acquaintance, he seemed relaxed and confident.

Isabel shook her head. 'It's perfect. Where's Mrs. Mead?'

'Still sitting with Connie. Now you're up, I will send her to her bed.' He waved a hand at the table. 'Please help yourself. There is no one here to serve you.'

Her stomach growled, and she tucked in gratefully to the simple fare.

'And how is Connie?' Isabel found herself unconsciously using the girl's diminutive name.

Sebastian shrugged. 'I sat with her a little this morning. She was sleeping.' He sighed and she caught the shadow of a rueful smile. 'She's still with us and that's what's important.'

'And Matthew?' she asked, looking around the room.

'He teaches at the grammar school, and he felt he would be more help out of the way.'

As he spoke, Mrs. Mead appeared at the doorway. She looked drained and grey with exhaustion, but there was defiance in the set of her jaw as she said, 'Just so you both know, I've sent for Dr Llewellyn.'

Sebastian's dark eyebrows drew together and in a low, controlled voice he said, 'Dr Neville will be here in a few hours, Mrs. Mead. There is no need to trouble Llewellyn.'

Even as he spoke, a knocking at the door announced the arrival of the doctor. He bustled into the house, his ancient wig askew and traces of gravy still at the corner of his lips. Without waiting for an introduction to the two new members of the household, he hurried upstairs, complaining about being interrupted in the middle of his dinner.

In the doorway, he stopped and turned to the crowd on the landing who had followed him up. He waved a hand at the dampened fire, the billowing curtains and the light covering over his patient, and his face grew purple with anger.

'What is the meaning of this, Mrs. Mead?' he thundered, rounding on the housekeeper. 'My every instruction has been wantonly disobeyed. If my patient has died, then on your head be it.'

Sebastian stepped forward. 'How dare you speak to Mrs. Mead in that tone,' he growled.

The doctor turned to face the tall soldier.

'And who, sir, are you? Are you a doctor of medicine?'

'I am Lord Somerton, Miss Alder's brother,' Sebastian replied.

The man's face dropped, and he took a step back into the room. '*Lord* Somerton? My apologies, sir.'

He bowed in a servile manner.

Sebastian's lip curled and he said in a tone of voice that dripped ice, 'But as you are here, doctor, you may as well see to your patient and make a proper diagnosis.'

'Bas?' The ruckus had woken Connie, who looked around at the assembled crowd with hazy, puzzled eyes.

The doctor listened to Connie's breathing, took her pulse, and pronounced, with some obvious displeasure, that the danger appeared to have passed. Isabel, standing behind Sebastian, allowed herself a smile of satisfaction.

'I will, of course, bleed her,' the doctor announced, reaching for his bag.

At this, Sebastian rose to his full height, towering over the little man and narrowly avoiding hitting his head on a beam.

'You will not lay another finger on her, you old charlatan. Now, out of my house.'

'Well, really!' The doctor began to protest, but his voice trailed off at the sight of Sebastian's thunderous brow.

Sebastian followed the man down and slammed the door behind him. Isabel heard him stomping back up the stairs two at a time.

'Thank God he wasn't here six years ago, or I would be dead,' he said as he re-entered the room, clenching and unclenching his hands.

Sebastian sat down beside the bed and picked up Connie's hand, raising it to his lips. It looked small and frail in his big, scarred hand.

Connie turned her head on the pillow.

At the sight of her brother, she smiled. 'It is you! I thought it was a dream. What are you doing here?'

His fingers tightened on the girl's hand. 'Mrs. Mead said I was allowed to sit with you and hold your hand. She also said I could adjust your pillows, offer you a drink of water, or read to you.'

He smiled and pressed her delicate hand to his lips, leaving Isabel with the suspicion that a secret joke had passed between them.

'Did she? Well, I would like a drink of water,' Connie whispered, her gaze not moving from her brother's face.

Isabel poured a glass of water and passed the glass to Sebastian. He raised Connie's shoulders, and the girl drank thirstily.

'Now then,' Mrs. Mead said, taking charge, 'you leave Miss Connie to me and both of you get yourselves some rest.'

'It's you who should rest,' Isabel said.

Mrs. Mead shook her head. 'I'll take to my bed this evening, my lady. For now, leave my girl with me.'

She shooed them both from the sickroom and shut the door behind them.

In the confines of the tiny landing, Sebastian loomed over Isabel. He took her hand and, even in the gloom, she sensed his gaze on her face, but could not bring herself to look into his eyes.

'How do I thank you? You saved my life and now Connie's. That is two debts I can't hope to repay,' he said. 'I won't forget what you did for me in London.'

Isabel bit her lip and looked down at the polished oak floor. 'I didn't think you knew that I had...'

'Sat with me?'

He placed a hand on either side of her face and raised her face to look at him. His eyes crinkled as he smiled and shook his head.

'To be honest it is all a blur but Bennet told me how you took charge. I remember your kindness to me then and I will remember your work today, Isabel.'

Isabel. She liked the way her given name sounded when he spoke it.

He let his hands drop and took a step back. 'Would you care for a walk, Lady Somerton? Little Benning is hardly London, but I feel the need for some fresh air.'

Chapter Twenty-Six

On her way to fetch her bonnet, Isabel glanced into the sick room. As she turned for the stairs, Sebastian looked up at her from the front hall, his brow creased with anxiety.

'How is she?'

'She's asleep,' she said, adding with a smile, 'so is Mrs. Mead.'

Sebastian held the front door open, and they stepped out into a bright, warm day.

'Mrs. Mead has been with us since Connie was a babe. I apologise if she has seemed a little high handed today,' Sebastian said.

Isabel shook her head. 'She has every right to be. It was very presumptuous of me to come in and tell her everything she had been doing was wrong. I shall try and make it up to her.'

They had reached the heart of the village, marked by a pleasant village green with a duck pond and, behind it, the pretty church that had probably been the Reverend Alder's living. Although no one was to be seen in the quiet village, somewhere she could hear children squabbling and the sound of chickens—the sounds of everyday life.

Isabel looked up as the clock in the church tower struck four.

'Good heavens. Is that the time? It's so peaceful here.' She looked up at the man walking beside her. 'I think Little Benning is lovely. And the cottage is charming.'

Sebastian glanced back at the little cottage, still visible from where they stood. 'It may be small, but it's mine, every stone in it bought with my hard-earned pennies and, I have to confess, it feels more real to me than Brantstone.'

'I can understand that. Everyone needs to belong somewhere, and I can see that in your heart, this is where you belong.'

He didn't answer for a long moment before saying, 'Any place where you have grown up and known happiness will always have a special place in your affections, but I haven't really lived here since I was sixteen. The army has been my home, and if I had remained just plain Sebastian Alder there would have been few enough jobs for army captains on half pay.' He sighed. 'Whatever line of work I could find would not have brought me back here, Isabel.' He paused. 'I hope that, in time, I will come to feel that I belong at Brantstone.'

She looked up at him. 'But you do belong at Brantstone, Sebastian. It may not feel like it yet but, even in such a short time, you have made your mark.'

'Do you think so?'

She nodded.

'Kind of you to say that but it's not home... not yet. What about you, Isabel? Where do you belong?'

She shook her head. 'I certainly don't belong at Brantstone. I never have.'

He raised an eyebrow and she added. 'Please don't mistake me. I like the dower house and I'm looking forward to living there. It is the first time in my life that I will have a place of my own, as you would say, a place to belong.'

He frowned. 'I must say no one would describe Brantstone as homely, but perhaps there is more to a sense of belonging than just the bricks and mortar. Is it about feeling wanted... and loved?'

She caught her breath. She had felt neither wanted nor loved for most of the years she had spent at Brantstone. If she had been, would she think of it differently?

He cleared his throat. 'I don't know why you came to Little Benning, but I'm glad you did, Isabel.'

Grateful for the change in subject, Isabel looked up at him and smiled.

'I was born to interfere.'

After the events of the last day, her original motives for accompanying him now seemed base and unworthy. This wasn't just about ensuring that Sebastian's sister would take her place at Brantstone and free her to move to the dower house, she had a glimpse of family and a happiness she had only dreamed of in the past.

Sebastian indicated a neat stone house beside the church.

'That's the Vicarage where we all grew up.' A frown creased his forehead. 'When Reverend Alder died, the new rector was on the doorstep within a week, demanding we vacate it. I had barely recovered my feet from the wound I'd taken at Talavera, and I had the responsibility for a grieving ten-year-old and an angry fifteen-year-old.'

'Oh, how awful. What did you do?'

Sebastian sighed. 'I tried to talk to the new squire, but the old squire had been dead a few years, and this man was a distant cousin with no interest in the village except what rents it brought him. The best he could do was offer me the cottage. It was in a shocking state of disrepair but, between us, we turned it into something habitable. That's all history now and once Connie and Matt come to Brantstone it will cease to be home.'

'What will you do with the cottage?'

He smiled. 'Oh, I have a notion, but I don't want to spoil any surprises, so I will keep it to myself for now.'

They had reached the lychgate to the churchyard, and Isabel followed him up the uneven flagstones towards the church. They entered the porch and stood looking at the heavy oak door. It stood open but Sebastian seemed hesitant to enter.

'This is where the Reverend Alder found my mother and I on Christmas morning. I was still a babe in arms and my mother near death.'

Isabel stared up at him. 'He found you here on the church porch?'

He nodded. 'What few warm things she had, mother had used to wrap me in. I suppose she must have been at the end of her resources and thought that, if she were to die, there was a chance that I might survive and be found by the Christmas churchgoers the next morning. It was sheer chance that the Reverend Alder found her in time.'

Isabel turned to look back at the tranquil village. 'What brought her here, of all places?'

Sebastian shrugged. 'My mother never talked about the time between my father's death and her rescue by the Reverend Alder, so I suppose I will never know.' He smiled a crooked smile. 'God, perhaps?'

They stepped into the soft light of the church and stood looking down the aisle towards the sanctuary. The building smelled of dust and damp, mingling with the scent of furniture polish and candles.

Sebastian entered a pew and kneeled, bending his head over his hands. Isabel slipped in beside him and, closing her eyes, said a brief prayer for Connie's speedy recovery. Sebastian straightened, and they sat together for a long time in silence, looking up at the altar. The late afternoon sun streamed through the fine stained-glass window of the crucifixion, spilling coloured jewels onto the stone flags.

'I still expect to see him,' Sebastian said at last.

'Your stepfather?'

He nodded.

'How did he die?' she asked.

'He'd gone into Chester for a meeting with the Bishop. A

runaway horse hit him as he was crossing the road. He died four days later.' He looked at her and rose to his feet. 'Come, Lady Somerton. There is a beautiful evening waiting for us.'

They walked back out into the sunlight and the peace of the old churchyard.

Chapter Twenty-Seven

It had occurred to Sebastian, as he had sat in the church, that this visit to Little Benning marked a transition point, a crossroads between his old life and his new. There could be no turning back now. He had a sense of a job unfinished. One more loose end to tie off.

He scanned the ragged lines of graves. 'Will you excuse me, Isabel, but while I am here, I should pay respects to my parents,' he said.

She looked up at him with understanding in her eyes. He had the odd sensation at times that this strange woman seemed to see into his soul.

'Of course,' she said. 'Do you wish to be alone?'

He shook his head. 'It's of no matter to me.'

He strode through the maze of crooked headstones and battered tombs, looking neither right nor left, to the quiet corner of the churchyard where John and Marjory Alder lay together in death as they had been in life. A posy of now dead flowers had been laid by the simple single gravestone. Connie's work, he suspected.

He laid his hand on the headstone and looked down at the well-tended grave.

'Did you know that, when a clergyman is buried, he is buried facing the west, not the east,' he mused.

'Why?'

He glanced at her. 'So that come judgement day, he will rise up and be facing his congregation.'

'That is reassuring.'

Isabel stooped to collect up the dead flowers, replacing them with a handful of wildflowers she had picked from around the churchyard. She kneeled for a moment by the grave as if in private prayer.

Laying her hand on the ground, she said in a low voice, 'I wish I had somewhere like this for William. I had no say in where he was placed. He went to that cold, unloving mausoleum.'

'And yet you visit him every day?'

Isabel looked up. 'How did you know?'

He cleared his throat. 'I've seen you. Isabel, forgive me for saying this, but it is easy to spend too long in the company of the dead.'

Anger flared in her eyes as Isabel rose to her feet to face him.

'What do you mean by that?' she demanded, her voice sharp with reproach.

Sebastian held out his hand. 'I apologise. I spoke out of turn. I have no right to judge you.'

'No you don't. Not when you still live with the ghosts of the past, Sebastian.'

She looked at him with those knowing eyes and Sebastian froze. Of course, the death of parents was a terrible loss, but it was part of life. The death of a child or the death of someone you loved more than life...?

Inez...

'Tell me about Inez, Sebastian.'

Inez...

For a long moment he stared at her, the name echoing in his mind. How could she know? All the memories came rushing back, and once more he smelled the dust and the blood of that terrible day. He put his hand on a nearby gravestone to steady himself and brought himself back to the present.

Isabel watched him, no doubt waiting for him to speak about the one thing in the whole world for which he had no words.

He swallowed, trying to make his voice sound neutral as he said, 'Coming home is not always a good thing, Lady Somerton. Sometimes there are memories that are best forgotten. How did you know... about Inez?'

'You called me by her name... in London, when you were ill,' Isabel said softly.

She made no further move towards him and he closed his eyes. He could not turn away now. She was entitled to an explanation.

He began, trying to keep his voice neutral, 'Inez Aradeiras was the daughter of a Colonel in the Portuguese army. We had married in Lisbon, and she was on her way to join me with the regiment. Her father had sent an escort, but they were overcome by a band of French marauders. They killed every man and...' He screwed up his eyes as he tried to contain the emotion that shook his voice, even now after all these years. 'Inez was murdered by the French.'

He stopped there. Isabel did not need to know the rest. How he had failed to protect the one person he loved more than life itself. How it had been his misfortune to come upon the scene—and the revenge he had exacted on her murderers when he had found them.

How he wanted to die—had tried to die.

'Harry Dempster and Bennet know the whole story, of course. They were there. The only other person I have ever told was my stepfather,' he glanced up at the church, 'here in this church, on the day I returned from Spain.'

He took a deep breath, remembering the day he had returned to Little Benning, still on crutches and in terrible pain. His faltering steps had taken him instinctively to the church, as if he needed to find a forgiving God, not the vengeful God of the Spanish churches.

His stepfather had been there and seated on the hard, stone steps to the sanctuary, in jerking phrases that barely made sense, even to his own ears, Sebastian had poured out his soul. Through it all the Reverend Alder had sat quite still, not one twitch of his face betraying any revulsion or horror or judgement at Sebastian's tale.

Instead, the good man had risen to his feet and, placing his hands on Sebastian's head, quietly pronounced absolution. As the words were murmured above him, the last wall of Sebastian's reserve broke, and he had wept in his stepfather's arms like a child.

He brought his gaze back to the woman who stood watching him. He hardly dared to meet her gaze, expecting to see pity, but when his eyes met her steady, unblinking gaze, he saw only understanding. She knew suffering and grief.

He rolled his shoulders, trying to slough away the memory of that awful day on a hot, dusty Portuguese road, but the stench of death now hung over both of them like a mantle.

What had induced him to confide in her, bring it all crashing back on top of him?

He shook his head. 'I have learned that you have to let the past go, or it consumes you.'

'How can you?' she said.

He looked past her shoulder. 'Anger, recrimination, and bitterness doesn't change what happened. I could spend the rest of my life consumed by rage and despair, but life is for the living, not the dead.'

'Did your stepfather teach you that?'

He allowed himself to smile. 'No. He gave me something more precious: forgiveness. For the rest... it was a realisation I came to by myself.'

'Then you have more generosity of spirit than I, Sebastian.'

She crossed the few short paces between them and stood

beside him, looking down at the simple grave. She looked up and her grey eyes searched his.

'If, as you say, the past belongs to the past, why has there been no one else in your life?'

He shook his head. To let himself love another as he had loved Inez? To fail again?

As he wondered how to respond to her question, he heard his name being called and, grateful for the interruption, he glanced back towards the lychgate. Matt leaned against one of the posts, his hand on his side as if trying to catch his breath.

A sudden fear gripped him. Had Connie taken a turn for the worse? Without a thought of Isabel, he ran towards his brother. As he approached him, Matt held up his hand.

'It's all right, Bas! The coach is back with Dr. Neville and I thought you should be there.'

'Excellent.' Sebastian turned to Isabel. 'Come, Lady Somerton, you will approve of Dr. Neville.'

Chapter Twenty-Eight

Doctor Neville pronounced the patient on the mend and commended Lady Somerton on her radical actions. In his opinion, her timely intervention had probably saved the girl's life.

He departed in the Somerton coach, assured by Sebastian of future patronage.

As darkness fell and the two women sat with Connie, Sebastian retired to bed. He found Matt, seated in a chair by the window of the little bedroom, looking out into the dark night.

Without looking around, Matt said, 'I'm glad you came, Bas. I felt so bloody useless.'

Sebastian frowned. 'Your father would turn in his grave to hear you use such language.'

Matt turned to look at him. 'Don't go all righteous on me, Bas. I know you are more than capable of bad language. In fact, I've heard you use worse.'

'Well, that was before...' Sebastian sighed, 'before I had to learn to be a gentleman.'

It was Matt's turn to smile. 'You were always a gentleman, Bas. Even when you were swearing like a trooper.' He smiled. 'We've missed you.'

'And I you. You have no idea how much.'

'I didn't want to worry you, but the doctor started making all sorts of dire prognostications and I knew you'd want to be here if...' Matt trailed off.

If Connie had died.

'You did the right thing, Matt. You two will always be my priority and, as soon as Connie's up to the journey, you're both coming to Brantstone,' he said.

Matt swallowed. 'I was hoping you'd say that. I resigned from the school today.'

'Did you indeed? Making a bit of a presumption, aren't you?' Sebastian smiled at the sudden alarm in his brother's face. 'Whatever good fortune has come my way is yours as well, Matt, but won't you miss teaching?'

'You *are* jesting? Not for one second! What about you, Bas? Will you miss the army?'

He shrugged. 'I must admit I am getting rather tired of being shot, but yes, it was my life for a very long time and a life I knew and understood.'

'Being a viscount is proving hard work?'

Sebastian raised his eyes heavenward. 'It certainly involves work, mostly on myself—my attire, my deportment, my speech... I could go on.'

'Well you look the part. I hardly recognised you. Face it, you were born to it, Bas. I always knew you were different from us.'

'Of course you did. It was no secret that I was your half-brother. One unexpected consequence. I have discovered a whole clan of relations we didn't know we had, including our grandmother.'

The shock on Matt's face made him smile.

He perched on the end of the bed and told Matt about his grandmother, Aunt Peggy and the rest of the family.

'I thought that, when you and Connie get to Brantstone, we shall hold a picnic for the whole damn lot,' he concluded.

Matt raised his eyebrows. 'A grandmother? Who would have

thought?' He added with wonder in his voice, 'Connie will be thrilled.'

Sebastian regarded his brother. 'I also want you to think about what you want to do with your life, Matt. I'm now in a position to send you to Oxford or Cambridge if that is what you would like.'

His brother stared at him. 'Do you mean that?'

Sebastian nodded. He knew that it had been Matt's long-held ambition to study mathematics at Oxford, but the family finances had simply not allowed it, so Matt had to be content with teaching, a profession he loathed.

'And Connie?' Matt asked.

Sebastian hesitated. The easy answer was that he could, at last, provide his sister with a dowry. Even low born as she was, with a good dowry, she could marry well. However, knowing his headstrong and independent-minded sister, that would be something to be broached gently.

'That will be up to Connie,' he said evenly.

'Now, how about you tell me about the lovely Lady Somerton?' Matt changed the subject.

'What do you mean "lovely"?' Sebastian asked.

'Are you blind, Bas? She has to be one of the most handsome women I've ever seen, and if you haven't noticed then you are not only blind but mad.'

Sebastian remembered his unworthy thoughts in the coach, when she had landed in his lap, and Harry's words came back to him.

'Matt, she is the respectable widow of my late cousin and she has been a good friend to me. That is all and ever will be,' he said, words aimed at convincing himself more than his brother. 'Lady Somerton has plans of her own. She is intent on doing good works in Manchester.'

'Good works in Manchester?' Matt's lip curled in derision.

'Don't sneer like that, Matt. Her motives are worthy, and I intend to do what I can to support her. As for you,' he said, changing the subject, 'don't mistake me, Matt, I still expect you to make your own way in the world.'

Matt gave a theatrical shudder. 'If that is how it is to be! You are a cruel taskmaster, Bas, but I think as a starting point I would like the opportunity to go to Cambridge.' He rose to his feet and clapped his hands together. 'So, when do we leave?'

'As soon as Connie is well enough to travel. All you have to do is send word and I'll dispatch the coach for you.'

Matt gave his brother a low theatrical bow. 'So be it, my lord.'

Long after Matt had fallen asleep and silence had descended on the little cottage, Sebastian lay awake with his hands behind his head, staring up at the ceiling and trying to ignore his brother's stentorian breathing.

Thoughts of Isabel kept circling in his head. Despite the hard years of marriage to Anthony and the grief at the death of her son, he suspected that lurking not far below the cool, collected surface of Lady Somerton was indeed a handsome woman, both physically and intellectually, and he wanted to get to know this real Isabel, if only she'd let him … if only he'd let himself.

If he closed his eyes, he was back in the coach with her slender body in his arms.

He muttered a curse under his breath. He was being a fool. She had been too hurt and too damaged by Anthony, and there remained the question of her husband's suspicious death. Could she be capable of murder?

He needed to resolve Anthony's death before he even thought of jeopardising the slender thread of friendship he enjoyed with Isabel—Lady Somerton.

The longer he stayed here, in such close proximity to her, the more difficult it would be for them to return to normality at Brantstone. Now Connie was on the mend, he could beat a tactical retreat, but could Isabel be persuaded to stay?

Chapter Twenty-Nine

Bennet was bored.

He had polished every pair of his lordship's boots until they shone like glass. He had rearranged his lordship's drawers and cabinets three times. He had starched and ironed his lordship's linen until it could stand by itself.

Mr. Pierce, on the other hand, viewed his lordship's absence as a holiday and installed himself beside the fire in the servants' parlour, with the London broadsheets and a steady supply of tea, only proffering advice and instruction to his apprentice when called upon to do so.

Freed of the strictures of military life, Bennet took himself off to the village public house. He settled into the snug beside the fire, pipe in hand, nursing a pint of ale and revelled in the unexpected freedom from duty.

On discovering that he was his lordship's valet, Wilkins and the locals were quick to share their thoughts about their new Lord Somerton. As he listened to the praise heaped on Lord Somerton, he felt inordinately proud of his officer. Up at the hall, the servants, too, approved of their new lord. Captain Alder had risen to his new position as if born to it. But then he had been born to it, he just hadn't known.

Mrs. Wilkins seemed especially enamoured of him.

'He praised my cooking,' she said, with a dreamy look in her eye.

Bennet didn't enlighten her. Sebastian would eat anything put in front of him.

The head groom, Thompson stumped into the parlour and demanded an ale. Bennet enquired if the man would care to join him.

Thompson stared at him. 'Who the 'ell are you?'

'That's his lordship's man,' Wilkins said.

'I avoid the stables,' Bennet said apologetically, but for answer, Thompson's mouth twisted in a snarl.

'Not in the mood for company,' he said and downed the ale. He procured a dark bottle from Mr. Wilkins and left, slamming the door behind him.

Wilkins shook his head. 'Got the black mood on him tonight, Molly,' he said to his wife.

'What do you mean?' Bennet said.

'He gets like this every now and then. You heard about his daughter?'

Bennet nodded. 'I heard tell she took her own life.'

Mrs. Wilkins sniffed. 'Oh, that was sad,' she said. 'Amy Thompson worked up at the house. Good girl, she was. Hard worker.'

'Drowned herself in the lake,' Wilkins put in.

Mrs. Wilkins looked around the room and lowered her voice. 'They say she was three months gone with child. Such a tragedy.'

This was news.

Bennet shook his head and made a suitable tutting sound. 'Who was the father?'

'Well, there are those who say it was his late lordship,' Mrs. Wilkins glanced at her husband, 'but that never sounded right to us, did it, Mr. Wilkins?'

Wilkins grunted a warning. 'Now, now, Mrs. Wilkins—'

Mrs. Wilkins leaned forward, dropping her voice to a

conspiratorial tone. 'I'm not one to gossip,' she said, 'but his late lordship... well... how do I put it? He was never one for the girls.'

Bennet took a large swig of ale. This was news to him, a juicy bit of gossip to share with Sebastian when he returned.

'What do you mean, Mrs. Wilkins?'

'Between us, Mr. Bennet, it was the pretty footmen up at the hall who were more at risk from his lordship.'

'But all I've heard is how his lordship was one for the ladies,' Bennet urged. 'Always off in London, womanising and the like.'

Mrs. Wilkins sat back. 'Well, you would, of course. Imagine if it had got about that his lordship weren't that way inclined. Can you imagine the scandal?'

'So if you don't think his lordship was the father of Amy Thompson's child, then who was?' Bennet returned to the subject.

Mrs. Wilkins sighed. 'She was a pretty girl but she set her sights high. If you ask me, it wasn't likely to be one of the staff.'

'A guest?' Bennet suggested.

Wilkins shrugged. 'We'll never know. The girl took her own life and that of her unborn child. Two sins. No Christian burial for poor Amy. It drove her mother clear out of her wits. Little wonder poor Thompson has his black moods.'

'They say her unshriven spirit haunts the lake,' Mrs. Wilkins put in. 'Old Tom,' she indicated an elderly man playing chequers by himself in a far corner. 'He says he saw her all dripping wet and wringing her hands.'

Wilkins snorted. 'Now you are being fanciful, Mrs. W. Nothing Old Tom sees that isn't accounted for by the ale. Enough of this tittle tattle. Back to work, woman!'

Bennet sat back and nursed his ale while he mulled over the intelligence imparted by the Wilkins. His new friends in the servants' hall were remarkably loyal, he reflected. There had been no murmur about the late lord's proclivities.

It would be interesting to find out a little more about the death of Amy Thompson. He set down the empty pot, picked up his hat, and, bidding the Wilkins good day, walked slowly back to the hall.

He had discovered the shortcut through the woods and, as the evening drew in, the trees closed around him.

'Want a drink?'

The slurred voice came from his right, and Bennet, his nerves already taut, started. He whirled around and peered into the dark. Thompson sat on a fallen tree trunk, his shoulders slumped, the bottle hanging loosely gripped in his right hand, between his knees.

As Bennet approached, Thompson raised the bottle and held it out to him. Bennet took the offering and swigged. A rough rum burned the back of his throat and he handed the bottle back as he wiped his mouth.

'Rough stuff that,' he commented, seating himself on the log beside the despondent groom.

Thompson lifted the bottle and held it to his lips. His throat worked as he swallowed the fiery drink.

'You know what today is?' Thompson slurred.

'No idea,' Bennet said, taking the bottle from the man's slack fingers. It was just about empty, so Bennet discreetly emptied the last drops onto the ground.

'It's a year since she died.'

'Your daughter?'

Thompson swung an arm behind him. 'There in the bloody lake. Parson wouldn't bury her in hallowed ground. I tried to tell him that she didn't take her own life.' He turned back to Bennet and poked a finger in his chest. 'I think she was murdered.'

'And why would you think that?' Bennet asked, keeping his tone neutral.

'I saw her body...' He paused and took a shuddering breath. 'My beautiful girl...'

He started to cry, great gulping sobs. Bennet sat quietly and waited for the sobs to subside.

'She had a massive wound on the back of her head,' Thompson said at last.

Bennet took a breath. 'What sort of wound?'

'Like someone had whacked her over the head with something heavy.'

'Could she have hit her head on something when she jumped into the lake?'

Thompson shook his head. 'Not where she was found. She didn't kill herself, Mr. Bennet.' Thompson hung his head, his big hands slack between his knees. 'She was happy. Her ma and I had told her that we'd stand by her. She had no reason to take her life.'

'Did she say who the father was?'

Thompson shook his head. 'There was rumours it was his lordship, but when I asked her she just laughed. Said the father was a real man and that he'd see her right.'

Bennet sat in silence, digesting this information.

'Come on, matey,' he said to the groom. 'Let's get you home.'

He put one arm around the big man, and they made a slow, weaving progress back to the stable block. The Thompson family had rooms above the stables, entered from a narrow stone staircase without rails that ran up the side of the building.

Drunk or not, Thompson managed the stairs without incident and threw the door open.

Peter Thompson, who had been sitting on a stool by the cooking fire, with a book on his lap, jumped to his feet. Bennet noted the boy secreting the book in the woodbox.

A low moan came from a pallet on the far side of the room, and Peter, casting a quick, disgusted look at his father, picked up the candle and crossed over to the bed.

'It's all right, ma,' he said. 'Mr. Bennet, his lordships' man's bought pa home.'

The woman in the bed mumbled something, a claw-like hand catching at her son's sleeve. Peter looked up.

'Ma'd like to meet you, Mr. Bennet,' he said, a frown creasing his young forehead.

Little in this life shocked Bennet. He'd seen life and death in every form, but even he took a sharp breath as he looked down on Mrs. Thompson. She looked like a woman already dead, her face shrunken against the bones of her skull. A line of dried spittle ran from the corner of her mouth and her body had convulsed into a rigor, the hands more claws than anything recognisably human.

He bent closer and looked into her eyes, seeing the light of life and intelligence, despite her terrible physical affliction.

'Pleased to meet you, Mrs. T,' he said. 'The old man's a bit the worse for wear. He'll 'ave an 'ead on 'im tomorrow.'

The woman choked, the corners of her mouth twitching, and something that could have been laughter flashed into the eyes.

'Good man,' she mumbled, her gaze moving from Bennet to the table where Thompson had slumped, his head buried in his arms.

'My girl,' she clutched at Bennet's sleeve.

'He told me. Don't fret yourself, Mrs. T.'

'Find 'im...' The hand tightened on his arm, the fingers digging into his flesh. 'He who killed 'er.'

Bennet put his own hand over hers and gently disengaged the twisted fingers. He frowned.

'You don't think she took her own life either?'

Slowly, the woman's head moved on the pillow. A negative.

'The new lord. I'll tell 'im. He'll help you,' Bennet assured her.

A tear ran from the woman's eye and the slack mouth trembled. Bennet laid her hand on her chest.

'Don't you fuss yourself, Mrs. T.'

He rose to his feet and gestured for the boy to join him at the door.

'How long's she been like that?'

'Since a few weeks after Amy died. She just fell down one day and she's been like that ever since.'

'And you and your pa are the only ones to care for her?'

The boy nodded, and Bennet put a fatherly hand on his shoulder. 'Keep reading those books, boy.'

Halfway down the stairs, he looked up at the youngster who still stood by the open door. 'Do you think someone killed your sister?'

Peter's gaze did not waver.

'Yes.'

Chapter Thirty

Isabel sat at the table in the little parlour enjoying the simple breakfast Mrs. Mead had prepared. The only sound in the room came from the deep-throated *tick tock* of the grandfather clock in the corner. Birdsong drifted in through the open window along with the smell of the late summer roses that bloomed prolifically in the bright, sunny little garden.

She held her cup in both hands and smiled. She had never felt such utter peace and contentment, as if she, in some way, had come home. She looked up as Sebastian entered the room, instinctively ducking his head under the lintel.

He wore his travelling clothes and carried a hat in his hand and her heart sank.

'You're leaving?' she enquired.

'Now I know Connie is on the road to recovery, I must get back to Lincolnshire. There's so much to be done and I dare not stay away too long.'

Disappointment tugged at Isabel as she set her cup back in its saucer.

'I will pack immediately.'

He stood looking down at her, twisting the brim of his hat in his big hands. 'Actually, Lady Somerton, I have another boon to ask of you.'

She smiled. 'Whatever is in my power.'

The time they had spent in each other's company and the shared confidences had brought them closer together and she saw him now as his men would have viewed him; a born leader who in his own quiet way instilled utter faith and confidence in his decisions. If he asked her to go into battle with him, she would have followed him without question.

If he asked her... anything...

She shook her head, dispelling the unworthy thoughts.

'Would it be too much of an imposition if you were to stay here a little while longer?'

Her heart gladdened. An imposition? There was nothing she would like more.

'Not at all. It would be my pleasure. There is little at Brantstone that cannot wait.'

Sebastian sat down at the table, and she poured him a cup of tea from the large pot.

'I thought that perhaps you could provide Connie and Matt with a little coaching on what is expected of them when they come to Brantstone,' he said.

A smile crept unbidden to her lips. 'You underestimate your siblings.'

He ran a hand through his hair, making it stand on end.

'I have had to learn so much myself and I think it is only fair they should know what to expect. I trust your judgement in these matters.'

Isabel felt a warm glow at his words. Compliments were rare in her life.

Sebastian looked around the little room. 'This is so far removed from Brantstone, Lady Somerton. I am sorry to inflict my own humble origins on you for a few days longer.'

'No!' she said rather too quickly. 'I love this cottage, Seb... my lord. I am quite content to stay as long as I am needed.'

It had been so long since she had felt needed or wanted.

His brown eyes fixed on her face and the corner of his mouth twitched.

'Would it be improper of me to address you as Isabel when we are alone? We seem to already be in the habit, but I would not like to be thought of as too familiar.'

'I have no objection, but only if you will allow me the same liberty,' she replied.

They smiled at each other and an unfamiliar glow rose within her chest. Her hand went to her throat as Sebastian straightened and his eyes drifted to the window. She followed his line of sight and her stomach lurched. The Somerton coach had driven up to the front door.

He stood up and turned for the door. 'I will say my farewell to Connie. Just send me word when she is well enough to travel and I will dispatch the coach for you all.'

'What about Mrs. Mead?'

He turned and looked back at her. 'I have offered to bring her to Brantstone but she has expressed a desire to remain in Little Benning. I will gift her the cottage and an allowance for her life.'

Isabel nodded. 'That is very generous.'

He shook his head. 'Nothing can truly repay the debt I owe her, Isabel.'

As he stepped into the hall, she said, 'Have a safe trip, Sebastian.'

He stopped and looked back at her, a smile lifting the corners of his mouth. He stretched out a hand, taking hers and lifting it to his lips. A thrill ran through her at the touch of his strong, calloused fingers.

'And thank you, Isabel. For everything.'

As he released her hand and turned away, she pressed that hand to her chest, and took a deep breath.

She heard his footsteps taking the narrow stairs two at a time and the floor creaked above her head as he crossed to his sister's bed.

Isabel looked up at the ceiling and smiled.

Chapter Thirty-One

As the coach rolled away from the little cottage, Isabel climbed the stairs to Connie's room. As she knocked and entered, she heard an audible sniff. She looked across at the bed in time to see Connie stowing a handkerchief beneath her pillow.

'The quicker you are well, the quicker you will see him again,' she said, taking the chair beside Connie's bed.

Connie smiled. 'Silly of me to cry, but I always seem to be saying goodbye to Bas.'

Isabel regarded the girl. Although pale and wasted from the fever, the likeness between this girl and her brothers was unmistakable. The quality in the men that gave them a rugged attractiveness, in their sister produced an ethereal beauty.

Connie smiled and looked around the room. 'Lady Somerton, you didn't have to stay. I am sure it must be perfectly beastly to be cooped up in this tiny cottage.'

Isabel shook her head. 'Not at all.' She folded her hands in her lap. 'Can I share something with you?'

Connie nodded.

'Not only am I glad to be of some use, but I like it here.'

'But it's so small compared to what you are used to. Brantstone must be very grand.'

'It is, but that doesn't make it a home. This cottage may be small, but this is a proper home, Constance.'

She refrained from saying that what made it a home was the invisible ingredient: love. There was no love at Brantstone.

Connie shook her head and smiled. 'Please don't call me Constance. The only person who calls me that is Bas, and only when he's cross with me. Everyone calls me Connie.'

Isabel smiled. 'Connie it is. And when we are alone, you can call me Isabel.'

'Oh, that wouldn't be right.'

'Please. I would be honoured.'

'Isabel,' Connie gave her a shy smile, 'I haven't thanked you for everything you have done for me.'

Isabel looked down at her hands. Two compliments in one morning?

'It was nothing,' she said.

'Oh no, Mrs. Mead told me what you did. I owe you my life.'

'Ah, now you are just exaggerating. It was your own sturdy constitution and Mrs. Mead's devotion that pulled you through,' Isabel said.

Connie's cheeks dimpled. 'I don't think so. Sebastian told me you looked after him too, after Waterloo.'

This time, the heat burned in Isabel's cheeks as her mind flashed to that night in London when she had sat with him in the dark hours.

'Again, Bennet did all the work.'

Connie smiled. 'Oh, dear Bennet. I am looking forward to seeing him again. He's been here a few times with Bas and he is such fun. But please don't underplay your role. You rescued Bas from that awful hospital and he said that when he was very ill you sat with him, like you did with me.'

Isabel cleared her throat, as her mind's eye played over the strong, muscular body she had nursed all those weeks ago in London.

'He wasn't so very ill. I just kept him company.'

Connie looked up at the ceiling. 'I don't believe you. I know what wound fever is. When he came back from Spain, after Talavera, he was very ill. Dr. Neville thought he would die. I heard him saying the wound had been badly treated. He had to operate again on our kitchen table. The doctor said Bas was lucky not to have his leg amputated. Afterwards, Mrs. Mead said I was allowed to sit with him and hold his hand and adjust his pillows, offer him a drink of water or read to him. So I did. I probably drove him to distraction.'

Isabel recalled Sebastian using those same words to Connie when she had woken the morning her fever had broken. That explained the joke between them.

'Sebastian really is the best of brothers, Lady Somerton,' Connie said.

'He is,' Isabel agreed. 'I wish I had a brother to care for me as much as yours do for you.'

Connie looked up, a smile dimpling her cheek.

'I am very spoiled.' Her face darkened. 'I feared the worst when I heard he had been wounded again. I couldn't bear to lose Bas. I am so glad you found him.'

'It was lucky for both of us. Brantstone needs its lord and I think he will be a good one.'

'So do I,' Connie said.

Isabel rose to her feet and circled the room. The walls were crammed with paintings, some in oil, and others watercolours or pencil sketches.

'These are very good.' She glanced back at Connie. 'Are they your work?'

A faint stain of colour rose to the girl's pale cheeks.

'Some, but not all. These days I paint miniature portraits and it gives me a little income. I'll show some to you when I am allowed out of bed.'

Hearing an echo of her brother in the impatient tone, Isabel smiled.

'You will get out of bed when I say.'

'I suppose, now I am Lord Somerton's sister, I won't be able to keep painting.'

Isabel shrugged. 'Maybe not for commissions.'

Connie's mouth tightened and Isabel saw her brother's stubborn nature in the glint of her eyes.

'I have no intention of becoming one of those fragile, useless little women who sit around painting vases of flowers, Lady... Isabel.'

'I will be starting a school in the dower house next year. Perhaps you can help me?' Isabel ventured.

Connie raised an eyebrow, and Isabel laughed. 'Yes, it is for those fragile, useless little women, but the school is just a means to an end.'

She told Connie of her plans for the financing of a charity school in Manchester. Connie's eyes widened.

'Oh, I'd love to help, but only if I can help with the other school.' She paused. 'If Bas allows me, of course.'

Isabel's mouth quirked. While gratified by Connie's response, she had conveniently ignored the fact that Sebastian had forbidden the school in the dower house. Perhaps with Connie's help she could persuade him to change his mind. She couldn't imagine Sebastian saying no to anything Connie set her mind to.

She turned back to the paintings on the wall.

'Those landscapes by the door are mine,' Connie said. 'The rest are mainly mother's. She was very good. Father told me that after her first husband died, she kept herself and her baby by selling paintings. I wish I'd known her, but she died when I was born,' Connie added wistfully.

'It seems you have inherited her talent,' Isabel said.

'We all have to some extent. Matthew does excellent lithographs and Sebastian, like me, is very good at people. The picture in the black frame by the fireplace is one of his.'

Isabel turned to inspect the pen and ink sketch of two small children; Connie and Matt, she surmised. The drawing, executed with perfect confidence in strong, clear lines, captured the essential characters of the two youngsters. She thought of the little sketches in the margins of the prayer book and recognised the same confident hand.

'The artist's eye seems to sit oddly with his life as a soldier,' Isabel said, more to herself than to Connie.

'Even as a soldier, he never lost the opportunity to capture a moment. Do you want to see some of his work?'

Isabel nodded, her curiosity about the soldier artist piqued.

Connie pulled herself up in the bed and pointed at the chest of drawers. 'In the bottom drawer of my chest you will find a book wrapped in a Spanish shawl. Can you get it out?'

Isabel complied, handing the parcel to Connie. The girl ran her hands over the bright embroidery of the fringed shawl.

'Bas sent me this from Spain,' Connie said. 'It's too beautiful to wear.'

She carefully unwrapped the parcel, revealing a small notebook. Its leather cover was stained and one corner appeared to be badly charred. She handed it to Isabel. 'You can have a look but don't tell Sebastian I have it.'

Isabel turned over the battered object in her hand.

'What happened to it?'

Connie bit her lip. 'When he came back from the war, after Talavera, it was like he had a terrible sadness inside. One day he lit a fire and threw a whole lot of letters and other documents onto it but this book fell out and I rescued it when he wasn't looking. I had taken a peek at it when he was ill and the drawings are so good. I couldn't bear to see it destroyed.'

Isabel looked down at the little book. The actions Connie described seemed at odds with the Sebastian she was coming to know. She sat down on the chair beside the bed and opened the book to the inscription on the first page.

My darling Sebastian. Christmas 1792. Mama.

Her heart lurched. It had been a gift from his mother to her son.

Like the portrait, the little sketches were done in pen and ink, executed in a hand that became more confident with time. The early sketches recorded life in Little Benning: the vicarage and scenes from around the village. She recognised the church and market square, peopled with the villagers, the character of each recorded with affection and accuracy.

A long gap moved the story to a troop ship bound for Spain and then to the Peninsula where the life of an army on active campaign came to vivid life. Sketches of encampments peopled with the soldiers, their women and children mixed with Spanish villagers, toothless peasants offering oranges or other produce for sale.

She recognised the face of Harry Dempster in several of the drawings and, as the war progressed, the face of a young woman, identified only in the first sketch as 'Inez, Lisbon, 1808', began to dominate.

Inez.

Isabel caught her breath. Here was the woman who still haunted Sebastian.

Inez appeared in various poses, even one of her asleep, her long, dark hair flowing over the bolster. Isabel turned to the last sketch of the young woman; a head and shoulders study, the hair carefully arranged to fall in ringlets around her oval face. He had caught the sparkle of laughter in the woman's dark eyes and her gentle smile. Her love for the artist spilled through his pencil and Isabel, struggled to control an emotion she had never encountered before ... Jealousy? She had never known what it was to love a man so much that it shone from your eyes like a candle in the dark and she yearned to share what Inez had known.

Connie leaned over to see what had caught Isabel's attention.

'Oh, that's Inez. I don't know who she is. Sebastian has never spoken of her in my hearing.' An unspoken 'but' lingered at the end of the sentence. Isabel raised her eyebrows encouragingly.

'When he was very ill, he called her name often, but...' Connie paused and then said, 'I think she must be dead.'

Isabel said nothing. It was not her story to tell. She hadn't needed words to know how Inez had died at the hands of the French. It had been written in the deep lines that grooved Sebastian's face even while he struggled to keep his tone neutral. Little wonder he could not speak of her to his siblings.

Inez, she thought, if only you knew that he still carries the memory of those beautiful, laughing eyes and your horrific death. Would you be angry? Would you want him to let you go and learn to love again?

She flicked through the blank pages that remained and on one page, unmarked in any other way, she found three words.

Sebastian had written '*Where is God?*' in such haste and fury that the ink from his pen nib had sputtered, casting drops of ink across the page like spots of black blood.

Isabel stared down at the page and traced the words with her finger—the cry of a man who had been forsaken. The words burned with his anguish and her fingers contracted. This little book held nothing but unhappy memories for the man who had consigned it to the flames. She hastily rewrapped it and laid it back in its hiding place and hoped Sebastian never knew of its existence.

The girl lay back on the pillows, watching her.

Isabel straightened her apron and said, 'I have tired you. I'll let you get some rest.'

Connie shook her head. 'No, it has been nice to talk to you. I am so looking forward to going to Brantstone but I have so many questions to ask you. I've never even visited a grand house before.'

'Then you really must get some rest and regain your strength, and we will talk later. We must get you well, if you are to be at Brantstone in time for the ball.'

The girl's eyes shone. 'A ball? A proper ball? How wonderful. I shall certainly be well enough for that.'

As Isabel turned to go, Connie caught her hand. 'Thank you for being Sebastian's friend.'

Isabel laid her hand over the girl's. 'And yours, I hope.'

Chapter Thirty-Two

Sebastian removed his gloves and handed them to a footman, conscious that Bennet waited at the bottom of the stairs, hopping from one foot to the other.

'Is something troubling you?' he enquired of his batman.

'May I have a word in private?' Bennet's eyes darted towards the footman.

'Can it wait? It's been a long journey and I would love a cup of tea.'

He would have liked an ale but he was learning.

Bennet didn't answer and Sebastian sighed. 'Very well. In my study, Bennet.'

Bennet closed the door behind them after a quick glance up and down the corridor. This nervousness in his long-time comrade made Sebastian uneasy.

'What is it?' he asked.

Bennet swallowed. 'You know as how we think his late lordship was murdered? Well, I think there may have been another murder, before his.'

Sebastian straightened. 'Good God, who?'

'Thompson, the groom... His girl, Amy.'

'Didn't she take her own life? Drowned herself in the lake?'

'Not according to Thompson. He said when they pulled her from the lake she had a head wound like she'd been hit on the back of the head. He told me she was happy. The man who was the father of her child was going to see her right. She didn't have a reason to take her own life.'

Sebastian turned and walked over to the window. He stood looking out over the gardens to the lake, his hands behind his back. Two possible murders within a few short months of each other. Coincidental? He thought not.

His reverie was short lived as the door burst open and Fanny came flying in with cries of, 'Cousin Sebastian, you're back! It's a disaster.'

Sebastian turned to face the girl who stood sniffing in the middle of the room, her eyes red-rimmed from weeping. She twisted a sodden kerchief in her hand, her full lips trembling.

'What's a disaster?' he enquired.

Fanny gave a shuddering sob and subsided against the shoulder of her brother, who had followed her into the room.

'The musicians we had booked to play at the ball have cancelled,' Freddy said.

'What are we going to do?' Fanny sobbed into her brother's coat.

Sebastian found himself unable to formulate a coherent response.

He snorted and stomped from the room.

Chapter Thirty-Three

❦

The ten long days since Sebastian had left Little Benning dragged. The big house seemed empty without Isabel and the increasingly difficult task of avoiding Freddy and Fanny, with their plans for the ball, had made Sebastian feel like a hostage in his own home.

He took to immuring himself in the study with the door firmly closed or going for long tours of his estate. In his spare time he devoured books and journals on farming. He now knew all his tenants and their families by name and had discussed plans for improving their holdings, renovating their cottages, and revolutionising the ancient farm practices.

Not all of his ideas would be greeted with universal enthusiasm, and, while he would rather bring them along of their own volition, for some of the older tenants, the power of position may be the only way he could ensure compliance. He understood that power. He was the lord and they would do as he ordered. It was a feeling not dissimilar to standing on a battlefield and giving an order to launch his troops into the thick of the fray, an exhilarating blend of fear and power. A heady mix to be used sparingly.

But now the long wait for his siblings to arrive was over. Young Peter Thompson had been stationed at the gate to keep a watch for the coach. From the window of the study, Sebastian could see the boy running up the drive towards the house, and his heart lurched with anticipation. Connie and Matt were here at last—his family.

'The coach'll be here any minute,' the boy announced, meeting his lordship in the front hall.

Sebastian gave Peter a shilling and, adjusting his neckcloth, which seemed to have come loose, he strode out of the front door to wait for his brother and sister.

As the coach turned on to the forecourt, Matt leaned out of the window, waving his hat, a grin from ear to ear.

'Bas!' he shouted.

A glimpse of Connie's best bonnet also appeared at the window as she pulled her brother back inside the coach. Sebastian smiled as he heard her scolding him.

'Matt, stop making such a fool of yourself.'

Lordly decorum quite forgotten, Sebastian bounded down the stone stairs to greet his siblings, lifting Connie from the coach before the footman had set down the steps and clasping Matt to him.

He turned back to the coach to lend his hand to Isabel. Her gloved fingers clasped his hand, and she smiled down at him. He gave her fingers a gentle squeeze, hoping the simple gesture conveyed a range of emotions, from how very pleased he was to see her to his thanks for everything she had done for his family.

'Welcome home, Lady Somerton.'

She rewarded him with a smile and a barely perceptible acknowledging pressure on his own fingers.

'It is good to be... home.'

'You look very well,' he heard himself saying, thinking as he spoke that a few weeks of homely cooking and bucolic living had given Isabel some colour in her pale cheeks and life in her eyes.

In the hallway, Connie spun on her heel, looking upwards at the mural of Diana and Actaeon sporting around the dome.

'Oh, Bas, this is beautiful. Is it all really yours?'

'Every stone and associated debt,' Sebastian said with a laugh in his voice.

'I am going to wake soon in my own bedroom in Little Benning and find this is all a dream,' Connie said. spreading her arms wide.

Sebastian put an arm around his sister's shoulders, delighted to have her by his side at last. He wanted to show it all to her, share his good fortune with his brother and sister.

'Wait until I show you the gallery and the stables. Did Lady Somerton tell you about her foal? Ah, Mrs. Fletcher.' He gestured for the housekeeper who hovered in the shadows of the stairs.

She came forward and bobbed a curtsey. 'Miss Alder, Mister Alder, welcome to Brantstone. You must be tired after your journey.' She gestured towards the stairs. 'Your rooms are ready.'

'Oh, I'm not tired at all,' Connie said and looked up at her brother. 'Bas, I've never known anything like it! The best room at the inn last night, and the inn keeper treated Matt and me like we were royalty.'

Sebastian beamed and turned to Isabel. 'I must apologise for my siblings. I hope you are not too worn out by their company.'

Isabel met his eyes. 'Not at all. I have thoroughly enjoyed every minute of the last fortnight.'

Impulsively, he took her hand, now free of the gloves, and bent and kissed her fingers.

'Thank you for your care, Lady Somerton. I am forever in your debt.'

'Well, well, who do we have here?'

Freddy and Fanny appeared, standing side by side at the door to the library, and the cheerful mood seemed to dissipate. Sebastian silently cursed the Lynchs. Their continued presence felt like a blight on the house, and it took a monumental effort to keep the ice from his voice as he effected the introductions.

Only a fool would have missed the fawning attention Freddy paid to Constance. Unused to the attentions of men of the world, Connie coloured prettily at his overblown compliments. The gorge rose in Sebastian's throat and he wondered how best to educate his sister in such matters.

'I am sure,' Fanny said, seizing Connie by the arm, 'that we shall be the very best of friends. Now, has Cousin Sebastian told you of the ball that is to be held here?'

Sebastian's teeth ground at the familiar use of *Cousin Sebastian*.

'Oh yes, Lady Somerton told me about it.' Connie looked at her brother. 'Bas, I have nothing to wear!'

Sebastian looked up at the ceiling. 'And so it begins...' he said with no malice.

He had already briefed Mrs. Fletcher to organise a modiste and a tailor to attend on Connie and Matt the next day.

Connie pulled a face at him. 'You know I wouldn't ask for a new dress unless I really meant it.'

Fanny patted her arm. 'If nothing can be arranged, we are much of a size and I am sure I will have something in my wardrobe that you will like. Come, let me show you to your room. It will be the yellow bedchamber, just near me. I can't wait to show you the house.'

As Fanny began to lead Connie up the stairs with a proprietorial air, the chill of disappointment settled on Sebastian's shoulders. He had been looking forward to showing Connie the house, anticipating her pleasure at the sight of her bedroom, which he had filled with yellow and white roses from the garden.

Isabel touched his arm and she looked up at him.

'Let me,' she whispered.

Walking to the bottom of the stairs, she called up at the two girls.

'Fanny, the tour of the house can wait. Constance needs a little rest after her recent illness and the stress of the journey. Allow Lord Somerton to show his sister to her chamber. Can you and Mrs. Fletcher arrange for some tea in the blue parlour?'

Fanny, masking the fleeting moue of disappointment that

curled her lips, relinquished her hold on Connie. She smiled at Sebastian and fluttered her eyelashes.

'Of course, Lord Somerton.'

Sebastian put his arm around Connie's shoulders and led her up the stairs, pointing out various sour-faced Somerton ancestors on the way.

'Close your eyes,' he said as he threw the door open.

'I can smell roses,' she said.

He had personally chosen the room for Connie, knowing she liked sunshine and light. The huge vase of the best of the summer roses stood on the chest, filling the room with their perfume.

She opened her eyes and, seeing the room, she squealed with delight, pressing her hands to her chest. At the sight of her incredulous face, love for his sister swelled Sebastian's heart. He wanted to fold her in his arms and keep her safe from all the evil of the world. He could not rest easily knowing a murderer lurked in the shadows of Brantstone.

'Oh, Bas ...' she turned to him, tears glinting on her eyelashes. She ran at him, throwing her arms around him. 'I have missed you so much.'

He held her to him. 'And I you, Connie.'

She looked up at him. 'We can be a proper family now.'

He nodded and dropped a brotherly kiss on her forehead. 'We can. Now I have one small welcome present for you.'

He fished in his jacket and pulled out a long, flat box and handed it to her. She took the box, turning it over in her hands.

'Open it,' he urged.

She unclasped the lid, revealing a delicate string of pearls with a diamond clasp and matching pearl earrings. A simple bit of jewellery, but, for a girl who had only her mother's wedding ring, it meant the world.

She kissed him again. 'You are the best of brothers,' she said.

He held out his arm. 'Come and take tea in the blue parlour and then I will show you the rest of the house.'

Chapter Thirty-Four

After supper, Sebastian and Matt retired to the study where a cheerful fire burned in the grate against the chill of the evening.

Matt swirled the brandy in his glass and took a sip. He closed his eyes and let out a long breath. 'I must say, Lord Somerton, life has dealt you a well-deserved hand. I still have to pinch myself to believe how it came about.'

Sebastian smiled. 'It's not as easy as you would think, Matt. First and foremost, I have responsibility for the lives and the livelihoods of the tenants—a responsibility my late cousin appeared to have done his best to shirk in his lifetime.'

Matt nodded. 'It sounds like your cousin was not greatly loved.'

Sebastian looked into the depths of the newly procured, expensive but legally imported brandy. 'I am struggling to find some redeeming feature in him,' he said.

'He had good taste in women,' Matt said.

Sebastian looked up.

'Having just had the pleasure of Lady Somerton's company for the last fortnight, I was not wrong in my first impression.

She is a treasure. You know the old pianoforte? She played it like it was the finest concert instrument. Beautiful and talented.'

'I'm glad you like her.' Sebastian maintained a neutral tone, but it pleased him to hear Isabel spoken of so highly by his brother.

'She doesn't talk about her husband much,' Matt pried.

'No. It was not a happy marriage,' Sebastian replied, cutting short any further comment.

'Those cousins of his are a strange pair,' Matt said. 'How on earth did you get saddled with that frightful duo?'

'I appear to have inherited them as a problem my cousin wasn't prepared to deal with.'

Sebastian toyed with confiding his thoughts on Anthony's death to his brother but decided not to cloud the younger man's judgment for the moment. Any insight Matt could offer was best untainted by Sebastian's growing unease about Freddy Lynch.

'On the other side of the coin, tomorrow you are going to meet your grandmother and a large assortment of aunts and uncles and cousins. I have organised a picnic in the grounds for the family. If the weather is foul, it will be a picnic in the ballroom.'

Matt shook his head. 'Fancy that, a whole family we never knew about. Connie is so excited.'

Sebastian nodded. 'All those years of thinking it was just us in the world, Matt.'

'So why did Lord Somerton cut his son off like that? Was it just because he loved the vicar's daughter?'

Sebastian sighed. 'From what I can gather, it was pride on both sides. Lord Somerton had betrothed his son to the daughter of an earl and our mother was betrothed to someone else. When they eloped, both fathers would have felt a terrible sense of betrayal and shame. But enough of the past. All the players in that sad drama are dead, and I think speculating on what might have been is a waste of time.'

'Quite right.' Matt rose to his feet. 'It's been a long day. I am looking forward to losing myself in that bed. I swear it would have filled my room at home.'

Sebastian smiled and bade his brother goodnight.

He sat for a while longer, finishing his glass of brandy and gazing into the fire, reflecting on what he recognised as a rare moment of contentment.

Chapter Thirty-Five

The next day dawned bright and clear, but before the guests were due to arrive, Sebastian took Matt and Connie down to the village to call on their aunt and grandmother. Peggy had burst into tears on seeing Connie.

'Oh, you are the spit of your mother,' she sobbed. 'I would have sworn it were Marjory herself walking up the garden path.'

Connie, in turn, had burst into tears on meeting her grandmother. While the women wailed, Sebastian and Matt stood by the door, waiting for the flood to subside. Sebastian stole a glance at his brother and noticed the younger man's eyes seemed moist.

Matt caught his glance, sniffed, and looked up at his brother with a rueful smile.

'You'd better become accustomed to the attention. Mother had five sisters. I believe we have upward of fifty relatives attending our luncheon party today,' Sebastian said.

'Good lord!'

Sebastian cleared his throat. 'Ladies? If you are ready to leave, my barouche is outside.'

Peggy dabbed at her eyes and blew her nose loudly on a sturdy handkerchief.

'Oh my. This is all too much, my lord. Who'd have thought it? Such a lovely girl.' She squeezed Connie's hand again and turned to her mother, saying loudly, 'Come along, mother. His lordship has his carriage for us.'

Matt helped both ladies, dressed in their Sunday finery, into the carriage for the drive back to the hall. Peggy, seeing some of her neighbours in the street, waved and bowed her head. Sebastian smiled. He had it in mind to offer to move his grandmother and aunt up to the hall where they could have rooms of their own in the east wing, but that was a surprise he would keep for another day.

The guests began arriving by mid-morning. Aunts, uncles, and cousins of all ages poured into the grounds of the hall.

With some reluctance, Sebastian had enlisted Fanny's aid and had to admit that when it came to organising social events, she had a rare talent. A long table had been set up underneath the largest oak tree in the garden, and Fanny had the footmen organising games of quoits, and shuttlecock and battledore as well as a game with hoops and mallets. Jugglers and acrobats had appeared, along with a small orchestra.

Fanny, showing unusual tact, wandered among the entertainment ensuring all was in order, but in all other respects, keeping a respectful distance. Of Freddy there was, mercifully, no sign. Isabel, at Sebastian's insistence that she would not be intruding, joined the party.

A comfortable chair with cushions had been arranged for his grandmother, and she sat like a queen in the shade of a tree, following the lively games and the interaction of her extended family with what eyesight she had left. She smiled beatifically at the happy noise around her.

Sebastian stood with one hand on the back of his grandmother's chair, watching Matt engaged in a rowdy game of blind man's bluff with some of the younger cousins. Connie sat on a stool at her grandmother's feet, holding the old woman's hand and listening with earnest attention to her grandmother's stories about her lost daughter, the mother Connie had never known.

Isabel, eschewing her usual dowdy black, had dressed in a gown of dove grey trimmed with lilac ribbons. Holding an elegant lace parasol she wandered across to Sebastian. He inclined his head, and she acknowledged the gesture with a smile. She had done something different with her hair. Little curls framed her face, and he liked the effect.

'Walk with me?' she offered.

Excusing himself from his grandmother, he crooked his elbow, and she slipped a hand around his arm. They circled the party, stopping to speak to guests. He led her up to the terrace, where they sat side by side on the wall, watching the festivities.

'I never imagined what it could be like to be part of a large family,' Sebastian said at last.

'Your grandfather, the Reverend Parker, cast a dark shadow over them all. If he were still alive, this,' Isabel waved a hand at the noisy party, 'would never be permitted.'

'My stepfather was a clergyman too,' Sebastian reminded her, 'but he loved life and felt it should be celebrated at every opportunity.'

She cast a sideways glance at him. 'And so it should. I think I would have liked your stepfather.'

'Everyone did,' Sebastian agreed.

'Lord Somerton, Lord Somerton...' Aunt Peggy came hurrying towards them. 'Oh, my lord, I am quite breathless. May I join you for a few minutes?'

'Of course, aunt. Sit by me.'

Sebastian indicated the wall, and Peggy lowered herself down beside him, fanning herself with her hand. Isabel excused herself to see that luncheon was ready to be served.

Peggy gave a deep, happy sigh.

'This is lovely, dear. The only time we were ever invited up to the hall was when the old lord used to throw a Christmas party for the village.'

'Then it is a miracle my parents even met,' Sebastian observed.

Peggy smiled. 'Young love does have its ways, my lord.' She shuddered. 'Oh, the row when they declared their love. I thought your grandfather would have a turn.'

'Surely it would have been a good match, at least from the good Reverend's point of view?'

'Aye, you'd think so, but your grandfather would not tolerate disobedience in anyone, however good the cause. He forbade Marjory's name to ever be mentioned in his presence.'

Sebastian sighed and his gaze strayed to Connie, now caught up in the game of blind man's buff. It occurred to him that he had put his sister in a very vulnerable position. The sister of a viscount with a dowry, she would be an attractive catch for any charlatan. Life had seemed much simpler when they were penniless.

'Now, I'm not one to gossip,' Aunt Peggy began. Sebastian smiled, Aunt Peggy was, he imagined, a veritable store of village gossip. 'But your cousin, Anthony, was not a good man.'

'In what way, aunt?' Sebastian enquired, with what he hoped was an ingenuous expression.

'There was that terrible scandal with poor Amy Thompson.'

'I know about that,' Sebastian said.

Peggy's eyes darted around the garden as if she expected Anthony to materialise from behind the shrubbery. 'They say he had his way with her and left her with child. The shame was too much for the poor girl.'

'Very sad,' Sebastian commented, recalling his conversation with Bennet. Of the many crimes laid at Anthony's feet, maybe getting poor Amy with child was not one of them, but it did not excuse the appalling neglect of his wife and the wasting of his estate.

Connie ran up to them, her bonnet hanging down her back by its strings and her face flushed from exertion.

'Sebastian, do come and play!' She grabbed his hand and hauled him to his feet.

The happy group surrounded him as Connie bound his eyes and turned him around three times for blind man's bluff.

After the last carriage had been waved off, Sebastian and his siblings retired to the blue parlour where the Lynchs joined them, to Sebastian's annoyance.

Connie collapsed into a chair with a dramatic flourish. 'I'm exhausted. Who'd have thought it, Bas? We have such lovely relations.'

Freddy bowed low as he offered her a glass of sherry. 'Of course, I hope you would consider my sister and me among that happy grouping?'

Connie looked up at him. 'Of course, Mister Lynch. You are both so kind.'

Sebastian's jaw clenched. He really must talk to Connie.

Freddy sat down and crossed his legs. His gaze flashed across to Sebastian as he spoke.

'And of course, we are both so grateful to Lord Somerton for his continued kindness to us, otherwise, my dear cousin Constance, we would be quite bereft.'

Connie's eyes flashed up to Sebastian and then back at Freddy. She gave him a charming smile and said, 'My brother is quite the most generous of men.'

'And may I say he is blessed with quite the most beautiful of sisters,' Freddy simpered in return.

'Enough of that, Lynch,' Sebastian growled. 'My sister has had quite enough compliments for one day. I don't want it going to her head.'

As Freddy looked at him and smiled, a cold shiver ran down Sebastian's spine.

Chapter Thirty-Six

From somewhere in the house, Isabel could hear music and laughter. Connie and Matt were having dancing lessons. Freddy had produced some ghastly French dancing master and they had all adjourned to the ballroom. The suggestion at breakfast that Sebastian may care to join them received a frosty response and his lordship had taken his broadsheets and retreated to the study.

As Isabel stood outside the door to the study, she wondered how many years it had been since laughter had rung down the corridors of Brantstone. Connie and Matt had brought life to the gloomy corridors.

She took a breath and knocked. At the gruff response, she opened the door.

'Am I disturbing you?' she enquired.

Sebastian shot to his feet, almost knocking his chair backwards in his haste.

'No, not at all. Come in.'

She entered the room and stood before him, her hands clasped in front of her black skirts.

'I came to tell you that I am planning to move to the dower house in the next few days.'

He stared at her for a long moment.

'Oh,' he said, followed by, 'Why?'

'I'm not needed here anymore. Your sister now takes precedence over me, and she will see to the running of the household.'

'But she's only seventeen. She doesn't know anything about running a household of this size.'

A small smile played at the corner of Isabel's lips. 'She is a fast learner, and it's not as if I will be far away if she needs advice.'

He cleared his throat. 'Is there anything I can do to assist you with the move?' he asked.

She shook her head. 'No, thank you. It's all organised.'

'You will need transport. Please take the small coach and the bays.'

'Sebastian, that is too generous...' she began, but he waved away her protests.

'Call it an indefinite loan,' he said.

'I will send for my saddle horse and Millie and the foal once I am settled,' she said.

He nodded. 'Whatever you wish, Isabel. You just have to ask.'

'Thank you.' She turned to go. As she opened the door, she stopped and turned back to look at him. 'We have all received an invitation to attend a supper at Lady Kendall's tonight. What shall I reply?'

Sebastian hesitated. If it were up to him, he would decline, but he thought about Connie and Matt and said with a heavy sigh, 'I suppose we should accept.'

Isabel nodded. 'I will send a response. The invitation includes Freddy and Fanny as well, but I will send my apologies. It would not be appropriate for me to attend while I am still officially in mourning.'

Sebastian gave her a sharp glance, but she schooled her face to complete impassivity.

It would never be appropriate for her to enter the home of

Lady Georgiana Kendall. The period of deep mourning would end in a few months, and Isabel would be breaking it with the Brantstone ball. For now it served as a useful excuse to escape an awkward situation.

Sebastian said, 'May I call on you when you are settled, Isabel?'

She turned to look at him and smiled. 'You will always be welcome, Sebastian.'

As she closed the door behind her, she paused with her hand still on the latch. She had anticipated the move to the dower house for so long but now the moment had come, she felt an unexpected sense of loss. Brantstone had been her home for ten years. There were memories here. Mostly unhappy memories that she had sought to escape but, since Sebastian Alder had come to Brantstone, the ghosts had begun to fade.

You are being ridiculous, she told herself.

Straightening her shoulders, she strode towards the stairs.

There could be no looking back, no regrets. The time had come for her new life.

Chapter Thirty-Seven

'Very fine, if I say so myself.' Pierce stood back from the mirror and looked admiringly at his handiwork. 'Don't you agree, Mr. Bennet?'

'He looks like a right toff,' Mr. Bennet agreed.

This was Sebastian's first foray into full evening wear, and he ran a finger around a stock so high and stiff that it almost grazed his ear lobe.

'It's very tight,' he complained.

'Meant to be, my lord. Meant to be! And, might I say, my lord, a very fine figure you cut. While his late lordship cut a dash, er... He didn't have the attributes you possess, my lord.'

Sebastian cast a nervous glance at his reflection in the mirror, in particular the tight white satin breeches, and hoped that the man referred to his shoulders and not other attributes.

'A more slender gentleman, his late lordship,' Pierce continued, happily expanding on his theme, 'suited to an altogether different style to yourself, my lord. Now if I may venture so bold, my lord, your stance...'

Standing in the properly affected manner, all the better to show off his attributes, Sebastian allowed himself the luxury of a last long look in the mirror. His own mother would have difficulty recognising her scruffy and disorganised son in the elegant figure that he now presented.

The Reverend Alder would merely have shaken his head. '*Vestis virum reddit,*' he would have said, quoting his favourite Roman writer, Quintilian.

Clothes maketh the man. We all wear uniforms, Sebastian thought.

In his army days, his uniform had been scarlet with buff facings. Now it was a well-cut jacket and satin breeches.

'When your lordship returns to London, we will be able to have some proper tailoring,' Pierce said, still primping the cravat.

'What's wrong with these clothes?'

'A quick job, my lord, hardly worthy of you.'

'It looks fine to me,' Sebastian said in a clipped tone that Bennet would have instantly recognised as a warning not to push Sebastian Alder into doing something he did not wish to do.

Pierce retired to the chest of drawers and returned with a diamond pin that he affixed to the fine linen folds of the cravat before allowing his master to escape.

The driveway to Fairchild Hall, home of Lady Kendall, had been lit by flares, and the front of the old house was brightly illuminated with red silk lanterns. Connie, leaning from the window, exclaimed at the show. Even Sebastian, alighting from the coach, had to admit that the effect had been carefully stage managed to give the visitors a sense of expectation.

They were met in the flagged front hall by a flunkey who took their cloaks and indicated the wide doors to the right from where the sound of music and laughter issued. Sebastian glanced down at his sister, dressed in a pretty pink gown, borrowed from Fanny. Her new pearl necklace graced her neckline, and her dark blonde hair had been swept up into a sophisticated knot, set off with pink ribbons and a white feather. If this was Fanny's work then he owed the girl his thanks. Connie looked beautiful.

He offered her his arm and she accepted it, her face flushed and her eyes sparkling with excitement. Her fingers tightened on his arm for a moment and he patted the gloved hand.

'Lord Somerton,' the footman intoned. 'Mr. Alder and Miss Alder.'

A sudden hush fell on the gathering as all eyes turned to the door. Lady Kendall, dressed in a green satin gown with a matching turban topped by a green feather set in place with an emerald the size of a quail's egg, disengaged herself from a group of guests and came forward.

Sebastian heard Connie whisper. 'Oh, my!'

Lady Kendall extended her hand. 'Lord Somerton. Welcome to my home.'

He bowed over the proffered hand and presented Connie and Matt. Connie curtseyed and Matt, resplendent in clothes borrowed from Freddy, seemed completely confident as he bowed to Lady Kendall. Isabel and, he grudgingly admitted, the Lynchs had done a fine job in preparing two youngsters straight from rural Cheshire for their new life. He felt inordinately proud of his siblings.

Across the room, Harry Dempster raised a hand in greeting before being drawn back into conversation with a woman in a scarlet dress. Matt looked around at the gathered crowd. Fans fluttered like a rabble of butterflies as his brother's gaze scanned the room.

Sebastian smiled and leaned in to whisper, 'You seem to be attracting attention, little brother.'

Matt cast him a cheeky grin and, taking Connie's arm, sallied forth. Lady Kendall tucked a small, gloved hand into Sebastian's arm and led him into the room.

'Your brother and sister are quite charming, Lord Somerton.'

'Thank you,' he replied. 'It was kind of you to invite us.'

'Not at all. I am sure you and your brother are everything the mothers of the county would wish.'

'And what is that?' Sebastian asked.

'In your case, a title and no inconvenient wife,' Lady Kendall replied, 'and your brother has a handsome face and, it is hoped, a generous allowance from your lordship.'

Sebastian laughed. 'The young rogue has to earn it first,' he said. 'I am packing him off to university.'

Lady Kendall raised a delicately arched eyebrow. 'Really? Is that something he wishes to do?'

'Yes. He has a talent for mathematics but I was never able to...'

He stopped, feeling the embarrassment rising to his face. He couldn't bring himself to say, 'never able to afford the cost'.

Lady Kendall took two glasses of champagne from a tray and handed one to Sebastian.

'May I claim a few minutes of your time in private, my lord?'

Sebastian glanced around the room, wondering about the propriety of a private audience with Lady Kendall. He ran a finger around his stock, which had become even more uncomfortable.

He followed her through the doors onto a terrace and into the night. She shivered in the cool night air, and Sebastian offered his jacket, which she declined.

'I will not detain you long.' She took a sip of champagne. 'I like you, Lord Somerton, and I wouldn't have you think ill of me.'

He started to protest, but she interrupted him, 'I do not wish you to be under a misapprehension about my relationship with your late cousin.'

Sebastian spluttered on his champagne. 'My dear Lady Kendall, your relationship with my cousin is of no interest to me.'

'Yes, but it matters to me. I know what people say and, more painfully, I know what Lady Somerton believes. You are an honourable man and I would like to share a confidence with you.'

'A confidence?'

She moved closer to him. Her exotic perfume wafted towards him in an intoxicating cloud of roses and spice.

'It suited both Anthony and me for our own reasons to be gossiped about in a certain fashion, but we were not lovers. Our relationship was purely platonic. People do not speak kindly of Anthony or his treatment of Isabel. The truth is that Anthony was a deeply conflicted man,' she paused. 'His own nature did not incline him to the female sex.'

Lady Kendall's revelation only confirmed the growing suspicion that the careful picture of a womanising, gambling rake Anthony had painted of himself was just an artifice, but it suited Sebastian to pretend ignorance.

'What do you mean?'

Georgiana Kendall put her head back and laughed, a soft, tinkling sound swallowed up by the dark night. 'Surely, Lord Somerton, you are a man of the world?'

'I am the son of a parson. I was brought up in a vicarage in a small village. I am not a man of yours or Anthony's world.'

'But you have been a soldier,' Lady Kendall said. 'Surely you must have seen such relationships in your time?'

Sebastian considered for a moment. He had been aware of certain particular friendships within the army, but as long as the parties had been discreet and it had not affected the morale of their company, it was something to which the senior officers, some of whom were similarly inclined, were prepared to turn a blind eye.

Lady Kendall drained her glass and stood for a moment looking into its empty depths as the sound of music, laughter, and bright chatter spilled from the open windows of the house.

'And you were happy to be complicit in maintaining this fiction? Even at a cost to your own reputation?' Sebastian asked at last.

She laughed. 'Oh, I know my reputation, Lord Somerton. In truth, I was being pursued by a man in whom I had no interest and it suited me to be known as Anthony's mistress. The man concerned would not cross Lord Somerton, and Anthony ...' She shrugged. 'At first, the pretence concealed his other life but, in more recent times, it can happen that some men can lean in either direction. I believe Anthony had come to love his wife.'

Sebastian gave a derisory snort. 'He had a strange way of showing it,' he said.

'I am not privy to the Somertons' private affairs,' she responded in a sharp tone. 'I know only what Anthony confided in me, Lord Somerton, and trust me when I say I believe myself to be his closest confidante. Anthony had fathered a child with his wife, a child on whom he doted and, in the months following the child's birth, he had grown to love his wife deeply, but he was not a man who knew how to demonstrate such affection. William's death was a bitter blow and Isabel's grief was so great that he felt himself inadequate to provide the solace she needed. His answer was to resume his former ways, but it masked a very different man and brought him no comfort.'

'If what you are telling me is true, then it is a sad story,' Sebastian said. 'I am certain, from what little she has told me, Lady Somerton had no idea of the depth of his feeling.'

'And I am sure you are correct. I counselled him to confide =in her and I believed he was about to do so. I would tell her myself.' Lady Kendall looked away, and her shoulders stiffened. 'Lady Somerton, quite rightly, shuns my company, which is a pity, because I would have greatly valued her friendship.'

'Why are you telling me this?' he asked.

She turned back to look at him and shook her head. 'I think sometimes when a person has a dark secret, such as that Anthony concealed, it leaves them vulnerable.'

'Do you think his death an accident?' Sebastian ventured.

She shrugged. 'He left here in high spirits. I have no reason to think it was anything more than just a tragic accident.'

But you haven't seen the saddle, Sebastian thought.

Before he could speak again, she moved closer to him, her hand resting on his arm. Her cloying perfume enveloped him, but he found himself unmoved by her advances, if that is what they were.

'We've been gone long enough, Lady Kendall,' he said.

She laughed. 'Indeed, even for a woman with my dubious reputation.'

She took his arm and led him into the next room, where card tables had been set up. As they entered, Sebastian heard Freddy's braying laugh. Beside him, Lady Kendall stiffened.

'When are you going to rid yourself of that odious man and his sister?' she asked in a low voice.

'As soon as I can, but it's not that simple. Why do you ask?'

'He is cheating at cards again.'

Sebastian frowned. Freddy sat at a table with three others. Nothing about his demeanour gave any indication that anything untoward was going on.

'What do you mean?' he asked.

'Watch his sister,' Georgiana whispered.

Fanny circled the table at a discreet distance. To Sebastian's eye there seemed nothing unusual about her.

Lady Kendall looked up at him and tapped her fan impatiently on his chest.

'She is sending him signals. See, she has just touched her fan to her ear.'

He watched Fanny for a few more minutes. The signals were subtle and, to the passing eye, benign. Freddy didn't seem to acknowledge them but his success at the hand he played indicated something was passing between brother and sister.

'I think you're right,' Sebastian said.

'Of course I am. It was Anthony who pointed their system out to me. Freddy's clever. He doesn't win every hand.'

'Should I call him out?' Sebastian said.

Georgiana shook her head and said with a laugh. 'You can't prove anything, any more than Anthony could. I have had ample opportunity in the past year to observe the Lynchs and I just wanted you to know what he was capable of. You can use it to your advantage when you need to. Now I see your delightful sister is looking for you.'

Connie and Matt joined them. Connie had a high colour in her cheeks and waved her fan in an indecorous way to cool her face. 'I've been dancing,' she said.

'Quite the sought-after partner,' Matt agreed. 'Thank heavens for the dancing lessons.'

'And what about you, Mr. Alder?' Lady Kendall said, fixing Matt with a winsome smile that would have made a stronger man weak at the knees.

Matt bowed. 'I hope, Lady Kendall, that you would honour me with a dance, if not this evening then at the Brantstone ball.'

She inclined her head. 'It would be my pleasure, Mr. Alder.' She turned to Sebastian. 'Tell me, Lord Somerton, has your sister made her debut?'

'Er, no,' Sebastian said. 'Is that something you'd want to do?' he enquired of his normally sensible sister.

Connie's bright eyes gave her answer. 'I think, Bas, if I am to fit in to this new world, it would be expected. Would you not agree, Lady Kendall?'

Lady Kendall gave her a long appraising look. 'When you come up to London for the season, I would be delighted to present you. I think, Miss Alder, you and I would enjoy a season in London.'

'When? Surely you mean "if". It was not my intention to go to London for the season,' Sebastian said, just to see the crestfallen look on Connie's face.

'Your brother is jesting,' Lady Kendall said, hitting Sebastian on the arm with her fan. 'Come with me, Miss Alder, and allow me to introduce you to some ladies of your own age.'

Matt and Sebastian stood watching Lady Kendall propel Connie through the crowd.

'I thought this was going to be a quiet little dinner party,' Sebastian remarked, more to himself than his brother.

'She's extraordinary,' Matt said, his face the picture of a moonstruck calf.

'She's not for the likes of you, so take that look off your face,' Sebastian said.

'Oh? Don't think I didn't see you sneaking off by yourself with her.'

'I wasn't sneaking. We were discussing business,' Sebastian said.

His brother raised an eyebrow. 'What business?'

It was on the tip of his tongue to confide in his brother, but Harry Dempster interrupted them.

'There you are, Alder. Did I hear my sister inveigling you to London?' Harry said.

Sebastian smiled. 'Your sister is a difficult woman to resist, Dempster.'

'As indeed is yours. You never told me that Miss Alder was such a beauty.'

Something in Harry's tone and the raised eyebrows disquieted Sebastian. Even when they had served together, Harry had a reputation for womanising that was the scandal of the regiment.

'I thought your taste was for married women, Dempster.'

Harry smiled. 'Indeed, they tend to be far less trouble.' He turned to Matt. 'We haven't met. Harry Dempster, an old comrade-in-arms to Lord Somerton. You must be Alder's brother.'

'Colonel Dempster?' Matt cast Sebastian a quick glance for affirmation.

'The same. My apologies for my absence. I had business in London, Alder. Anything of interest happen while I was gone?'

'Just the arrival of my brother and sister,' Sebastian smiled.

Matt drifted away to partner a pretty girl in a blue dress, and the two men wandered back into the gaming room, where Freddy had now accumulated quite a purse.

'Never play cards with Lynch,' Harry said in a low voice.

'So your sister has warned me.'

'He's clever enough not to win all the time, but it looks like he has excelled himself tonight.'

'Hopefully he is saving to leave Brantstone,' Sebastian remarked drily.

'If you'll excuse me, I might join that other table,' Harry said. 'What about you?'

Sebastian shook his head. 'I don't gamble.'

'I forgot. Something about your vicarage upbringing?'

'No, more to do with years of not having the means, Dempster. The only opinion my stepfather ever voiced on the subject was to say, "Don't gamble with money you can't afford to lose" and I never had any money I could afford to lose.'

'Sound advice,' Harry said and drifted away towards a table of gentlemen engaged in a game of Commerce.

Sebastian accepted a glass from a passing footman and stood back in the shadows, watching Freddy. He wondered if he was imagining it, but it seemed to him that Freddy played with an air of desperation, as if he needed to win above everything. He made a mental note to enquire of Bragge how far the investigation into Freddy's past had advanced.

※

IN THE COACH RETURNING TO BRANTSTONE, SEBASTIAN TRIED to ignore Fanny's incessant babble about the evening. He lapsed into a reverie as he recalled the interesting conversation with Lady Kendall and tried to reconcile Anthony's deadly secret with the public man.

' ... And then, of course, your friend, Colonel Dempster...' Fanny said, nudging Sebastian.

At the mention of his friend's name, Sebastian turned to look at her.

'What about him?'

'He is quite charming, cousin Sebastian. Didn't you notice

how he escorted me into supper and ensured I had everything I needed?'

'This Dempster, does he have expectations, cousin?' Freddy asked from his shadowed corner of the coach.

'Expectations?' Sebastian enquired. 'What do you mean?'

'Oh, Harry's father is very wealthy,' Connie said, ingenuously.

Sebastian glared at her in the dark. She had been giggling with Fanny, evidence she may have imbibed one glass of wine too many.

'Dempster is a full colonel on half pay. His father is hale and hearty and he has no expectations of improving his lot for some time,' Sebastian retorted in a clipped tone.

'Pity,' Freddy said. 'However, I am sure such a handsome and charming fellow will do well.'

'And what about you, Freddy. Did you do well at the tables tonight?' Sebastian enquired.

Freddy's teeth gleamed in the darkness as he smiled. 'Tolerably well.'

'You seem to be having quite a bit of luck when I saw you,' Matt interposed, in innocence of Sebastian's knowledge of Freddy and Fanny's connivance at cheating.

'I am known to be lucky. There have been times when my skill with cards is all that has kept poor Fan and me from debtor's prison,' Freddy said with a heavy, theatrical sigh.

'Just a week 'til our own ball,' Fanny chirped, diverting the subject with surprising skill.

The high stock around Sebastian's neck tightened. He slumped down in his seat with his arms crossed.

'Oh!' Connie exclaimed, her hand flying to her neck. 'Oh, Sebastian, your necklace!'

'What about it?'

He heard the edge of tears in his sister's voice as she said, 'It's no longer around my neck. The catch must have broken.'

After a deal of fussing and checking of clothing and reticules, which ended with Connie in floods of tears, she concluded that it must have fallen off while she was dancing.

'Oh, Bas,' Connie wailed, falling into his arms. 'The first pretty thing I have ever owned, and I lost it.'

'I have no doubt one of Lady Kendall's staff will find it,' Sebastian said.

He patted her ineffectually on the back and smiled into the dark. The lost necklace gave him a good opportunity to return to Fairchild Hall the next day.

He had some questions for Lady Kendall about the night of Anthony's death.

Chapter Thirty-Eight

❦

Sebastian dismounted from Pharaoh and handed the reins over to the Fairchild Hall stableboy, who ran out to meet him. Lady Kendall's footman met him at the front steps and showed him into a small parlour that had not been open the previous evening. Lady Kendall reclined on a daybed in a loose, frothy robe of muslin and green ribbons.

A flush of embarrassment rose to his face. Even he knew a lady should never receive a man in such a state of 'deshabille'.

'My pardon, Lady Kendall,' he said. 'I could have sent one of my footmen on this mission.'

'But you came yourself. How sweet.'

Lady Kendall waved at a chair and sent the footman away with an order for tea. She lifted the pearl necklace from a little box by her day bed.

'Is this what you are seeking?'

'Yes it is. Thank you.'

Lady Kendall let the necklace play through her fingers. 'A pretty thing, but the clasp, alas, is broken.'

She passed it to Sebastian, who wrapped it in a handkerchief and stowed it in his pocket as the footman returned with a tea tray. Lady Kendall dismissed the man and poured for them both. She lay back, placing a hand languorously across her brow.

'I fear I am getting too old for parties.'

The cup rattled in Sebastian's saucer as he set the dainty thing down on the table.

'Forgive me, Lady Kendall, but something in our conversation sparked curiosity in me. I would like to ask you some more about the night Anthony died.'

'Of course. What would you like to know?'

'What was the occasion?'

She frowned. 'No occasion. He turned up unannounced and took supper with Harry and me. We played cards for a little while, and then he left.'

'Alone?'

'Yes.'

Harry had mentioned that he had been visiting his sister. It had been a passing comment but Sebastian made a note to examine his friend more closely.

'What was Anthony's mood?'

She made a dismissive gesture with her hand. 'He was in no particular mood. It was just a pleasant social evening, as I'm sure Harry will confirm. Why are you asking? Do you think he may have taken his own life?'

Sebastian looked at her. 'No. I just want to be clear in my own mind that what happened was an accident.'

'Is there any suspicion that it wasn't?'

Sebastian ignored the question. 'Did you see him leave?'

She shook her head. 'He took his leave of me before midnight and I presume the rest you know. And before you ask, yes, he had consumed a deal of wine, but not enough to make him a danger.'

Sebastian nodded and rose to his feet. 'Can I see your stables?'

Lady Kendall laughed. 'Most men of my acquaintance would enquire about another room in my house.'

Sebastian stared at her blankly. She rolled her eyes and shook her head.

'Lord Somerton, you are a delight. Dear Isabel would be a fool to let you pass her by.'

'Isabel?'

Lady Kendall rose from her daybed and Sebastian stood. She crossed over to him and laid a hand on his chest.

'Lord Somerton, I pride myself on being a judge of human nature. Now let us go and inspect my stables but first I should change.'

She took an inordinately long time before rejoining him, dressed in a simple, long sleeve gown of Indian printed cotton. She carried a paisley shawl, which she threw over her shoulders as they walked to the stables. These stood a little way from the house and were a fraction of the size of those at Brantstone.

Lady Kendall summoned the stable lad who had taken Pharaoh, and Sebastian asked if he remembered the night the late Lord Somerton had visited.

'Aye,' the boy said slowly. 'Was only me here. I were just seeing to the coach horses when he arrived.'

Sebastian indicated Pharaoh. 'On that horse?'

The boy nodded. 'He's a fine 'orse that one. His lordship gave orders for him to be left saddled. Said he wouldn't be long.'

That seemed to contradict Lady Kendall's claim of a long evening of wine and cards.

'Did anyone else come to the stable that evening?'

'Not that I saw. I finished with the coach 'orses and spent the evening polishing the tack.' He pointed at a room at the end of the stables.' I musta gone to sleep cos I didn't hear 'im leave.'

'So anyone could have entered the stable without you seeing?'

The boy nodded and lowered his head, shooting a quick sideways glance at his mistress.

A clatter of hooves on the cobbles announced the arrival of Harry Dempster. He flung himself easily from the back of his horse, handing the reins to the boy.

'Good morning, Somerton,' he said as he approached them. 'What brings you out to the stables? Are you coming or going?'

Sebastian patted his pocket. 'Just collecting some lost property.'

'Lord Somerton was asking me about the night poor Anthony died,' Lady Kendall said.

'Oh God, yes. That was the night I called in on my way to Yorkshire. I arrived late and left early. Didn't hear about Somerton's death for days. We played a couple of rounds of Loo, if I remember, Georgie?'

'I was telling Lord Somerton that he seemed quite his normal self.'

'Took a few coins off me,' Harry agreed.

The stableboy came forward, leading Pharaoh and Sebastian swung into the saddle. He looked down at Harry and his sister.

'Why would Lord Somerton have jumped the hedge at Lovett's Bridge?' he asked.

Lady Kendall shrugged. 'It was his customary route home. If you cut across the fields behind the farm, it takes a good fifteen minutes off the journey back to Brantstone Hall. He took that route every time.'

'Did everyone know that?'

Lady Kendall shrugged. 'I assume so. It is common local knowledge.'

She raised her hand in farewell as Sebastian swung himself into the saddle. He acknowledged her gesture and kicked Pharoah into a canter, only slowing when he reached Lovett's Bridge. Here, he paused, considering the shortcut to Brantstone. The horse seemed to sense his discomfort or perhaps, in its own way, it recalled the night Anthony had died. It shifted beneath him, its ears lying flat. Sebastian patted the glossy, black neck.

'It's all right, old chap, we'll take the long way, but I think we'll pay another visit on our way.'

Chapter Thirty-Nine

'Am I disturbing you?'

Isabel looked up from polishing the table and her eyes widened. Sebastian stood in the doorway to the dower house, attired in moleskin breeches and an elegant cutaway coat of red wool. He carried a riding crop and gloves and his hair looked windswept, but then it rarely looked tidy even with the best haircut.

She hastily smoothed down her skirts and tried to look like a dowager viscountess, not the hired help. She wore her oldest gown of dark blue cotton gingham with a large apron tied over it. She had tied her hair up in a scarf, and she was sure there was a smudge of dirt on her cheek.

'No, not at all. Have you been out riding?' she enquired.

He nodded. 'I rode over to Fairchild Hall to collect Connie's necklace.'

'You could have sent one of the lads,' Isabel said.

'I could have done,' he agreed, 'but I wanted to go myself.'

The breath left her body as if she had been hit, and she looked down at the duster she held in her hand. Lady Kendall again. Always Lady Kendall.

'Fortunately, the missing necklace had been found,' Sebastian added.

'Connie will be pleased. She seemed very upset this morning at breakfast. What a shame that it spoiled her evening.'

Sebastian nodded, and a slow smile spread across his face.

'She did very well for her first foray into polite society. I was very proud of her.'

'I have every confidence in Connie. What brings you here?' Isabel enquired.

'You mentioned at breakfast you planned to spend the day at the dower house so I thought I should come and see if there is anything I can do for you.'

She patted her hair and was alarmed to find a spider web adhering to her fingers.

'No, nothing. I just need to clean a few things up, rearrange the furniture...'

She broke off and looked around at the shabby, outmoded furniture, covertly wiping the spider web on her apron as Sebastian circled the room.

'The proportions are lovely,' he said, more to himself than to her.

'It was the original house, built in the reign of Queen Anne, I believe. Your great-grandfather built the big house sixty years ago to replace it.'

She looked up at the ceiling painted with a mural of Greek Gods, noticing, with annoyance, that here and there the paint had flecked off.

'It's old and a little shabby, but I like it.'

He turned around to look at her. 'Is there anything you want from the big house?'

'A few pieces of furniture, all of which I brought with me on my marriage. That's all.'

'Nothing of sentimental value?'

She shook her head. 'No. The contents of the big house are

for show, not sentiment. Come into the garden. That's the heart of this house.'

She threw open the large double doors that opened onto a terrace. Sunlight streamed in and, still holding the doors, she lifted her face up to the sun.

'What a glorious day,' she exclaimed.

As they stepped out onto the terrace, Sebastian said, 'This is charming. Old-fashioned, but perfectly suited to the house. I wouldn't change a thing.'

She found herself smiling. 'Really?'

'Really... Maybe I would strengthen that parterre and perhaps a row of pencil pines against that boundary.'

'What do you know about gardens?' she teased as they strolled the overgrown paths.

He shrugged. 'I understand what works. The gardens of the big house need to be redesigned. They don't make the most of the view down to the lake.'

'The lake?'

She looked up at his profile. This man seemed riddled with contradictions; a soldier with the soul of an artist.

Sebastian kicked at a weed. 'I'll send some of the gardeners down to help with bringing this garden back into shape.' He looked sideways at her. 'Can you spare me some time? I'd like to show you something.'

She glanced back at the house, thinking of all the things she had planned to do that day, and decided a stroll with Sebastian was far more to be preferred. Fetching her bonnet and shawl, she found Sebastian waiting for her on the front steps.

They set off in the direction of the lake. He prowled beside her, reminding her of a cat moving easily on long legs, with only the barest hint of an uneven gait. She cast a furtive look sideways, taking in his profile with the strong nose and sensitive, well-shaped mouth. He had the height and the figure to carry off the high, immaculate stock and cut away jacket. She thought of the strong, well-muscled chest beneath his clothes and for a moment, her wanton imagination took her into the bedchamber.

She shook her head, banishing the wicked thought. She had no right to think such thoughts. Far better to keep their friendship at a distance.

As they walked, he outlined his thoughts about the garden.

'That sounds grand,' she said.

He gave a snort of laughter. 'Just dreams in the air. There are other priorities before I can lavish any money on the garden.'

At the edge of the lake they stopped to admire the vista across to a grove of trees where the dome of a small summerhouse peeked through the surrounding foliage. Isabel sat down on the grass and drew her knees up. Sebastian lowered himself down beside her. He sprawled full length, propped up on his left elbow.

She leaned her chin on her knees. 'I am terrified of water. I saw a child drowned in Jamaica, and in my nightmares I always imagined the sea as some sort of ravenous beast, pulling innocent children to their death, just as this lake did Amy Thompson.'

'Even as an adult?'

She nodded. 'I look at this beautiful lake and imagine it is full of weeds and dead things.' She shivered, wrapping her arms around herself. 'It's as if her ghost haunts it.'

He looked up at her. 'She drowned herself I am told.'

Isabel nodded. 'So they say. I never understood it...'

She frowned. The time had come for honesty.

'Sebastian, may I confide in you?'

'Of course.'

'Anthony came to see me a few days after Amy's body had been found caught in that stand of willows.' She pointed to a stand of willow trees bowing gracefully over the water. 'He was almost manic with distress. He had heard the gossip. They were saying she was with child, his child, and it was his rejection of her that had led to her suicide.'

She looked away. She had never confided in anyone before, and to do so would cost her dearly.

'Go on,' Sebastian urged.

'He told me things.' She took a deep breath. 'About himself. Terrible, shameful things. Things for which he could be hanged... but he could not have Amy's death on his conscience. He was not the father of her child.'

'Isabel,' Sebastian said softly, sitting up. 'I know all about Anthony.'

She turned to look at him, her eyes wide with shock. 'How?'

He sighed. 'Gossip.'

She looked down and humiliating tears pricked the back of her nose. 'So everyone but me knew? All the years I had been married to him, I had assumed his lack of interest in me was because...' She stopped herself from saying any more.

The shame at her own naivety and her anger at Anthony for his duplicity welled up inside her, and the hot, angry tears began to roll unbidden down her cheeks.

She steeled herself, trying desperately to will them away. Sebastian sat up and put his arm around her shoulders, and drew her into the curve of his body. She made no protest. It felt good to be held. He pressed a large, clean white kerchief into her hand, and she mopped at her face.

'You don't have to say any more,' he whispered.

'But I do,' she gulped. 'That's why I never understood about Amy. Anthony swore he never touched her and, given what he told me, I believed him.'

Sebastian looked down at her, a small frown creasing his brow. 'There is no doubt she was with child?'

Isabel nodded. 'The doctor confirmed it.' She gave a great shuddering sigh and let her hands fall in her lap. 'I don't know why I'm telling you all this.'

'Because it is something you have kept to yourself for too long, Isabel. There's no shame in it and, for what it's worth, I believe Anthony did care for you in his own complicated way.'

She gave him a scathing glance. 'How would you know?'

'Georgiana Kendall told me,' he said.

She pushed away from him, a band around her chest tightening as she said the hated name between gritted teeth.

'Georgiana Kendall …' she began, trying to find the words to express her feelings.

Sebastian laid his hand over hers. 'They were not lovers, Isabel. She was under no illusions about Anthony's preferences. She was just part of the picture he painted about himself.'

Isabel looked away, her humiliation complete. Georgiana Kendall had known something of such importance while she, his wife, remained in ignorance, torturing herself with her own imagined inadequacy.

'How she must have laughed at me,' Isabel said, the tears beginning again. She shook her head. 'In some ways it was easier to believe that they were lovers, but once I knew the truth and understood that he could talk to her in a way he could not talk to me, it felt like as much of a betrayal than if he had taken her to bed.' She dashed away the tears. 'Sebastian I am such a fool. I knew he only married me for my dowry. I hadn't realised it was also for the veneer of respectability it gave him. I was just a part of that same picture.'

Sebastian took her chin between his fingers and tilted her face up to look at him. His thumb gently stroked her tearstained cheek.

'Isabel, I am no apologist for Anthony, but you are the one who was so quick to tell me to put the past behind me. I can only give you the same counsel. There will be someone, somewhere, who will care for you the way you should be loved.'

She looked into his brown eyes and saw something she had never seen before. Compassion, yes, but something else—desire. All she needed to do would be to let her reserve go, close her eyes, and feel his lips on hers. The thought sent a warm rush flooding through her, and her betraying body softened, leaning in towards him.

He could kiss her... she could kiss him. Her lips parted, her eyes closed and his breath caressed her cheek, warm and sweet. If she just let this happen, it would change everything. Her plans, the school...

The school!

She pushed him away and jumped to her feet. Caught off balance, Sebastian fell backwards. He lay on his back and to her surprise he began to laugh.

'I deserved that. Please forgive me, Isabel. I would not risk your friendship for anything.'

He held out his hand and she grasped it, not that he needed any assistance in rising.

He rose smoothly to his feet as she said in a voice, husky with her confused emotions, 'Nothing happened, Lord Somerton.'

For a long moment they stood looking at each other. He swallowed and looked down at their still clasped hands. His fingers relaxed their grip and he ran the hand through his disordered hair.

She handed him back his soggy handkerchief.

'I am grateful for the loan of your handkerchief.' He cleared his throat and glanced back the way they had come. 'I am keeping you from your home, Isabel. Let me walk you back.'

'I can make my own way...'

He crooked his arm. 'Please, I insist...'

She looked up into his face, seeing the contrition in his eyes. Once again, that warm rush seeped through her bones and she bit her lip and took a deep breath. She could not, would not, allow these feelings. Not again... not ever.

'No, thank you, Lord Somerton,' she said and, turning, she hurried away, before he saw the tears that coursed down her cheeks.

Sebastian watched her go, her proud, stiff back disappearing around a hedge.

'Damn it!'

He swore and hit his leg with his hat.

What was it about her that aroused feelings in him that he had not felt since… since Inez.

He needed to walk off his frustration and anger with himself, so he turned and strode along the path leading around the lake, following it up to the summer pavilion in the trees. It was a pretty little folly, built of once white marble in the style of a circular Roman temple. A statue of Diana frolicked in its centre and marble benches lined the sides.

He sat down on the steps and looked down at the house, the view obscured by the foliage. Thinking about improving the view distracted him from thinking about Isabel. In a tree nearby, a cuckoo called, and a soft breeze brought the scent of the new mown hay drifting in.

'What was I thinking …?'

He had behaved like a boor, like the commoner he was. He had compromised the one person whose good opinion he valued most. What had been done could not be undone and he had to face Isabel again, see the reproach in her eyes.

Her good opinion anchored him to his new life. More than that, it also represented a thread of hope that he could love again—that he was learning to love again—and he had thrown it all away.

'Do I dare?' he said aloud, looking up at the few wispy clouds in the blue sky.

Anthony had much to answer for, and the damage he had done to his innocent young wife could never be forgiven, but could it be mended? Did he dare risk his own heart again to woo and win Isabel? It would have to be done slowly. He had seen the fear in her eyes, like a frightened deer that realises the man with the gun is a foe not a friend but, before that, he had seen something else. Yearning? Desire?

There was no impediment to any match between them. They were both widowed, they were both of the same class, whatever that meant. But they were both damaged.

The cuckoo in the trees called again.

'You're right,' he said to the unseen bird. 'I think it is possible, but I must tread carefully.'

Chapter Forty

Sebastian walked back to the big house, and dispatched Peter Thompson to collect the horse from the dower house.

Entering his bedchamber, he found Connie sitting in his favourite chair reading a report from Bragge that he had brought upstairs to read at his leisure. She looked up and, from her blotchy face, he guessed she had been crying.

'Connie?' He pulled the little package from his jacket. 'I have your necklace. The clasp broke, so I will send it in to the jeweller in Lincoln to have it repaired.'

'Oh, Bas.' She took the package from him and her lower lip began to tremble.

A second weeping woman in one day was a bit much, Sebastian thought reaching for his kerchief. He let his hand drop, remembering the piece of cloth was already sodden from Isabel's tears.

He sat down on the footstool and took her hands between his.

'Now, now, what's the trouble?'

Connie sniffed. 'I had a terrible fight with Fanny,' she said. 'I found her in my bedchamber. She had my earrings, Bas!'

'What did she say?'

Connie's nostrils flared. 'She said she was looking for the gloves she lent me last night and happened to see the earrings and was just having a look at them.'

Sebastian sensed an unspoken 'but', so he raised an eyebrow, which was all the encouragement Connie needed to continue.

'But I had returned her gloves, and I had made sure the earrings were back in their box. I'd already lost the necklace. I didn't want to lose the earrings too.'

'Do you want me to speak to her?'

The anger had begun to die in Connie's eyes. She had never been a girl to hold a grudge for long.

'No. I think I said everything that needed to be said, but she called me a common little piece who thought, just because my brother had come into a title, I could act like lady of the manor.'

Sebastian rose to his feet. 'Only one common little piece in this household and that's Fanny,' he said darkly. 'And when Isabel retires to the dower house then yes, you, as my sister, take her place—as the rightful lady of the house.'

Connie stood up and threw her arms around him. 'You are the best of brothers, Bas, but leave Fanny alone. I slapped her good and hard, as only a common little piece can.'

Laughter rose in his chest and he squeezed his sister.

'They'll both be gone soon, Connie. I promise.'

Connie gave one last sniff and let her brother go. She looked around the room.

'This is a bit florid for your taste, Bas.'

'I thought you might like to have a go at redecorating it, but I don't have the money to spare for it at the moment.'

'Are things dire?' She picked up the report she had been reading.

'Not in the sense that you and I would understand them, Connie, but dear Anthony seemed to leak money from every pore.'

'Do you mean the regular payments of one hundred pounds a month?'

Sebastian nodded. 'Bragge can't account for them. It seemed to be a private payment Anthony made outside of the usual payments.'

'They started in March last year. Maybe he was being blackmailed?' Connie suggested.

Sebastian stared at her. 'What do you read?'

'Evil novels, brother.'

Sebastian looked back at the paper. Blackmail would explain the payments. *Ridiculous!* He set the report down again.

'Isabel said at breakfast that she is hoping to move into the dower house in the next day or so,' Connie said.

'I know. I just paid a call.'

'Would you be violently opposed to me helping her with the school?'

He ran a hand through his hair. 'She is not still planning to open a school in the dower house?'

'She told me she was.'

'That damned woman! I told her I would make good her jointure.'

'Maybe she doesn't want you to make good her jointure. Maybe she would prefer to be independent.'

Sebastian stared at his sister. 'You don't understand,' he began.

Connie grinned. She crossed to her brother and pushed him lightly in the chest.

'You like her, don't you? I knew it!'

Sebastian opened his mouth to protest but ended up subsiding onto the stool. He buried his head in his hands.

'Not a word, Connie. I've already made a prize idiot of myself with her once. I'll not do it again.'

'Why not? I don't know who Inez was, but she has been dead a long time. Isabel is lovely and lonely. I fail to see where the problem lies.'

'There's no problem, Connie. Just... damn it... she's still in mourning and we've only known each other a short time.' He held up a warning finger. 'You're interfering in something you have no business in.'

Connie merely smiled. 'I am interfering because I can clearly see two stubborn people I love who are incapable of admitting how they feel about each other.'

'What do you mean?'

'I've got eyes in my head, Bas, and I would wager my necklace that she feels the same way about you.'

Sebastian looked away, unable to meet his sister's appraising gaze.

'She has her own plans, and you're correct, she desperately wants to be independent. I have no right to interfere in her life.'

'Hmm,' was all the answer his sister gave him.

'What should I do?' he asked, looking up at her.

'I think,' Connie said slowly, 'that you better say something soon or you will lose her to the school and Manchester.'

She crossed to the door and opened it. Before leaving, she turned and looked back at him with a smile.

'There's the gong. I will see you at dinner, Bas.'

Chapter Forty-One

Freddy folded himself into the chair across from Sebastian, crossed his legs and steepled his fingers.

'I gather our dear sisters had something of a contretemps this morning,' he said.

Sebastian said nothing for a long moment. 'What of it?'

Freddy rolled his eyes. 'The female of the species is an unpredictable beast.'

'Well, I would thank your sister to mind her own business in future and respect Connie's privacy.'

Freddy held up a placatory hand. 'Oh, *bien sur*, my dear cousin. I have spoken most firmly with her and told her she is to apologise forthwith to Constance. We can't have these petty domestic squabbles disturbing our peace, not with the ball only a few days away. I am sure by tomorrow morning all will be forgiven and forgotten.'

Sebastian held his peace. Connie may well forgive, but she would be unlikely to forget.

'On another matter, dear cousin,' Freddy continued, 'I am conscious that dear Fan and I have overstayed our welcome. I am happy to advise that I have an expectation of good fortune in the weeks to come.'

'May I ask from where?'

Freddy tapped his nose. 'Ah, now dear cuz, that would be telling. However, that by itself may not suffice and you have mentioned a settlement from Anthony's estate. Are you able to clarify that position any further?'

As he was still waiting on Bragge's report on the Lynchs, Sebastian said with absolute honesty, 'I am awaiting a report from my man of business, Lynch. When I am in receipt of that I will be only too pleased to discuss your future.'

Freddy rose to his feet. 'That is excellent news. Are you looking forward to the ball?'

Sebastian glanced at his desk where a stack of bills for the costs of this extravagance grew by the day.

'I will be pleased when it is over.'

Freddy smiled. 'Indeed, I am sure we all will, but I promise you a night to remember, my lord. A night to remember.'

As the door closed behind Freddy, Sebastian stared into the fireplace.

Why had Fanny been nosing around in Connie's bedroom? Only one reason came to mind, and he summoned the housekeeper.

'Do sit, Mrs. Fletcher.' Sebastian gestured at the chair so recently vacated by Freddy.

She coloured. 'Oh, sir, I never...'

'Please,' Sebastian smiled at his housekeeper.

She complied and sat as rigid as a poker with her hands clasped in her lap.

'Am I in trouble, sir? Has something displeased you?'

Sebastian stared at her. 'Good God, no, Mrs. Fletcher. Please take your ease. I wanted to ask you if you have been aware of any petty pilfering going on in the house?'

Her hand flew to the brooch at her neck.

'Oh dear, what have you heard?'

'Nothing. It's just a question. You're not in trouble, Mrs. Fletcher.'

She glanced at the fire. 'Well, of course everyone blamed young Amy Thompson,' she began.

Sebastian had not been expecting this response. He leaned forward. 'What do you mean?'

'Small things went missing. Small but valuable. A silver spoon here, one of his lordship's tie pins. Little things, easily missed.'

'And why was Amy Thompson blamed?'

'She worked in the house as a house maid. She had access to all the rooms where things had gone missing.' Mrs. Fletcher twisted her hands. 'She started buying herself new things. Just little pretties, mind. Nothing fancy, but not the sort of thing a maid would be able to afford. His lordship instructed me to find the culprit and, naturally, the finger of suspicion pointed at Amy. She denied it, of course, became quite distraught, and, a few days later, she went and took her own life. So sad.'

'Was she the culprit?'

Mrs. Fletcher gave a small shake of her head. 'I don't believe so, sir. I went through all her things myself and there was no evidence of pilfering. I've come across thieves in my other positions and it's my experience that they like to keep little souvenirs. A few months after his lordship's death, it began again. Why, only last week, two little silver saltcellars disappeared. We've searched high and low for them so, to answer your question, the thief was not Amy Thompson.'

'Thank you, Mrs. Fletcher.'

Sebastian sat back in his chair and the woman stood.

'Was there anything else, sir?'

He shook his head. 'No, you must be very busy with this ball.'

She smiled. 'Oh, I am sir, but it will be such fun to see the house come to life again. It's been a sad place for too long.'

After she had left, Sebastian stared at the ceiling. An accusation of theft might give Amy Thompson a reason to take her own life. An unfounded accusation. Poor girl.

If he was right in his suspicions then there was a good chance the silver saltcellars were still in the custody of the thief and he had a fair idea who the thief may be.

Never mind. It could wait until after the ball. Everything would change once the wretched ball was out of the way.

Chapter Forty-Two

Isabel raised her hand to knock on the door to Lord Somerton's bedchamber. She could hear the low growl of Sebastian's voice from within, interspersed with encouraging noises from both Bennet and Pierce.

As she opened the door, she beheld Sebastian standing in the middle of the carpet, looking impeccable from the carefully coiffed hair on his head to the polish on his dancing shoes. She took a deep breath and thought of the Sebastian she knew with his hair disarrayed, his neckcloth untied and those old boots. While he would turn heads and set a few hearts aflutter tonight, of the two, she infinitely preferred the latter.

He glanced at her and managed a watery smile.

'Do I pass?'

She smiled in response. 'You look every inch a Somerton.'

Pierce added a diamond pin to the neckcloth and stood back, a pleased smirk on his face.

'Very fine, my lord. Don't you agree, Mr. Bennet?'

Mr. Bennet concurred, and Isabel cast the little corporal an amused glance. Like his master, he appeared to be falling into the ways of the house with ease and dressed and emulated Pierce in every way.

'Are you ready? Your guests are assembled,' Isabel said.

Sebastian ran a finger around the stock.

'I feel worse than I did before Waterloo,' he said.

'Mercifully, we have not invited the French infantry tonight,' Isabel said.

He held out his arm, and she tucked her hand into the crook of his elbow. It had begun to feel a comfortable and natural act between them.

'You look very lovely tonight, Isabel,' he paused, 'if I may make so bold.'

Warmth flooded her cheeks. She had taken a great deal of trouble with her wardrobe. Conscious she was still officially in mourning, she had dressed in a new gown of black satin trimmed with jet beads. Lucy had worked hard on her hair, twisting it into a complicated knot and enhancing it with a turban of the same black satin, trimmed with a curling black feather.

'Thank you, my lord. I have no doubt my presence will scandalise a few of the more conservative of our neighbours.'

'Anthony has been dead nearly a year. Time to start living again,' Sebastian said.

She looked up at him, conscious of his gaze on her face. The brown eyes, softened by the shadows, filled her with a confidence she hadn't felt in years. It felt as if something momentous would happen tonight.

At the head of the stairs, Sebastian hesitated, pulling back into the shadows at the sound of the gathering crowd in the brightly lit hall below. Beyond from the ballroom, came the sound of bright chatter and music. Beads of sweat dappled his brow.

'Sebastian, it is only a ball,' Isabel whispered. 'Besides, you have already met many of your guests at church and the horse auction and the other night at Lady Kendall's.'

He gave a rueful smile. 'That was different. I was not the centre of attention. They had other diversions.'

'So what did you do before battle to calm your nerves?'

'Psalm 23,' he said and closed his eyes, his lips moving as he silently recited the comforting words.

When he opened his eyes, he straightened his shoulders and, looking down the stairs, said, 'Forward, Lady Somerton.'

Fanny, dressed in a gown of blue and silver that Isabel had not seen before, cut her way through the crowd to meet them at the foot of the stairs.

'There you are, cousin Sebastian. Everyone is waiting for you.' She drew back and looked him up and down. 'My, you do look fine. Now, do come and let us greet your guests.'

Fanny stepped forward, Isabel moved in close beside Sebastian.

'Thank you, Fanny,' she said. 'It will be my pleasure and duty to affect the introductions.'

Isabel did not miss the flash of annoyance that clouded Fanny's face for an instant.

The girl turned to Sebastian, her eyelashes fluttering as she said, 'Cousin Sebastian, I do hope you will take the first dance with me. My card is quite free.'

Sebastian turned and looked at her. 'My dear Miss Lynch, I told you that I don't dance.' He swept a hand towards the ballroom. 'Besides I can see plenty of young men who would be more than happy to oblige.'

Fanny pulled a face. 'Oh yes. The war wound.'

Sebastian patted his right thigh. 'Pains me something fearful if I so much as try a cotillion.'

Fanny glowered, but before she could retort, a young man with a badly pocked face had approached her. Lacking any excuse to decline his offer of the first dance, she took his proffered hand and, with a toss of golden curls, sailed into the ballroom.

'The war wound doesn't seem to inconvenience you unduly in other matters,' Isabel observed with an arched eyebrow.

'Oh, I could manage a cotillion if forced into it,' Sebastian admitted with a smile, 'but not just yet.'

'Come, you are keeping your guests in the most terrible suspense.'

As they entered the room, a silence spread across the gathering like a blanket across a bed. Glancing up at Sebastian, Isabel felt a surge of pride. His nerves did not show in the confident way in which he stood, allowing the eyes of the assembled company to conduct their evaluation of his worth and person. She could hardly credit that this was the same ragged soldier she had pulled from the fetid hospital in London. His own natural charm and some hard work by Pierce had produced a man who looked as if he had been born to the role.

'Ladies and gentlemen, I would like to thank you for the welcome I have received since my arrival. I apologise that I have not been able to receive you all in person but I hope to get a chance to make your acquaintance this evening.' He spread a hand across the room in a gesture of munificence. 'In the meantime, I bid you a warm welcome to my home.'

A smattering of applause met this speech. Sebastian introduced Matt and Connie, who looked delightful in a new gown of green silk, and with Isabel at his elbow to smooth the introductions he moved through the assembly. As he passed, the fans fluttered and Isabel caught snatches of the whispered conversations as the women compared their impressions.

Seeing Harry Dempster standing alone, Sebastian quickened his pace. Harry wore full dress scarlets and Isabel had to admit he looked magnificent. He didn't have Sebastian's height and his hair was a lighter brown but he had a litheness and elegance to his carriage and a confidence in his former rank that made him every bit the subject of covert female attention as was his lordship. And he knew it.

Sebastian clapped his hand on his friend's shoulder with an obvious sense of relief.

'Dempster, so glad you could come.'

Harry bowed to Isabel. 'Lady Somerton, your servant.'

'Is your sister here?' Sebastian enquired.

Harry gestured at the dance floor where Lady Kendall danced with one of the neighbours. She wore a high-waisted dress of deep midnight-blue satin, cut low enough to intrigue the men and scandalise the women, whose fans waved furiously as she passed. A magnificent drop of sapphires hung about her creamy throat and her thick, auburn hair was curled and coiffured around a simple blue ribbon.

As Isabel watched the woman circle the dance floor, the familiar stirrings of the green eye of jealousy tugged at her. Why couldn't she be more like Georgiana Kendall? So full of life and laughter and easy with all she met.

'Somerton!' Sebastian was hailed by a portly man. 'You must meet Sir John Dawlish. He's got some radical ideas on farm improvement. Just the sort of thing you were talking about at Lady K's the other evening.'

With only time to briefly acknowledge Isabel and Harry, Sebastian was hauled away.

'You look very lovely tonight, Lady Somerton,' Harry said in a low voice.

Without looking at him, she found her voice. 'How kind.'

'Would you consider a dance?'

She looked up into his handsome face and shook her head. 'I think not. I am still officially in mourning.'

Isabel opened her fan, making a pretence of watching the dancers. She sensed Harry's presence behind her, his breath on her hair. On the far side of the dance floor, Sebastian bent low to talk to a group of elderly matrons.

'You haven't taken your eyes off my old comrade,' Harry observed.

'What do you mean, Colonel?' Isabel hid her embarrassment with her fan.

'He is wed to a ghost, my dear Lady Somerton.'

Isabel took a steadying breath. 'Inez?'

'He told you? Do you know how she died?'

'Just that she was murdered by the French. Some of it I can guess.'

Harry's lips tightened. 'It took some persuasion, but they had just wed with the Colonel's consent, and Inez was on her way to join him when her coach was ambushed by a patrol of French soldiers. I will spare you the details, Lady Somerton, but it was a bad business, and the tragedy is that it was Alder who had the misfortune to find her. Would have destroyed a lesser man. It shook me to the core.'

She turned to look at him, seeing the grim line of his mouth. 'You were there?'

He nodded.

Isabel had read newspaper reports of terrible atrocities in Spain. A young, beautiful woman, such as Inez, would have met a fearful end. And for Sebastian to have found her? She gave an involuntary shudder.

'What was she like?'

'Inez Aradeiras was a truly lovely girl. She nursed the wounded, and I never heard a bad word about her. Alder was besotted with her. And she with him.'

Isabel felt a stab of pain. She would much rather have heard about a harridan. Little wonder the memory of this paragon of Portuguese virtue made it hard for any living woman.

'He tracked the murdering swine down and killed him, you know,' Harry continued. 'Didn't bring Inez back, and he took to the bottle. Then came Talavera. Wouldn't be the first soldier who sought a way out in battle.'

It took Isabel a moment to pick up the implication of his words. 'Are you saying he deliberately put himself in danger at Talavera?'

'Led a suicidal charge that should have killed him, but the good Lord had other plans.'

Isabel shot a glance across the room to Sebastian as all the pieces of Sebastian's past fell into place. Matt had joined him and they were engaged in conversation with another of their neighbours, Sebastian's handsome head bent towards an elderly woman as if she were the most interesting person in the room. She tried to imagine what he had been through and wondered how he could appear so... normal. For that, she concluded, the credit had to go to the Reverend Alder.

The conversation in the churchyard at Little Benning came back to her. He had found the solace and forgiveness he sought from his stepfather's gentle counsel, but was Harry right? Would he always be wed to a ghost?

She turned to excuse herself, but Harry had already left her side and was leading Fanny out onto the dance floor.

Chapter Forty-Three

Sebastian excused himself from the gossipy woman and waylaid a passing servant for a glass of champagne. Across the dancers, Isabel still stood where he had left her, Harry Dempster at her shoulder, engaged in conversation.

He began to make his way around the floor, pausing for the most cursory of greetings, only to find his way barred by Freddy.

'Our Isabel and your old chum seem to be getting on well, don't they?' Freddy leaned forward and said in a conspiratorial whisper, 'I have heard that the good Colonel is a little stretched for cash. Perhaps a widow's jointure would be useful?'

Sebastian scowled. 'That is insulting to both of them, Lynch.'

Freddy held up a hand in protest. 'I merely meant they make a handsome couple.'

They did. Even Sebastian had to concede that there was something about both of them that seemed matched.

'I think Isabel is entitled to some happiness in her life,' Sebastian replied stiffly.

'Watch yourself, Somerton, Lady Kendall is heading this way and she has her eye on you,' Freddie said.

The crowd parted to let Lady Kendall pass. She approached him in a miasma of perfume that threatened to choke him.

'My dear Lord Somerton.' She held out her hand and he bowed low over it.

'Lady Kendall, may I say you look enchanting tonight.'

Sebastian's eye was drawn to the magnificent sapphire necklace and he wondered about her late husband. He must have left her well provided for. As if guessing his thoughts, she smiled and her hand went to the sapphire necklace, letting the perfect stones fall between her fingers as they played in the light of the candelabra.

'Thank you, Lord Somerton. Oh, Mr. Lynch, I didn't see you there.'

'Lady Kendall. Your servant, ma'am,' Freddy said.

Lady Kendall spared him a quick smile and a cursory acknowledgement of his presence before turning back to Sebastian as the band struck up the next dance.

'A waltz, Lord Somerton? My card is quite free.'

Sebastian opened his mouth to protest but she had already taken his arm, and he had no choice but to lead her out onto the floor. Despite his protests to Fanny, he could dance, quite well. The pain was not so much physical as emotional. Dancing always brought back memories of the ball in Lisbon, where he had met Inez.

For once, Inez was forgotten as the familiar rhythm took them both around the dance floor. Out of the corner of his eye, he noticed that Freddy had led his sister out, moving with a grace and elegance that surpassed any of the other men.

Lady Kendall glanced at the Lynch siblings, and a small frown puckered her eyebrows.

'Quite why Anthony put up with Freddy Lynch I never understood. It was almost as if the odious creature had some hold over him.'

'They were cousins,' Sebastian said without conviction.

'If there is any family resemblance, I am afraid it eludes me. I did ask him once but he changed the subject.' Lady Kendall smiled up at Sebastian. 'On a more pleasing subject, Lord Somerton, your sister is a picture tonight. You must be very proud of her.'

Lady Kendall indicated Connie on the arm of the pimply young man. He hadn't seen much of his sister over the past week but he had been aware, from the accounts that were crossing his desk, that a veritable army of dressmakers, hat makers, shoemakers and glove-makers had been kept very busy. If the green dress was any indication of her new wardrobe, their efforts had been well worth it. She looked as if she had been born to the life.

He brought his attention back to Lady Kendall, who continued, 'You have quite a treasure there. I shall look forward to presenting her in London and I will not take no for an answer, Lord Somerton. A pearl such as your sister cannot be left to moulder in the country. I take it she has a dowry?'

'Really, Lady Kendall—' Sebastian began to protest, but Georgiana Kendall laughed.

'It was a foolish question. I am sure you will see your sister properly provided for. I think an earl at least for Constance.'

'God help the earl who has to put up with my sister. But in all seriousness, Lady Kendall, I will never force Constance to wed against her will,' Sebastian said.

'What romantic notions you have, my lord,' Georgiana Kendall said. 'Very well, we shall have to find an earl for her to fall in love with.'

The dance ended, and before she had left the floor, Lady Kendall had been claimed by another.

'I thought you said you didn't dance!' A gloved hand insinuated itself around Sebastian's elbow and he looked down at Fanny. 'I must insist on the first dance after supper, Cousin Sebastian.'

Masking his annoyance, Sebastian filled in Fanny's card. Glancing up, he saw Isabel slipping out of the doors to the terrace. He excused himself from Fanny's cloying attentions and followed her.

She stood leaning her gloved hands on the parapet wall,

looking out over the gardens, lit for the festivities with brightly coloured lanterns. He came up softly behind her.

'It's cold out here,' he said.

She started and looked around. 'Oh, Sebastian. I didn't hear you.'

'What were you thinking about?'

She shook her head. 'I do not like large gatherings of people.'

'I must agree with you,' Sebastian said. 'I will be glad when this evening is over.'

She turned to face him, the light from the windows catching an impish smile on her face.

'You dance very well for a man with a French musket ball in his leg.'

Sebastian returned a rueful smile. 'So Pierce says. He has been giving me tuition.' He paused. 'I would like to dance with you.'

'Oh, I think I have scandalised the matrons enough for one night just by my presence. Perhaps Lady Kendall will oblige you again.' She paused and looked up at him, her eyes, unreadable in the dark, scanning his face. 'I'm curious, Sebastian, what do you think of Georgiana Kendall?'

Sebastian blew out his breath while he struggled to find the right words.

'It's all right, Sebastian, you don't have to be polite. She quite literally swept you off your feet, didn't she? You know, if circumstances had been other than what they are, I would have liked to have been her friend. In fact, I admire her.'

'Do you?' he said, unable to hide his surprise at the echo of the words he had heard from Lady Kendall.

'She has turned her widowhood to her advantage. It is said she has even caught the eye of Prinny in her time.'

'The Prince of Wales?'

'Her secret is keeping them dangling.'

'Is that what turning widowhood to advantage means? I

think your plans for a school have more to recommend them than being the mistress of rich and powerful men.'

'There is not much in life for a lone woman. In the absence of social charms, a school is the best I can hope for.'

He shook his head and said in a voice husky with emotion, 'I think that you have so much more to recommend you than a woman like Lady Kendall.'

He reached out to touch her cheek, and she leaned against his hand. His thumb gently stroked the line of her jaw and, when she didn't draw back, he tilted her face up to his and ventured a kiss. Their lips met in a brief touch, and when she didn't withdraw, he slid his hand around the back of her neck, his other hand sliding around her shoulders, drawing her nearer to him.

She gave a deep shuddering breath and brought her hand up to rest on his chest, not pressing him away but slipping up around his neck. He drew her into the shadows, away from the light of the ballroom.

'Isabel,' he whispered into her hair. 'I think it is quite possible that I am falling in love with you.'

He heard her sharp intake of breath, but she made no attempt to pull away from him. He breathed in her now familiar scent of rosemary.

'Sebastian, this is utter madness. We barely know each other.'

'I feel like I have known you a lifetime, Isabel. I have confided things in you that I have shared with no one else.' He kissed her forehead, the skin beneath his lips soft and warm. 'Unless I am a complete fool, I don't think my feelings are unrequited.'

'Sebastian, I—'

'Bas, are you out here?' A shadow fell across the terrace as Matt stepped outside.

Sebastian swore under his breath. He jumped apart from Isabel and strode to his brother, throwing an arm across his shoulder and turning them both back towards the ballroom before Matt could see with whom he had been trysting.

'Apparently, you are supposed to lead us into supper. Fanny's in a terrible tizz,' Matt said.

'Who am I supposed to lead into supper?'

'I think Fanny is expecting you to do the honours with her.'

'In that case, I shall find Mrs. Bracks. She is an agreeable old thing.'

One look at Fanny's sulky mouth confirmed Matt's opinion that she had been expecting him to lead her into supper. He let out a sigh of relief that he had negotiated that particular trap. Harry Dempster substituted for him and Fanny looked a little cheered as he paid her the attention she craved. The niceties of who would be seen to escort whom into supper quite defeated him. He was relieved to see Isabel on Matt's arm. She caught his eye and smiled, the secret smile of a person who knew something that no one else in the world except Sebastian would understand.

Sebastian could hardly concentrate at supper, his head full of thoughts of Isabel and that brief, private moment on the terrace. For the first time, the memory of Inez receded, and all he could see was Isabel's serene oval face.

Plans for a proper wooing and courtship jostled through his mind. He would be everything to her that Anthony had failed in, and he would make her happy. From that first moment when she had leaned over him in the hospital, he knew he had found his soul mate.

Chapter Forty-Four

After supper, Fanny claimed Sebastian for a cotillion, which he could hardly refuse after his dance with Lady Kendall. In contrast to Isabel's fragrance of rosemary, Fanny smelt of rosewater and stale perspiration. She nattered brightly about the guests but failed to elicit more than a few polite grunts from him.

As the dance came to an end, she did not relinquish her hold on him. Her fan fluttered open and she began to fan herself furiously as she leaned against him.

'I feel a little faint,' she said in a small, tight voice.

Sebastian refrained from commenting that the second serve of raspberry ice he had seen her consuming might account for her indisposition.

'Please help me, cousin. A little fresh air...' she said, leading him towards the door.

He scanned the guests to try and catch the eye of some helpful matron on whom he could foist his fainting burden, but no one seemed to be looking his way.

For someone about to swoon, the grip on his arm felt like a vice. As they entered the library, her knees buckled, and he caught her dead weight. Sweeping her up in his arms, he carried her over to the daybed beneath the window.

She groaned, and he began to chafe her hand.

'I'll fetch someone...' he began as her eyes fluttered open.

Her fingers closed over his hand. 'No, no. Just sit with me. I will be fine presently.'

'Can I fetch you a drink?' Sebastian made to rise again. He could hear voices in the hall outside the library door.

Fanny only tightened her grip, pulling him back down beside her.

'Fanny, will you let me go? I will be back presently.'

'Don't leave me!' She clutched the sleeve of his jacket as if she was drowning.

Sebastian looked to the door of the library, wondering how to summon assistance, and was relieved to hear Freddy's voice saying, 'And of course, the Somerton library has a famous collection of monographs ...'

Fanny sat bolt upright at the sound of her brother's voice. Sebastian, half rising, his concentration on the door, had no time to deflect the sudden movement of her left hand. Something sharp raked down his left cheek and, as the door opened, she began to scream, a great rending scream that made his ears ring.

Sebastian leaped to his feet, staring down at her in horror as she pulled at her hair and her bodice. A woman in the crowd at the door gave a loud exclamation and Sebastian saw, with mounting horror, the tableau Fanny had presented: the screaming, distressed girl with her torn gown and disordered hair and he... His fingers went to his cheek and came away sticky with blood.

He took a step back from the couch as two women rushed towards Fanny, folding her in their motherly arms. Freddy moved behind the couch, placing a solicitous hand on his sister's shoulder.

'He... he attacked me,' Fanny said between gulps, pointing an accusing finger at Sebastian.

'I never touched her...' Sebastian began to say, but his words were lost in the clamour of approbation.

Beyond the crowd, Isabel stood at the door, straight and still. He mouthed her name, but she turned on her heel, her place taken by Matt and Connie. They, in turn, stared at him and the crowd fussing over Fanny. Matt's eyes asked the question and Sebastian answered with a look of complete despair.

'Fanny, dear, let these good women take you to your chamber. I will deal with his lordship,' Freddy said in a loud voice, the last two words heavy with venom.

Too shocked to move, Sebastian became aware of a flash of scarlet as Harry entered the room. His friend moved to his side, followed by Matt and Connie.

Fanny, still sobbing hysterically, was helped from the room and the rest of the crowd ushered outside by Freddy. At the door, Freddy turned to look at Sebastian. His gaze rested on Sebastian's supporters.

'I must speak with Lord Somerton alone,' he said.

Harry stepped forward. 'Whatever you have to say, Lynch, you can say in front of us.'

'Very well.' Freddy walked back into the room, straightening the ruffles at his wrist with deliberate care. 'I will say what I have to say. You, sir, have outraged my sister, an innocent girl in your care and protection.'

'I didn't touch her,' Sebastian said with gritted teeth.

'Then how do you explain your face?' Freddy indicated the cut that dripped blood onto the immaculate white of Sebastian's stock.

'She had something in her hand,' Sebastian replied. 'I would never—'

Harry cleared his throat. 'We believe you, Alder, but it doesn't matter what we think. It is what the world is going to think.'

Realisation dawned on Sebastian.

'You mean ...?'

Matt glanced at Harry. 'The colonel's right, Bas. As far as the world is concerned, you have outraged the modesty of an innocent girl.'

Sebastian turned slowly to face Freddy, the whole staging of the scenario now crystal clear.

'Innocent? The whole thing was carefully planned, wasn't it, Freddy?'

Freddy, still absorbed with his linen, looked up. A muscle twitched in his cheek. 'My dear Somerton, how dare you make such an accusation? I know only what my eyes told me: my sister, distressed and deshabille, in your company. I expect you to address the situation as a gentleman.'

Sebastian glared at the man. 'So, tell me, as you have been some weeks in the planning of this, what am I, as a *gentleman*, expected to do?'

'He means,' Harry said, his mouth a grim line, 'that you must marry the chit.'

'Marry her?' Sebastian turned to his friend, his heart sinking.

'You have ruined my sister's reputation, Somerton, of course you must marry her,' Freddy said.

Sebastian sank down onto the couch. Connie sat down beside him and began dabbing at his ruined cheek with a kerchief supplied by the colonel.

'Marry her?' Sebastian repeated. 'I would sooner return to the field of Waterloo.' He looked up at Freddy. 'You have played me for a fool, Lynch. You and that dim-witted sister of yours were never going to accept any offer of settlement. Nothing less than a title for your dear sister. Isn't that what you said?'

Freddy straightened, his fingers going to the pin in his cravat. 'I can see you are overwrought, Somerton. We will speak in the morning when you have had time to consider your situation. This unfortunate incident has regrettably brought the evening to an end, so I will see to your guests and bid you all a good night.'

Numb with despair, Sebastian buried his face in his hands as Freddy left the room. Connie slipped her arm around him and laid her face on his shoulder in a comforting gesture he appreciated.

'We believe you, Bas,' she whispered, her own voice sounding close to tears.

'I should have seen this coming,' he said at last, shaking his head in despair.

'They seemed so nice,' Connie said in a wavering voice, and her brow furrowed. 'But she did try to steal my earrings.'

'Looks are deceiving,' said a voice from the doorway.

They all looked up to see Isabel standing framed by the light from the hallway. Sebastian rose shakily to his feet.

'Isabel...'

'I suggest we all go to bed,' Isabel said without meeting Sebastian's eyes. 'I will take Fanny with me back to the dower house tonight. In the circumstances, it is hardly proper she stays in this house. Colonel, thank you for your help. I am sure his lordship appreciates your friendship. God knows, he is going to need his friends in the next few days. Good night.'

She gave Sebastian a last pitying glance and walked away.

Sebastian sank back on the sofa. Had it only been a couple of hours earlier when he had kissed Isabel and told her he loved her? Only a few hours since his future had a contained a promise of happiness with a woman he loved by his side?

'Isabel is right,' Connie said softly. 'I think we should all go to bed. The world will seem much brighter in the morning.'

She sounded so like her father that Sebastian gave a bitter laugh. The world would be no brighter in the morning. He would still face the grim prospect of a lifetime with Fanny. He wondered if challenging Freddy to a duel would satisfy honour, but it wasn't Freddy's honour at stake. It was his, and if he considered himself an honourable man, he had no choice but to marry Fanny. The Lynchs had set a fine trap, and he had walked blindly into it.

After seeing Fanny settled into the guest chamber, looking for all the world like a well pleased cat, Isabel sought the sanctuary of her own bedchamber. Shutting the door behind her and turning the key in the lock, she took a deep, shuddering breath, gasping as a physical pain gripped her. Laying a hand against her chest, she put out the other to support herself against the post of her bed.

This, she told herself, *was what people meant when they talked of a broken heart.*

A little voice inside her cried out, *He said he loved you.*

And I should have said I loved him, she answered the little voice*, but I didn't, and now it is too late.*

She had allowed herself to hope. For a few fleeting moments she had imagined a life with Sebastian, and it had seemed like a warm sun on the cold, barren plain of her life. In her heart she had already shed her widow's weeds and donned brightly coloured gowns. She would dance with him, feel her hand gripped in his strong hand. They would have been happy here at Brantstone... a brood of strong, handsome children...

She gave a strangled cry and sank to the floor, leaning her head against her bed and allowing her grief to overwhelm her.

Chapter Forty-Five

❦

Isabel stood at her window, looking out at the parkland with dulled eyes. The grey fingers of dawn washed the colour from the landscape and a light fog shrouded the trees, matching her mood. She had hardly slept and her future now appeared as grey and bleak as the weather.

A few deer appeared in silhouette against the grey light of the skyline. They looked up and then started, scattering in all directions as a dark horse, ridden hard, appeared out of the mist. She was not the only early riser.

Isabel stiffened as the horse came to a halt at the gate to the dower house. She pressed a hand to the cold, unforgiving pane of the window and her breath caught in her throat as Sebastian raised his hand in acknowledgment.

She turned abruptly and, stopping only to pull on a pair of shoes and an outdoor coat over her nightdress, ran down the stairs and out of the front door, startling the maid who had risen early to set the fires.

Sebastian had dismounted and waited for her, Pharaoh's reins looped over his left arm. He put out his right hand as she ran towards him. She wanted to throw herself into his arms but the memory of the previous night slowed her footfall. If he touched her she would die. She stopped just out of his arm reach and pulled the coat around her, holding herself tightly.

His hand dropped and he stood looking at her, his face haggard with exhaustion and strain.

'Isabel, I wanted you to know that I didn't... They...'

Her chin came up. 'I know, but it makes no difference what I may think, Sebastian. They have played you for a fool and you must live with the consequences. The wedding should take place as soon as practicable if you are to have any hope of salvaging what is left of your reputation.'

'I don't give a damn for my reputation,' he said with ferocity.

'Well, you should. What the world thinks of you affects all of us within your sphere, most particularly your sister.'

His lips tightened and he looked up, over her head.

'I will find a way out of this.'

She gave a low, humourless laugh and shook her head.

'There is no way out. It was cleverly planned and expertly executed.'

He brought his gaze back down to meet hers. Seeing the naked despair in his eyes, her resolve weakened and she took a faltering step towards him. She caught her breath and straightened her shoulders.

'I know one thing: I cannot remain here,' she said. 'As soon as this matter is settled, I will remove myself and go to my friend, Lady Ainslie. She will take me in and we will proceed with our plans... somehow...' She heard her voice take on a high, almost hysterical note.

His hands, by his side, clenched and he looked away.

Every fibre in her being cried out to touch him, to put her hand on his arm, tell him that she was still his friend and she would comfort him. In the darkest hour of the night, she had wondered if she could defy society's expectations of her and become his mistress, but she knew in her heart that he would not want that. He was a good, honourable man and, once he had made a commitment to another woman, however unwanted, he could never come to her.

His brown eyes met hers. 'This is your home, Isabel. I will not let a chit like Fanny drive you from it.'

She smiled and shook her head. That 'chit' had already driven her from the man she loved. She would not stay. She could not. To do so would be to face daily humiliation.

He turned back towards his horse and leaned his head against the horse's neck.

'You must do what you think best,' he said, his voice heavy with defeat.

He gathered Pharaoh's reins in his right hand, swinging himself with ease into the saddle.

He looked down at her. 'Just one thing before I go. Do you recall the saddle you gave Anthony?'

She nodded. 'Yes. I gave it to him for his birthday. I thought —' she broke off.

The saddle had been a peace offering, a thanks for the few happy months they had enjoyed with the new baby. That had been before William's death.

'When Anthony had his accident, did you give an order for the saddle to be destroyed?'

She looked up at him and shook her head. 'No. I didn't even think of it. Why? What has happened to it?'

Sebastian shook his head. 'I'll explain later. Tell Miss Lynch I will see both her and her brother in the library at noon.'

Without waiting for a reply, he put his heels to the horse. Pharaoh, obedient to his touch, sprang away, and she watched man and horse until they rounded the bend in the carriageway that ran between the dower house and the big house.

She wrapped her arms tighter around herself, feeling that if she didn't do so, she would shatter into a thousand pieces on the ground.

Chapter Forty-Six

Sebastian stood in the chaff room looking down at the dusty saddle he had laid on the table. He glanced up as the door opened and Thompson walked in. The man's gaze fell on saddle.

'Where did you find that?' he asked.

Sebastian shook his head. 'It doesn't matter. This is the saddle the last Lord Somerton was using the night he died?'

Thompson crossed to the table and ran a hand across the bow of the saddle with its delicate reproduction of the Somerton arms.

'Aye. Never seen a saddle like it before or since. His lordship told me it were the best saddle he'd ever used.'

'Who gave the order for it to be destroyed?'

Thompson frowned. 'I don't rightly remember.'

'Think, man!'

Thompson brightened. 'Her ladyship.'

Sebastian's heart sank, but Thompson ran a hand through his thinning hair.

'No, wait. It were Mr. Lynch what brought the message. He said her ladyship never wanted to see the saddle again. I told the boy—' Thompson broke off, his mouth tightening in a grim line. 'I'll give him what for when I see him.'

'No,' Sebastian said. 'You will not give him what for. What the boy did was to preserve some very important evidence.' He held up the cut end of the girth. 'Look closely and tell me what you see.'

Thompson held up the strap to his eyes. He set it down and looked at Sebastian, the colour draining from his face.

'It's been cut.'

Sebastian nodded.

He could almost see Thompson thinking through the ramifications of the discovery.

'There are stories that Lord Somerton was the father of your daughter's child,' Sebastian stated.

Thompson's eyebrows shot up. 'No! I mean ... are you saying I did this, my lord? I assure you I checked the saddle meself that very afternoon and there was naught wrong with it then.'

Sebastian shook his head. 'I'm not saying you are involved, Thompson, but what has struck me is that there are two suspicious deaths here at Brantstone within a short time of each other. Your daughter... and Lord Somerton. Is it possible they are related?'

Thompson shook his head. 'It weren't Lord Somerton who fathered Amy's bairn.'

'And you know that for certain?'

Thompson gave a disgusted snort of laughter. 'A pretty girl like my Amy wasn't to his lordship's taste. I came across his lordship when he weren't but a boy, sportin' in the hayloft with one of the young footmen from the house. No, it weren't Lord Somerton.'

Sebastian looked down at the saddle. Some nagging instinct told him the key to unwinding the tangle lay in this inanimate object.

'Thompson. I would like you to take this saddle and find a new place to secrete it.'

'My lord?'

'And replace an old saddle in that chaff bin.' He pointed to the bin where Peter had kept the saddle hidden.

Thompson looked mystified but kept his peace. 'Of course, my lord.'

'One last thing, Thompson. Did you see Lord Somerton's body?'

Thompson nodded.

'What were his injuries?'

'His neck was broken. That'd be what killed him, but he also had a broken leg and several smashed ribs.'

'No other wounds?'

'What do you mean?'

'Like those you saw on your daughter's body?'

Thompson's face darkened. 'No, my lord. Just a snapped neck.'

Sebastian sighed. 'Thank you, Thompson. I'll leave this with you now. Hide it well and not a word to anyone.'

Thompson nodded.

Sebastian walked back to the house, feeling the enormity of his predicament settling on his shoulders like a black carrion bird.

Chapter Forty-Seven

Bragge stood in front of the large table that served as Sebastian's desk and cleared his throat.

'I don't think you will like this, my lord,' he said.

'What do you mean?' Sebastian enquired.

'Had I come to you with my report earlier—' He handed over a sealed document.

Sebastian broke the seal and scanned the contents, the anger rising in his chest as he took in the importance of the words in front of him.

'Why in God's sweet name did you not bring me this yesterday?' he demanded, handing the document to Matt, who stood beside him.

Bragge looked down at his toes. 'I thought it could wait another day. I didn't want to disturb you,' he mumbled.

Sebastian shook his head. Possession of the facts disclosed by Bragge's report could have changed the whole course of the previous night's events, but the damage had been done and still needed to be undone.

'You know what it says?'

Bragge nodded. 'My informant advises me that, while the late lord's mother did indeed have a cousin by the name of Lynch, he can find no record of there being any children of that name. The lady concerned died in her early twenties, unmarried and childless.'

'So they are imposters?'

'It would appear so, my lord.'

Matt glanced at Sebastian. 'Then who are they?'

'And more importantly, what did they have over Anthony that he took them into his home?' Sebastian wondered aloud.

Bragge shook his head. 'My informant says only that Frederick Lynch appeared in society circles not long before his late lordship took up with him.' He paused. 'What do you intend to do, my lord?'

'You are my man of business, Bragge, you tell me. Regardless of what I may or may not know about Frederick Lynch and his sister, the fact remains that, before a number of distinguished witnesses, I was caught in the act of dishonouring Miss Lynch.'

Matt leaned on the desk. 'Damn it, Bas. This proves they were lying about their relationship to your cousin. They are villains, the pair of them. You can't go through with it.'

Bragge looked uncomfortable. 'Money, my lord?'

'Money is really what this is all about, Bragge, but it does not salvage my now irretrievably damaged reputation. Matt, this is not just about me, it is about you and Connie and Lady Somerton. You will all be tarred with the same brush as me, unless I can clear my name properly.'

'How are you going to do that?' Matt asked.

Sebastian shook his head. He checked the clock on the mantelpiece. 'They will be here shortly so, for the time being, I will have to play along with Freddy Lynch's scheme. Matt, leave this to me and Bragge. I just need to write a note to Harry.'

Matt opened his mouth to protest but one look at his brother's steely eyes and he left the room.

Chapter Forty-Eight

❦

Obedient to his summons, Freddy, with Fanny on his arm, entered the library on the stroke of midday. The girl leaned against her brother, her face pale and drawn, the picture of outraged innocence. Sebastian, standing by the fireplace, spared her no sympathy. He thought only of the vicious slash that now marred his face, marking him as a boor and degrader of women.

He looked from one to the other. If any of his soldiers had seen him, they would have been in no doubt that trouble would follow. Fanny gave her brother a nervous glance. Freddy, in his turn, raised his chin in a pugnacious fashion, but even he could not meet Sebastian's cold eyes.

As Freddy reached for a chair, Sebastian spoke, employing a tone of voice he had not had cause to use since his army days.

'I didn't say you could sit.'

Freddy stepped back from the chair as if it had burned him.

'You sent for us, Somerton?'

He produced a handkerchief from his sleeve and patted his upper lip where a few tell-tale beads of sweat had gathered despite the chill of the room.

'Yes, I sent for you. To tell you, I have no intention of playing out your little game.' He glanced at Fanny whose chin wobbled. 'I am not the fool you played me for, Lynch. You think you may have trapped me into marriage with your sister, but that is as far as it will go. If it's money you want, name your sum and be done with it.'

The siblings stared at him as if they had never seen him before in their lives.

'Sebastian... Lord Somerton...' Freddy began in a jovial tone, as if all that Sebastian had said was some enormous joke they would laugh over later.

The words died on his lips as he looked into Sebastian's face.

'But Sebastian...' wailed Fanny, her protests, like her brother's, dying in the light of his lordship's cold eyes.

'Name your sum, retract your statement that I assaulted you, pack your bags and leave,' Sebastian said. 'Bragge here has recorded an agreement for your signature.'

'And if we don't agree?' Freddy's chin came up.

Sebastian shrugged. 'You may both pack your bags and leave anyway. I can live with a ruined reputation. I doubt your sister can.'

Fanny began to sob. Beyond proffering her his handkerchief, her brother made no move to comfort her but glared at Sebastian, his arms crossed.

'But I want to marry you. I would do anything to make you happy. I will give you an heir...' Fanny sniffled through Freddy's handkerchief.

'You mean, not only marry you but share your bed? The answer is no, Miss Lynch. Nothing will induce me to partake in any charade of a marriage.'

At that, Fanny dissolved into a flood of tears. This time her brother put a solicitous arm around her shoulders.

'No need to be so heartless, Somerton,' he said.

'Do you really expect me to spare Fanny's tender feelings, Lynch? Whatever your plan was, she is as complicit as you are.'

'But I love you!' Fanny wailed.

'Spare me!' Sebastian spat. 'Right now, I have nothing more to say to either of you.'

The muscle in Freddy's cheek twitched. 'On the contrary, Somerton, we still have a great deal to say to each other.' He cast a meaningful glance at Bragge and added, 'In private.'

Bragge looked uncertain and Sebastian reluctantly indicated he should leave.

'And you, Fan.' Freddy smiled at his sister. 'Wait for me in the blue parlour. I won't be long.'

Neither man moved until the door had firmly closed behind Bragge and Fanny.

'Well?' Sebastian demanded.

This time, Freddy sat unbidden. Crossing his legs, he flicked his ruffled cuffs and smiled in a manner that made Sebastian cringe.

'That was a fine speech, cousin, quite worthy of dear Anthony,' Freddy said.

'I am not your cousin,' Sebastian said between gritted teeth.

'No indeed, you are shortly to become my brother,' Freddie observed. 'I've heard you out, Somerton, I think it is time you heard what I had to say.'

'There is nothing I want to hear from you.'

Sebastian crossed to the window. He turned his back on Freddy and stared, without really seeing anything, out of the window.

'Regardless of your wishes, I am certain society will be agog to hear that, as well as monstering my precious sister in your short time at Brantstone, you have also compromised the virtuous widow, Isabel.'

Sebastian's stomach lurched, and he reached for the window ledge to steady himself. 'What new concoction of yours is this nonsense?'

Behind him, Freddy laughed. More a high-pitched giggle worthy of Fanny.

'Ah now, this I don't have to invent. I have the evidence of my own eyes. You and your precious Isabel forgot that a house has eyes and I just happened to be looking from my window and saw you rolling in the hay with the lovely Lady Somerton like a pair of randy farm hands. I can produce two witnesses to the fact. My man and his sister were both with me at the time.'

A cold chill ran down Sebastian's spine. Did Freddy mean those few snatched moments by the lake? Nothing had happened, but to the casual observer ...

The jolt hit Sebastian as hard as a physical blow beneath the ribs. He felt the air leave his lungs as the enormity of what Freddy had said hit him. Even without the glimmer of truth around it, once Freddy's evil tongue had spread the vile whispers, Isabel would be ruined. No respectable family would entrust their daughters to her school, and no man would risk her reputation to save her from a long and lonely widowhood. Sebastian, his own reputation tarnished beyond redemption, would be powerless to save her.

'What do you want?' he said between clenched teeth.

'I want what your late cousin allowed me as the price of my silence.'

Sebastian turned to face him. 'Would that be the one hundred pounds a month that Anthony was paying to someone?'

Freddy smirked. 'You know about that? I think, in the circumstances, that should be increased to two hundred pounds a month and, of course, I would expect you to do honour by my sister as your wife.'

'There is no money. Anthony left this estate destitute.'

'Then you will just have to find it, Somerton. Anthony did. Dear Cousin Anthony, so generous to a fault.'

Sebastian resisted the urge to grab the man by the orderly folds of his neckcloth and throttle him. He steadied his breath and considered Freddy for a moment, trying to read the implacable face.

'What did you have over Anthony?'

Freddy's eyes widened. 'Now that would be telling, Cousin

Sebastian. Let's just say he was enamoured of a friend of mine and made the mistake of writing him letters, which, unfortunately for Anthony, came into my possession.'

'How?'

Freddy met Sebastian's gaze with equanimity. 'Sadly, my poor friend succumbed to consumption, but he left the letters as an insurance policy, you may say. You never know when such things will be useful.'

'But Anthony's dead. They can't hurt him.'

'No, but they could certainly hurt poor Isabel. Betrayed by one man and impugned by another. Time to reconsider, dear Cousin Sebastian?'

'You are no more Anthony's cousin than you are mine,' Sebastian snarled. 'I don't know who you are, but I know one thing for certain: you and your sister are imposters. Not only have you inveigled your way into this house, but you have been systematically pilfering valuables from Brantstone since your arrival.'

Freddy raised an eyebrow. 'And can you prove that?'

Sebastian had no tangible evidence, just Connie's encounter with Fanny. He had ordered both Freddy and Fanny's rooms searched but had found nothing.

'Fanny was caught red-handed by my sister,' he said.

'A misunderstanding, nothing more. And you think that would be sufficient for a court of law? You are naive in the extreme, Sebastian Alder.' The name was said with venom, emphasising Sebastian's lowly birth.

'An innocent girl died with her name besmirched by your thieving, Lynch.'

Freddy raised an eyebrow. 'My, you have been busy, Somerton. What a distrustful person you are. If you mean Amy Thompson, it was not the thieving that besmirched her name.'

'Were you the father of her child?'

A look of genuine astonishment crossed Freddy's face. 'Me? Hardly.'

'Then who...?'

Freddy rose to his feet and smiled enigmatically. 'I really have no idea. Now, I must go and comfort my poor sister with the reassurance that you will be married by special licence within the week. I will see you at dinner.'

'You will see me in hell,' muttered Sebastian.

As the door closed behind Freddy, he slammed his fist into the desk.

'Damn you!'

The door opened, and Matt came back into the room, accompanied by Harry Dempster.

'How did it go?' Matt asked.

Sebastian shook his hand, trying to restore the feeling to his tingling fingers.

'Badly,' he said.

'You didn't hit him, did you?' Matt enquired.

Sebastian shook his head. 'Sorely tempted as I might have been, it didn't go that far.' He looked at his brother. 'I need to talk to Harry, Matt. Can you excuse us?'

Matt left the room and Harry sat himself in the chair recently vacated by Freddy.

'Bad business,' Harry said after Sebastian had finished recounting his interview with Freddy. 'Do you think he did Somerton in?'

'Why would he? Somerton was paying him regularly. He had a comfortable place to live. Anthony's death ended all of that.'

'Perhaps Somerton had offered him more? In the event of his death.'

Sebastian considered that notion for a long moment. 'Surely not. No doubt Anthony would have been in mortal fear of exposure.' Sebastian raised a hand to his throat. 'It's a hanging offence, Dempster. More likely Anthony had decided to withdraw his favour.'

'Again, why? If Lynch was blackmailing him, he must have known that odious little swine would have no hesitation in calling his bluff. Just as he called yours.' Harry ran his hand across his chin. 'What are we going to do, Alder?'

'We? This is my problem, not yours.'

Harry gave a rueful smile. 'Never could resist a challenge!'

Sebastian allowed himself a smile in response. 'Your selfless support is appreciated, old friend. The key to this is the saddle.'

'What saddle?' Harry asked.

'I've got Anthony's saddle. It clearly shows the girth strap was tampered with.'

Harry's eyes widened. 'You mean...?'

'Not quite cut through but sufficient to break if any force was put on it. I've an idea to draw the killer out, but we're running a risk.'

Harry grinned. 'The riskier the better.'

Chapter Forty-Nine

To Sebastian's chagrin, Freddy took his accustomed place at supper as if nothing untoward had occurred. He shook out his napkin and smiled beatifically at the three Alders and Harry Dempster, who had joined them for the meal.

Connie glowered at him from across the table. 'Where's Fanny?' she asked.

'Poor Fan is quite overwrought so I accompanied her back to the dower house. I must say, Lady Somerton has made it most agreeable. Quite homely,' Freddy said.

Sebastian looked down the table at the man, wondering if Freddy now had designs on the dower house.

'Lady Kendall called this morning, Sebastian. I received her as you were otherwise engaged,' Connie said.

'Thank you, Connie,' Sebastian replied.

'I like Lady Kendall,' Connie continued, and he smiled at her gratefully. Her chatter brought some normality to the situation. 'She is very keen to present me in London.'

Freddy set his soup spoon back in the bowl. 'Oh, but you will have your own new sister-in-law to perform that function!'

'I would rather have Lady Kendall,' Connie flashed back.

Freddy did not push the point.

'Matt, remind me in the morning to talk to Thompson,' Sebastian said over his soup.

Matt looked up. 'What about?'

'I was down in the stables this afternoon and thought I'd do a bit of an inspection of the chaff room.'

'Why?' Matt asked unhelpfully and Sebastian regretted not taking his brother into his confidence.

'I thought some of the oats were mouldy,' he said.

'My dear Somerton,' Freddy put in, 'the standard of the oats is hardly your concern.'

Sebastian shot the man a hard glance. 'It is when mouldy oats can give a horse colic.' He turned back to Matt. 'I am damned if I didn't find a saddle hidden in one of the chaff bins.'

'A saddle? How extraordinary,' Connie said. 'Did you look at it?'

'Of course I did. I wonder if we don't have a thief in our midst. It was rather a nice saddle engraved with the Somerton coat of arms. I hadn't seen it before.'

Out of the corner of his eye, he noticed Freddy's knife hovered over his meat before he forked the slice of beef and asked in a casual tone, 'What did you do with it?'

'Thompson wasn't around so I put it back where I found it. If one of the stable hands is stealing, I thought it best not to arouse suspicion. I'll take it up with him tomorrow morning.'

Freddy folded his napkin and straightened in his chair. 'Absolutely the right decision. Leave it 'til the morning. I thought a game of cards tonight, gentlemen?'

Sebastian shot him a sour look. 'I've had enough of playing games with you, Lynch. I didn't get much sleep last night so I shall retire.'

Matt yawned. 'I'll play a couple of hands with you, but I won't be far off bed myself.'

Sebastian and Connie rose from the table, leaving Freddy and Matt with the remains of the bottle of wine.

Connie took his arm as they climbed the stairs. 'I've hardly seen you all day, Bas. Are you all right?'

He smiled down at her.

'I really am tired,' he admitted.

At the top of the stairs she threw her arms around him. 'I hate Freddy and I despise Fanny. I abhor what they have done to you.'

He kissed the top of her head. 'Don't lose sleep over me, Con. I am sure something will work out in the end. Now go to bed and I'll see you in the morning.'

He waited until her bedchamber door closed and allowed himself a small smile. He had an hour to make the necessary arrangements.

Chapter Fifty

Harry let out a breath. 'I don't think he's coming,' he whispered, shifting his weight. They had been secreted behind barrels in the chaff room for a couple of hours and were both stiff and cold.

'Shh,' Sebastian responded, stiffening as, over the familiar sound of the horses moving restlessly in their stalls, he heard booted feet on the cobbled floor of the stable.

Harry nodded and raised his pistol.

They had left the door to the feed room ajar and it squeaked on its hinges as an unseen hand pushed it back. In the dark, Sebastian glanced at Harry and laid a hand on his sleeve. He had been expecting only Freddy but three figures entered the room.

Freddy's man, Jenkins, the large, silent man whom Bennet uncharitably referred to as 'the dumb ox', set a lantern down on the table, illuminating the room and the faces of the other two men, Freddy and Matt. Seeing his brother, it was all Sebastian could do not to let out an audible groan. What in God's name was Matt doing with them? His orders to Matt had been only to engage Freddy in cards and a few drinks. He had been quite explicit that Matt was not to get any further involved.

Insubordinate brothers, he thought, grinding his teeth.

He had counted on Freddy coming alone and he did not need his inebriated brother caught up in this matter, nor, for that matter, Jenkins. Why would Freddy have brought a witnesses? He could have slipped into the stables unseen and dealt with the incriminating evidence without anyone knowing.

Matt looked around the room. 'So, which bin do you think it's in?' he asked, his words slurring.

Freddy gestured at the chaff bin furthest from the door.

'Start there, Jenkins,' he directed his man.

Freddy was no fool. He would have worked out that anything concealed in the more convenient bins would have been easily discovered. The big man shambled over to the bin and Sebastian heard the soft rustle of the chaff as Jenkins rummaged in its depths. Finding nothing, he moved to the second bin and gave a grunt of satisfaction as his questing hand found the sack.

Freddy looked down at the hessian bundle Jenkins thumped onto the table. When he pulled the sacking away to reveal an old, battered saddle, he swore.

'Wassa matter?' Matt asked.

Sebastian stepped out of the shadows, his pistol held steady in his hand and pointed straight at Freddy.

'Found what you were looking for?'

Freddy whirled to face him. The light from the lantern cast his fine features into a hard relief and Sebastian could almost see his mind grappling for a logical explanation for his actions.

'Your brother thought it would be a lark to find the saddle,' Freddy said in a light tone. He gestured at the saddle on the table, 'I hate to disappoint you, Somerton, but that's not Anthony's saddle.'

'That's because the saddle I found has been secured elsewhere,' Sebastian said.

'Now who's playing games,' Freddy said with a laugh. 'I wouldn't have thought hide and seek was in your nature, Somerton. Now, do be a sport and put that weapon down. What is so special about an old saddle anyway?'

'The interesting thing about the saddle I found is the fact that the girth was cut through. Not enough to snap immediately but enough to fail when put under strain, such as taking a fence. Of course, a sharp-eyed groom would notice the cut, but apparently the distressed widow gave an order for the saddle to be destroyed on the morning of Anthony's death before it could be inspected.'

'Dear me! Are you suggesting our dear Isabel cut the girth?' Freddy ventured.

'I think that is what the killer would have liked the curious to think, except that the order relayed to the stable hand came from you, Freddy, not Isabel.'

'Of course it did. She was too distressed to deal with so trivial a matter, so she asked me to relay her orders. I would be prepared to swear to that.'

'Your word against hers?'

'If you are implying that Anthony's death was foul play then dear Isabel had more motivation than anyone else in the house to want Anthony dead.' Freddy sounded more confident as the conversation progressed.

Sebastian shook his head. 'However abominably Anthony may have treated her, she's no killer and, in a court of law, it would be her word against a proven imposter, blackmailer and card cheat.'

'Bas? Whatcha talkin' about?' Matt interposed.

'Get out of here, Matt. This has nothing to do with you,' Sebastian said, not letting his eyes, or his aim, leave Freddy.

Matthew uttered a short exclamation, his eyes widening in surprise. 'I don't think I can,' he said, his voice high and the words no longer slurred.

Freddy smiled and Sebastian let his gaze move to Matthew. Jenkins stood behind his brother with a knife at his throat.

'Drop your pistol, Somerton,' Freddy suggested. 'Oh, and Dempster, I think you should probably get out here too. I'm certain Lord Somerton did not come alone. That is why I brought my own insurance with me.'

The knife tightened on Matt's throat, drawing blood. Matt yelped.

Behind Sebastian, Harry uttered a violent oath and stepped out into the light, laying his pistols on the barrels.

Freddy took a step back out of the immediate light thrown by the lantern. His hand slid beneath his jacket and withdrew holding a pistol.

'I was afraid this would happen. It seems, Jenkins, that my plans may have gone a little awry.'

Jenkins gave an interrogative grunt and Freddy waved his pistol at Sebastian and Harry.

'You two, I want you face down on the ground with your hands behind your back. Jenkins, you can pass that idiot boy over here while you tie these two up.'

When neither Sebastian nor Harry moved, Freddy glanced at Jenkins.

'If you don't start doing as I ask, my man here will start making your brother's life extremely unpleasant. He knows how to kill a man slowly.'

In answer, Jenkins moved the knife to Matthew's ear, cutting a nick. Matt gave a sharp cry and squirmed in the man's grasp as the wound began to bleed, staining the pristine white linen of his neckcloth with bright blood.

Sebastian and Harry complied. From the supine position Sebastian found himself in, all he could see of Matt were his booted feet, stumbling across the floor as Jenkins dragged the young man across to Freddy.

Jenkins set about his work quickly and effectively, securing Sebastian's wrists behind his back and then his ankles. To make certain there was no risk of escape, he ran a rope between Sebastian's wrists and ankles, forcing his knees to bend into an agonising position. While Jenkins secured Harry, Sebastian rolled onto his side to relieve the cramp in his limbs and to give him a better view of Freddy.

Freddy held his pistol to Matt's temple and, even in the dim light, Sebastian could see the sweat on his brother's forehead and the fear in his eyes.

'Why did you kill Anthony?' Sebastian tried to keep his voice level and neutral as if lying trussed on a dusty floor was of no consequence to him.

Freddy gave a theatrical heave of his shoulders. 'I didn't intend for him to die, just come off the blasted horse and break his leg.'

'That doesn't answer my question.'

Freddy gnawed his lower lip for a moment before replying, 'The bastard had stopped paying me.'

'Why?'

Freddy gave a snort of derision. 'Said he had run out of money. Told me he had invested everything he had in some gold mine, and it had been a fraud. He said he didn't care what happened to him anymore. Told me to do my worst.' Freddy laughed. 'Not sure he anticipated what my worst could be.'

Jenkins grunted to signify he had secured the two men.

Freddy's voice became clipped and efficient as he issued his orders.

'Excellent. I regret we are going to have to take leave of your generous hospitality, Somerton. Pity to disappoint Fanny. She had such high hopes of a happy marriage. Jenkins, the small coach and the bays are stabled at the dower house. Go and hitch them up.'

Jenkins gave a low growl and stomped out of the room.

'Excellent man, Jenkins. I found him in London and saw his value at once. He had his tongue cut out for some misdemeanour to his lord and master. You are an upstart, Somerton. You have no idea of your place in this world. You wouldn't have the guts to cut out a man's tongue for talking back to you.'

'You're right, Lynch, I wouldn't. But don't mistake me, I have killed men without compunction.'

For the first time, the smile left Freddy's face, and he pushed the pistol harder into Matt's temple.

'And so have I. Now, what am I going to do with the three of you?'

'Let my brother go, Freddy. This has nothing to do with him.'

In answer, Freddy pushed Matt to his knees, keeping the pistol at the back of his head.

'Who are you?' Sebastian asked, desperate to keep Freddy talking.

Freddy shook his head. 'If you are so curious, Somerton, my father was a farrier in Bristol. My mother died in childbirth, and my father drank himself into an early grave. Fan and I were left on our own. Let's just say I worked my way up from the gutter where he left us.'

'How much does Fanny know?'

His mouth worked as he framed his answer. 'I love my sister and she deserved a better life than that she was born into.'

'It was all for Fanny?'

Freddy didn't answer and, for a moment, Sebastian almost believed that Freddy's motives were born purely out of love for his sister, and then he remembered the card party and the well-honed team that guaranteed Freddy's wins. The petty thievery had probably netted the Lynchs a tidy sum over the years. Fanny had been no innocent in Freddy's plans and schemes.

Freddy tossed his head. 'This is so annoying! It all started with that silly unpleasantness over the Thompson girl. He blamed me for that. Can you credit that?'

'Did you kill her?' Sebastian's blood ran cold.

'No.' Freddy sounded indignant. 'I told you I had nothing to do with her death, but, for some reason, Anthony seemed to think I did. As if I would succumb to the charms of a servant girl. I blame Isabel. Anthony was besotted with the infant, and, as for his fawning over Isabel, really it was all too distracting.

Then he had the gall to threaten to expose Fanny and me as imposters and, most hurtful, blackmailers.'

'Does Isabel know any of this?'

'Of course not, but he was going to tell her. He told me so himself that day. Said he wanted us out of the house by the next morning. So you see, Somerton, he had to be punished, and he made it so easy. That night, he rode over to see Lady Kendall. All I had to do was follow him. I found he'd left his horse saddled in a deserted stable. I cut through the girth and slipped away—' Freddy stiffened and swung his pistol to the door. 'Who's there? Come out and show yourself or Alder dies.'

'Don't hurt me!' A small, very young voice came from the doorway, and young Peter Thompson took a small step into the room.

'The wretched boy I gave the order to,' Freddy snapped. 'It was you, wasn't it, you little urchin. You decided to keep the saddle?'

Peter's lips trembled as he nodded his head. With Freddy distracted, Matt took the opportunity to lash out jerking his elbow back into Freddy's knee. The pistol discharged with a blinding flash as Matt rolled away from Freddy and made a bolt for the door where the petrified boy stood.

Freddy gave a cry of anger and produced a second pistol from his jacket. Before Sebastian could shout a warning, the pistol discharged. Matt gave a sharp cry and fell forward onto the ground.

Freddy reached the door in a bound, seizing Peter by the scruff of his neck. He kicked at Matt's prone body and relief flooded Sebastian as he heard his brother groan.

Looking back at the two bound men, Freddy shook his head.

'Why did you have to make this so difficult?' he complained, raising his eyes to the ceiling. 'Now I suppose I should get out of here before the whole household descends on us. You ...' he kicked Matt again.

Matt rolled over and pulled himself into a sitting position, clutching his right arm. Freddy jerked his head in the direction of Harry and Sebastian.

'Over there with the others.'

Matt complied, dragging himself across the floor until he sat with his back against the chaff bins.

Peter Thompson began to cry as Freddy's fingers tightened on his shoulder.

'Sorry, my lord. I was just checking on Millie and the foal when I heard voices. This is all my fault.'

'No, it's not, Peter,' Sebastian said.

Freddy looked around the room, his gaze lighting on the three men. A nasty smile curled the corners of his mouth. His grip firmly on Peter's arm, he walked over to the lantern that still burned on the table, collected the discarded pistols and picked up the lantern.

'Good evening to you, gentlemen.'

Propelling Peter before him, he left the room, shutting the door behind him. In the silence, Sebastian heard a key turn in the lock. He held his breath at the sound of rustling hay on the other side of the door. Freddy laughed. A chilling sound in the dark silence.

Harry spoke first. 'Can you smell smoke?'

Chapter Fifty-One

Isabel woke with a start. She lay awake, her senses at attention, straining her ears, but heard only silence, punctuated by the distant tick of the grandfather clock that stood at the head of the stairs.

She breathed out and turned over, but even as sleep began to claim her, the unmistakable sound of scuffling and whispered voices in the corridor outside her room caused her to sit bolt upright. She swung her feet off the bed and as she lit the night candle on her dressing table, the door burst open. Freddy, holding Fanny by the arm, entered the room.

Isabel straightened. 'How dare you!' she began, but her bravado faltered when she saw the fear on Fanny's face and the wild look in Freddy's eyes.

Her hand went to the bell pull only to be stayed by the sight of a pistol in Freddy's hand and another tucked into his waistband.

'Don't move, Lady Somerton.'

'What is the meaning of this?' she demanded, trying to keep her voice calm and controlled.

Freddy thrust Fanny down on the daybed.

'He's killed Sebastian,' Fanny wailed.

Killed Sebastian?

Isabel made a dive for the door, but Freddy caught her by the arm and pulled her in towards him. She felt the cold muzzle of a pistol against her throat.

'That's far enough, Isabel.' He flung her towards the daybed. 'Sit.'

Isabel complied. Beside her, Fanny snivelled. Her lip trembled and a fresh spill of tears coursed down her face.

'No one was meant to get hurt.'

Isabel turned to her. 'What do you mean?'

'It was that stupid saddle. If Sebastian had never found it, none of this would have happened,' Fanny sniffed.

Isabel caught her breath. 'The saddle? Anthony's saddle?' She glanced up at Freddy. 'Why? What did Sebastian find?'

Fanny's voice rose to an almost hysterical pitch. 'Anthony promised! He promised to make a generous settlement for Freddy and I, but then he laughed and said he'd never made such a promise and that he would turn us out onto the street. Freddy was so angry. Freddy didn't mean to kill him. When he cut the girth, Anthony was just supposed to fall and hurt himself.'

'What do you mean he cut the girth?' Isabel looked from Fanny to Freddy.

'Yes I cut the girth,' Freddy said. 'He was about to throw us out on to the street, expose us as blackmailers and imposters so I needed to remind him I was not to be trifled with. We need to get out of here. Fanny, pack a bag.'

'But I was supposed to marry Sebastian. I was going to be Lady Somerton,' Fanny protested. 'You always spoil everything.'

Freddy moved to the window and said with a grunt of satisfaction, 'The stables are well alight. He'll be dead by now, and his brother with him. Your precious Sebastian is probably charcoal by now, Isabel.'

'No,' she murmured in disbelief.

Nausea rose in her throat as a golden glow lit the dark sky, casting the room into moving shadows. Freddy grasped her by the arm and propelled her to the window.

'Take a look, Lady Somerton. I left dear Sebastian and his comrades trussed up like pigs on market day.'

Isabel stared at the golden-red blaze rising above the tree line. Sebastian ... dead? She took the thought and pushed it to the back of her mind. Later, she would rail against the unnecessary death, but now she had her own foe to face, and she needed to keep her wits about her.

She looked back at Freddy. 'What are you going to do?'

'Sadly, I think the first thing is to depart this place and find somewhere a little more conducive to my health,' Freddy said.

'Where?' Isabel asked.

'Oh, probably the continent,' Freddy said thoughtfully. 'But, make no mistake, Lady Somerton, you're coming with us. Get dressed. I have the coach downstairs. Oh, and do make sure you bring your jewels, Isabel—all of them.'

Isabel looked into Freddy's eyes. There would be no reprieve, no mercy. He had killed once, twice, if what he said about Sebastian was true, and he would so again. The thought of Sebastian dead numbed her. He'd been in her life so short a time, and yet now she couldn't even begin to comprehend a world without him.

Freddy watched as she stuffed the contents of her jewel box into a soft bag, which he took from her. She pulled on the gown, cloak and bonnet Fanny proffered and, with Freddy's pistol in her back, they made their way silently down the stairs. Fanny dashed for her bedroom, returning with a bandbox that clinked with the metallic ring of a number of metal objects roughly thrown in together.

As she descended the stairs in the dark, Isabel nearly fell over Peter Thompson. The boy had been tied by his hands to the banisters with a dirty piece of cloth twisted around his mouth as a gag. She kneeled down beside him and boy turned a tearstained face to her as she undid the cloth around his mouth.

'Has he hurt you?' Isabel asked.

The boy shook his head. 'No, but he's killed his lordship. Shut him in the chaff room and then set fire to a pile of straw by the door. It's all my fault, my lady. I should never have kept that saddle,' he wailed.

'Nonsense, Peter—' Isabel began but, before she could say anything more, Freddy hauled her up by the arm.

'What about the boy?' Fanny asked.

Freddy shook his head. 'He's served his purpose. Lady Somerton is a far more valuable hostage.'

Pausing only to replace Peter's gag, Freddy hustled the women out of the house. The carriage, with Jenkins on the driving box, stood waiting by the front door. Freddy pushed Isabel inside, and the coach began to move off before the door had shut.

Chapter Fifty-Two

Beyond the door to the chaff room, Sebastian could hear the crackling of flames. Acrid smoke had begun seeping into the room.

He coughed and swore. Beside him, Harry groaned as he flexed, trying to loosen his bonds.

'How did we get ourselves into this, Alder? Been in some tight spots before, but I think this takes the prize. We must be losing our touch.'

'Roll over with your back to me,' Sebastian ordered.

His friend complied and, with his fingers, Sebastian worked the knots on Harry's wrists. They had been well tied by an expert hand, but he gradually got purchase and, as the ropes began to loosen, Harry freed himself. He shook off the ropes and began on Sebastian's bonds. When he had been freed, Sebastian turned to his brother who sat slumped against the wall, like a broken toy.

'Matt!'

Matt didn't move and Sebastian bent over him. Even in the dark, he knew from long experience that Matt had probably lost a good deal of blood and needed to have the wound tended. First they had to get out of this room. Flames were now licking around the doorframe and the room had filled with smoke. In a moment the chaff room would be ablaze.

From beyond the door and outside in the stable yard he could hear screaming horses and the shouts of men and women.

'The window,' Harry coughed and pointed to the small window set some five feet off the floor.

'Pull the table over,' Sebastian said.

As Harry manoeuvred the table over to the window, Sebastian searched the room for a club. He found a wooden spade and, being the taller of the two men, climbed onto the table. Swinging the spade at the window, he knocked out the glass.

He heard Bennet's familiar voice above the rabble.

'There he is. Praise be... Quick, you, fetch a ladder.'

Sebastian jumped down from the table and crossed back to his brother.

'Matt!' He slapped Matt's pale cheeks.

Matt groaned but didn't open his eyes.

'Matt, look at me.'

Matt coughed and his eyelids flickered. It took Harry's help to haul his brother's dead weight up and onto the the table. Bennet's face appeared in the window.

'Rope!' Sebastian choked.

Bennet disappeared. A stout end of rope coiled through the window.

'Here, my lord!' Bennet said.

Sebastian tied it under his brother's arms and pulled him to his feet.

'Matt, I need you to wake up.'

Matt moaned and his eyes fluttered open.

'You're going through that window, understand? Bennet?'

'I'm here, sir!'

Sebastian shouted instructions at his corporal and, with Harry to aid with the pushing and Bennet, Thompson and the men below pulling, they managed to haul the semiconscious man up and across the lintel. Sebastian gave one final shove and Matt's legs disappeared out of the window.

Flames had eaten the door and were now creeping with long fingers along the ceiling beams.

'You go,' Harry ordered.

Sebastian didn't have time to argue. With a monumental effort, he hauled himself up and over the sill. His hand scraped on a piece of broken glass but there were strong hands on the other side ready to pull him out, and he tumbled to the ground.

'Thank God! We had no idea you were in there. Are you hurt, my lord?' Thompson bent over him.

Sebastian looked back at the stable that was now well alight, the flames licking up into the rooms occupied by Thompson and his family.

'Your wife... We must get her out.'

Thompson nodded. 'Already done, my lord. She's safe. Can't find my boy though.'

'Freddy Lynch has got your boy.' Sebastian coughed, his lungs screaming for air as Harry fell to the cobbles with an audible thump. 'Has anyone seen him or his man, Jenkins?'

Bennet, his face streaked with soot, looked down at him and shook his head.

'Lynch? I've not seen him.'

Sebastian grimaced. Freddy must have slipped away in the dark with his hostage as the alarm was being raised. He looked around the courtyard, now filled with people and horses.

'Where's my brother?'

'They've carried him to the house,' Bennet said.

Harry held out his hand. 'Going to lie there all night, Alder?'

He took Harry's hand and rose to his feet. He shook his head. 'I'm a fool, Dempster. How could I have underestimated Lynch so badly?'

Harry put a hand on his shoulder. 'You had no way of knowing quite what a villain the man was.'

Sebastian raised his voice and addressed the throng and repeated his question. 'Has anyone here see Lynch or his man?'

The men gathered around him shook their heads.

'Lynch was going for his sister,' Harry said.

Sebastian stared at his friend. Fanny was at the dower house with Isabel.

Isabel!

He turned and set off at a run with Harry and Thompson behind him.

His heart jerked as he found the front door to the dower house wide open. Inside, he stopped and stood for a moment in the front hall, trying to adjust his eyes to the darkness. He heard a moaning sound and fixed on a huddled figure on the stairs.

For a brief moment he thought it was Isabel, but the boy, Peter, looked up at him over a gag, with large, frightened eyes. Sebastian unbound him and Peter flung himself at his father who had followed Sebastian into the building.

'He took Lady Somerton!' The boy's voice was muffled by his father's coat.

'How long ago?'

The boy shook his head and turned to look at him. 'Not long. My lord, the stables! He set the straw on fire. I thought you were dead. The horses...'

Before Sebastian could respond, the boy took to his heels, running back towards the burning building with Sebastian behind him. Sebastian's only thought was to find Pharaoh and take off after the coach with Freddy and his hostage aboard.

By the time he got back to the stables, flames licked high into the night sky from the roof. The whole household had been turned out and a bucket line ran from the wells, but the buckets of water barely impacted the inferno. The noise of crashing timbers was almost deafening.

'How many of the horses have they got out?' Sebastian shouted at one of the grooms.

'All of them except Lady Somerton's mare,' the man yelled back.

The fire had not yet reached the far end of the stables where Millie and her foal were stalled. It would break Isabel's heart if her gentle mare were to die in such a horrible manner.

Peter looked up at him, his face anguished.

'My Lord, we've got to get her out.'

The boy turned and sprinted towards the burning building.

'Peter! Stop him, Bas.'

At the sound of Connie's voice, Sebastian turned to see his sister running towards him.

'He's gone inside!' Connie screamed as she reached him.

Sebastian snatched up a blanket from the pile being used to beat at the flames.

Thompson caught his sleeve.

'My Lord, you can't go in there! He's my son, I'll go after him.'

'Stay here!' Sebastian commanded and ran towards the building, pausing for a moment in the doorway to wrap the blanket around his head and shoulders.

The smoke that billowed out towards him was so thick that Sebastian could hardly see. Above him, wood cracked and the roaring of the flames almost sent him back. Drawing the blanket around his mouth, with his eyes watering, he groped his way along the stalls until he could make out the shadowy figures of the boy and the horses in the furthest stall.

Peter wrestled with the terrified horse. The mare, docile as she was, plunged around her stall in panic as the boy tried to secure a lead rope to her.

Coughing, Sebastian grabbed the boy's collar and hauled him out of the stall. Peter had managed to get the rope around the mare's neck, but the mare's eyes rolled and she pulled against the rope as he tried to lead her out. Her foal leaned against her, nickering in terror.

Sebastian slackened his hold and held the mare's nose, looking into her eyes, making soothing noises.

'Come on, old girl. Only one way out of here. Trust me.'

Grunting, he picked up the foal, knowing Millie would follow her foal to hell and back. The mare's eyes rolled white and terrified in her head, but as he moved towards the door to the stall, she followed. Peter sat on the ground outside the stall, coughing.

Sebastian set the trembling foal down and hauled the boy up, flinging him bodily across the mare.

'Keep low and hang on for your life,' he said hoarsely.

He collected the foal again and pushed on towards the exit.

As they neared the stable door, the roof above him cracked and a burning beam crashed to the ground behind him. The rope in his hand jerked out of his grasp. The mare screamed and Sebastian turned, seeing the beam had come down between him and the mare. The little horse had reared, depositing Peter on the floor, and now she backed away from the flames that separated her from her baby, screaming.

Sebastian bolted for the door, pausing only to thrust the foal at the nearest person he could find, before turning back into the inferno. He pulled the blanket from his shoulders and began beating at the flames and kicking at the burning timber, clearing enough to get through to the small corner where the semi-conscious boy and terrified horse cowered against the wall.

Tearing a strip from the tail of his shirt, he tied it around the mare's eyes. Her nostrils flared, but no longer seeing the licking flames, she seemed calmer. Sebastian threw the boy across her back again. Giving a quick tug of the leading rope, he pulled the singed blanket over himself and, holding his breath, he ran for his life as the roof timbers buckled and collapsed around him.

Dimly, he heard the sound of cheering as he emerged into the stable yard with horse and boy. He fell to his knees, gasping for breath, and the world went black.

Chapter Fifty-Three

Wedged in a corner of the rocking coach, her hands and feet securely bound with cords from the coach's curtains, Isabel could only just make out the shadows of her travelling companions. She shifted her weight to try and find a more comfortable position but nothing helped.

'Are you uncomfortable, my dear Isabel?' Freddy's voice came out of the dark.

She ignored the question.

'Where are you taking me?'

Freddy took a moment before answering. 'A little jaunt to the seaside. We can pick up a fishing boat or coastal trader that will take us to France for the price of one of your earrings.'

'And me?'

Freddy shrugged. 'Oh, I think you may need to come with us, dear Lady Somerton.'

'Why? What purpose would that serve?'

Freddy shrugged. 'You make a useful hostage, and maybe I enjoy your company.'

'You don't think that they will have already connected the fire in the stables with your disappearance? And when ...' she paused to deal with the catch in her throat, ' ... when they find Lord Somerton's body, they will certainly put up a hue and cry for you.'

It felt easier to say 'Lord Somerton' rather than Sebastian. When she thought of Sebastian, she wanted to howl with grief.

Freddy snorted. 'Fanny, bind her mouth. I've heard enough from her ladyship for the moment.'

His perfect consonants had slipped into a coarser accent, betraying origins that were far from gentlemanly.

Fanny complied, with whispered apologies to Isabel before subsiding into her corner of the coach opposite her brother. A grey light had begun to creep in through the gaps around the curtains and Isabel squinted through the narrow gap, trying to make out something of the landscape, but all she could see was the lightening sky and wondered, for a moment, if this might be the last sunrise she saw on this earth.

After the first mad flight from Brantstone, the coach's pace had slowed, the horses no doubt exhausted. They would need to be rested.

The coach rolled slowly on for a few more yards and stopped. She heard the man jump down from the box and the coach door opened. Jenkins's ugly face appeared at the door, and he grunted unintelligibly, gesticulating at the front of the coach.

Freddy sighed. 'Very well, Jenkins. The next inn we come upon, we'll rest the horses.' He glanced back at the two women. 'My travelling companions could probably do with some breakfast.'

As the coach jerked off again, Freddy leaned across to Isabel.

'Now, my fine lady, I am going to untruss you and, if you are a good girl, you can refresh yourself and have something to eat. Just promise me you'll behave.'

Isabel nodded and gasped with relief as Freddy undid the gag and bonds. She shook her hands, trying to restore some feeling to her numb fingers.

Freddy handed his spare pistol to Fanny as the coach clattered into an inn yard.

'One thing you should know about our Fan: she is a dead shot with the pistol. Ain't you, Fan?'

'I am,' Fanny agreed. 'Freddy taught me.'

The door swung open. Freddy jumped down first, looking around the quiet inn yard before striding into the inn.

'Fanny, you don't really want to shoot me, do you?' Isabel said in a low voice.

Fanny's chin came up. 'I can't let you go, Isabel. He'd kill me as well. You don't know him.'

Isabel had no chance to say anything more as Freddy appeared at the door again. He took the pistol from Fanny, concealing it underneath his cloak.

'I've taken a private parlour. We have an hour, and you,' he addressed Isabel, 'don't even think of crying out.'

He twitched back the fold of his cloak to reveal the pistol trained on her. As she climbed down, he took her by the waist, and the muzzle of the pistol pressed against her ribs.

'Lean ean on me as if you are faint. That's it.'

In such close proximity, he smelled rank and she wondered if it was the scent of fear. Holding her close, Freddy marched her into the inn and upstairs to a small, private parlour where a breakfast of bread, cheese, bacon, and small beer had been set for them.

'Eat up, ladies. It may be a while before we get a chance to eat again.'

Isabel complied. She recognised that nothing would be served by a refusal to eat. She needed all her strength to keep her wits about her. Fanny, however, picked at the food, prompting an angry outburst from her brother that reduced the girl to tears.

'Finish it, Fanny,' Isabel urged in a low voice as Freddy strode across to the window.

Fanny raised her head and turned her miserable face on Isabel. Isabel smiled encouragingly. Fanny's faith in her brother must have been sorely shaken by the events of the previous night, and she could see the girl was genuinely frightened. If she could win Fanny's confidence, there was a faint hope that, between the two of them, they might be able to overcome their tormentor.

But Freddy, no doubt instinctively alert to the danger of letting the two women have any time alone together, ensured that they were not afforded an opportunity for conversation, even escorting Isabel to the privy. After an hour's respite, they were back in the coach.

Isabel noticed that the bays were still hitched to the coach, their heads drooping with exhaustion. Even if Freddy could have changed them, leaving two such recognisable horses would make their tracks easier to follow, but their progress from here would be slow. That gave her hope

In the coach, Freddy tied her hands, this time in front of her, leaving her feet free.

'Where are we going?' Isabel asked as he fastened the knot.

Freddy cast an irritated glance. 'Suffice to say, I know of a small harbour and a friendly fisherman who'll not ask too many questions.'

In the gloom of the curtained coach, Isabel sat back and considered this intelligence. Freddy had not appeared to be in possession of it before their stop, so it could only have been gleaned from someone at the inn. If anyone was in search of her, which by now they would surely be, Freddy had left a considerable clue. He would be hoping they could make good their escape before his pursuers caught up with them.

She closed her eyes. Like food, she needed rest if she were to keep her wits about her. The coach moved at a walking pace, and she closed her eyes. Visions of Sebastian lying dead in the burning stable and her own possible death at the hands of this monster kept her from sleep. She choked back the threat of tears.

I cannot show any weakness, she thought.

A sharp, frustrated cry from Freddy, accompanied by a rapping on the roof, startled her into full consciousness.

'Get on, you fool. We need to reach the coast by the turn of the tide.'

Isabel peered around the curtain. It had begun to rain, no doubt turning the road to mud. She thought of the two beautiful bays, labouring to pull the coach.

'Freddy, you'll kill the horses,' she protested.

'Do you think I care about horses?' he snapped. 'It's my neck or theirs.'

The coachman's whip snapped and the coach creaked into a faster pace, lurching from side to side. Isabel, with her hands bound, could not prevent herself from being flung against Freddy, seated on the opposite seat. He caught her by her forearms and leered into her face.

'I've wondered what it would be like to kiss you, and here you are throwing yourself at me,' he said.

She squirmed in his grasp but could do nothing when he kissed her on the lips, a wet, grasping coupling, accompanied by his tongue, which he tried to force between her tightly clenched teeth. When he broke away, laughing, she spat in his face. He rewarded her by slapping her across the face and throwing her back in the corner of the coach.

'Bitch!'

'Freddy, please,' Fanny said.

Freddy laughed.

The momentum of the coach seemed to be getting stronger. Isabel braced herself as the coach lurched to the right. She heard a sickening crack from the rear axle and a loud, animalistic cry from the driver. A horse screamed as the coach began to topple onto its side, but the momentum did not cease. The panicked horses, still attached by the traces, must have broken into a wild gallop, dragging the stricken coach, now fully on its side.

The occupants churned inside the broken coach as if caught in a river in spate. As she scrambled to get a finger hold on something, anything, to stop her wild tumble, Isabel heard Fanny screaming.

This was it. She was going to die.

She closed her eyes and let her body go slack as the coach came to a shuddering halt.

Chapter Fifty-Four

Sebastian woke with a headache, a sore throat, and a sore hand. He lay staring up at the silk bed hangings as the events of the night seeped back into his consciousness with sickening clarity.

What was he doing lying in bed when Isabel remained in the hands of a madman?

He sat up, coughing, and cast a disparaging glance at his bandaged right hand.

'Sebastian?'

He turned his head and smiled at the sight of his sister in the chair beside his bed.

'Connie?' His voice sounded hoarse, and the act of talking caused him to cough.

She stretched and smiled. 'The good lord in his wisdom built you tough, Sebastian Alder.'

'What time is it, Connie? How long have I been asleep?'

Connie glanced at the window where daylight clawed its way around the folds of the curtains.

'At least eight,' she said.

'I've lost hours!' Sebastian said.

'Harry put together a search party, Bas, but they came back

an hour ago—no trace of the coach in the dark. Where are you going?' she added as Sebastian swung his legs out of the bed.

'I've got to rescue Isabel.'

Sebastian stumped around the room, trying to find where Bennet and Pierce hid his clothes. He gave a groan of exasperation and sank into the chair and buried his face in his hands. 'I'm an idiot, Connie. I underestimated Freddy's capacity for evil.' He looked up at his sister, seeing the distress in her face. 'Where's Harry?'

'Downstairs. When I last saw him, he had his breakfast plate piled high.'

Sebastian nodded. 'Tell Harry I'll be down in a few minutes—and can you find Bennet? I'll take him along as well. I'll need Pharaoh saddled and ready as soon as possible.'

'M'Lord, you're surely not thinking of going after the man yourself?' Pierce chided him from the door.

'Clothes, Pierce. Now! Where's Bennet?'

Pierce opened his mouth to utter another protest but Sebastian fixed the man with a cold glare.

'Mr. Bennet is with young Mr. Alder, sir,' Pierce replied.

Still half dressed, Sebastian threw open the door to Matt's bedchamber. His brother, deathly pale, appeared to be asleep. Bennet sat in a corner, polishing Matt's boots.

'Get the pistols, Bennet.'

Bennet's eyes gleamed. 'Action, sir?'

'I hope not, but I need you. Snap to it, Bennet, I'm leaving now.'

As Bennet scuttled from the room, Matt turned his head on the pillow.

'Bas? Give me a few minutes, I'll come with you.'

Sebastian crossed to the bed and put a hand on his brother's shoulder. 'You're not going anywhere.'

Matt screwed up his face in pain. 'Damn it. Why did he shoot me, Bas.'

'I should never have put you in so much danger, Matt. You rest easy, I've got to go.'

Matt plucked at his sleeve. 'This is my fault. I let him dupe me into going in search of the bloody saddle. Somehow, he made it sound like it was all my idea. I heard everything he said, Bas. I don't think anyone could have guessed how evil he truly was.'

Sebastian shook his head. He knew. He had seen evil firsthand. Inez had not died easily.

He cursed himself for passing out. A bit of smoke, that was all, and now Isabel was in the hands of a man who had killed once.

Was every woman he loved doomed to suffer?

'We'll talk later, Matt.' He turned and, pulling on his jacket, ran from the room.

In the daylight, the route taken by the fugitives proved easy to follow. A coach driven like the furies was after it attracted plenty of attention, even from those who should have been in bed. It soon became clear that Freddy was heading for the Wash and, no doubt, a fishing boat to the continent.

More fool Freddy for taking such a readily recognisable coach and pair, Sebastian thought grimly.

The search party stopped at an isolated inn, partly because it seemed an obvious post for the fugitives to pause in their headlong flight and partly because they were tired and hungry and their own horses needed resting.

Despite the ample bandaging, his hand hurt, and an exhaustion he had not felt since his army days tugged at his mind and body.

Obedient to their request for haste, the landlord obliged with a hearty meal that the men set about with a vengeance. Sebastian questioned the man about the coach.

'A gentleman and two ladies? Aye, they stopped here about nine this morning. Stayed about an hour. I counselled 'im to stay longer but he were set on 'is way. Didn't even change the horses though they was done in. Them poor beasts.' The landlord shook his head.

Sebastian checked his watch and caught Harry's eye. If Freddy had left this place around ten and it was now midday, they were now only a few hours behind him and, if he was now travelling slowly with tired horses, they could well overtake him by late afternoon.

'And the ladies… Did they appear to be well?' Sebastian asked

The landlord frowned. 'Well, now you mention it, one of 'em seemed poorly. Himself all but had to carry her in.'

Isabel! Had that fiend hurt her?

'What do you mean?' he asked in a neutral tone.

'Well, he had his arm around her, holdin' her close. Couldn't see her face. She kept the hood of her cloak up.'

'Did you serve them food?'

'Aye, but he wouldn't let me in the room. Insisted it was all set out afore the ladies alighted.'

'Did he say where they were bound when they left here?' Harry asked.

'Well, I'm guessing it would be Lidiford on the Wash,' the landlord said with utter certainty.

The men stared at him.

'How can you be so sure?' Harry asked.

The innkeeper shrugged. 'I saw him talkin' to young Bob over there.' He pointed out of the window at a swarthy lad, mucking out the stables. 'Bob's from Lidiford way. He'd know all the fishin' villages on't Wash.'

Three sets of forks clattered onto empty plates.

Shouting instructions to Harry to settle the account, Sebastian, with Bennet scuttling in his wake, all but ran from the room.

'Young Bob' confirmed that he had advised the fine

gentleman that he'd find a boat at Lidiford that would be willing to take him across to the continent if the price was right.

The three men swung into the saddles of their barely rested horses and, putting their heels to the beasts, regained the road. Through the rain and the mud, they followed the tracks of the coach in the direction of the sea.

Chapter Fifty-Five

Isabel lay still as the memory of the helter skelter ride in the damaged coach came back in jerky pictures. Slowly, she opened her eyes and looked up at the grey, lowering sky. She lay on her back in the open, rain stinging her face and eyes.

She gingerly turned her head. The shattered remains of the coach lay on its side some yards away. One of the horses still stood in the traces, its head lowered, its sides heaving. Its comrade had fallen beside it and lay unmoving.

She must have been flung out—or dragged—from the wreckage.

She did an inventory of her limbs: feet, legs, hands, arms and, tentatively, her neck. Her wrists were still bound and her right wrist hurt but, as she could move her fingers, she guessed it was nothing worse than a sprain. Her head hurt and she wondered if she had banged it just before the coach came to rest.

Awkwardly, she pulled herself into a sitting position and looked around her. She saw no sign of the coachman. Jenkins must have been thrown when the coach had first shed its wheel. She hoped he was dead.

A dark figure moved in the wreckage of the coach that

resembled nothing more than a pile of shattered tinder wood. Freddy emerged, hauling Fanny with little gentleness up through the broken remains of the door that now stood open to the heavens. He jumped down and carried the girl's inert body over to where Isabel sat.

Ignoring Isabel, he laid Fanny down and kneeled beside her, his hands moving over his sister's face. Isabel read what seemed to be genuine distress in his furrowed brow as he looked up at her.

'Is she dead?' he asked Isabel, his voice hoarse with emotion.

'Untie me and I'll tell you,' she said without sympathy in her voice.

He glanced at her bound wrists and, with shaking fingers, complied. Isabel flexed her sore wrist and decided it was not badly hurt. Gathering herself together, she bent over Fanny's inert body. A strong pulse beat in the girl's throat.

She looked up at Freddy and nodded. 'She's alive.'

Freddy's shoulders relaxed for a moment before he frowned again. 'But she's badly hurt, isn't she?'

Isabel ran her hands along the girl's limbs, lifting the torn skirt to reveal what her fingers told her. Fanny's right leg, below the knee, was already swollen and fell at an unnatural angle.

'Her leg's broken,' Isabel said.

Freddy's face crumpled in genuine emotion, but just as quickly as he had revealed himself, he resumed his inscrutable demeanour and looked at her.

'Are you hurt?'

She shook her head. 'No.'

'Good. Get to your feet. We haven't a moment to spare.'

She stared at him. 'What do you mean?'

'We're still a few miles from the coast.'

'Then you go on. I'll stay here with Fanny.'

His lip curled, all trace of concern for his sister gone as he said, 'Someone will find her soon enough.'

Isabel looked around at the desolate marshy land. The chances of imminent help for the girl seemed remote unless a search party was on their tail. A small spring of hope welled in her heart. Surely there had to be a search party.

Freddy yanked her to her feet and told her to fetch the travelling blanket and some cushions from the coach. As she leaned into the smashed carriage searching for these objects, Freddy carried his sister back into the shelter of the coach.

With some ingenuity, he rigged up a rough shelter from the broken coach panels. Wrapping his sister in the blanket, he bent and kissed her on the forehead.

Only when he was satisfied Fanny was as comfortable as she could be, Freddy got to his feet and pulled his pistol from his belt, waving it in the direction of the coach.

'Fetch your jewels.'

She found the bag under a torn cushion and handed it to Freddy. He tucked them into his jacket before retying her wrists in front of her. He looped a second cord around the bindings so he could pull her along like a dog on a lead.

'Freddy, there is nothing to be gained from taking me with you. I will only slow you down. You will move faster without me.'

He looked at her, and a smile curved the corners of his lips.

'Isabel, you really don't understand your position, do you.' He moved closer to her and tucked a curl of her disordered hair behind her ear. 'Your value to me is priceless. God willing, we will reach the coast before our pursuers catch us, but if they don't, sweet Isabel, you are a valuable hostage. I will see you dead before I give myself up to be hanged.'

Her stomach lurched. She had no doubt Freddy would carry out his threat.

He jerked at the cord. 'We've no time to waste. Move, Isabel.'

When she didn't respond, he grabbed her arm and pulled her towards the muddy road. Trailing her bedraggled skirts, Isabel had no choice but to let herself be dragged along through the mud and the rain to what now seemed an even more uncertain fate.

The small threads of hope to which she had been clinging began to fade.

Chapter Fifty-Six

Sebastian swore aloud as his horse laboured through the mud. After the heavy rain, the track which passed for the road to Lidiford was mired and difficult going. They could follow the erratic path of the coach with ease but the men were making poor time. The horses struggled through the mud, each footstep adding another layer of cloying mud to their hooves and legs.

Bennet, riding ahead of the party, drew his horse to a sudden halt. The little corporal jumped down and ran over to inspect a dark shape half submerged in the flooded ditch beside the track. As Sebastian and Harry drew level, they could see it was the body of a man. The broken wheel and axle of a coach protruded from a large, water-filled pothole.

They pulled the body from the ditch and Harry turned the man over. Sebastian shook his head as he looked down into the heavy, uncompromising face.

'Jenkins.'

'His neck's broke. Nothing we can do for the poor bastard.' Bennet rose to his feet.

The trail left by the broken carriage stretched ahead of them.

Dreading what he might find, Sebastian indicated for Bennet to remount and they followed the mangled vegetation and freshly carved ruts until the wrecked carriage came into sight.

Sebastian reined Pharaoh in, fighting back a wave of nausea as the sight recalled another coach: a dead coachman sprawled on the dusty road, the escort of Portuguese soldiers lying tangled in pools of their own congealing blood, their bodies thick with flies, and Inez's broken and bloodied body...

He flung himself off his horse and was violently ill on the side of the road.

'Alder?' Harry's hand fell on his shoulder.

Sebastian shook off his friend's hand, his heart leaping in hope as he heard a woman's voice coming from behind the wrecked coach.

'Help me!'

Isabel?

With Harry following, he ran around to the back of the coach while Bennet dealt with the surviving coach horse. For a man who didn't like horses, Bennet had a good way with them.

Sebastian's heart fell when he saw Fanny, not Isabel, lying under a roughly constructed shelter that did little to keep out the persistent drizzle. Despite Freddy's attempts to provide his sister with some sort of shelter, the rain had soaked the blanket in which she had been wrapped. Her lips were blue with cold and shock and she looked up at them with grey-ringed eyes, her teeth chattering as her fingers plucked at the sodden blanket.

Sebastian looked down at her and, for a moment, he felt genuine pity, but then he recalled what this girl had done to him and the pity vanished. Lynch had probably relied on the rescuers stopping to give the girl aid and slowing down their pursuit of him. Every precious moment wasted on this girl put more time and distance between him and Isabel.

'Where are you hurt?' Harry knelt down beside her.

'My leg,' she moaned.

Harry lifted the blanket and her skirt away, revealing the truth of her statement. The lower part of her right leg twisted at an awkward angle through the torn stocking, the bruising and swelling clearly visible.

Sebastian stood over her, chafing with impatience. 'Where's your brother, Fanny?' he demanded. He had no more time or sympathy to spare for this lying, cheating girl.

'I don't know,' she sobbed.

'Where were you heading?'

'A village with fishing boats,' Fanny said unhelpfully.

Sebastian crouched down. He took Fanny's chin between his fingers and twisted her head so she looked straight at him.

'And Isabel? Was she hurt?'

Fanny's tear stained face crumpled again. 'I don't know. They went when I was unconscious. I woke up and found myself all alone. How could he just leave me?'

'Because your brother is a cold, heartless killer,' Sebastian said, releasing his grip on her.

'Steady on, Alder,' Harry reproved.

'You don't know him. You don't know why he had to do the things he did,' Fanny protested without conviction.

Sebastian rose to his feet and looked down at the girl. 'We're wasting time! Bennet, ride back to the nearest village and get help for Fanny. Colonel Dempster and I will continue on to Lidiford, if that's where he's heading.'

'Don't leave me!' Fanny's hand clawed at his boot.

He gave her no more than a cursory glance, knowing his disgust was written on his face.

'Bennet will be back soon enough. Coming, Dempster?'

Harry picked up Fanny's hand. 'Sorry, Miss Lynch,' he said. 'Just hang on a little longer. Corporal Bennet will fetch help for you.'

Sebastian snapped. 'She'll be fine for another hour. I can't do this without you, Harry! Are you coming?'

Harry rose to his feet in one swift movement, and they swung into their saddles and looked at each other with grim purpose written on their faces. Being on foot made Freddy a much easier target. They just had to make it to Lidiford before the turn of the tide.

Chapter Fifty-Seven

'Please, Freddy. I must rest.' Isabel clutched at the man's arm as she tripped over another puddled rut, sending her to her knees.

He had marched her through the unrelenting rain, dragging her unmercifully across the mire and the mud until she was soaked through to the skin. Her stout boots were sodden and heavy, and her feet felt like blocks of ice. They had encountered no one and had seen only distant dwellings. In this wild, desolate place, Isabel felt her hope fading.

Freddy turned and looked down at her. Water dripped from a lock of his rain-darkened hair on to his nose. He looked as exhausted as she felt. He jerked on the cord, dragging her back to her feet.

'I can see the village,' he said.

Isabel raised her head, her teeth chattering with the cold, her thoughts immediately turning to warm food, a fire and dry clothes.

'Is there an inn?'

Freddy looked down at her. 'An inn? By now, Isabel, I'll have half the county on my heels. No, first we have to find the fisherman the boy told me of.'

'For pity's sake, Freddy!'

'I'll find somewhere dry first,' he conceded.

Towing his reluctant charge, Freddy skirted the village. It was a poor place without a church or an inn that Isabel could see, the rough dwellings gathered around a tidal creek that ran out into the Wash. Behind the village, a few meagre agricultural lots provided the sustenance for the villagers.

About half a dozen fishing boats were anchored in the estuary, the angle of list indicating that they rested on the mud flats. They would wait until the tide rose and carried them out to sea.

That thought sparked hope in her heart again. They would not be sailing until the tide had turned. That gave her rescuers a little more time to find them.

Freddy led her down to the dunes and she saw what had attracted his attention: a hut, no more than a few bent boughs covered with whatever debris could be found. It looked like the sort of thing children would build. He pushed aside the leather skin that served as a door. A rough hearth in the middle of the floor set with an old cooking pot and a kettle, a low stool, a few cracked plates,you and a bed of sorts laid over rough planking gave the simple dwelling a rustic humanity.

Freddy thrust her down on the bed and pulled a stinking—and no doubt vermin-infested—blanket around her shoulders. Despite its odour of rotting fish and sweat, Isabel huddled into its warmth

'Can we light a fire?' she suggested, through chattering teeth.

'Don't be a fool! I don't want to attract attention.'

'But somebody lives here,' she protested

Freddy kicked at the roughly made hearth. 'There's been no one here for days.' He looked around the hovel. 'Lie down on the bed.'

Isabel stared up at him, her heart hammering in her chest. He surely didn't intend—?

Freddy's lip curled. 'Don't look at me like that. Believe me, I've no interest in what's beneath your skirts. I'm just going to secure you while I find the man I'm looking for. I would hate for you to go running off.'

Rope of varying kinds seemed to be in plentiful supply, and he bound her ankles. To make doubly sure, he ran a rope from her wrists to her ankles and gagged her with a strip of cloth torn from her petticoat. When he was done, he covered her with the verminous blanket.

Trussed like a Christmas goose, Isabel could do no more than watch helplessly as the leather flap fell across the door. She forced herself to close her eyes and try to sleep, but the cramps in her bound wrists kept her wakeful. She wondered about the time. The dank weather made it almost impossible to judge. It could still be an hour or so until full tide—still time for a search party to catch up with them.

Whoever came, it would not be Sebastian. For the first time she allowed herself to think of him, his terrible death: burned alive in the stables. Her eyes filled with tears, and she sniffed, wishing she could blow her nose.

Eventually, she must have dozed, only waking when someone shook her shoulder. She woke with a start, hope fading when she looked up into Freddy's cold blue eyes. He sat down beside her and began to undo the ropes that bound her.

'We've about an hour,' he said as he worked. 'I've paid the man well. He'll have his boat standing off the beach at six.'

As he untied her wrists, she flexed her fingers, tentatively rotating her sore wrist. It did not appear to be swollen or badly injured, but it still hurt.

He thrust a hunk of bread at her, and she tore into it hungrily. As she ate, his fingers stroked the back of her neck. Her skin crawled but she couldn't risk aggravating him.

'It will be all right, Isabel. I'll take care of you, just like I always took care of Fanny. Everything I did was for her.' His tone had become light and musing.

She turned her face to look at him. 'What was it you did for Fanny?'

His fingers dropped from her neck. 'Everything. They wanted to send us to the workhouse but I took Fanny and ran away to London to make my fortune. We were rescued by a man.' He gave a twisted, humourless smile. 'He ran a house for other gentlemen. I don't suppose you know of such places.'

'A molly house?'

Freddy turned to look at her and she could see shock in his eyes. At first, Isabel thought his surprise might be caused by the fact she knew about molly houses, but his lip curled back in a sneer.

'What do you take me for? This house catered for the needs of gentlemen, not the common rabble.'

'And you... you provided services to these gentlemen?'

He looked away. 'I was only sixteen and I had Fanny to think of. They put her to work in the kitchen. She was only a little thing and I don't think she ever had any idea what went on upstairs.'

For the first time, Isabel felt a flicker of sympathy for Freddy. A desperate boy with a pretty face must have been easy prey for a procurer.

'The money was good, and it had some perks. I learned to cheat at cards, and I learned how to be a gentleman. All useful skills.'

'That's where you met Anthony?' The pieces of the puzzle were beginning to fall into place.

In a small, tight voice, she asked, 'Was he ...? Was he your lover?'

Freddy looked down at his hands as if inspecting his fingernails. 'He frequented my house, but he had his favourite and it wasn't me. Then he stopped coming, and I didn't think anything more about him 'til I went to a soiree with one of my clients and saw him with you.'

Isabel drew away from him. 'Me?'

'You wouldn't remember. Those were the days when you were

trying to be a good wife, laughing, and being the lady. Were you in love with Anthony?'

Isabel turned her mind back to those early years of their marriage. She had tried to be the wife she thought Lord Somerton wanted. The gall rose in her throat. She had no inkling of this secret life; his predilection for men. He had never been an enthusiastic lover but how would she have known any better?

'Did you not wonder what he did on those trips to London after you retired to the country?'

There had been the stories that had filtered back to her of his womanising. Had that, too, been a charade played out for public benefit?

Freddy stretched out his legs.

'He drifted back to us,' he said with a smile. 'Anthony wanted to resume the friendship with my friend. He wrote some lovely letters but the poor boy was dying of consumption and gave them to me for safekeeping. You should see the letters, Isabel. Your darling husband laid his heart on the page. When my friend died, I made it my business to help poor Anthony in his grief. We became very close and of course I had his letters.'

So that was it. Letters. Were the letters that Freddy had in his possession enough to hang her husband for sodomy?

'Then he wanted it all to end.' Freddy's face screwed up like a small child deprived of a treat.

'I wasn't going to let him go that easily, so Fanny and I came to live at Brantstone.' He smirked. 'Anthony was not pleased but he came to accept the situation.'

'You were blackmailing him with the letters?'

Freddy smiled. 'They would have hanged him. He was very explicit.'

'Were you and he,' Isabel swallowed, 'lovers under my roof?'

Freddy's lips twitched.

'No. Believe me when I say it was not my natural inclination and now I was free of the house I could pursue my own interests. It all went wrong when he found where I had hidden the letters and destroyed them. He was going to throw Fan and me out onto the street, and when I threatened to tell you, he said he'd already confessed everything. He said there'd been too many lies. He wanted to start all over again but it was too late.'

Her blood ran cold and she forced the next words out through tight lips.

'Is that why you killed him?'

'I didn't intend for him to die. It was supposed to be a warning.' Freddy sighed. 'And then that upstart Alder came along. He was never going to cooperate, so he had to die.' Freddie yawned and stretched. 'Move over. I think I will rest for a short while.'

Freddy rose to his feet and, grabbing Isabel's wrists, bound them together in front of her, tying the end of the rope to his own wrist. If she moved he would know.

He lay down on the narrow pallet beside her. His close proximity, the stink of his body, and the smell of long dead fish that clung to the shack began to overwhelm her. Her stomach heaved and the bile rose in her throat. She took a deep breath, forcing herself to breathe through the nausea.

'We've wasted enough time, Isabel. There'll be plenty of time to talk when we are on a ship for the continent. A whole lifetime to get to know each other properly. Where do you want to go first? I've always wanted to see Italy,' Freddy mused with his eyes shut.

Isabel lay rigid beside him. She held her breath. If she let him sleep, he might miss the tide. She screwed her eyes tight shut and prayed.

Chapter Fifty-Eight

Sebastian shivered as another blast of cold rain slewed off the marsh, penetrating his saturated cloak and sending cold, watery fingers down his back. He dismounted and waited for Harry to catch up with him. Harry's horse had begun to favour a leg over the last mile, so he had dismounted and had to lead it on foot.

Pharaoh, as cold and weary as his master, threw his head up and whinnied. Sebastian leaned forward and patted the horse's sodden neck.

'It's all right, old boy. This is it.'

Through the rain and driving wind he could see the dark, squat shapes of buildings rising out of the bleak, miserable landscape.

'I can see the village. Not far now,' he said as Harry joined him.

Harry nodded and Sebastian spared his old friend a second glance. Harry looked exhausted. The events of the last twenty-four hours had tested both of them. Without needing to speak, the two men led their horses into the village of Lidiford. Although the ragged collection of rough dwellings hardly deserved so grand a title as 'village'.

A quick glance at the water showed them the tide was nearly in and the fishermen were aboard their craft readying the little boats to sail.

From the shoreline, Harry hailed the nearest boat. A scraggly bearded man leaned over the rail, his hand to his ear as Harry shouted through the wind and rain, 'We're looking for a man and a woman that may have come this way.'

The man scratched his beard and looked up at the leaden sky.

'Strangers?'

'Aye,' Sebastian said.

'We don't get many strangers down here.' The man rubbed his nose. 'Don't know about no woman, but I did see a man talking to Tom Parkins.'

He indicated a boat that had begun to set its sail.

Harry thanked the man and they set off on foot down the bank.

'Hey, you!' Sebastian shouted across the water.

The man on the boat looked across at him but did not respond. He turned his back and continued hauling up the sail.

'We're looking for a man and a woman who are seeking passage across the channel,' Harry called out.

The man kept his back resolutely to the shore, and the little boat began to slip out along the channel towards the estuary.

Harry and Sebastian exchanged glances and, without speaking, ran back to the horses. They swung into the saddles and turned the horses to follow the patched sail as the boat met the sea on the turning tide.

Chapter Fifty-Nine

Isabel lay braced and alert next to Freddy as the minutes ticked past with agonising slowness. Her heart fell as he jerked awake, sitting up and pulling his watch from his pocket. He swore and, extracting a knife from his boot, sawed at Isabel's bonds, leaving the gag in her mouth.

He hauled her to her feet and pulled her towards the entrance. When she resisted, a blow from his left hand sent her sprawling.

'I don't have time for nonsense, you stupid bitch. I slept too long. If we don't hurry we'll miss the boat.'

With her ears ringing and the taste of blood in her mouth, she could do nothing except let him pull her to her feet and push her out of the doorway.

Running now, Freddy dragged her across the dunes and down towards the seashore. The wet sand marked the retreating tide.

Freddy swore again and stopped dead, waving an arm in the direction of a little boat, its red sail raised, that traversed the estuary out of a creek mouth and into the broad water. Isabel's heart lurched. Was this their transportation? Were they too late?

Hope kindled for a moment and then extinguished as the man on the boat waved an acknowledgment.

Freddy pulled her down to the water's edge, propelling her towards the water, which lapped at her ankles, filling her boots. She shook her head, resisting his restraining hand. He responded by putting his arm around her shoulder, drawing her closer.

'He's going to bring the boat in close. You'll get a little wet, my dear, but I don't think that will matter. When we reach Holland, you can have all the dresses you desire.'

He pushed her forward, and she stumbled, going down on her knees in the cold water.

He cursed and pulled her to her feet. 'Get a move on,' he said.

A shout from the man on the boat, carried on the wind, reached them, and Isabel could see the man pointing down the beach. She turned to see where he indicated and gave a joyful gurgle as she saw two horses, emerging from the estuary onto the sand. The riders kicked their horses into a gallop and would be on them within a few breaths. Her heart soared as she recognised the black horse—Pharaoh. Surely only one man could ride that beast with such assurance.

Freddy's gaze moved from the horsemen to the boat and back again. He pulled out his knife and, with one hand under Isabel's chin, tilted her head back, exposing her throat. He held the knife against her throat as the horsemen drew to a shuddering halt some fifteen yards from where Isabel and Freddy stood knee deep in water.

Isabel raised her eyes, hardly daring to hope.

He was alive ... alive.

She closed her eyes, hardly daring to open them again in case this was a vision—an apparition. But it was Sebastian, hatless, his dark hair plastered wetly to his scalp, his face lined with exhaustion.

''Bastian ...' She gurgled his name behind the gag that bound her.

'Don't come any closer,' Freddy shouted, his words disappearing in the rain-laden wind.

'Isabel!' That low, well-beloved voice.

She must have moved. Freddy's knife bit into the flesh of her neck, and warm blood trickled down her neckline.

'Stay very still, Isabel, and you won't get hurt,' Freddy said, his mouth so close to her ear that she felt his breath. 'The boat is just offshore. We're going out to meet it.'

Isabel cried out in alarm, struggling within Freddy's grasp as she tried to communicate to him that she could not swim and had a fear of water. Memories of a small, dark face, struggling in the grip of the blue waters of Jamaica, came back to her, and her breath came in strangled bursts, tears starting in her eyes.

He ignored her and, tightening his grip on her, walked backwards into the water, his eyes on the two horsemen.

Icy cold water lapped around her legs, dragging at her skirts. She tried to pry Freddy's hand away from her neck, but his grip was immutable.

A wave crashed against them. Isabel's feet gave way, upsetting Freddy's balance and forcing him to loosen his grip on her. He gave a cry of frustration and seized her wrist, dragging her through the waves.

They were in deep water now, and the little boat seemed no closer. Freddy gave up on his efforts to hold on to Isabel and released his grip on her, kicking away from her in his effort to strike out for the boat.

Freddy now became the only thing between Isabel and certain death. She thrashed at him, clawing, struggling to hold on to him, but he pushed her away and already weakened by the day's headlong events, Isabel's strength began to wane. Every grab for air rewarded her with a mouthful of water. The water monsters dragged at her skirts, tugging her down into their cold, grey lairs. Fear and panic sapped her strength.

Distantly, she could hear Sebastian calling her name, but he couldn't reach her now. Instead, she heard the gurgling laugh of a small child, and she smiled, seeing her son William's golden hair and soft smile. She stopped struggling and reached for him, letting the water monsters claim her for their own.

Chapter Sixty

As Freddy began his headlong plunge towards the boat, Sebastian could do little except watch. He knew Freddy was quite capable of plunging the knife into Isabel's neck if he or Harry so much as twitched.

He tensed as a wave knocked Freddy and his hostage off their feet. Freddy's grip on Isabel appeared to loosen. Now was his chance. Sebastian turned Pharaoh's head, and the horse plunged willingly into the water, his ears pricked. Like most horses, Pharaoh liked water. He capered like a young foal, pulling resentfully against Sebastian's hand, but Sebastian held him steady.

Glancing behind him, Freddy plunged on, dragging Isabel through the water like a broken doll. They disappeared from view as the waves crashed over them, and next time Sebastian saw Freddy, he appeared to be alone, striking out for the boat with a firm stroke.

'Isabel!' Sebastian screamed into the wind, but no answer came.

A wave crashed against the horse's chest. As it passed, a dark shape floated face down in the calm water between the waves, only ten yards from him.

A cry of pure, physical pain escaped from him, and he forced the horse onwards. She couldn't have drowned, not in so short a time, but as he reached her, the cold fear grabbed his heart. Isabel floated face down, unmoving, her skirts swirling around her, her loosened hair drifting like seaweed, her arms outstretched.

Sebastian seized her by the back of her gown, hauling her across the bow of his saddle. He no longer cared if Freddy reached the boat or not. He had Isabel, and that was all that mattered. Without a backward glance, he turned the horse's head back to shore.

Harry had already dismounted, and he took Isabel from Sebastian as he slid off the horse. Together, they laid her gently on the sand.

Sebastian's heart clenched as he smoothed back the wet, tangled hair from her pale face. Her lips were a faint bluish colour, and dark circles ringed her closed eyes. Hardly daring to trust himself, he felt for a pulse but could feel nothing except the frantic beating of his own heart.

He looked at Harry. He needed Harry's calm right now.

'You try.'

Harry placed his fingers on the pulse of Isabel's neck. He frowned and then a slow smile spread across his face.

'She's alive.'

Harry rolled her onto her side and thumped her back. Isabel coughed, retching up sea water. She fell back on the sand, her eyes fluttering open.

Sebastian picked up her hand and began to chafe it, trying to restore the circulation to her frozen limbs. She looked up into Sebastian's eyes and smiled.

'You're not dead,' she whispered.

'And neither are you.' His voice gruff with emotion.

News of the excitement on the beach must have spread through the village, and a crowd of strangers surrounded them filling the void with shouts and cheers.

A large, motherly woman elbowed her way through the gawking crowd.

'You must get her to some warmth. There's no inn here but ye're welcome to come to my home.'

'Thank you.'

Sebastian acknowledged the generous offer and took off his heavy Garrick overcoat. He wrapped Isabel in its damp folds. Even wet, it was some protection from the cold. He rose to his feet with Isabel in his arms, but the distance back to the village was too great for him to carry her, so he set her on her feet, letting Harry support her as he mounted Pharaoh and lifted her in front of him, folding her closely in his arms.

Before they set off, he cast a quick glance out to sea where the sail of the fishing boat bobbed just above the horizon.

'Did he make it to the boat?' he asked Harry.

Harry shook his head. 'I don't know. Personally, I hope he's gone to hell.'

Isabel shivered, and Sebastian looked down at her. 'It doesn't matter anymore. He's gone. Come, my lady, let's get you to a warm bed.'

''Bastian,' she whispered.

He pressed her closer and kissed the top of her head.

Isabel was alive and he was never letting her go again.

Chapter Sixty-One

The woman, who gave her name as Mother Shipton, had one of the larger cottages in the village. A cheerful fire crackled in the hearth of what looked to be the one living room. Sebastian set Isabel down on a chair beside the fire. She clung to him, shivering so much that her teeth chattered. He folded his arms around her, trying to instil some warmth into her.

The old lady bustled in after them. 'Sir? Do 'e have a name tha's willing to share?'

'Of course, I'm sorry. Lord Somerton, and this is Lady Somerton.'

The woman's eyes widened, and she bobbed a curtsey, glancing around the sparse room.

'Oh, my lord, I'm sorry I can do no better for ye.'

Sebastian shook his head and smiled at her. 'It will do us fine. We just need somewhere to dry off and rest.'

'Then let's get her leddyship upstairs and into a warm bed.'

Sebastian lifted Isabel into his arms and carried her up narrow stairs to a sleeping chamber. The room was dominated by a large bed surmounted by a headboard on which were carved scenes of the sea life of the village. Intricate carvings of shells and pebbles twisted in a border around the scenes of little boats crashing through waves that beat into a bleak shoreline.

'You leave her leddyship to me. I've a clean nightgown here and I'll find ye some dry clothes as well. Ye'll not be leaving before daybreak so ye're both welcome to my bed.'

Realising her error, Sebastian opened his mouth to explain 'Lady Somerton' was not his wife, but she shooed him from the room, before he could speak.

He returned to the warm, homely kitchen, where he found Harry sitting in a chair beside the fire, pulling his wet boots off. Harry looked up. Now the excitement had passed, his friend looked drawn and grey with weariness and Sebastian realised that every bone in his own body ached with sheer physical exhaustion.

'I've seen to the horses.' Harry gave him a rueful smile and ran a hand across his eyes. 'You and I have been through some adventures, Alder, but today was a close-run thing.'

Sebastian crossed over to the fire and stood in front of Harry. Steam rose from his damp clothes, almost scalding his skin. The sting reminded him he was alive.

'How's the hand?' Harry asked.

Sebastian looked down at the dirty bandage encircling the cut on the palm of his hand. He had spared it no thought for the last few hours. Now it started to throb.

'It's fine,' he lied.

Harry ran a hand over his unshaven chin. 'If you let me take Pharaoh, I'll ride back to the nearest civilisation and send a message on to Brantstone from there. You'll need a coach for Lady Somerton.'

'You need to rest too, Harry,' Sebastian said. 'I know you were out looking for them most of the night, and it's already been a hard day without another couple of hours ride.'

Harry rose to his feet and clapped his friend on the shoulder.

'You're alive. Lady Somerton is safe. Your reputation is

restored, and the imposters are discovered. I'd call that a good day's work.'

'A man is dead, my stables are razed, my coach destroyed, one of my best coach horses dead, and the villain has evaded capture. Something of a pyrrhic victory, I'd call it.'

Harry smiled and glanced out of the window as he pulled his boots back on. 'It won't look so bleak in the morning. I'd better get going before it turns dark on me.'

'Travel safely.'

Harry grinned. 'There'll be a warm inn and a good supper for me in a couple of hours. You enjoy a well-earned rest.'

With a wink, he turned on his heel and went back out into the appalling weather.

'Oh, has your friend left already?' Mother Shipton appeared at the door with a neatly folded pile of clothes in her hand.

'Yes. He's gone to send a message to my home, but it will be tomorrow before they get a coach to us. I hope you don't mind us intruding on your hospitality.'

'Not at all. 'Tis an honour to have such a fine gentleman and lady with me.' The old woman handed over the clothes. 'These belonged to my Jos. He were a big man like you, so they should fit. If you give me your wet things, I'll dry 'em by the fire along with her leddyship's clothes.'

Sebastian looked around the little room, wondering where he could get changed.

'I'll see to some broth for your good lady. There's nowt you've got I haven't seen before.'

Giggling to herself, she turned her back on him and Sebastian stripped off his sodden clothing. The simple clothes that had once belonged to her 'Jos' fitted well and reminded Sebastian of another time, not so very long ago, when he would have called such clothes his own. He sank into a chair by the fire.

Mother Shipton took the pile of wet clothes and set his sodden boots to dry by the fire while Sebastian downed a very good fish broth with fresh bread that she set in front of him.

When he had put the wooden bowl to one side, the old woman produced clean bandages and redressed the wound on his hand, slathering a vile-smelling unguent on the cut. Sebastian's nose twitched and the old woman chuckled.

'Aye, it smells bad, my lord, but I guarantee within a day ye'll not know ye've been hurt.' She pointed at the stairs. 'You go and be with your lady, m'lord. I'll not disturb you.'

Chapter Sixty-Two

Isabel closed her eyes and sank back against the feather bolsters in Mother Shipton's bed, letting the events of the past twenty-four hours circle and collide in her tired mind. Surprisingly, she felt no urge to sleep. She was warm and dry, and the excellent fish broth had revived her.

She threw back the bedcovers and, holding up the voluminous folds of what was probably Mother Shipton's best nightdress, padded over to the little window. It had gone dark, and only the lights from the other dwellings in the village illuminated the night. Rain still pattered on the panes, but the worst of the storm had passed. She wrapped her arms around herself, remembering the howling wind and the crashing waves and how close she had been to death.

She heard the front door shut and watched as Harry, his head bent against the wind, walked out into what passed for a street. He disappeared around a corner, and she turned her attention back to the events of the day.

Had Freddy made it to the safety of the boat, or had he drowned in the attempt? Unless his body washed up on the shore, she might never know. Images of Freddy's wild eyes as he dragged her to what could have been her death clawed at her, and she closed her eyes, consigning them to a dark place.

Sebastian had pulled her from the sea. Sebastian had saved her life and she had nothing to give him in return except her love, and she would give that gladly.

Sebastian.

A smile twitched the corners of her mouth and she hugged herself tighter. Sebastian—alive, his dark eyes full of love and concern as he bent over her on the beach.

More than anything in the world, she wanted him here to hold her. She wanted a chance to say those precious words that had been on the tip of her tongue on the night of the ball.

As if on cue, a firm rap sounded on the door.

'Come in,' she said.

He paused in the doorway, his eyes widening at the sight of the peculiar garment that enveloped her.

'Good lord, what on earth are you wearing?'

She held out the nightdress and smiled. 'I think this night-dress would hold four of me.'

He took a step into the room, closing the door behind him. He came to stand beside her, his hands behind his back as they both looked out of the window into the dark, damp night.

Her nose twitched. A strange, slightly fishy smell seemed to be emanating from Lord Somerton.

'Sebastian, I hate to be personal, but you do smell a little... odd.'

He looked down at his bandaged hand.

'I'm afraid Mother Shipton took it into her head to dress the cut on my hand. She slathered this stuff on before I could stop her. I did have a go at trying to wipe it off, but the smell lingers, I'm afraid.'

Isabel put a finger to her nose. 'Oh, dear.'

'And I am afraid we have something of a dilemma, Lady Somerton.'

'A dilemma?'

'Mother Shipton seems to think we are man and wife.'

'Oh?'

'And there is nowhere else for me to sleep except in this room, without appearing somewhat strange,' Sebastian said.

'What are we to do?' Isabel responded, trying to keep the edge of laughter from her voice.

If a night in this man's arms loomed, she felt not one jot of guilt or embarrassment at the thought.

'Hmm... There is always the chair,' Sebastian observed, looking at the rickety object. 'I could sleep on the floor if you don't mind lending me a bolster and blanket from your bed. Don't worry, I'm quite used to sleeping on the ground.'

Isabel looked up at him in disbelief. The answer for her was simple. She wanted him in the bed with her, Mother Shipton's unguent notwithstanding. She wanted to curl up in his arms and whatever followed, she would welcome.

But how did one seduce a man? Lady Kendall seemed to have no difficulty with obtuse members of the opposite sex. She would know exactly what to do or say, whereas Isabel felt as ignorant as a nun.

'Lady Somerton, you have a face like a book.' Sebastian smiled, and she could see he had been teasing her.

'Sebastian Alder—'

He shook his head and laid a finger on her mouth, turning her to face him. He cradled her face in his hands, tilting her face upwards. Her knees turned to water, and she leaned in against him, the warmth of desire suffusing her body. In his eyes, she saw the answering hunger.

'Isabel.' Her name sighed from his lips as he bent to kiss her.

She pressed against him, opening her mouth to receive him, feeling the heat run through her as his lips brushed hers. She meshed her fingers in his hair, holding him to her. He pressed her close to him, and she realised he wanted her as badly as she wanted him.

She tore at his borrowed shirt, pulling it over his head as he fumbled with the buttons on his breeches. With a growl, he scooped her up in his arms and carried her to the bed.

He threw her backwards onto the bed and crouched over her, looking down at her, his eyes blazing with desire.

'Off with that appalling piece of cloth,' he croaked, tugging the shift over her head.

'You are more beautiful than I ever imagined,' he whispered, but the smile faded as he touched the myriad bruises and scratches that were the legacy of the headlong flight and the coach accident.

'Oh, Isabel,' he said, and she caught the underlying growl of anger. 'If I could have caught that man.'

She shook her head. 'He's gone, Sebastian. He can't hurt either of us now. The bruises will fade and the tale will become a good one to tell at supper.' She touched the bandage on his hand. 'And you have another scar to add to your catalogue.'

Ignoring the lingering smell of the unguent, she kissed his hand, and Sebastian responded with soft, gentle butterfly kisses, on her lips, her throat, her breastbone, seeking out the soft place at the base of her throat.

'Bas,' she whispered.

'Shh.' He placed a finger on her lips. 'No words, Isabel.'

She closed her eyes, as they came together, two broken souls who were finally learning to heal and to love.

※

LATER, SEBASTIAN LAY BESIDE HER, ONE ARM FLUNG ACROSS HIS forehead as Isabel curled up against him, resting her head in the comfortable circle of his other arm. She dared not speak, dared not spoil the moment of exquisite closeness with another human being.

She propped herself up on her elbow and he stroked her hair as she bent her head and touched his golden flesh with her lips, tracing the line from his neck to his naval, tasting the residual saltiness. She'd nursed him when he'd been ill, and she thought she knew the hard, muscular planes of his body, but there was much more to discover.

His chest rose and fell as he sighed, his fingers stroking her neck. For a moment, she had a memory of Freddy doing something similar and stiffened. Sebastian sensed her disquiet and stopped, looking at her with a frown creasing his brow.

'Isabel?'

She shook her head. Freddy had gone, swallowed up by the sea or halfway to Holland. He could never touch her again. This man—this dear, honourable man—was the love of her life, and she would surrender herself to him without hesitation.

She smiled at him. 'Nothing.'

'I meant what I said the night of the ball. I love you, Isabel. What I didn't get a chance to do was to ask you to marry me.'

'You were going to ask me to marry you?' Isabel sat up.

'Yes. What would you have said?'

She looked at him and slowly shook her head. 'I don't know what I would have said. That night already seems like a lifetime ago. The world has changed for us, Sebastian. What I might or might not have done a few days ago means nothing now.'

She ran her fingers across his forehead, twisting the locks of dark brown hair that fell across his forehead.

'I only know that when I thought you were dead, Freddy could have killed me and I would not have cared.'

He cupped her face in his hand. 'Say it, Isabel.'

She knew what he wanted to hear. The words she had never spoken in her life.

'I love you, Sebastian Alder.'

A slow smile caught the corners of his mouth. 'Was that so very hard?'

She shook her head. 'Not for you.'

His finger strayed down her throat, and he pulled her down on top of him.

'You smell of the sea,' he whispered. 'This will be how I will always remember you: my sea nymph.'

'Hardly,' she laughed. 'I nearly died out there.'

'But you didn't. Now kiss me, sea nymph.'

Chapter Sixty-Three

A weak grey daylight broke fitfully over the little fishing village. Sebastian opened his eyes and looked out through the dusty window at the lowering sky and then down at the woman in his arms. They had both been so tired that they had hardly shifted their position all night. He kissed the top of her head, and she stirred, snuggling deeper into his embrace.

He loved the way she fitted so well into the curve of his body, as if she had always belonged there. He traced the line of her nose and kissed her.

'Let's stay here forever,' she murmured, rolling onto her back and stretching like a contented cat.

'Take up fishing and live the life of a peasant?' he suggested. 'Nothing wrong with living simply. I was always very happy in Little Benning.'

'I was happy in Little Benning too,' Isabel agreed.

He stroked her cheek. 'Unfortunately for us, my darling girl, that is fantasy. The reality is that I have responsibilities now that extend beyond just keeping my brother and sister clothed and fed. I now have tenants and servants who rely on me.'

She turned to face him, her face so close to his that their foreheads touched. 'You are a fine Lord Somerton, Sebastian.'

'And you were already a fine Lady Somerton.'

She smiled. 'What do you mean?'

'I am asking you again to marry me, Isabel. You didn't give me an answer last night.'

She touched his face and smiled.

'Yes.'

His heart swelled, and he buried his face in her hair, overcome with the emotion that flooded him. He kissed her with such passion that he thought he would lose himself in her, but any thought of making love again was interrupted by a gentle knock on the door.

'I hope I haven't woken you,' Mother Shipton's voice called from the far side, 'but I've got some breakfast set for ye and your clothes are dry. I'll just leave 'em outside the door here. Come down when you're ready.'

Sebastian flung his arms over his head and groaned.

'I suppose the day must be faced.'

'This has been our own little world, Sebastian. Will our normal world be the same?'

He swung his legs out of the bed and sat up, looking down at her slender body, half concealed by the bedclothes. The nasty bruises on the delicate flesh looked so much worse in the daylight and his anger rose at the thought of Freddy and the damage he could have wrought—had already wrought.

'Nothing will ever be the same again, my dearest, and that is a good thing,' he whispered, stooping to kiss her again

Dressed and tidied as best they could manage in their salt-encrusted clothes, Sebastian and Isabel ate a simple breakfast of bread, cheese and small beer. Sebastian hadn't shaved in two days and, although Isabel had tied her hair back, long salt-stiffened wisps escaped around her face.

She pulled a face, trying to tidy the curls away. Sebastian thought she had never looked so beautiful.

'It needs to be washed in fresh water,' she said. 'I long for a proper bath.'

'It will be some hours before the coach reaches us, Lady Somerton. Would you care for a walk along the beach?' Sebastian asked

Every bone and muscle in her body ached, but Isabel agreed, and they stepped out into the cool day. He wrapped his arm around her, folding her into the voluminous Garrick, and together they walked down through the dunes to the scene of the drama of the previous day.

The rain had cleared and the sea had withdrawn far into the Wash, leaving a broad expanse of glistening sand. The little fishing boats were back, listing on the sand and mud and waiting for the next high tide. Sebastian stopped on the side of the creek to ask about the boat that Freddy had commissioned to take him to France.

The man he addressed scratched his beard and looked out at the boats on the creek bed.

'Not back yet,' he said.

Sebastian turned back to look at Isabel. There was no need for words. The grim look on Isabel's face was reflected in his own. It would appear that Freddy had escaped.

'There's no justice,' Isabel whispered, slipping her hand into his, 'but he's gone. Nothing more we can do.'

Sebastian squeezed her hand, his heart overflowing with love for her ...her courage and her stoicism.

Hand in hand, they walked along the shore. Out of sight of the village, Sebastian pulled Isabel down beside him on the sand. They sat side by side, looking out to sea.

'Did you find Fanny?' Isabel asked.

Sebastian nodded. 'She was feeling a little sorry for herself, but she should live.'

'I wish I could feel some pity for Fanny, but I don't,' Isabel said.

Sebastian gathered her hand in his and kissed her fingers.

'You can't force yourself to feel an emotion, Isabel, but if you can't feel pity, at least forgive her.'

'I hear your stepfather in those words, Sebastian,' she said.

'Possibly.'

'Did you forgive the murderers of Inez?'

Sebastian picked up a piece of driftwood and drew patterns in the damp sand while he considered the answer.

'Yes,' he said at last. 'If I hadn't forgiven them, the hatred would have consumed me.' He looked up at the sky and added, 'Mind you, I killed them first.'

'Sebastian!' Isabel pushed him and he fell back on the sand, pulling her with him.

He rolled over until he was on top of her and kissed her. She put her hands around his head, pulling his face down towards her, and they kissed long and hard, exploring each other in a different way to their passionate lovemaking of the previous night.

When they were spent, they lay side by side on the sand, looking up at the clouds scudding across the sky.

'Freddy told me that he used to work in a place that serviced the needs of gentlemen. He had been procured at the age of sixteen,' Isabel said.

'A molly house?' Sebastian said as the snippets of Freddy's life fell into place.

Isabel nodded and related what Freddy had told her of his early life and the reason for the blackmail.

When she had done so, she shuddered. 'I almost felt sorry for him. A young man with the responsibility for a much younger sister has few options.'

'There were other ways he could have made a living,' Sebastian pointed out. 'He chose his path because it was an easy assurance of quick money and provided ample opportunity for adding to the purse through other means, like blackmail.'

'I was so naive. It never occurred to me that Anthony was so deeply unhappy. I just thought he didn't want me.'

'Did Freddy tell you why he thought Anthony had to be punished?' Sebastian asked.

'Anthony found the letters he had been using for the blackmail and refused to pay him. Freddy maintains he didn't intend for him to die, but then he had no conscience when it came to burning you alive, so I'm not certain I believe him.'

Sebastian put his hands behind his head. 'My stepfather once told me that there are four reasons men kill: love, hate, self-defence and money. Freddy had been blackmailing Anthony, and the money had dried up, but there was more to it than that. Freddy wanted the trappings of wealth. He craved respectability. Anthony was about to take all that away from him and throw him back on to the streets. As for your husband, I think Anthony was tired of leading his duplicitous life. He'd confessed to you and probably intended to work something out that would suit you both. From what Freddy and Georgiana Kendall both told me, he really did love you. I just don't think he knew how to show love.'

A tear dribbled down Isabel's cheek and she dashed it away.

'He was so different when William was born. For a little while, I thought that we had reached that amicable relationship. That's when I gave him the saddle. But after William died, he just turned on me. How is that love?'

'Grief affects people in different ways, Isabel. I can't answer for his actions.'

To prevent her from interrogating him further, he silenced her questions with his lips, and Isabel settled herself into the curve of his arm, her head resting against his shoulder. He kissed the honey-coloured hair, tasting the salt on his lips and pushing all thoughts of Freddy and Anthony away. He had been given another chance at love, and he was determined he would not lose this person or let the dark past shadow their future happiness.

'Alder! Put that woman down!'

He heard his name on the wind and sat up to see two figures coming up the beach towards them. Isabel also sat up, her face pink with embarrassment. She tried to secure her wayward hair, but even Sebastian could see it needed a good wash and a comb. Nothing she could do would make her look anything less than a bedraggled sea nymph, and he loved her more for it.

They struggled to their feet, brushing sand from their clothes as Harry and Matt reached them. The younger man looked deathly pale and his arm was in a sling. Another figure, her blue dress flapping in the wind as she struggled to hold her bonnet, came running up the beach behind the men.

Connie threw herself not at Sebastian, but Isabel.

'I am so glad you are all right. I feared the worst when I heard that monster had taken you! Did he hurt you?'

Isabel returned the girl's warm embrace.

'No, he didn't hurt me. Just a few bruises.'

Connie turned to Sebastian, standing on tiptoes to give him a warm, sisterly kiss.

'I thought I told you to wait in the coach,' Matt chided.

Connie turned and gave her brother a hard stare.

Sebastian laughed. 'Surely you didn't entertain the notion your sister would listen to a word you say, Matt.' He drew them both towards him, folding them in his arms. 'I can't tell you how pleased I am to see you both, and you, Harry. What news?'

Harry shook his head. 'Bennet has seen Miss Lynch lodged with a widow in Hazlemere, and her leg has been set.' He glanced at Matt. 'We stopped on the way and found Miss Lynch in a distressed state, as you can imagine. Is there any news of her brother?'

Sebastian shook his head. 'In the absence of a body, we can only assume he made good his escape.'

'With all my jewellery. Enough to set himself up in some style,' Isabel observed. 'I think Fanny may well have seen the last of her brother.'

Harry patted his coat. 'We found a box full of Somerton silver and expensive trinkets in the ruined coach and I have a signed statement from Miss Lynch giving her account of matters as she knows them and exonerating you, Alder, of any responsibility towards her.'

'It's always nice to know I am not a rapist,' Sebastian observed drily. He glanced out to sea. 'I'm anxious to get back to Brantstone. Both Lady Somerton and I could do with a hot bath and some clean clothes.'

'You do look rather disreputable,' Matt said with a cheeky grin. 'Did you sleep well?'

'Very,' Sebastian replied with a smile. 'Now, has anyone got any money I can leave with old Mother Shipton for our board?'

Chapter Sixty-Four

A week after the turbulent events at Lidiford, Sebastian stood at the end of Fanny's bed and looked down at the miserable young woman, who sniffled into her handkerchief. He tried to dredge up some shred of pity for Fanny Lynch, but the memory of how close he had come to being forced to marry the wretch made him push his stepfather's spirit behind him. He might be able to find it in his heart to forgive her, but he would never forget.

Fanny looked up at him with red-rimmed eyes.

'Have you,' she began in a tremulous voice, 'come to take me home?'

Sebastian stared at her. 'Home?'

'To Brantstone?'

'I don't know where your home is, Fanny, but it's not, and never has, been Brantstone. Your presence there was based entirely on lies and deception.'

Her lip wobbled. 'I didn't know!' she wailed. 'Freddy only told me that Lord Somerton had offered us his home and would look after us.'

Sebastian might have felt inclined to believe the woman's credulity, had he not remembered the very active part Fanny had played in Freddy's deceptions, from the cheating at cards through to that ghastly night in the library.

'As it is, I am considering turning you over to the constable. You will be lucky not to hang for the amount of silver you have stolen from me.'

'You wouldn't do that.' The tears stopped and Fanny sat bolt upright. 'I will be transported to New South Wales and never see Freddy again.'

Sebastian hesitated. Much as he disliked Fanny, he hated to be the bearer of bad news.

'Freddy is dead. His body was washed up on a beach near Lidiford two days ago.'

Genuine tears welled anew in the large blue eyes and spilled down her pale cheek as she fell back on the bolsters.

'Dead? Not Freddy, not my brother... Sebastian, you are all I have now. You have to help me.' She clutched at his sleeve but he stepped back out of her reach. 'Don't turn me over to the constable. Please. I've said I'm sorry for what we did. Freddy's always looked after me. I don't know what to do without him.'

Sebastian refrained from the angry words that sprang to mind. Fanny did not need to be reminded that her brother was a murderer who would have—should have—died at the end of a hangman's noose.

He glanced at Fanny's nurse, who stood by the door, her arms folded, her face impassive.

'This is what I will do for you, Fanny. I won't hand you over to the constable. You will be looked after here and, when you are well enough to travel, you will be given the sum of fifty pounds and an introduction to a respectable lady in London who can find a position for you as a lady's companion. After that, it is up to you what path you choose to take.'

'But, Sebastian—'

He hardened his heart. 'I'm sorry. I will do no more for you.'

'And very generous, his lordship is. You should thank the lord for your good fortune,' interjected the woman who was caring for Fanny, and evidently knew the better part of the story.

Fanny cast her an uncertain glance. She looked down at the sodden piece of cloth in her hand.

'Yes. It is more than I deserve. Thank you, Lord Somerton.'

For the first time, Sebastian caught a glance of the potential the young woman could have in the right circumstances, but he would not dictate her future. That was entirely Fanny's decision.

She looked up at him and, for the first time, a smile caught at the corners of her mouth.

'When is the wedding?'

He raised an eyebrow. 'In the new year. How did you...?'

'I guessed. I always thought you and Lady Somerton were meant for each other. I really rather liked Colonel Dempster,' the corners of her mouth drooped. 'Do you suppose...?'

Sebastian glared at her, and she subsided into silence.

He put on his hat and, inclining his head to acknowledge Fanny's nurse, left the room and the last of his responsibility to Fanny Lynch behind him.

Chapter Sixty-Five

Bennet took a long draught of his pipe and closed his eyes, feeling the warmth of the late autumn sun on his face. He had found a sunny corner of the kitchen garden to take his ease, and he considered that life had definitely taken a turn for the better.

'Mr. Bennet.'

He opened his eyes. Peter Thompson stood in front him, holding a battered tin box out before him.

'What'cha got there, boy?'

Peter swallowed. 'The men who was tearing down the stables found it hidden behind a loose brick in a wall,' he said. 'I think it was Amy's. I used to see her with it when she thought no one was looking.'

Bennet considered the object, a sad remnant of the girl's life.

'Nice it was found,' he said.

Peter held it out. 'I want you to take it to his lordship,' he said. 'There's things in there. I don't know what they are, but he will.'

'What sort of things?'

Peter just shook his head and shoved it at Bennet before turning on his heels and running away.

Bennet looked at the object on his lap and opened the lid. The contents looked like the sort of detritus he would expect of a young girl's life: ribbons, dried flowers, the sort of cheap trinkets pedlars at a fair would sell and, hidden in a corner, a small, apparently insignificant object.

Bennet fished it out and held it up.

He let out a low whistle.

※

SEBASTIAN POURED TWO GLASSES OF FRENCH BRANDY AND handed one to Harry. Harry swirled the liquid and took an appreciative sniff of the fumes that rose from the glass.

'When's the wedding?' he enquired.

'March,' Sebastian said.

Harry cocked an eyebrow. 'Have to say, old chap, I'm a bit hurt you haven't asked me to stand by you.'

Sebastian set his glass down. 'I have my reasons.'

Harry frowned. 'What do you mean?'

Sebastian crossed to his desk and opened the cigar box that stood on the table. He stood looking down at the little silver button... an officer's button from the 40th Regiment of Foot—the number 40 encircled by a laurel wreath.

He handed it to Harry.

Harry tossed it in his hand. 'Collecting buttons from the old regiment, Alder?'

'So you recognise it, Harry?'

'Of course I do. It's an officer's button from the Fortieth. Hanging on to it for sentimental reasons, Alder?'

'It's not mine. It was found in a box, hidden behind a brick in the old stables.'

Harry stiffened and set the button back on the table, recoiling from it.

Sebastian continued. 'The box belonged to a housemaid here at Brantstone, Amy Thompson. Did you know her, Dempster?'

The faintest hesitation gave lie to the words that followed. 'How the hell would I know a housemaid from Brantstone?'

'Perhaps you can tell me? Did she accompany her father over to Fairchild Hall? Did you see her in the village? Did you meet her at Brantstone?'

Harry picked up the button, turning it by its shank. His shoulders sagged and he shook his head.

'I saw her at the church one Sunday when I was staying with Georgie. She was lovely, Alder. Really lovely.' He let the button, with its betraying number 40, drop back on to the table.

Sebastian sighed and retrieved the small but significant object. Only one officer, other than himself, would have worn the insignia of the Fortieth Regiment of Foot in this neighbourhood. He knew as soon as Bennet showed it to him that he had found Amy Thompson's secret lover. Had he also found her killer?

He looked down at the button in his hand. It carried such a weight. A man's life, but it had already cost a life—two lives.

'You have the death of two on your conscience, Harry. Amy carried your child.'

Harry flung himself out of his chair and walked across to the window, running his hands through his hair.

'It was an accident, Alder.' He turned to face Sebastian, his face crumpled in distress. 'There's not a day goes by when I don't think about it... what I did...'

'What did you do?'

'We used to meet in the pavilion up behind the lake. When I was staying with Georgie I'd send the girl a ribbon. That was our secret signal. Different colour for different days. The last time...'

Harry covered his face with his hands, his shoulders convulsing as he struggled to control his emotions.

'She told me she was with child. She started making all sorts of demands. I couldn't think straight.'

Sebastian regarded his friend without sympathy.

'Plenty of men find themselves in your situation, Dempster. They don't resort to murder.'

Harry dropped his hands and stared at Sebastian.

'Murder? It wasn't murder. I panicked. I admit I lost my temper. I think she thought I was going to hit her. She took a step backwards and slipped. I couldn't stop her. She fell backwards and hit her head on the corner of the marble bench.' His breath came in short bursts as if he had been running. 'I can still hear the crack. I didn't know what to do.'

'Was she still alive?'

Harry shook his head. 'No.' He took a great shuddering breath. 'I waited for hours, hoping it was all a terrible mistake, but she just lay there, cold and dead, with her eyes wide open. I carried her body down to the lake and I put her in. There wasn't even any blood, Alder. No trace that it had ever happened.'

'So you threw her away and you went on with your life,' Sebastian said without disguising the disgust in his voice, 'leaving her family to mourn; her mother to suffer an apoplexy, her body to be buried in unconsecrated ground with all the world thinking she had committed the sin of suicide?'

'She was only a housemaid!' Harry all but screamed.

Sebastian didn't answer. He held out his hand, palm open with the incriminating silver button.

'When did you lose this?'

'After one of our trysts,' he said. 'I was wearing a uniform on my way to a party. I know I'm retired, but the ladies do like a uniform. It was annoying to find the button missing but I just thought a thread had come loose.' He scowled. 'If I had known the chit had purloined it...'

'She loved you. She was carrying your child and you threw her away like a piece of refuse, Harry.' Sebastian could not keep the disgust from his voice.

Harry looked away. 'I'm not proud of myself.'

'She thought you would marry her.'

Harry shook his head. "That was never going to happen but I

would have done the right thing and seen she and the child wanted for nothing.' He turned his gaze back to Sebastian. 'What are you going to do?'

Sebastian shook his head. 'What are *you* going to do, Dempster? You have twenty-four hours before I report this to the Chief Constable. If what you say is true then you won't hang... or you can be the coward I think you are and run. The choice is yours.'

Harry stared at his friend. 'That's it? You would turn me in? After Spain, after Inez... after everything we have been through together? God damn it, Alder, you're no saint. You've killed!'

Sebastian's gaze did not waver. 'When I have killed, it has been in battle, Dempster. I don't have the death of an innocent woman and her unborn child on my conscience, but I counted you my friend. For Inez if for no other reason, I owe you the chance to do the honourable thing.'

Harry gave a snort of laughter. 'Honour? God, Alder, I lost my honour years ago. Did you know I was all but cashiered from the army? It was all done quietly, my reputation intact.'

'What did you do?'

'Gambling debts. Not just a few guineas here and there. Debts I could never hope to repay, even if my father dropped dead tomorrow.'

Sebastian narrowed his eyes.

Harry sighed heavily. 'You may as well know the whole story. I founded a company: The Golden Adventurers Club. Forged some convincing reports of gold mines in Guinea and promised a fortune to be made. It was so easy to gull the investors. I soon made my fortune back, paid off my creditors.'

'And the investors?'

Harry's smile made Sebastian's flesh crawl. 'Oh dear, the mines were a failure. As far as the investors knew, a legitimate investment had been badly made. They didn't make a fuss, didn't dare risk their own reputations.'

'And Anthony was one of them. He put everything he owned

into that investment in one last gamble to rid himself of Freddy. Did he know it was you?'

'No. I covered my tracks well. Even pretended to be one of the fools caught by the collapse.'

'Anthony lost everything, including Isabel's jointure in that venture.'

'Well more fool him,' Harry said, his swagger and confidence returning.

Sebastian rose to his feet. 'Get out of my house, Dempster. You have twenty-four hours to examine your conscience.'

Harry straightened his shoulders and, without looking at Sebastian, walked over to the door.

As he put his hand to the doorknob, he said, 'Your problem is you are too trusting, Alder. You see good in people where there isn't any to be found.'

'Get out before I change my mind.' Sebastian turned his back.

He heard the click of the door and waited a long moment before he let out his breath. He knew the decision Harry would make. He would run, like the coward he had shown himself to be.

Tomorrow he would exercise his powers as magistrate and give an order for the body of Amy Thompson to be buried within the churchyard with a proper Christian funeral. He had already housed the Thompson family in a grace and favour cottage on the estate and found a proper nurse for Mrs. Thompson.

He could not bring Amy back to life, but he could give her some peace and dignity.

Chapter Sixty-Six

Isabel looked at the card on the silver tray and picked it up, her fingers playing with the sharp edges for a minute. Her maid shifted uneasily, anticipating the response, but Isabel nodded.

'Show her in.'

She rose to her feet as Lady Kendall entered the room wearing a soft, green-sprigged dress and green pelisse.

Isabel extended her hand. Lady Kendall's green eyes flashed in surprise, and she took the hand in her own green-gloved fingers.

'Thank you for seeing me,' she said.

'Please take a seat.' Isabel indicated the chair across from her. 'Roberts, some tea for my guest.'

'I came to offer my felicitations on your betrothal to Lord Somerton. He is a fine man,' Lady Kendall said as the maid closed the door behind her.

Isabel allowed herself a gentle smile as she thought about Sebastian.

'He is. I am fortunate,' she agreed.

Lady Kendall fidgeted. To see Georgiana Kendall discomfited

was a novel experience for Isabel. She looked at the woman curiously.

'What can I do for you?'

'I have come to make my peace with you, Lady Somerton. Anthony is dead, so it falls to me. The knowledge that I knew your first husband may not have been what you thought him to be has plagued me,' Lady Kendall began delicately.

Isabel looked down at her hands.

'I know all about my late husband's unhappy life, Lady Kendall. Seb... Lord Somerton tells me that your relationship with my late husband was no more than platonic. Is that true?'

Georgiana Kendall's shrewd eyes held hers, but she was prevented from answering by the reappearance of the maid with the tea tray. Neither woman spoke while Isabel poured tea and handed a bowl to her guest.

Lady Kendall took a delicate sip and looked up. 'It is quite true. Anthony loved only one woman in his life, Lady Somerton, and that was you.'

'Sadly, I don't believe he truly knew how to love a woman,' Isabel said.

'Maybe not,' Georgiana responded. She set the bowl back on the saucer. 'But I would not have you continue to think the worst of me... or of him. His feelings for you were confused, but genuine. I was but a friend to Anthony. No more.'

Isabel cocked her head, looking directly at the woman. 'Just a friend' had not been the impression conveyed by either party, but it no longer mattered. Anthony was dead, and, in his memory, she could forgive this woman.

'I came to tell you that I am selling my home in Lincolnshire and moving away from the area. Too many memories, Lady Somerton. With Harry's unexpected departure for the colonies, I find myself craving some bright company, so I intend to move back to London.'

Sebastian had told Isabel of Harry Dempster's sudden decision to seek adventures in the far-off colony of New South

Wales. She wondered if there was more to the story than Sebastian was prepared to tell her, but she had learned not to pry. If he wanted to confide in her, he would do so in his own time.

Isabel allowed herself a smile. 'Our company is not bright enough for you?'

Lady Kendall's lips twitched. 'In honesty, my dear Lady Somerton, there is a certain recently widowed earl currently in London with whom I wish to get better acquainted.'

'Ah, I see.'

Isabel felt a pang of regret. All the time she had thought of Lady Kendall as her rival, only to see that she could have been her friend.

'I hope it is not any antipathy on my part that drives you away, Lady Kendall,' she said.

Georgiana smiled. 'Not at all. I would like us to part as friends, you and I.'

Isabel nodded. 'I think we will probably never be friends, Lady Kendall. We are too different, but I would not like to think of us as enemies.'

Lady Kendall set her cup down and looked at Isabel with an unblinking gaze. 'I hear that you are establishing a charity school in Manchester?'

Isabel nodded. 'I am. It has been a long-held dream of mine.'

'I would like very much to donate to your effort,' Lady Kendall said.

Georgiana, Lady Kendall, may just as well have hit Isabel in the stomach. All the breath left her body and her mouth dropped open.

'Donate? But why...?'

'If a difference can be made to the lives of even just a few women, Lady Somerton, then I will think the money well spent. I will instruct my lawyer to set up an annual donation that should be enough to assist with the running expenses of the establishment. I want no acknowledgment, except a yearly report of your activities.'

'That is extraordinarily generous of you...' Isabel began but Lady Kendall waved away her gratitude with a gloved hand.

'I have been fortunate in my life. This is just a small way I can repay the many blessings.'

Georgiana Kendall rose to her feet. 'Thank you for the tea. I will now take your leave. I return to London in the morning. I wish you every well-deserved happiness.' She bobbed a respectful curtsey. 'Good day to you, Lady Somerton.'

With a twitch of her green skirt, Lady Georgiana Kendall left the room, leaving the lingering scent of her perfume. Isabel stood for a long moment, staring out of the window of the dower house. She turned and hurried to her room to fetch her hat and coat and, ignoring the cold, autumnal wind, she strode out of the dower house gate and up the hill to the mausoleum.

Holding her bonnet, she stood looking at her husband's name on the memorial.

'Anthony!'

The name rose in the wind and was carried away across the grass. She laid her hand on the cold marble inscribed with his name.

'Anthony, I'm sorry that it had to be the way it was. Forgive me for not understanding.'

She sank down to her knees and touched the letters of her son's name, overwhelmed with a peace and contentment that she had thought she would never feel again.

Epilogue

15 MARCH 1816

Among the gravestones of the Brantstone church, a few hardy daffodils and primroses braved the first breath of spring. The faintest green softened the grey branches of the yew trees that marked the boundary and inside the little church, Isabel and Sebastian pledged their undying love for each other.

So many people crowded the church that those at the back were forced to stand, and as the happy couple left the church, it was to cheers and whoops of delight.

Later, much later, after a grand party in the ballroom—attended by as many of the tenants, villagers, and neighbours as could be fitted into the room—the new Lord and Lady Somerton slipped away.

In an acknowledgment of the change in their lives, Sebastian had announced that they would occupy a much smaller bedchamber than the overblown room that had been Anthony's. For months, Sebastian had been deep in secret consultation with Connie about its redecoration and, while Isabel had initially been a little miffed not to be included, she allowed him his plots and plans, trusting if not to his taste, then to that of his sister.

They stood outside the door, hand in hand.

'Close your eyes,' Sebastian ordered.

Isabel complied. The door swung open with a creak, releasing the subtle scent of snowdrops, one of her favourite flowers. Sebastian took her hand, leading her into the room.

'You may open your eyes now.'

Isabel complied, and her mouth fell open in surprise as she found herself looking at the bed. Not one of the grand four-posters that graced the other bedrooms, but a familiar scene of seashells and seaweed and little boats carved with a firm but naive hand on the headboard.

'It's Mother Shipton's bed!' she exclaimed

'No. It's only the headboard,' Sebastian said. 'When I explained why I wanted it, she was only too happy to sell it to me. I hope you like it.'

She turned to look at the rest of the room, decorated in soft blue with landscapes of sea and sand hung on the walls.

Isabel turned to her husband, tears of happiness springing into her eyes.

He put his hands on her shoulders and drew her in towards him. Every time he touched her, she thought she would shatter into a hundred pieces. She wanted to be with him all day, every day. As they kissed, she let her mind fly away to the future.

She was once more Lady Somerton, but how different her life would be with this man. She had found hope and happiness and a new life with a man she loved and who loved her. She knew now what it was to be truly content and loved.

Sebastian slid his arms around her, lifting her up and carrying her over to their new bed. Tonight they would come together as man and wife and, in time, God willing, there would be a child: Lord Somerton's heir.

A chance to download the prequel to
LORD SOMERTON'S HEIR...

The idea for LORD SOMERTON'S HEIR was born on the battlefield of Waterloo on a flying visit in 2005. As it turned out, this particular story starts not with Waterloo, but in the days after Waterloo, but I had always wanted to look at Sebastian's experience of the battle.

A more recent visit to Waterloo on the eve of the bicentennial in June 2015, sparked the kernel for this story...

SEBASTIAN'S WATERLOO
A short prequel to Lord Somerton's Heir

Before Lord Somerton*, he was just plain Captain Alder, a penniless career officer in Wellington's army.
As Napoleon makes his last great bid for power, he will meet an Iron Duke and an indomitable force of English and allied troops in the fields just south of a little village called Waterloo.
For Sebastian Alder, the events of June 18, 1815 will change his life forever...

If you click use the QR CODE below, you can download SEBASTIAN'S WATERLOO...

(You will be asked to sign up to Alison's newsletter but we hope that you will join us!)

Alternatively it is available to purchase directly from Alison Stuart's bookstore on her website

A SHORT EXCERPT FOLLOWS...

SEBASTIAN'S WATERLOO

CHAPTER ONE

THE VILLAGE OF WATERLOO, BELGIUM 17 JUNE 1815

'Are you married?'

Sebastian jerked his head up at the unexpected question. He looked across at his commanding officer and stuttered, 'No.'

He had been married once... briefly... and in a way he still thought of himself as a married man, despite the six long years that had passed since Inez's death.

Major Arthur Heyland laid his pen on his writing box and smiled, but even in the dim light of the lantern, there was no humour in his smile. 'Consider yourself fortunate, Alder. No one to worry about you.'

That was not strictly true, Sebastian had a brother and sister who would certainly worry about him.

'You, sir?'

Heyland nodded. 'Married twelve years.'

'Children?' Sebastian prompted, not from any great interest, but conversation of any kind helped pass the time.

This time, there was humour in the smile, a genuine warmth he rarely saw in his commanding officer.

'Six... and one due any day,' Heyland replied.

Sebastian did the mental calculation. Quick work in only twelve years of marriage, most of which had been spent on active service.

As if sensing his unspoken question, Heyland said. 'Mary followed the drum, and it broke my heart to leave her in Wales, but she's... well she could hardly follow in her condition. She's a capital girl, my Mary.'

He sat back and scratched his nose with the end of his pen.

'You know the life she has led, Alder, all without complaint. She has borne me four boys and two girls...' he paused, the corners of his mouth turning down, 'and the one I may never meet.'

There was no answer to the last. Both men lapsed into silence, unbroken but for the steady lashing of rain on the window of their billet.

'This rain will be the very devil on the morrow,' Heyland said, changing the subject.

'If it is for us, then the French will have it just as bad,' Sebastian responded.

Heyland looked down at the letter he had been writing.

'I'd been given permission to retire on half pay,' he said without looking up. 'We have enough to live comfortably. Mary and I...' he broke off with a shuddering breath.

Sebastian said nothing. There was nothing he could say. He had been a soldier as long as this man, they had both seen service on the Peninsula, both been wounded several times. The prospect of battle held no illusions of grandeur or glory. If Heyland had some premonition that tomorrow would be his last day on earth, then Sebastian had seen it before, and he had no comfort, no platitudes to offer.

Death came at its own behest, and even as he had charged the walls at Talavera, crying its name, death had laughed in his face. Now... he took a deep shuddering breath... now the thought of death terrified him. He had not seen serious action since

Talavera, and in that time his life had changed. His stepfather had died, leaving him with the responsibility for his siblings, a responsibility he took on willingly.

'I have a younger brother and sister,' Sebastian volunteered. 'Orphaned...'

He made a pretence of inspecting his sword for rust, conscious that Heyland gave him a long, lingering glance of complete understanding.

If Heyland had been about to say something, a knock on the door interrupted him. Sebastian's orderly, Bennet, entered, carrying two metal pannikins.

'That smells like real food,' Heyland remarked, taking the pannikin Bennet offered him.

'Chicken,' Corporal Bennet announced with a degree of pride in his voice.

Sebastian took his pannikin, but in truth he had little appetite. Only common sense told him he needed to eat.

'Where did you steal it, Bennet?' he asked.

His orderly looked offended.

'Didn't steal 'nuffin, sir, and I resents the implication. This came for you, Major Heyland, sir.'

Bennet handed a folded and sealed paper to Heyland.

As Sebastian hastily consumed the gelatinous mess Bennet had produced, without tasting it, Heyland broke the seal and scanned the contents.

He waited until Bennet had left the room before he said. 'Our orders for tomorrow, Alder. We are to be held in the reserve under Lambert and be in place at the farm Mont St. Jean by 9 in the morning.'

Sebastian nodded and rose to his feet. 'I'll pass the orders on,' he said, 'and make sure the men are rested.'

Heyland ran a hand over his eyes. 'God knows they must be exhausted after that march from Ghent. I know I am, and I had a horse.'

Sebastian left his commanding officer to finish his letter to his wife in private and went in search of the rest of the officers of the 40th Regiment of Foot. Some were already asleep. He apologised for rousing them, but they had the responsibility to ensure their men were settled for the night, had eaten, cleaned their muskets, and would be ready to march at seven.

'In this weather?' one of the younger officers complained, glancing at the open door and the pouring rain.

'Count yourself lucky you have a dry bed and a meal in your belly,' Sebastian snapped. 'I am betting there are men out there who have neither. See to your men... now!'

If you click follow the QR code below, you can download
SEBASTIAN'S WATERLOO...
(You will be asked to sign up for Alison's newsletter but we hope that you will join us!)

Alternatively it is available to purchase directly from Alison Stuart's bookstore on her website

Acknowledgments

I would like to thank everyone who helped in Lord Somerton's journey to publication, particularly my writing group, *The Saturday Ladies Bridge Club*, who lived through all its ups and downs, my beta readers Sasha, Kandy and Judy and *Hearts Through History*, the Historical chapter of *Romance Writers America*, who awarded *Lord Somerton's Heir* the 2012 Romance Through the Ages Award (for an unpublished manuscript).

Books by Alison Stuart

Australian Historical Romance
THE POSTMISTRESS
THE GOLDMINER'S SISTER
THE HOMECOMING

The Guardians of the Crown Series
BY THE SWORD
THE KING'S MAN
EXILE'S RETURN

The Feathers in the Wind Collection
AND THEN MINE ENEMY
HER REBEL HEART
SECRETS IN TIME
FEATHERS IN THE WIND (BOX SET)

Regency/World War One
GATHER THE BONES
LORD SOMERTON'S HEIR
A CHRISTMAS LOVE REDEEMED (Novella)

BOOKS BY A.M. STUART

The Harriet Gordon Mysteries
SINGAPORE SAPPHIRE (Book 1)
REVENGE IN RUBIES (Book 2)
EVIL IN EMERALD (Book 3)
TERROR IN TOPAZ (Book 4)
AGONY IN AMETHYST (Book 5)
THE UMBRELLA (Prequel novella)

Printed in Great Britain
by Amazon